PURSUIT
The American Way
By
Thomas Holladay

I0636365

This is a work of fiction. Similarities to real people, places, or events are entirely coincidental.

PURSUIT: THE AMERICAN WAY

First edition. November 17, 2021.

Copyright © 2021 Thomas Holladay.

ISBN: 978-1736914021

Written by Thomas Holladay.

Also by Thomas Holladay

The American Way
Deliberate Justice
Pursuit: The American Way

Standalone
Treasure
The Birthday Box
Meadowlarks
Comes the Call: For God and Country

Watch for more at www.thomas-holladay.com.

This book is dedicated to my wife, Wilma, and our daughter, Micvhelle Trixie. Thank you for your never-ending support and patience. I dearly love you both.

Chapter One

"I DON'T SEE ANY YANKEES," said little Melanie, peeking between the drapes at the front parlor window of Winterbridge Manor. "Oh, look! There's white smoke over at McAdams Hall. Those Yankees must be there right now." She spun to look at Allison, eyes wide with fear. "Are they coming here?"

"I hope not, honey. I hope we're far enough off the road so they can't see us." Allison Mosby stood behind her daughter and looked out across their cold, baron rows of what had once been cotton. "I so wish your daddy was here."

"I miss my daddy." Melanie hugged her mother then looked up. "He's all I wished for for Christmas." She looked straight up. "Santa, please bring my daddy home."

"We won't have much of a Christmas this year, honey."

"If Santa brings my daddy . . ." Melany hugged her mother's legs, eyes wide with hope.

Allison Mosby and her seven-year-old daughter, Melanie, had lost weight during this damnable war, but both had remained healthy, as had their darkies.

What would we do without them?

Before going up to Virginia to join his brother's regiment, her husband, Franklin, had invested nearly all of their available funds in Confederate bonds. All that remained was a small iron box of gold coins hidden under the marble hearth of their upstairs bedroom fireplace. She'd not touch that. Whichever way this war ended, they'd need something for replanting their fields, for rebuilding their lives.

All the cattle and pigs on Winterbridge Manor had been appropriated over the past three years to feed the brave men of the Confederacy.

Winterbridge slaves had remained. They seemed happy to have been owned by the Winston family, and by Franklin Mosby. Most of them lived in cottages down along the Savannah River.

With cotton exports barricaded by those damn Yankees, she'd allowed their slaves to grow crops for food and to fish and trap for game. They'd brought catfish, rabbit, or squirrel up to the house near every day last summer, along with potatoes, corn, carrots, and greens.

This winter had been leaner and meaner but they still had corn and potatoes.

On cold days, such as that day, she and Melanie spent their afternoons in the west facing bay window where late sun kept them warm. They dared not show those damn Yankees smoke from a fire.

As a precautionary measure, they'd blocked both chimneys in the cookhouse around back. Smoke from cooking filled that big room and seeped through the walls, making it very hard for Yankees to see from the road below. John Jackson Youngblood, their plantation overseer, said the slaves out there complained about smoke burning their eyes and noses, but that they understood the why of it all.

Always keeping busy with useful tasks, Allison and Melanie had been working on a patchwork quilt for Melanie's bedroom.

"Is that my daddy?"

A stocky, red bearded man in a Confederate officer's uniform stepped out of the Georgia pine forest near their lower cotton field and walked brusquely into the barn.

"No, Honey. Your daddy's a mite taller, and thinner."

2

Allison's right hand went to her throat, fearing this man might bring bad news about her husband. He might have been wounded or taken prisoner.

Lord, keep my Franklin safe.

John Jackson always left the barn door open during the day. He'd been born at Winterbridge, and he had an excellent education; better than most white folks. His skill with mathematics made him a natural for overseeing the manor house and generally running their entire plantation.

Most plantations hired white overseers, some of whom whipped their slaves for whatever reason that suited them. Franklin, and the Winstons before him, held whippings to be inhumane. If one of their slaves had turned lazy or spiteful, they'd been sold or traded, straight away. That had always been enough to keep the others thoughtful of place and time.

Allison's daddy owned only two houseslaves. They'd never been beaten but they'd never received any education either. Her daddy believed them to be inferior to white people. He treated them like he did their dogs and horses. He didn't treat them mean but neither did he respect them as human beings.

Growing up, she'd never thought about any of this.

Since marrying Franklin and living at Winterbridge, she'd grown to agree with the Winstons. Darkies were people. Like their pastor said, slavery was one of life's callings. Those who were slaves should be good slaves. Slave masters should, likewise, be good masters. These were God's creatures under less fortunate circumstance. After all, there once had been a lot of white slaves in these here American states, north and south.

Winterbridge slaves worked hard, worshiped God, held their own Christian services down by the river, and revered their masters. Nobody could ask for better.

John Jackson, with his wife and daughter, shared two rooms in the barn and stayed busy. Right then, he'd probably be in back of the barn chopping firewood, one of his daily tasks. His wife and their infant daughter would be in the cookhouse baking cornbread.

Even during this damnable war, life at Winterbridge had been stable, largely because of John Jackson Youngblood and his wife.

The stocky, Confederate officer marched out of the barn and looked up at the manor house. He stopped and stared at Allison. She hadn't before noticed a splash of what looked like blood across the hem of his gray coat. He adjusted his tight-fitting hat and marched toward the house.

"Maybe he knows my daddy." Melanie dashed through the double doorway into the entry hall before Allison could stop her.

A sense of dread had momentarily cemented Allison's feet to the floor. "No." Allison rushed after her daughter.

Melanie yanked open the front door before Allison could stop her.

The stocky, red-bearded man filled the doorway. He did not remove his hat. The blood on his coat looked fresh. His dirty face, tight uniform, tangled beard, and large hands spoke a certain truth. This could not be a southern gentleman.

Allison stepped forward slowly and backed Melanie between her legs.

Dirty teeth showed from behind the man's bushy, filthy red beard. "Well now . . ." He stepped toward them. The knife in his hand appeared from nowhere. "Ain't you a pair of pretty bells?" His accent was that of a Yankee.

Allison stepped back and pulled Melanie around behind her. "What do you want?"

"I can cut a hog from belly to jaw, slow as you like. I enjoy the squealing." He took two quick steps and snatched Allison's arm above her elbow, pinching a painful nerve, so painful it choked her

4

scream. He yanked her close. His stinking breath surrounded him. "Who else is in the house?"

"Captain Franklin Adam Mosby, my husband, is serving with his regiment in Virginia." She immediately regretted her answer.

His eyes narrowed. "You don't want to watch me gut that little girl, you'll show me where it's hid."

She glanced toward the grand staircase.

"You and me is going upstairs alone." He looked at the coat closet. "What's in there?"

"No." Allison tried to pull away but he pinched her arm at the bone, more pain than she'd ever before felt. "Melanie, do you remember me telling you about your uncle?" She forced a smile and pushed Melanie back into the parlor. "We need to go talk upstairs. You go in and work on your quilt. Okay?"

"He's my Uncle John?"

He grinned. "That's right, little one. Now, go on."

Melanie smiled, curtsied, and turned back into the parlor.

The man in the gray, Confederate uniform dragged Allison up the stairs. They stopped at the top, looking down the long hall past four open doorways. "Which is it?"

Allison led him through the last door on the right. "Promise you won't hurt us, and I'll give you what you want."

"Okay. I promise I won't hurt you. Why would I want to hurt anybody?"

She pointed at the carved marble fireplace. "Lift and slide that stone hearth aside."

He hurled her onto the floor and closed the bedroom door. He noticed the skeleton key, locked the door, and pointed the knife at her face. "Get up on that bed where I can see you. You make a sound, I'll go down and gut that pretty little daughter of yours."

"What you want is under there." She pointed at the left end of the hearth.

He aimed his knife at her face, motioned toward the bed, and waited.

She climbed onto the foot of the bed and sat, trembling from the cold and from her fear.

He looked back and forth, moved quickly to the fireplace, bent, lifted the hearth, and slid it out of the way, as if the heavy stone was a feather. Seeing the iron box brought a smile. He pointed the knife at her again. "Now, crawl back against that headboard and take them clothes off."

He pointed his knife toward the head of the bed, grabbed his uniform collar with his left hand, and swiped his knife down the front of his tunic. His brass buttons bounced and skidded across the wood-plank floor. He fanned his knife toward her face. "Sharp, ain't it?"

"What? Why? You've got what you wanted. Take it and go before my brother comes back."

He shifted and his tunic dropped off his left shoulder. He shifted again and freed his left arm. He switched the knife to his left hand, shifted, and his tunic dropped to the floor.

Allison stayed at the foot of the bed, crossed her arms, and grabbed her shoulders. "No!"

"That's okay. I'm happy to cut that dress off."

Allison's left hand shot out, blocking her view of his face.

He said, "Don't you make a sound." He kicked off his boots, dropped his pants, and kicked them aside. He was a powerfully built man.

Allison crawled backward and stopped against the headboard. She had nowhere to hide.

His filthy chest peeked from behind curly red hair. His dirty teeth sneered from behind his matted red beard. He kneed his way onto the bed, grabbed the hem of her dress, and dragged her close. His breath smelled of rotting teeth.

He cut the hem of her dress and slowly cut the fabric away from her legs. He dropped his knife to the floor and stared at her open-crotch knickers. "Oh, I like that."

He flipped her onto her stomach and tore off her clothing until she lay naked. He bent down, found his knife, and pressed the cold flat of it against the inside of her thighs, slowly spreading her legs. "Lady, you got real pretty skin. Real blonde hair, too." His husky voice barely whispered.

Franklin . . . Warm tears slid down her nose onto the pillow.

"You make a sound, I'll do bad things to that little girly downstairs."

ALL NIGHT RAIN HADN'T driven off the smell of charred wood from up river, where Yankee soldiers had left a wide path of destruction.

These vindictive Yankees held Savannah intact, too valuable a port to destroy. Savannah had also become world famous for her beauty. Yankees, under Generals Sherman and Geary, had struck a deal with Savanna's mayor, Dr. Richard Arnold. If the Yankees met with no resistance, the city would not be destroyed. Near everything had been destroyed upriver. According to rumors, the Yankees hoped to break Georgia's fighting spirit.

Maybe they had.

Georgia's wonderful rail system had been completely destroyed. Steel rails had been raised, heated, and bent beyond any possible use.

Samuel Greenwood, the long-time manager of Winston Dry Goods & Mercantile, a large warehouse and store near the Savannah River docks, appreciated the mayor's surrender. Beautiful Savannah, the city of his birth, would not be raised to the ground as Atlanta had been.

Rumors abounded. Sherman would deliver the city to Abe Lincoln as a Christmas gift. It would still be Savannah, still in the great State of Georgia, but Lincoln's Union Army had taken her.

So be it.

Moses Broadback walked up from the shadows of the warehouse where he'd been sleeping on baled cotton since boyhood.

"Moses, why are you still here?" Samuel pulled open the shade on one of the storefront windows, lighting empty shelves once jammed with trade goods. "Don't you know the Yankee general set all you Nigras free?"

"I don't belong to no Yankees. I'm Winterbridge property." Moses, and others, somehow took pride in being Mosby slaves. And why not? The Winston family of Winterbridge Manor had been educating their slaves for two or more generations, kept them well housed, well fed, and properly clothed. They lived much better than most hired factory workers in northern states. Samuel had read all about it in a Savannah newspaper.

The slaves of Winterbridge Manor had a reputation of being the best kept property in all of Georgia. After the Winston family died off, their relative from Virginia, young Franklin Mosby, had inherited Winterbridge and all that went with it; including Winston Dry Goods & Mercantile, Winston Hotel, money in the bank, and loyal, hard working slaves like Moses.

Out on Fahm Street, a burly man with snarled red hair and beard drove a familiar looking wagon into early morning sun, heading down toward the river. His well tailored suit looked two sizes too small, and, like the wagon, looked familiar. A little girl sat next to him, clutching her coat tight, shivering from the cold of morning.

"Mr. Greenwood, isn't that wagon from Winterbridge Manor?" Moses leaned closer to the window for a better look.

The burly man driving the wagon turned sharply. His angry eyes immediately focused on Samuel.

A cold chill rushed up Samuel's back. "Isn't that little Melanie seated next to him?"

"Yes, sir. I reckon it is."

"Moses, follow that wagon with charcoal and your sketchpad. Be sure not to let him see you."

DONALD THORNE CLIMBED down from the wagon slowly, being careful not the tear the double-breasted jacket, too tight for his heavy arms and shoulders. Suspenders held up the pants, too tight to button at the top. "You wait here." He left the girl on the wagon bench and stepped into the shadows of an open livery.

A Yankee corporal strolled from darkness into shaded daylight. Long yellow hair framed his clean-shaved face. Thorne had never seen him before.

Thorne poked a thumb over his shoulder toward the horse and wagon. "How much for the horse and wagon?"

The yellow-haired corporal leaned around Thorne to look at the horse and wagon. "You selling?"

"That's what I said." Thorne stepped out of his way.

The corporal walked outside to examine the horse's legs, hooves, eyes, and teeth. He checked the wagon, racked all four steel-rimmed wheels, and turned back inside. "Give twenty Yankee dollars for the horse and thirty-five for the wagon."

Thorn's eyes narrowed. "What you trying?"

"Yeah. I know. Both the horse and wagon are in top condition. I'm not authorized to pay more." He squared up to Thorne. "Why are you selling, anyway?"

"I never favored this damn war. I grew up in New York. My father died and my mother married a southerner with a small farm. I was twelve when we moved down here to Georgia. We never owned slaves, but you Yanks burned the place down anyway. They clubbed me unconscious, then raped and murdered my wife." He stared hard into the corporal. "I got no reasons to stay. We're headed to California."

"Did we catch the deserters who did such a thing?"

"Not so's I've heard." He poked a thumb toward the wagon. "Thank God, my little girl's okay."

"If they find the ones who did such a thing, they'll shoot 'em on the spot, or hang 'em. You mark my words." The corporal looked again at the wagon and horse. "Well, like I said, I ain't authorized to pay more. Wish I could"

Thorne nodded, went out, grabbed the heavy canvas satchel from under the wagon seat, and dragged the child off the bench. He settled her onto his right hip, stiff as a wooden doll, and carried her inside.

The corporal smiled and walked back into the shadows.

Thorne followed him to a small, lamp-lit office in a stable filled with too many horses and very few wagons.

He stood the kid on the floor and bent close. "Stand right here and don't you move. Keep both them eyes on this here." He set the heavy canvas bag at her feet. "Guard it real close." He turned back into the office doorway.

The corporal opened a drawer, pulled out a metal cashbox, and set it on the desk. He fingered into a hip pocket for the key and turned it into the lock.

Thorne reached to the small of his back and pulled his knife, hiding it while the corporal pulled a wad of Yankee folding money from the box. Seeing the money, Thorne stepped close, grabbed the corporal's long yellow hair, yanked his head back, and stabbed the side of his neck.

He pushed hard and shoved the sharp blade forward, cutting through the corporal's windpipe. Bright red blood shot from both sided of his severed throat. None of it hit Thorne's new, tight-fitting suit.

The corporal jerked, sucked air through the open hole in his neck, and his knees buckled.

Thorne flung the corporal sideways, being careful not to bloody the money. He stepped on the corporal's twitching arm, reflexively moving toward his blood spurting throat, and carefully slid the money from his twitching grip.

He cleaned his knife with the corporal's yellow hair, pulled the rest of the folded money from the cashbox, and organized it with what he already held. He stuffed the money into his breast pocket, picked up the cashbox, and dumped the coins into his hand. No need counting it, heavy as it was; mostly gold and silver.

He pulled the corporal's new Navy Colt and slid the weapon into the suspender loop of his unbuttoned trousers. He turned, stepped out of the office, and found the kid backing toward the wagon.

He carefully returned his knife to the small of his back, adjusted his coat sleeves, dropped the coins into the canvas bag, and picked it up. He grabbed the kid's arm, yanked her up on his way out, and set her on the wagon bench. He set the bag under the seat, climbed up, released the foot brake, and slapped the reins. He guided the horse toward the river, toward the boats, toward his preplanned escape route.

NEARING DARK, FAR DOWN river, speaking to boat people all along the way about buying passage south, he'd finally found a small, sloop rigged fishing boat with a two-man crew. They were loading nets onto the boat, preparing to set sail. Thorne reined in, set the brake, glanced at the kid, climbed down, and strolled toward the sloop.

One of the men turned his way. "Help you mister?"

"Me and my kid need to get on a southbound ship. The Yankees burned our home, raped and killed my wife, clubbed me, and left me for dead." He rubbed the back of his head and winced.

"We don't take no government paper. You got silver or gold?"

"I do." He turned back, reached under the wagon seat, and dragged out the heavy canvas satchel. He set it on the ground, opened it, and pulled out a leather purse, leaving the loose coin from the livery at the bottom of the bag. "How much?"

"Gold or silver?"

"Gold coin from the Georgia Railroad and Banking Company."

"Take you to Key West for three hundred dollars."

Chapter Two

LONG GONE. Mike Zabel smiled, remembering his real name and titles: Major, the Count Mikhail Diebitsch-Zabalkansky. That name had long since passed. He'd completely adapted to San Francisco's steadily growing population.

Billy Cahill, Abe Warner, Charlotte King, and a few others still sometimes called him Count Mike, but he'd become Mike Zabel to everybody else, including himself.

Molly, his wife, called him Michael.

After James King of William's death, Jim's widow, Charlotte, had given Jim's Olympic Club lifetime membership to Billy Cahill. In the past few years, Billy had grown from being a type-setter to become the star reporter for the Daily Evening Bulletin. It had been a long time since Major, the Count Mikhail Diebitsch-Zabalkansky had taught Billy to read and write, and Mike had arranged Billy's first job at the Bulletin.

Mike's small investment group met regularly at the Olympic Club Gym. John Downey, a founding member of the group, had served as California's governor from 1860 to 1862, after which he'd returned to Southern California. He'd sailed all the way up from San Pedro for this special meeting. John tossed the heavy medicine ball to Abe Warner, another founding member.

Warner still owned the Palace, often called the Cobweb Palace, due to Abe's refusal to clean the spider webs from the rafters. Abe's long-held superstition, that killing spiders brings bad luck, prohibited any cleaning of the ceiling joists, which had become a jumbled mixture of spider webs and cobwebs.

Mike had grown used to the spiders, having worked at the Palace for the past ten years. He still ran the gambling side, he still ordered the good European wines, and he still collected his share of the profits.

He and Abe Warner had become close friends.

Abe tossed the ball to Mike and Mike tossed it to Billy Cahill.

Billy had been given a voice in Mike's investment group, as proxy for Charlotte King of William. Billy turned and handed the ball to Colonel William Tell Coleman, another founding member.

Coleman had formed both of San Francisco's Committees of Vigilance, first in 1851, and again in 1856, both times to clean up the city. After the trials and hangings of Charlie Cora and James Casey, Cora for shooting U.S. Marshal William Richardson, a shooting Mike felt at the time had actually been in self-defense, and Casey for the cold-blooded murder of James King of William, a murder Mike had witnessed, Coleman had formed the local People's Party. His new political party now controlled the city government and had joined Abe Lincoln's national Republican Party.

Coleman puffed hard, set the heavy leather ball on the floor, and sat on it. "I'm ready for a steam."

All of them were soaking wet with sweat.

John Downey and Billy Cahill pulled Coleman to his feet and Abe led them all into the adjoining rooms.

Stripping off his sweaty workout costume, Billy said, "We received some wires of interest during the past few days. The Union Army has taken Atlanta and now controls Georgia, from Atlanta all the way to Savannah. General Sherman has wrapped Savannah in a big red bow, figuratively speaking, and presented it to President Lincoln as a Christmas gift."

They all wrapped towels around themselves and followed Warner into the otherwise empty steam room.

Everybody but John Downey found a seat. He had the floor by default. "Mike, why in thunder did I come all the way up here? What's going on?"

Mike smiled and said, "Yes, John, as to why I've called this meeting so early in the morning." His Russian accent had given way, sounding more and more American, at least to his inner ear. "As you all know, the U.S. Congress has finally authorized funding for the Central Pacific Railroad to start laying rails over the Sierra Nevada Mountains. We own substantial shares in the San Francisco and San Jose Railroad. Central Pacific Railroad is now purchasing many smaller lines, like ours, and our stock is due to increase in value." Mike waited for input.

"What do you recommend, Mike?" Warner always needed to be the one.

"Since the San Francisco and San Jose Railroad first completed their tracks two years ago, they've laid more rails and purchased more engines, and they still can't keep up with public demand. This is a good time to sell, if that's what you all choose to do." He again waited for a response.

Warner glared at Mike, always impatient. "What do you recommend, Mike?"

Mike held up a hand, still more news. He looked at Billy.

"Yes, well . . ." Billy paused to organize his thoughts. "Most of the war correspondents in the east think Sherman's march through Georgia will break the will of the Confederacy to continue the fight. Their rail system has been destroyed and the north has garrisoned Atlanta and Savannah. I think the war will come to an end in a matter of months, if not weeks." He looked to Mike.

"The U.S. Congress has also established a national currency and opened the First National Bank. Branches are spreading across northern states and are required to post bonds with the U.S. Treasury backed by gold or silver, which affects our Comstock Mining investment. The new railroad will be able to ship our silver from the mine directly to the U.S. mint, here in this city. This means the silver shipments will be easier to protect." Wagon shipments had experienced trouble with bandits. Guards had been killed. Everybody knew this.

"You're talking years, here." John Downey finally found a seat next to Abe Warner.

Mike smiled at Warner, hoping he'd remain calm. Warner and Downey had nearly come to blows in the past, always friendly quarrels.

Mike said, "Our investments have paid steady dividends over the past few years. I'd like to keep our rail stock and roll it into Central Pacific Railroad. I think we should buy Central Pacific stock right now and grow our shares. I'm not personally considering the sale of Comstock shares."

Coleman said, "What about the others?"

"I spoke with Preslova yesterday. They want to convert their dividend stock to purchase additional shares in Central Pacific."

"And?" Warner's face glowed red. He needed to get to the Palace. They all wanted Mike's clear recommendation.

"The other Russians and I have already done this. If any of you want to follow, I can handle the paperwork."

They looked at each other, man to man. Billy Cahill jumped in first. "The widow is in. She said to do whatever you recommend."

Mike said, "As a former military man, I think it certain; America's Civil War is over. The Union will be preserved. There is no better time than the present to invest in America's future. Rail travel is that future."

The others mumbled among themselves and nodded their collective agreement.

Mike took a confirming glance from each of them. "Very good. Bring your stock certificates to our offices at the exchange. You'll all be issued Central Pacific stocks as soon as they come across my desk." Mike stood. "Meanwhile, I've purchased tickets to San Jose and back for tomorrow. Let's meet at the depot at 8:30 tomorrow morning." He looked at Abe. "We'll open the Palace after lunch, if that's okay."

Abe nodded. He would start his chowder early.

The rest of what Mike had planned would wait until he firmed up a couple of additional opportunities.

LITTLE CHAI WON YO had been waiting for his mom to wake up for a whole day. Her still face felt cold to Won Yo's touch. His mom had been sick and hot for the past three days. The stench from her and her bed, wet with brown waste, tortured his empty stomach.

Won Yo could not remember his father.

Won Yo had nowhere else to go.

Their small hut always felt cold inside. Now, at the end of the day, it felt colder. He went outside and sat in late afternoon sun. Maybe he'd feel warmer.

That big, familiar man stood across the road, watching Won Yo like before. He always stood just below Parker House, one of the glittering gambling houses of Portsmouth Plaza. He wore a heavy, warm looking coat.

Won Yo wanted to be warm too, but this big man frightened him. He knew not why.

The man stepped farther away from Parker House, late sun at his back, his face a dark shadow, and crossed the narrow road toward Won.

Won Yo thought to jump up and run but couldn't. He was too cold to run.

A wide smile crossed the big man's face, already very close. He knelt and reached inside his coat. He seemed friendly for such a big man. "Here, you look hungry." He pulled out and unfolded a piece of cloth, offering Won Yo a slab of bread with a piece of pan-fried fish.

Won Yo snatched the food and ate it, fast as he could.

"You look cold. Is your mother sick? Let me take you to a warm place. I can give you more food to bring home to your mother, and a nice, warm blanket."

GENERAL, THE COUNT Boris Romochka-Krestyanov had been in direct service to the Romanov Dynasty for all of his adult life. He'd served in combat with Alexander in the western wars with Poland and, since Alexander's ascension to Czar of all of Russia, he'd been reassigned to the Grand Duchess Catherine Mikhailovna, a 33-year-old, single woman. She'd filled herself with hate since learning of the death of her brother, the Grand Duke Nikolai Nikolaievich. Had he lived, he would now be Czar. Without the hate lines etched into her face, she might have remained beautiful.

At 65 years of age and being a combat veteran, General, the Count Boris Romochka-Krestyanov, no longer liked to travel outside Russia. Under her command, he had no choice.

Lady Catherine's thirst for vengeance had taken them halfway around the world. Though modern steamships and railroads had greatly diminished the time necessary for travel and had eliminated most of the hardships and dangers, he still hated international travel.

He missed his wife and sons.

Late in the day, it was already getting dark. With the ship rolling across Pacific swells, he spread his feet and stood at her cabin door. He braced against the ship's motion and knocked softly.

A full minute passed before the door cracked open. Sacha Varvarinski, Lady Catherine's attractive hand maid, smiled. Her typical greeting.

The general said, "Tell her we are approaching our destination. Only a few hours more. The captain says we are entering the bay of lights. He thinks you might both appreciate the view. He says it is very spectacular." The general could not imagine it being more spectacular than St. Petersburg.

The duchess, Lady Catherine, yanked the door wide-open, always dressed in black. Her eyes displayed her unrelenting rage. "Yes. I want to see this." She stepped back, inviting the general to enter.

He stepped in and Sacha closed the door.

Lady Catherine's eyes asked that question for what seemed the hundredth time.

The general said, "Yes, Highness, our identities remain unknown. We travel as merchants."

She allowed herself a slight smile. "We will always speak in the English, from this point forward." She motioned to Sacha.

Sacha opened the door and they both followed the duchess out onto the deck. The soaring mountains of the California coast felt very near and had no visible lights.

She said, "What lights?"

The general said, "Madam, we are on the port side, looking north." He'd been directed to always address her as Madam in public. "Let us move to the south facing side of the vessel." He led the ladies around to the starboard side where city lights sparkled across the bay from the still distant city.

The duchess snapped, "This is spectacular?"

The general said, "No, madam. St. Petersburg is far more exciting. Even New York is better than this." The general did find this particular display of lights to be warm and inviting. The rise of the hills with their lights added to the sparkle of lights reflecting across the bay. Neither St. Petersburg nor New York had the spectacle of glittering hills. He dared not say this.

"He knows we are coming?" Lady Catherine had repeated this question over and over, so many times.

"Yes, madam. I sent a telegram from Panama." He'd answered her question over and over, so many times.

THEIR HOUSE ON RUSSIAN Hill had been completed nearly two years earlier, yet Molly still felt out of place. She missed the White Chapel Saloon, her boardinghouse down on the Barbary Coast. Still, she did agree with Michael. This house was a better home to raise their son, James Michael Zabel, so much like his father, that wicked, wonderful man. She'd grown to love both of them more than she'd ever thought possible.

Jimmy had a governess. That man would have it no other way. He didn't trust the new public education system, yet in its infancy, and Molly had not sufficient education to make up any deficiencies. And, of course, that man was too busy.

His choice of Coira Macauley, a Scottish Highlander in every way, had not proven to be pleasant for Molly. She looked down on Molly's poor Irish background and her inferior education. Proud, arrogant, superior, and oh so sure of herself, was Coira Macauley.

To be fair, Coira had always acted in a polite manner, even if Michael had gone off, God knows where. Coira let it be known, with stern expressions of regret, that she did not approve of the way Molly and Michael coddled and spoiled Jimmy. Gratefully, the woman never dared say a word. The worst of it was the way Coira looked down her long nose at Molly.

Not at that man. No! And not at their son. Not even at Raul Perez. Only at Molly.

It was hard for Molly to believe an eight-year-old child could wield such power over his own existence, not to mention the existence of others. How Coira Macauley had managed to guide him through six hours of proper education, six days a week, remained a mystery.

He'd soon know more than Molly.

Would he look down on her too?

The little stinker.

Whenever Michael wasn't around, which was most of the time, Raul Perez kept things in balance. Not even Coira faced up to Raul, small in stature but powerful in his presence. Their bedrooms were at opposite ends of the ground floor. Raul slept opposite Michael's office, near the street entrance. Coira slept behind the kitchen, close to the alley entrance and stable. This probably kept them from tangling with one another.

Jimmy and Coira spent most days on the third floor. Jimmy would be at his mathematics, with Molly and Raul returning from their daily business down at the White Chapel Saloon. This was Molly's time for cooking the dinner.

Raul came in from the stable, having fed and brushed Gypsy, their carriage mare. He crossed to their new gas stove, brought all the way from London, and lifted a cast iron lid to smell Molly's pot roast. He smiled, his eyebrows shooting up and down. He liked meat and potatoes, as did Michael and Jimmy.

Her pot roast always smelled good. A sheet of fresh biscuits would go into the oven the moment that man arrived home. Always hungry, he was. The biscuit batter was still rising with the yeast.

Recognizing the particular sound from the back door, Raul slid the bench toward the wooden icebox, stepped up, lifted the lid, and hopped aside.

The iceman opened the back door and carried in a fresh block of ice. "Evening, ma'am." He hoisted and lowered the block of ice into the top of the icebox, dropped the lid into place, and sniffed. "Hmm. Wish my little woman could cook like that."

Molly pulled the coins from her apron pocket and handed them to the iceman. "I'm sure she's a better cook than the one in this house."

Always well fed and rosy cheeked, the iceman glanced at the money, put it into his trouser pocket, smiled, turned out the back door, and closed it.

Raul cranked an ear and marched toward the front hallway.

Molly followed, wiping her hands on her apron.

Raul turned up the gaslight in the entry hall and opened the front door, three steps above the sidewalk on Hyde Street.

A well-dressed Chinaman stood on the middle step. He took off his dark brown derby hat and climbed onto the small porch. He stiffened, turning the hat nervously in both hands. "I am looking to speak with Mike Zabel. He lives here?"

Raul stood firmly in the doorway. "What is this about?"

Molly turned toward a sound from the kitchen. *That man.*

Mike crossed into the entry hall and smiled. He stroked Molly's back in a soft embrace and tried to push her toward the front door. She stood fast and he stepped around her onto the porch. "Han, thank you for coming."

The Chinaman bowed low at the waist and Michael stood him back up, turning him toward Molly and Raul. "This is Han Wok. I've invited him to join us for dinner." He pulled Han into the entry hall and closed the door.

Rapid footsteps thundered down the stairs. Jimmy jumped over the last tread and flew into Michael's outstretched arms. "Daddy!" He hugged his father's neck.

Michael lifted and twirled him, tucked him under his arm, and marched into the dining room.

Chapter Three

GENERAL, THE COUNT Boris Romochka-Krestyanov guided Lady Catherine down the boarding plank onto California Street Wharf.

Grigori Balakirev, the general's special advance investigator, waited under a gas streetlight with two large carriages. He clicked his heels toward the general, pivoted, and bowed at the waist toward Lady Catherine. He spoke in Russian. "Your Highness, welcome to America's city of lights."

Lady Catherine glared angrily and General Krestyanov.

The general stepped close to Balakirev and spoke softly in English. "Why do you violate my orders? We are to speak always in English, and never are we to recognize madam's royal station. Our identities must not be known."

Balakirev blinked and lowered his head, acknowledging his mistake.

"Have you secured adequate lodging?"

Balakirev snapped to attention and clicked his heels. He had.

Krestyanov pulled Balakirev to one side, making room for Sacha to assist Lady Catherine into the nearest carriage. He spoke softly to Balakirev. "No bowing or saluting, or snapping of the bootheels. Treat us as equals, when in public."

Balakirev's lips pursed with a quick nod. His lifetime of service and training made this difficult.

Luka Varvarinski, Sacha's older brother, and Lady Catherine's personal bodyguard, loaded luggage onto the second carriage.

Lady Catherine spoke privately with Sacha.

Sacha curtsied and joined her brother in the second carriage.

Krestyanov and Balakirev climbed into the front carriage and sat opposite the duchess. Reins snapped and the carriage lurched forward.

Balakirev said, "The drivers know where to go."

Lady Catherine glared at Balakirev, awaiting his report.

Balakirev cleared his throat and stared at her folded hands, not daring to look directly at her. "We have two suites on the mezzanine level of the Cosmopolitan Hotel. This is on Montgomery Street, well above the filthy peasants of the Barbary Coast and Chinatown."

The general pressed a soft elbow into Balakirev's arm. "What is the report from your investigations?"

"Major Zabalkansky is now known as Mike Zabel. He has done well for himself and is well connected. He now lives on Russian Hill, on Hyde Street." He looked up at the general. "Has the czar not quashed the warrant?"

The general looked into Lady Catherine's night darkened face, impossible to read. "He has. He wants no trouble with America."

Lady Catherine said, "My nephew, Alexander, need not know why we are here. I am not sure he even knows of our trip abroad. He busies himself in Western Europe, trying to raise Russia's status." She cared nothing for the czar's foreign intrigues, only her own.

The general said, "What of those previously assigned to protect the grand duke?"

"Colonel Preslova and the duke's bodyguards have rooms at the St. Francis Hotel. It is not far from the Cosmopolitan. They are part of an investor group managed by Major Zabalkansky. They have invested the grand duke's gold. Of this I am certain."

AFTER SUPPER, MIKE, Jimmy, and Raul helped Molly clear the dining table, while Coira Macauley sat and sipped tea. This irritated Mike, but he said nothing. Running the house was Molly's responsibility. Coira irritated Molly more than she did Mike, and Molly could certainly speak her mind. Why she hadn't yet done so also intrigued Mike. He'd never stopped unfolding the mysteries of Molly, and had always relished each new unfolding of his wonderful wife's deep thoughts.

From the kitchen, Raul said, "I'll go feed and brush Jasmine," Mike's mare.

Mike grabbed a serving tray with a fresh pot of tea and two cups, led Han Wok across the entry hall, and into his office. He turned up two gas wall sconces and fanned toward the chair opposite his desk.

Mike poured tea and sat behind his desk. He leaned his elbows on his desk, sipped tea, and studied Han. "We're buying stock in Central Pacific Railroad. You supplied Chinese labor in building the San Jose Line, so I wanted to talk with you first."

Han waited for more.

"Before we lock in our investment, I will try to secure a contract to supply labor. We will bare the cost and add the total to our stock purchase. This will save them from laying out cash, and should enhance our bid."

Han leaned forward in his chair, eyes wide with questions. "How many labor you need? When can you need these?"

Mike suppressed a smile, remembering his own early clumsiness with English. "The Civil War in the east will end soon. I am certain of this. This will end slavery."

Han nearly slid off his chair, shaking his head so hard. "Chinese not slave. Not same like African in America. Chinese is pay to come America."

Mike put up his hand and smiled. "Take it easy. None of what I've read addresses Chinese labor. The California Legislature is slow

25

to take up this subject. They are not sure how it works." He stared at Han, wanting him to explain.

Han picked up his tea, slid back in his chair, and sipped, not willing to explain without specific questions.

"As I understand it, Chinese immigrants sell themselves into seven years of servitude in exchange for passage, food, and lodging."

Han nodded, *Yes*. He thought for a moment, and then he shook his head. "I do not buy or supply prostitutes. I am good Christian man."

Mike moved on. "We should plan on supplying a labor force of one thousand workers for bidding purposes. We will need gang bosses who speak English and Chinese." He waited for a response.

Han nodded. "Okay. I need bring more from Hong Kong. Most mans who work to San Jose Line already earn freedoms."

"You need anything from us yet?"

Han stared at the ceiling, thinking.

Mike said, "We still need to win the bid. We'll bring them over after that."

"Long sail on. Many work to do in China, get them ready. Long sail on."

"How much more to bring them across by steam?"

Han blinked and sipped. "I check and tell you."

"If it comes to that, we'll pick up the difference. It depends on timing. Sail might work. I don't know yet."

Han nodded and sipped.

"We'll supply field tents, work tools, and food. You'll supply cooking utensils, clothing, and bedding."

Han nodded. "Okay, we bring many family, keep here in Chinatown. They work in many restaurant and laundry."

"Sure. Okay. What do you think, one English speaking Chinese boss for every fifty workers?"

"Some more, some less. Depend on boss." He thought about it. "Twenty gang boss can work okay?"

"That's one for every fifty workers," *like I said.* "What about medicine and injuries."

Han blinked and stared at Mike. He hadn't considered the possibility.

Mike said, "This line will be crossing the tall mountains." He pointed toward the east.

Han blinked at Mike.

"I have a Chinese doctor friend. I'll try to get him here when the time comes. We'll pay for this. We want these future American citizens to be well treated."

Han nodded his agreement, leaned forward, and set his empty teacup on Mike's desk. "Cholera is break out in Chinatown, below Portsmouth Plaza. Sisters of Mercy no take China patient."

"Saint Mary's Hospital on Stockton?" This surprised Mike. This was the county hospital intended to care for the poor. It had been funded by the state legislature.

"Yes. Maybe is sisters." Han flinched. "Maybe somebody no like Chinese."

"I'll talk to Dr. Cole. Not tomorrow. Day after tomorrow."

Han said, "There is some young boy go missing; three by now."

GRIGORI BALAKIREV HAD spent all day with General Krestyanov and the duchess, delivering his complete report, and showing them some of what he'd learned of San Francisco, like where to dine, the theater, and the opera house. He'd departed their company before their evening of dining and vodka. They would never invite him for this. No Romanov would ever think of such an invitation.

He would much rather be assigned to the Czar's personal guard, as he had been under Czar Nicholas II. Working advance security for a czar had been noble and good. Security under the duchess had strained his professional integrity. Since the death of her brother, Grigory had been reassigned to her protection at the personal request of General Krestyanov. Grigori would not mind this, except she often mistreated those in her service because of her perpetual rage. Perhaps he would follow Colonel Preslova's path and simply slip away.

Niet.

Preslova and his two companions had been found, thanks to Gregori's hard work. Major, the Count Mikhail Diebitsch-Zabalkansky had been found, thanks to Grigori's hard work.

The sun had long gone when his taxi turned onto California Street and sped downhill toward the docks. At the sound of horse hooves on wood, Grigori leaned out the window, watching for Duncan Frack's blacksmith shop.

He tapped the front wall of the taxi.

The taxi stopped and he climbed down. He paid the driver and turned toward a small brick and wood building locals called the Forge.

The blacksmith who'd owned the building had been shot dead over a game of cards. Duncan Frack, the other card player, had claimed the building as winnings. Duncan and his Mexican lady had immediately moved into the already furnished rooms above the shop.

Had it not been for Duncan's help in finding Count Zabalkansky and Colonel Preslova, Grigori Balakirev would never go down to the Barbary Coast; too much gambling, too much drinking, and too much prostitution. Worse, crimpers like Shanghai

Kelly might club or drug a man and put him out to sea against his will.

Grigori pushed through the half-open, weathered-wood door, passed through the vestibule, passed through another door, turned at the stairs, and entered the shop.

Duncan's heavy wool coat, broadbrimmed hat, and outer garments hung on hooks under the stairs.

Duncan kept a coal fire going at the brick-hearth firepit all of the time, making it too warm to ever need a coat.

Grigori removed his overcoat and hung it next to Duncan's.

Duncan turned and smiled. "Just in time."

"This again? Why you do this?"

Duncan glanced at the small, naked, Chinese boy huddled at the hearth. "I like it. You need to try some of this. I get . . ." Duncan spread his arms and shivered with excitement. "I get stimulated. I get . . ." He smiled. "It gives me power. I can't explain it. It just does."

Duncan moved easily for a big man, powerfully built for his height. "These Chinese boys . . . Their skin is so . . ." He stroked the little boy's back. "Like silk."

Duncan slowly unbuttoned the top of his long underwear and turned back to the young boy. "Did you get enough to eat? Are you warm enough?"

Tears streamed from the child's eyes. Fear choked his speech. "What you want? Ooh!" This was a cry for help. "What you want with Won?" The boy looked to be between five to eight years old, not yet big enough for work.

Grigori turned toward the door, not wanting to watch, but he couldn't help himself. He turned back. "Why you do this? He is child."

Duncan turned his back on Grigori. "You should try some of this, Grigori. I know you'd like it."

"I already don't like. I have two sons, five and seven. I miss them."

Duncan turned back, stepped close, and looked down at Grigori. "I got my reasons. I think you want to watch this."

"I thought we will talk about bringing Count Zabalkansky before the general and the duchess."

"Your count Mike is well connected and hard to get at. And, he's plenty tough. We need to bring him to us, alone. What I do to these boys will be known to him. We'll see to that. When we take his wife and son, he'll panic." He poked Grigori's shoulder. "He'll come running."

Grigori blinked and stepped back. Duncan's logic seemed clear. Grigory could not find fault with this plan.

Tears of fear sheeted down the child's face. "What you do?"

Grigori wanted no part in the terrible act soon to be committed. "What about your woman?"

"She knows never to come down here. She likes it when I go upstairs, strong and ready." He again poked Grigori's shoulder. "This power is real." He looked at the boy. "She likes it fine." He turned back to Grigori. "I'd wager your duchess knows this kind of power."

Chapter Four

AT 8:45 A.M., MIKE and Abe Warner departed one of about fifty taxis lined up on the brick street in front of San Francisco's Mission Station, and merged into a squeeze of travelers coming and going on another crisp, foggy morning.

A half block down the line, John Downey and Billy Cahill climbed down from another taxi and dodged between other travelers toward Mike and Abe.

The train whistle blew once, the signal to board.

Abe led the way to the loading platform amid the crush of boarding passengers.

Mike guided the group onto the second of four passenger cars and ushered them to their assigned seats.

The train whistle blew a second time and the train jerked noisily forward.

Abe smiled and shook his head. "God, I love this. It's only my third time."

Mike liked it too.

Picking up speed, already moving quickly past buildings, John Downey said, "The feel of steam powered locomotion is an elixir for the spirit. Rail transportation is our future, gentleman."

Either caustic or sarcastic with every Downey pontification, Abe said, "Aha! Our brilliant narrator explains it all . . . again."

Abe and Billy laughed and looked away, not trying to be mean. They couldn't help themselves.

John, of course, did not like it.

Mike pushed down on John's bouncing knee, calming his famous temper. "I spoke with Han Wok last night about providing labor for Central Pacific. We will negotiate the purchase of their servitude and bulk it in with our investment dollars. We will also make an allowance for tents, food, and medicines. I have sent a telegram to my friend, Doctor Chiang Po. We will negotiate a monthly fee for his services."

Abe nudged Mike's arm. "I, for one, have always appreciated your thoroughness."

John's knee jumped back into motion as he leaned close to Warner's pointed nose. "What, you think the rest of us don't?"

"You . . ." Abe squared to John, both still in their seats.

Mike put a hand on each of their shoulders to keep them apart. "We will make the cost of this labor a part of our cash bid for rail stocks. This will save them money on their initial investments. It should strengthen our position. I've already spoken with the governor. He's working with Secretary Seward to finalize a budget with the U.S. Congress. Federal funds will pay for up to half of the total cost. The railroad will be built, gentlemen. Of this I am certain."

John leaned back, relaxing.

Mike knew these men and what they were thinking. John knew the federal government would make sure the railroad would be finished. Politicians loved throwing other people's money around, often throwing good money after bad. They could never admit they'd made a mistake.

John stiffened with a thought. "Seward won't like slave labor."

Mike smiled. "Chinese labor is not technically slavery. They trade their labor for passage, food, and shelter. It's voluntary, not forced."

John shook his head. "Seward's more antislavery than Abe Lincoln."

Abe Warner squirmed in his seat, ready to verbally pounce. "I'm giving Mike my approval so he can place the bid. What are you . . ."

"I'm just saying . . ."

Mike kept Abe from standing.

Abe said, "Saying what?"

Mike smiled into Abe's conjured rage. "I cannot guarantee it will work, but I need your approval to make the bid. I have already received this from Colonel Preslova."

"Oh." John twitched, acting like he had never before heard of this. "Okay. Go ahead."

"Billy?"

"The widow said to follow your lead."

Mike appreciated her reliance on his judgments but, at times, it seemed an uncomfortable burden. What if something went wrong? "Why don't you ask her and the kids to join us for a train ride? I'll bring Molly and Jimmy."

Outside the train, three horsemen rode fast, steadily getting closer to the train. Their hats dropped below the windows.

Mike braced off Abe's bony shoulder and stood. He leaned toward the window for a better look.

He stood into the aisle and said, "Everybody keep your seats and stay still, so nobody gets hurt. We're being robbed."

A squat man stepped into the forward doorway of the passenger car holding a twin-barreled shotgun chest high, aiming it at Mike. His broadbrimmed hat had been pulled low over a flour sack with jagged mouth and eye cutouts.

Mike eased back into his seat.

A tall, broad-shouldered man in a dark wool coat and broadbrimmed black hat stepped into the car from behind his shotgun toting partner. He wore the same type of flour sack mask. He pulled off his hat and held it out with his left hand. His right hand gripped a Colt revolver, fanning it side-to-side. He looked at

33

Mike and his eyes held a hint of recognition. "Put your guns under your seats and nobody gets shot. Then drop your valuables into this here hat. Somebody puts nothing in here will get clubbed good and hard." His gun hand twitched, aiming it at Mike.

Mike pulled his hip holstered revolver and set it on the floor.

Abe and John both pulled their shoulder holstered revolvers and set them on the floor.

Others on the fast-moving passenger car did the same.

Mike reached slowly to his inside pocket and dragged out his coin purse, unintentionally exposing his gold watch chain but not his shoulder holstered Colt.

Switching from side to side, collecting purses and pocket watches, the tall bandit stood between Mike and the other bandit, making it impossible for Mike to move. The shorter man's chest high shotgun would certainly kill somebody.

The big man reached Mike, held out the hat, and Mike and the others all dropped their purses into the nearly full hat. The big man motioned with his gun.

Mike delivered his gold watch and chain, a long-held gift from Molly.

Abe and John pulled and delivered their silver watches and chains. Billy shook his head and opened his jacket, showing he had nothing.

The big mad backhanded Billy with his pistol, not very hard.

Billy's eyes darkened with anger, something Mike had never before seen from his longtime friend.

The big man moved to the next row of seats.

Abe, John, and Billy stared at Mike, demanding he do something.

Being a special investigator for the state police, Mike grinned into their stares and looked at the shotgun. *What can I do?*

The shorter bandit held his shotgun close to the head of a wet cheeked woman in the first row. At that range, it would remove a big chunk of her skull.

Mike knew this rail line. They must be nearing the wide curve above San Mateo. He tensed, planning his move. He turned slowly and looked toward the rear.

The big man had only a few more passengers before he reached the rear door, no doubt working their way toward the caboose. There would be a safe back there.

Mike turned slowly forward.

The squat man stood at the forward door, his eyes and shotgun trained at Mike's face.

Good.

The passenger car lurched and swayed through the San Mateo curve.

The squat man reached up to grab the overhead luggage rack for support, pointing the shotgun skyward.

With fluid motion, Mike dropped to one knee in the aisle, pulled his shoulder holstered revolver, pulled back the hammer, took careful aim, and squeezed the trigger.

BOOM!

The squat man's eyes flashed with surprise, as the bullet smacked a black hole through the flour sack, an inch under his left eyehole. Bright red blood sprayed the door behind. The man's jaw hit the back of the woman's seat on his way to the floor. The shotgun went down with him, still cocked.

Mike spun for the bigger man but he'd already gone.

Billy and John craned to look out the closed windows.

Mike jumped to his feet, close behind Abe, and pressed his head to the window glass.

The bigger man tumbled down the gravel slope, hat held tightly to his chest, not spilling a single trinket or coin.

Abe yanked the emergency cord.

The train broke hard.

Billy reached for John, too late.

John tumbled forward down the aisle.

A woman on horseback towed two horses toward the big man.

The train slowed quickly, still rounding the curve.

Mike's view became blocked by rail cars. He rushed through the open rear door.

With the train slowing to a stop, Mike jumped down to the gravel base and stepped away from the train. He quickly reached a line of sight beyond the end of the train.

The big man handed the hat to the woman, too far away for a revolver. He grabbed reins of both spare horses and mounted one. They turned toward San Francisco, kicked their horses, and rode quickly into tall brush.

Mike walked back to his car and climbed aboard. He holstered his Colt and nudged his way forward. "Step aside, please. Take your seats."

Only about half of the passengers sat, but they all stepped aside.

John Downey, Abe Warner, and Billy Cahill followed Mike to the forward door. Mike rolled the dead man onto his back and removed the hat and flour-sack mask. "Does anybody recognize this man?" Mike did not.

The others shook their heads.

John glared at Mike. "You said trains never get robbed. They took my Comstock watch."

OVER THE PAST EIGHT years, Weaverville had been good for Chiang SuLin and Chiang Po, her father. After that terrible fire, Winston Bray had built a bigger house on her uncle's property. This house had been built of brick with two bedrooms, a real kitchen, a big room for dining and reading, and a front room for her father's medical clinic.

Following public hearings, her uncle's gold mine had been returned to them. It still provided small but steady income, even after they split with two Chinese men who did the labor.

SuLin still heard from her count, married now with a son. His wife, Molly, sent a letter every Christmas to report news from the city. SuLin's only sadness came from still being single and pure, twenty-four years old already. She had so many questions about what it meant to be in love, to be with a man.

Someone knocked at their front door.

SuLin covered her pot of roasting rabbit, wiped her hands on her apron, and hurried through the dining room.

Po worked at the table in his clinic, preparing herbs and refilling his supplies.

She brushed past him and opened the door.

The telegraph runner, a teenage boy, handed her a small envelope and smiled. "Telegram from San Francisco, for you, ma'am." He turned off the porch and hurried back down the trail.

Early winter snow fell from a stone-gray sky, and a clean, pine scent filled the air.

Her heart skipped.

She closed the door and stood near the window for better light.

My count. She tore it open.

"To Chiang SuLin STOP We have cholera in Chinatown STOP Can you come STOP Mike."

MIDMORNING THAT DAY, Donald Thorne finally departed *Golden City*, a steamer up from Panama. He tucked the heavy canvas satchel tight under his left arm and dragged the rebel brat onto Pacific Street Wharf.

The kid hadn't spoken for nearly three weeks after leaving her plantation. Her silence had ended as soon as they'd boarded the train in Panama. She'd been asking for her mommy and daddy ever since.

He'd told her that her daddy died in the war and that her momma got too sick to take care of her.

He grinned with the memory of her momma. As far as this little brat knew, he was her uncle on her momma's side. He sometimes wished he'd done away with the brat and left her with her momma. The thing of it was, in a few more years, she'd be a prime moneymaker. He'd make a fortune, as long as she never got knocked up. This pretty little rebel would be as irresistible as her momma had been.

He looked at her bright eyes, at the way they looked back at him. He never thought he'd like a kid, but there she was. She'd crawled under his thick skin.

There it is. He'd seen the advertising banners off the side of *Golden City*, and he'd heard the barkers on that sloop, shouting out for Tommy Chandler's Boardinghouse.

He knelt on the wharf and pulled the child close, smiling nice as he could. "This place might be our home for a while. The owner might not like kids, so you need to be quiet. Okay?"

Her stubborn little chin poked out and her eyes fixed on his. "Do I get a new dress? Mine's dirty, and it smells bad." She'd worn the same dress since Savannah.

He smiled. "Sure." He gave her a little hug, stood, and pulled her inside.

The main room looked clean enough. Some ladies in bright colored frills leaned over a table in the far corner, a gossiping bunch of clucking hens. Boxing billboards and fliers covered the wall behind the bar, all of the man standing under them. He'd aged some.

"You Tommy Chandler?"

Chandler looked up from his newspaper. "I don't allow kids. We cater mostly to men off ships."

Thorne thumped the heavy satchel onto the bar and lifted the brat up next to it. "This here's gold coin, worth its weight. You got a problem with that?"

"Gold's always good here. How long you want a room?"

Thorne said, "I need to be able to lock it."

"I only have one room available. It's got four beds. If I can't rent the other two beds, it'll cost you extra."

"I need to be able to lock it."

"I'll have a lock put on, later today. You'll need to pay for that."

"Fine." Thorn looked over at the corner table. "Any of your girls baby sit? I can pay."

"You need to ask them."

"She needs bathing, a new dress, and someone to care after her."

"You need to ask them."

Thorne turned.

Two of the ladies stretched their clothing from too much to eat. One looked maybe fifty. The one in the far corner filled her slender dress nicely, looking Thorne up and down. She smiled at the brat.

"She'll do."

Chapter Five

ON APRIL 9th, 1865, with cold snow still on the ground, twenty-nine-year-old Captain Franklin Adam Mosby stood in the forest next to his thirty-one-year-old brother, Colonel John Singleton Mosby, known as the Gray Ghost for his guerilla tactics in command of the 43rd Battalion of the Northern Virginia Cavalry Regiment, proudly serving under General Robert E. Lee and Major General James Ewell Brown "Jeb" Stuart.

Franklin worshipped his older brother, always a leader, always pushing forward. He'd once been convicted for shooting the son of an innkeeper, a much larger man who'd been known as a bully. While in prison, John studied the law. At the early age of twenty-two, upon release from prison, he'd registered with the Virginia Bar and opened his own law practice in Howardsville, Virginia.

About that time, when Franklin had just turned twenty, their mother received word of the death of her favorite uncle, Jacob Forsythe Winston. His wife and two children had succumbed to scarlet fever years earlier. In his will, he'd left his various properties to his favorite niece, Belinda, John and Franklin's mother. She'd immediately transferred everything to her two sons, and John had signed everything over to Franklin. Nobody wanted to move down to Georgia. They all loved the serenity of life in Virginia.

Being the youngest, it had fallen on Franklin to make the move. Having an adventurous nature made it easy. Looking back, it had become his life's greatest blessing.

In early 1856, at the young age of twenty, Franklin had boarded a train and headed south to Atlanta. He'd switched trains in Atlanta and arrived in Savannah early the next morning, where he'd quickly found the office of Elias Thornton, the attorney who'd sent word to his mother.

It took more than an hour for Attorney Thornton to read the will and deliver deeds to Winterbridge Manor, a plantation just west of Savanna, Winston Dry Goods, a warehouse and store in Savannah, Winston Hotel in Savannah, and savings certificates from two banks.

Unexpectedly a wealthy young man, Franklin had been both surprised and delighted. Feeling a duty to do so, he'd immediately notified his parents and his brother John. They'd congratulated him on his good fortune, and they'd all refused to consider any sharing of his newfound wealth. It all belonged to Franklin.

Attorney Thornton had taken him two blocks from his office to the Winston Hotel, a small hotel near the river. The three-story, red brick building of simple design now belonged to Franklin. He'd checked in for the night.

Thornton, being a true southern gentleman, had invited Franklin to dine at his home. He'd sent a carriage at 6:00 p.m.

The evening breezes had been cool but not cold. Riding in an open carriage, enjoying the canopy of spring budding trees, Franklin had marveled at the natural and manmade beauty of Savannah. Most impossible to believe, was that the people seemed more congenial than did the citizenry of Virginia. He'd since come to the realization that Virginia had too many politicians.

He would never forget that most fortuitous day and evening; the evening when he'd first met seventeen-year-old Allison Thornton, beautiful, bright, and very outspoken. He'd immediately fallen in love.

After a year of courting, only meeting when properly chaperoned, they'd been married at the Independent Presbyterian Church of Savannah on Bull Street. Ten months later, she'd given birth to their beautiful daughter, Melanie. He'd not seen them since Christmas, 1863, a short Christmas leave for officers. Trains and connections had still been running through Atlanta.

Before the war, big brother, John, had argued against secession, but he'd joined the Confederacy out of loyalty to his beloved Virginia, his friends, and his neighbors. He'd started as an infantry private and sharpshooter. Under J.E.B. Stuart, he'd become a scout. A year later, he'd called for volunteers to form a special guerilla unit. They'd since become known as Mosby's Raiders. His call for volunteers had fetched Franklin into the war.

General Lee and Colonel Stuart had found John so effective, building his raiders to more than 1,900 mounted troops, they'd promoted him to the rank of colonel.

Upon reporting to his brother's command, Franklin had been commissioned captain and assigned as his brother's adjutant.

Hiding in the forest that day, a thousand yards from the Wilmer McClean residence in the township of Appomattox Court House, John, Franklin and more than 1,000 remaining raiders were near starvation.

General Sheridan's Union soldiers had them surrounded and cut off from supplies. With the fall of Georgia, the heart to fight on had fallen out of the south, though many remained loyal to the cause of maintaining the gracious southern culture.

That which remained of Lee's once proud regiment stood in the open field outside the McClean residence, vastly outnumbered by the Union troop formations to their direct north.

Mosby's Raiders hid in the forest in bewildered silence, watching General Robert E. Lee, the general they had so proudly served, dismount from his white charger and step to the ground in front of the house.

Lee's second in command, Major General J.E.B. Stuart, dismounted, and both officers marched slowly up the steps to waiting Union officers. Lee and Stuart, in full dress uniforms, looked far more elegant than did any of the Yankees.

The Union staff followed Lee and Stuart inside and left the front door open.

A few minutes later, General Ulysses S. Grant arrived with two other Yankee officers, dismounted, climbed the steps, entered the house, and closed the door.

Twenty minutes later, Lee and Stuart walked out onto the porch. Stuart fanned his hat in a circular pattern and put it on, the signal they'd been waiting for. Their terms of surrender had been accepted.

Confederate officers would be allowed to keep their horses and sidearms, and all of Lee's regiment would receive rations.

John turned to face Franklin. "That's it, then."

They moved deeper into the forest and were quickly surrounded by what was left of their Battalion of raiders.

John climbed onto a tree stump. "You'll all get fed. Officers will keep their horses and weapons. Enlisted men will surrender their sidearms, but you may keep your rifles and horses. Just tell the Union officers that the horses are your own private property, and that you'll need them for spring planting. After you've eaten your fill and surrendered your sidearms, you'll all be free to return to your homes."

Captain Jefferson asked, "What about you, Colonel?"

"They've put a five-thousand-dollar bounty on my head. I think I'll stay in the woods for a while."

Major Hollister smiled and said, "Are those Yankee dollars, Colonel?"

This brought soft laughter from those near enough to hear.

Franklin said, "Weren't we all supposed to be pardoned?"

"I'm sure there's no problem with you and the rest. I'm the only one with a bounty. Hopefully, it will soon be rescinded. Maybe it already has been."

Major Hackenbush stepped close. "About that, Colonel. Many of us want to fight on. No retreat, no surrender. We can rejoin our boys in the south, regain our strength, and we can still win."

John slowly removed his cavalry hat, pulled his handkerchief, and wiped inside the sweatband, visibly drained of his usual vitality. "Major . . ." His disappointment showed in his gaze upon Hackenbush. "You were there last night when this very subject was discussed."

John replaced his hat, tucked his handkerchief into his glove, and scanned full circle, making eye contact with many of his men. "Boys, the war is over. General Lee has surrendered with terms we all discussed last night. General Stuart has given the signal. Our terms of surrender have been accepted. All you boys will be allowed to keep your rifles for the purpose of hunting game, not Yankees."

Soft murmurs swept through the pines.

"Officers will be allowed to keep their sidearms. All of you can keep your horses. They're your private property since before the war. General Grant knows they'll be needed for spring plowing."

John looked at Major Hackenbush. "General Lee was asked about fighting on, and about rejoining the rest of the army to the south for a guerilla war. The general told us how bad this would be for our beloved Virginia, and for the rest of the south. He knows we'd be hunted as criminals, and as traitors. He knows there'd be no Confederate Government to feed, arm, and support us. He knows we'd be forced to steal from our fellow countrymen just to survive. I don't think any of you want to do that." He stared down at Major Hackenbush.

Hackenbush had attended the previous night's meeting. He removed his hat and stared at his boots.

John slowly turned on the tree stump, looking at his men. "You've been the finest, bravest men I've ever had the pleasure of knowing. Your valor is not in question. You've been loyal, brave, and noble. Now is the time to go home and rebuild your lives. It won't be easy, but it will be far better than living as outlaws, away from your families, and away from your homes. The war is over. Go home and rebuild."

FRANKLIN TRAVELED ALL day and into the night getting to his parents' home in western Virginia. After kisses and hugs from his mother and a long, tugging handshake from his father, his mom's worried eyes searched Franklin's. "Where's John?"

"He's fine. He's gone into hiding. There's still a bounty of five-thousand Yankee dollars on his head, dead or alive."

His father said, "Damnable Yankees. If the war's over, it should be over. His surrender ought to be enough. He stood against secession before the war, for heaven's sake."

Mom said, "We want both of our sons back."

Franklin said, "He doesn't dare visit here, or try to see his wife and daughter. He's trying to get word to General Grant."

Mom said, "Why on earth would he want to see him?"

Franklin said, "The word among General Lee's staff officers is that Grant is a fair man."

A pig squealed loudly from out back, probably getting his throat slit.

Mom glanced out the rear window, turned back with a smile, and wrung her hands with her apron. "You hungry, honey?"

Chapter Six

AFTER LEAVING HIS PARENTS' home, wearing his cleaned and pressed Confederate officer's uniform, Captain Franklin Adam Mosby followed the roads southeast toward Georgia.

Without the railroad, much of which had been destroyed by General Sherman, he rode southeast through Virginia and the Carolinas for two weeks, dejected, defeated, dirty, and hungry. His horse, Domino, named for her black coat and white markings, didn't mind the slow travel. She had plenty of spring grass and water. For Franklin, the slow pace proved a burden. His impatience for home had been forced to give way. Railroad travel had become unpredictable to impossible.

On his second day in Georgia, he was greeted by still proud folks, still friendly to Franklin's Confederate uniform. Only their eagerness to share what little they had had kept Franklin from starvation.

Nearing Atlanta, fear struck deep. Burned buildings and angry faces greeted him at every turn. His regiment had received word about Sherman's march through Georgia but he hadn't expected to find such destruction. Rails had been pulled up, piled onto bonfires, bent, and twisted beyond any possibility of future use.

Dear God . . .

What would he find at Winterbridge Manor? What about his wife and daughter? He'd heard the stories of Yankee stragglers raping and murdering? To Sherman's credit, when caught, these criminals had been shot or hanged.

Winterbridge wagons had been hauling cotton into the warehouses, the mills, and the ports of Savannah for more than a hundred years. With the war drawn to a close, would his plantation be able to return to its former productivity?

Dear God...

Winterbridge Manor lay well off the highway. The Yankees might never see Winterbridge. *I pray not.*

Domino slow-walked around a curve in the gravel road and Franklin stiffened.

A command tent had been set up with a roadblock two hundred yards ahead. Two Yankee soldiers stood on the road with rifles, looking his way.

Nearing the roadblock, Franklin buttoned his tunic, straightened his hat, pulled rein on Domino, and stepped down to the road.

A Yankee sergeant leveled his rifle and pointed it directly at Franklin's belly. "Where you coming from, Reb?"

Franklin broke a slight but friendly smile. He wanted no trouble. "I served in the army of Northern Virginia under General Lee."

"You was at Appomattox?"

"I was."

"You'll need to surrender your horse and sidearm." The Yankee aimed his rifle at Franklin's nose.

Franklin looked overhead at the telegraph wire. A drop wire led to the command tent. "We were told otherwise, sergeant. According to . . ."

The sergeant pressed the butt of his rifle to his shoulder and pulled back the hammer with an angry shout. "You will surrender your sidearm and horse."

Franklin slowly lifted his hands in surrender. His friendly attitude had been replaced by fear.

A whiskered major stepped through the flap of the command tent and climbed onto the road. "At ease, sergeant."

"Sir?" The sergeant kept his rifle tight to his shoulder and turned his stare to his commanding officer, questioning the order.

The major held eye contact with the sergeant, put his hand on the rifle barrel, and gently pushed it away from Franklin's face.

Franklin slowly lowered his hands.

The major swung his back in front of the sergeant and stepped closer to Franklin, examining his uniform and looking into his eyes. "You rode with General Lee?"

"Yes sir, I did."

The major said, "I took a class of his at West Point. He was a true gentleman."

"Yes, major. He still is."

"A mite confused with his loyalties, says I." His tight smile did not invite debate.

"Not anymore. He's ordered us to go home and get on with our lives. Since we all brought our own horses in the beginning, General Grant has allowed everybody to take their horses home. We'll need them for spring planting."

The major's steel bright eyes narrowed with intensity. "Some of you rebels don't follow orders too well."

What? Franklin had heard nothing.

The major detected Franklin's doubt and turned to his sergeant. They stared at each other for what seemed an hour, probably 30 seconds, and the major turned back. "We've had problems around here with rebel raiders. They're stealing horses and food stores. Even shot one of my men."

"I hope, sir, that he will recover."

The third Yankee soldier moved to Domino's hind quarter, examining the brand. He stepped away and shook his head. "She's not one of ours."

The major blinked back anger and leaned closer to Franklin. "Maybe you haven't heard the worst. President Lincoln's dead. He was shot by a rebel named John Wilkes Booth. Andrew Johnson's now the president of these here United States of America." He pointed down at the road, at Georgia soil.

Franklin stepped back, stunned, with no idea what to say.

The major crossed his arms and stared into Franklin. "Policy toward you rebels is a might uncertain right now. Where you headed?"

"Savannah."

The major blinked and shook his head, a slight smile. "You're a lucky man. General Sherman spared Savannah. The mayor down there surrendered and promised there'd be no trouble. Far as I know, his word proved true. There's been no organized trouble in Savannah." He waited for Franklin's response.

Franklin had nothing to say.

"You headed straight through?"

"I want nothing more than to get home, sir."

JOHN JACKSON YOUNGBLOOD had recovered from the knife cut across his upper chest. The blade had barely missed his throat, after he'd been knocked unconscious from behind.

On Christmas Day, the plantation darkies had set a cot on the family plot so as John could oversee the burial of Mistress Allison. They'd all loved her so.

They'd laid her under two leafless oaks on the rise above the river. Nice view from there. Across the river, the western end of Hutchinson Island looked far off. South Carolina was too far off to see through the mix of trees.

All seven slave families had attended her burial; thirty-two darkies aged six to eighty-one, all of them weeping and carrying on.

I don't know. They'd possibly been crying more about what might happen to them than over the death of Allison Mosby. They'd asked many times about their futures.

John had no idea what might happen.

Here on Winterbridge Manor, they'd always been allowed their own vegetable gardens along the river, long as they kept up with the plowing, planting, and harvesting of cotton and corn. Anyone who didn't do their work got sold at auction. None of the families here wanted that. Winterbridge had always provided a good life for darkies.

Now was April, going on May, with still no word on the war.

They'd all heard of General Lee's surrender, someplace up in Virginia, up where Master Franklin went, but still no definite word on the end of the war.

As soon as he'd gotten up and was able to move, John had gone into Savannah to see Moses Broadback and Mr. Greenwood. He'd told them of the murder of Mistress Allison, and showed them the scabbed cut across his upper chest.

They'd both assured him how lucky he was to be alive, and Moses had showed him charcoal sketches he'd done of the man who'd killed the mistress and taken little Miss Melanie. The sketches showed a strong resemblance to Melanie. Sketches of the bearded man sitting next to her on Master Franklin's wagon, wearing one of Master Franklin's suits of clothes, m"Sir?"ost likely resembled the murderer, much as Miss Melanie's sketches resembled her.

John asked, "She's still alive then?"

"Yes. But she's been taken." Moses told of how he'd followed them all the way downriver to a fishing sloop bound down to Key West, how he'd overheard mention of a place called San Francisco, of how this murderer had paid Confederate gold coin for their passage from a heavy canvas satchel.

John said, "The master's gold got took." Winterbridge had no money for planting.

There'd been no market for cotton for the past two years, Yankee blockades and such, but Winterbridge slaves had still cleared and planted. Master Franklin's mules had still hauled bulk into his warehouse in Savannah, near full to overflowing. Black mold had started showing on bails touched by rain.

Work to be done.

War over or not, Winterbridge Manor had supported every man, woman, and child. Slave or free, John knew they'd all want to stay. They'd be happy to sharecrop, from then on.

Master Franklin had discussed possible sharecropping with John two Christmases past. They'd even discussed that option as far back as the attack on Fort Sumter, over yonder in Charleston, that being the first beginning of the war.

None of the Winterbridge slaves knew what freedom might mean. After Fort Sumter, they could have chosen to be free at any time. The master had given them the option. All had elected to stay.

There had been evidence of bad treatment on other plantations, the whippings, the sweat boxes, some forced to fight to the death with other slaves for the purpose of whites gambling. None of that happened here. Nor had Winterbridge Manor ever seen dog fights or cock fights.

John had long since decided to stay on at Winterbridge, no matter what.

Eager for any news, John had taken turns with other slaves, watching the road through their fields, while weeding freshly planted corn crop. Maybe some Yankees would come to burn them down, like they'd already burned some of their neighbors. Maybe some no-count runaway slaves would come to kill and rob.

What . . . A gray rider on a black horse rode slowly up the rise toward him, a black horse with white markings.

"Domino?"

John took two steps and broke into a run. Other slaves bled from the fields onto the road, following Domino up the shallow rise.

The gray rider dismounted and took off his hat, more whiskered than before the war.

Gathering slaves mumbled and stared down at their feet. Some gazed over the top of Master Franklin's head. None dared look straight at him, fearing he might be a ghost.

Master Franklin smiled, relieved. "John Jackson, you're surely a sight for these tired eyes." He threw an arm over John's shoulder, giving him a short hug. "The Yankees passed over Winterbridge Manor?"

Master Franklin's visible gratitude nearly dropped John to his knees. He didn't yet know what had happened.

John backed away and stared at Domino's hooves, unable to speak of it.

Master Franklin turned slowly, looking at the other slaves. "The war is over. Winterbridge Manor no longer owns any of you. You're all free to go wherever you want."

May Bell, one of the house darkies, said, "What we going to do? Where we going to go?"

John said, "We all want to stay, sir. We'll do the sharecrop plan, like you promised."

Master Franklin smiled, a mite shy. "Won't be much in wages. Yankees are sure to demand a war tax. Mistress Allison will want to continue your educations, I'm sure." He turned and looked toward the manor house. "Where's the mistress and my Melanie?"

"Sir . . ." Tears flowed down John's cheeks. He wiped them away but more followed. He turned and led Franklin to the small graveyard where generations of Winston family headstones lined the ridge. All faced the river. Allison's grave had been adorned with a finely crafted headstone, much more elaborate than those of the Winston family.

Franklin fell face down on the already grassy mound. His sobs near crushed John's chest.

FRANKLIN WOKE THE NEXT morning, stretched out across Allison's grave, alone, tired from not much sleep. John hadn't yet explained what had happened. Franklin's imaginings hadn't allowed sleep until shortly before dawn.

He stood, brushed off his uniform, and walked slowly toward the house. Without Allison, it didn't feel like home.

Melanie. He still had her.

Seeing him coming, May Bell spun off the front veranda and rushed toward the cookhouse.

All right, then. Franklin needed to eat something. He took a chair at the small table on the veranda and emptiness overwhelmed him.

May Bell brought pealed orange wedges, two split apricots, and a pot of hot tea with one cup.

One cup.

"May Bell, where's my daughter? Is she in Savannah with her grandparents?"

May Bell leaned back and blinked, surprised by his question. "Sir, she got took by the man who kilt Mistress Allison."

"What?" Franklin leaned over the table and braced to stand.

"Sorry, sir. I thought John Jackson already told you."

"No, he did not." He leaned back in his chair with no place to go.

May Bell poured his tea and hurried toward the cookhouse.

He sipped tea without looking at the fruit.

A minute later, May Bell delivered steaming biscuits and gravy. Her soft voice shook. "Good to have you home, sir."

He had no appetite for food. "You see what happened May Bell?"

"No sir. I was in the cookhouse with Sissy and Jasper. Jasper had just brought in some chopped wood."

"Who put up Mistress Allison's gravestone?"

"Her daddy come out, sir. He never knew till after. He don't like her being already buried."

Franklin choked back stomach acid and hot tea, momentarily unable to speak. He sucked air, swallowed, and sipped tea. "Was there no coffin, May Bell?"

"Oh, yes sir. Jasper and Clarence cut one from a oak stump. Took near two days of burning out and carving but it sure did look proper. Gave me and Sissy time to clean and dress the mistress real fine."

"Was she . . ." Franklin couldn't say it.

May Bell looked away and hugged her belly, shaking her head. She wouldn't go there.

"Tell me, May Bell, was the man cruel? Did she suffer?"

Tears flooded down May Bell's cheeks. "Oh, sir, what that man done." She dropped to her knees and shook from sobbing, still hugging her stomach.

"Tell me, May Bell."

"Oh, sir." She gagged on her sobs. "He violate the mistress real bad." Her hand pressed toward her pelvis. "He cut her womb open wide, sir. I think after he done raped her." Her head shot up, tears flowing. "Then he gone and cut her neck." May Bell touched her fingers to her throat and looked away.

Franklin stared up at the wood slat ceiling over his veranda. *Why, dear Lord?* Franklin's deep grief drifted toward rage. "Was there no preacher, May Bell?"

"No, sir. John was too bad hurt to go into Savannah."

"Could nobody else go?"

May Bell looked away, ashamed to speak of their collective fear of leaving Winterbridge Manor. "John only woke up the morning she got buried. We carried him out on his cot to oversee her burying. He off and on slept when we sung her some gospel songs. Was three days later, when he went into Savannah. Her father come out, next day."

"He supplied her gravestone?"

"Yes, sir. It come later. Him, some deputies, and some Yankees looked all over Savannah for little Melie. He never went into the store to see Moses. Never look at them drawings. Never heard what Moses Broadback heard."

"What of Allison's mother?" *What? Moses? Sketches . . .* May Bell's words finally slammed into the back of Franklin's brain.

"Her momma died last year, sir. Moses come out to tell how she got took away by the consumption. The mistress and little Melie went to help put her into the churchyard."

"What about Moses?"

John Jackson climbed onto the veranda with something to say.

Franklin motioned to a chair. "Have you eaten yet, John?"

"Yes, sir. Ate some hominy and catfish." He helped May Bell to her feet and sat across from Franklin, nervous about something.

"What is it, John?"

"I was unconscious when that man come onto the manor house and . . ." He lowered his head.

"What?"

John wouldn't look at Franklin. He looked out toward the barn and pointed to the back of his head. "He hit me here and dislocated my senses." He turned back and looked down at his shaking knees. He hesitated then pulled open his shirt to show a long, pink scar across his upper chest. "He cut me and left me for dead." Tears flowed down his high cheeks. "I'm so . . ." His lips quivered, unable to say more.

"Easy, John. I will not allow you to blame yourself for this."

John leaned forward, suddenly eager to speak. "I went into Savannah soon as I could. Mr. Greenwood and Moses Broadback saw Miss Melie on your wagon with a man wearing your clothes. Moses followed them downriver. They boarded a fishing sloop bound for Key West, said something about San Francisco. Moses did up a bunch of sketches. I tried to say so yesterday, but you was . . . I was . . ."

Fresh hope rushed through Franklin, renewing his energy. "It's okay, John. One day won't make much difference." He chomped down slices of fruit before slurping biscuits and gravy.

"May Bell, lay out some fresh clothes and draw me a bath. Then pack my bag for travel."

May Bell rushed into the house.

Franklin turned back. "John, you'll need to be master for a while. Mister Greenwood will purchase seed and take care of any taxes. Whatever he pays you should be split into equal shares. You keep two shares for yourself. Don't let me come home and find a dirty house or rundown fields."

John winced like he'd been slapped.

"Sorry, John. I know you'll do right. I guess I've been an army officer for too long."

"That murderer took up the hearth upstairs. I set it back but your gold's been took."

"I thought sure that would be used up by now." He would need to find money from somewhere. "Get Domino fed, brushed, and saddled . . . please."

Chapter Seven

SAM GREENWOOD'S BACK faced the door when Franklin entered his store. He turned to stock sacks of salt and jerked back, surprised by Franklin's presence. He stumbled around his stock cart, regained his balance, and gripped Franklin's shoulders. Moisture filled his eyes and he blinked. "Franklin. We didn't know if . . ."

Franklin embraced the older man, a dear friend. He patted Sam's back and pushed him to arm's length, something hard to say. "War's over, Sam. Allison's gone and Melanie's been taken." He looked into Sam, knowing Sam had information about Melanie.

Sam stiffened and turned toward the warehouse. "Moses, can you come up here?" He turned back to Franklin. "We put him on salary two weeks ago."

Franklin smiled. He liked that.

Moses Broadback cracked open the warehouse door, peeked through, and disappeared back into the warehouse.

Sam said, "He's got something to show you."

Franklin twitched with anticipation. "So said John Jackson."

Moses pushed through the warehouse doors carrying a worn canvas portfolio. His face creased with anger and grief. He handed the portfolio to Franklin. "We wasn't sure what to do, Master Franklin, city full of Yankees and all. Mister Greenwood sent me behind your wagon. I brought your mule and wagon back to the manor after they sailed. The man just left them there on the road."

Franklin turned, set the portfolio on the central cutting table, and opened it. Light flooded in from the storefront windows. He slowly spread several charcoal sketches on parchment, studying each one. He said, "Melanie's hair got long. She looks scared." He swallowed and blinked back tears at seeing the fright in his normally fearless daughter's eyes. He cleared his throat and brushed away his tears. "You've become a fine artist, Moses."

Moses pointed. "This here is of the fishing sloop, the one he took Miss Melanie onto. That was the last drawing I did when I followed."

Two winter bare trees in the foreground framed a sixty-foot fishing sloop, giving it scale. Franklin's suit coat stretched tight across the back of the heavyset man dragging Melanie up the boarding plank. No mistaking her identity with the lifelike quality of these sketches.

The second sketch showed a heavyset man with bushy beard and hair on the front seat of one of Franklin's flatbed wagons. Melanie sat at his elbow.

The third parchment held large, detailed sketches of his daughter's frightened face and the face of the bearded man. His angry eyes stared straight at Franklin.

"You draw these from memory, Moses?"

"Yes, Master Franklin. I done some that-a-way. I outlined first, when they was near, then I drew them in later."

Franklin said, "I'm not your master anymore. You're free to address me any way that pleases you."

"Yes, Master Franklin." Moses studied his sketches, carefully placing each back into the canvas portfolio.

Sam said, "That's the spitting image of that fellow, a mite shorter than you. Heavy set. No fat I could tell of. Hair red as swamp lily."

Moses nodded.

"Moses, I'd like to take you with me and hunt this man down; get my daughter back."

Moses looked at Sam Greenwood, eyes wide. He wanted to come.

Sam nodded, "Of course. We'll make do."

Franklin said, "I don't know how much I can pay. The murdering varmint robbed the manor before he left." He looked at Sam. "Do we have any funds in the bank?"

Sam shook his head. "Not much. Cotton's selling again, though. I got an auction scheduled for day after tomorrow. Moses has been putting up notices. Some of our stock has black mold but John Jackson brought in sixty-two wagon loads last fall. That's still in prime condition."

Franklin told Moses, "I'll pay what I can. Your job here will be waiting when we get back, should you favor coming back." Franklin shrugged. Who could know what the future holds.

Sam nodded at Moses, *of course.*

Franklin asked, "Moses, did you ever take a wife?"

"No, sir. I been sleepin' here in back." He poked a thumb toward the warehouse.

Franklin said, "Sam, I'll need all the money we can raise. You'll need to pay whatever taxes get imposed on the manor and the store. The hotel can pay for itself. I'll speak with Elias about that. There's sure to be a heavy war tax, so set aside fifty percent.

"John Jackson and the others will share-crop Winterbridge Manor while I'm gone. They'll need shares from the auction to live on. You'll need to buy seed and take your share. I'll need the rest."

"Of course."

Franklin looked at his store's mostly barren shelves. He still had one rack of new suits and a few folded shirts. "Get Moses suited up with two changes of new clothes. I need to go see some people. I'll stay in the hotel until we sail. I can't sleep at the manor without . . ." He leaned on the folding table and looked at the floor. "Dear Lord." He missed them so.

Franklin closed the portfolio and tucked it under his arm. "Moses, ride Domino out to Winterbridge and leave her with John.

Ask him to choose someone to help here in the store. I'm sure he'll have plenty of volunteers. John can bring the two of you back here this afternoon."

Franklin carried his portmanteau and the portfolio of sketches two blocks to his hotel and entered the lobby.

A Yankee corporal stood behind the registry desk. "Help you, mister?"

"Is Jonathan Sessions about?"

The corporal shook his head. "Never heard of him."

"He's the hotel manager."

"Oh, him." The corporal nodded. "We haven't seen him since last year."

Franklin stood staring, with no idea how to proceed.

"Something I can help you with?" The corporal tried being polite, but his arrogance denied that possibility.

"I own this hotel. What's going on?"

Recognizing Franklin's southern accent, probably having heard the owner had gone off to fight Yankees, the corporal's attitude changed, no pretense at politeness. "I wouldn't know about that. This here establishment got commandeered last December."

"Well, who would know something about that?"

The corporal shook his head, disinterested and belligerent.

"Are there any rooms available?"

The corporal sneered. "All taken, Reb."

FRANKLIN HAD BEEN TO the home of Elias Thornton many times, the home where he'd first met Thornton's daughter, Allison, a long walk on a cool, pleasant, spring day. He passed through the brick framed iron gate into the front courtyard, rounded the stagnant fountain, climbed the front steps, and used the heavy brass knocker.

He waited a full minute before knocking again. After another minute of waiting, he followed the brick pathway around the side of the house, through the porte-cochere, toward the carriage house, and turned onto the rear terrace.

Elias Thornton, Franklin's lawyer, father-in-law, and friend, sat alone at the far end of the terrace, gazing into his unkempt acre of oak and pecan forest. Disheveled, unshaved, and looking tired, he did not sense Franklin's approach.

"Elias?"

Elias's head pivoted slowly, at first not recognizing Franklin. He blinked and rocked back a little. "Franklin? That you, boy?"

"Yes, sir." Franklin set the portfolio on the small wrought iron table and dropped his portmanteau underneath.

Elias stood, pulled Franklin in, and wrapped him with both arms. "Good to see you, son. Didn't know if you were . . ." He pushed Franklin away and looked more closely. "Yes, it is you."

Franklin smiled. "Yes."

Elias looked past Franklin, sat, and gazed back into his forest. He blinked a few times, sniffed, looked across the table, and motioned to another chair, refocusing his mind.

Franklin walked around the table and sat. "Sorry to hear of Mrs. Thornton."

Tears welled in Elias's eyes. "I've lost my women-folk."

"Yes. We both have."

"That futile war took everything I cared about." Elias glanced blankly at the portfolio on the table. "What's this?"

"Thank you for Allison's headstone."

"I wanted to bring her into the church yard to lie with her mother." He glared at Franklin, suddenly angry. "Those nigger loving Yankees took everything I ever cared for. It was your damn niggers kept me from bringing Allison home." Tears rolled down his cheeks into his whiskers.

"The man who killed Allison and took Melanie nearly killed John Jackson Youngblood. He came in and told Sam Greenwood soon as he could."

"You've got enough niggers to have sent another. I could have brought her into Savannah for a proper funeral."

Franklin stared at his father-in-law, thinking what to say, not recognizing what Elias had become. He'd filled his life with hate. "They were afraid to come into Savannah, what with all the Yankee soldiers."

Elias nearly climbed out of his chair onto the table, leaning forward with such intensity. "Afraid of what, nigger loving Yankees?"

"I think they were more afraid of you and what you might do."

"What?" Elias jumped to his feet, kicking his chair back with the backs of his knees.

Franklin remained calm, no need to bicker with Elias. "I'm glad she's at Winterbridge. She loved it so."

Elias crossed his arms and paced, stewing with tensions not yet unleashed. "Me and two deputies scoured the city for a week, searching for Melanie." He stared down at Franklin with tears streaming into his stone-gray whiskers.

A yet unidentified quandary had been tearing at the back of Franklin's mind for two days. And here it was, slamming into his face. "And, you found nothing."

Elias blinked. His hands doubled into fists. "It must have been a runaway nigger. We'll probably find my little Melanie face down in the swamp."

Blood rushed to Franklin's head and he stood, leaning into Elias. "You're so blind with hate you never bothered to look where it might have helped."

"What are you talking about? Your niggers said they never saw anybody. That's how I know it's a runaway. They're protecting one of their own."

"I arrived yesterday. I already know more than you and all your deputies." Franklin tapped hard on the portfolio, picked up Elias's chair, shoved it to the table, and motioned for Elias to sit.

Elias blinked at Franklin's growing anger, adjusted the chair, and sat.

Franklin sat opposite and shoved the portfolio closer to Elias.

Elias opened the cover and looked at the first sketch, the back of the man lifting Melanie onto the sloop. "What is this?"

"Sam Greenwood and Moses Broadback saw Melanie and this man on one of my wagons."

Elias turned a sheet and looked at the close-up sketch of Melanie. "That looks like my granddaughter." He picked it up and studied it. "Looks just like her. She's frightened."

"It is her. She is frightened. Look at the next one."

Elias set Melanie's portrait aside and picked up the close-up of the bearded man.

Franklin said, "That's the man killed Allison and took Melanie."

Elias studied the portrait. "That's not a nigger."

"No, it is not. Sam said his hair is red as swamp lily."

"Sam Greenwood drew these? I never knew he could even draw."

"No. Moses Broadback drew these portraits."

"Your nigger at the store drew these?"

"Yes! He followed them to the livery where the man killed a Yankee soldier. Then he followed them downriver to where they boarded this sloop. They're headed for San Francisco by way of Key West. They've probably crossed Panama by now. If you'd thought to ask, you might have taken a steamer down to Key West and brought Melanie and this murderer back."

Elias looked through the portraits. He wouldn't look at Franklin. "I didn't know. How could I know?"

"When I left to join my brother's regiment, you promised to look after my interests. That should have included the store and the hotel."

"I..."

"I get back, my store's nearly broke and my hotel's been commandeered by Yankees. If you'd have been looking after things, Sam might have brought you this straight off. He never thought to do so, because he doesn't know who you are." Franklin leaned back, thoroughly disgusted with his father-in-law. Airing it out had clarified his thinking.

Elias blinked and looked away. He slowly turned back, his eyes seeking forgiveness. "What do you want me to do?"

"Get my hotel back. I'm taking Moses to San Francisco but I need money."

THE PRESBYTERIAN CHURCH on Bull Street looked the same as the day he'd married Allison, a beautiful church in the most beautiful city Franklin had ever known. He walked to the rear of the church and followed the brick path under two spreading oaks to the pastor's house. He took a deep breath and knocked.

A colored maid cracked open the door and poked her face into sunlight. "Yes, sir?"

"Is Pastor Dixon in?"

The door opened wide and the pastor stood behind his maid. "Franklin Adam Mosby. Thank the Lord, you're back." He pulled the maid aside. "Come in, Captain."

They shook hands.

Pastor Dixon pulled Franklin inside, closed the door, and nodded at his maid. "Claudette, could you bring some tea into the parlor?"

She turned and disappeared through a side door.

Pastor Dixon pulled Franklin into the parlor and swung the door half closed. He pointed to a stuffed chair and Franklin sat. The pastor sat opposite, leaned his elbows onto his knees, and clasped his hands.

His mournful stare into Franklin looked like he might be acting. "We were gravely distressed over the death of your dear wife." He had nothing more to say.

"Did you attend her burial?"

"No. We didn't learn of it until after." He nodded several times. "Done is done. We held a memorial service in her honor the following Sunday. Most all of the congregation attended, those not fighting in the war, that is. Elias, her father, he didn't attend. His grief was beyond . . ." He shook his head and looked away.

A soft knock at the door preceded Claudette. She swung the door wide and carried in a tray crowded with a teapot, cups, and a dish of biscuits. She set the tray on a small table and poured two cups of tea. She offered one to Franklin.

Franklin shook it off. "Not right now, Claudette. Thank you."

She returned the cup to the tray, handed the other cup to the pastor, left the room, and closed the door to a crack.

Franklin leaned forward and stared at the pastor. "What else can you tell me?"

"They found a Confederate uniform upstairs in your house, a major, I think. They also found an unclothed, rotting corps not far from your house, with a Yankee private's uniform nearby. They figure it was a Yankee deserter. Nobody thought to make a connection. Elias had already convinced the sheriff of a runaway slave. I think he was wrong, but nobody wanted to say it."

"Why didn't you speak up?"

The pastor sipped tea, thinking what to say. "I don't know." He shrugged. "Why? What have you found out?"

Franklin said, "The varmint killed a Yankee livery sergeant. He was wearing my clothes at the time. You were probably correct about it being a Yankee deserter."

"Oh, we heard about that. The livery man, I mean." The pastor sipped tea and looked into his cup, not at Franklin.

Franklin said, "He nearly killed John Jackson Youngblood."

"That's your boss darkie?"

Franklin nodded. "Moses Broadback, over at the store, he sketched the murdering kidnapper's likeness. We're going after them."

"Kidnapper? Melanie's with him?"

"As far as we know."

The pastor blinked his surprise. "I've thought some about this situation." He set his tea down, stood, laced his fingers behind is back, and paced. "At Allison's memorial, I spoke of the kind of woman your wife was."

He returned to his chair, pressed his hands over his knees and leaned closer to Franklin. "For some of us, life is about what we get out of it, what we take from it, and what we learn in that process. If we're lucky, we pass this knowledge onto others before we carry this knowledge to the grave. If we put a mind to it, we write about those experiences.

"Allison lived for what she could bring to others, never a worry for herself. If somebody wronged her, or said bad things about her, she always forgave. This made others feel the worse for it, if they were the ones speaking poorly behind her back. Everybody who knew her loved her."

"Yes." Franklin's shoulders shook. Warm tears ran down his cheeks and dripped onto his knees. His words caught in the back of his throat. "That Yankee deserter killed her and took our Melanie."

"What would Allison want you to do? Would she want vengeance?"

Franklin stood and leaned over the pastor. "Are you worried about that man?"

The pastor looked up into Franklin. "No, Franklin. I'm worried about you."

66

Franklin stepped back, turned away, and thrust his hands onto his hips, thinking how to say it. He turned back. "During the war, I came to grips with losing my life. I'd resigned myself to it, having seen so many others die for our *glorious* cause. I knew Allison and Melanie would survive. I knew, with or without me, they would survive, maybe even thrive.

"On my way back, after General Lee's surrender, I passed through Atlanta. The destruction, the burned-out buildings, the torn-up railroad, and, worse, the burned down plantation houses between here and Atlanta, broke my heart. The stories of southern women being raped and murdered struck fear into my bones. Seeing this, day after day, hearing the stories, I came to grips with the possibility of returning to see Winterbridge Manor in ashes. I never once thought of harm coming to Allison or Melanie." He fanned air in front of his face, pushing away the images. "I dared not to think such a thought."

He wiped away tears. "When I rode up the road off the highway and saw my home in one piece, my heart soared. My home had been spared."

Franklin sat, clasped his hands, and watched his tears fall to the floor between his feet. "I slept that night on her grave. Actually, I couldn't sleep." He wiped away the tears, stood, and faced the pastor. "If the Yankees truly shot or hung those rapist murderers they caught, if they can affect justice, why can't . . ." He slapped air. "Enough. I came here to seek your help. I wanted to pray for the safe return of my daughter."

The pastor put up his hand. "Okay. We will, Franklin. We will. Come to church on Sunday. I'll call the entire congregation to prayer. We'll petition God's forgiveness and . . ."

Franklin stood, slapped the pastor's hand aside, and leaned over his gaping face. "I'm going after my daughter."

Chapter Eight

GEARS CLANKED LOUDLY and both side wheels reversed, building speed, slowing *Calisphere's* approach to the ferry landing at Broadway St. Wharf. Chiang SuLin and her father, Chiang Po, had boarded *Calisphere* at Harper's Landing two hours earlier.

The ferry nudged into the wharf and ropes flew, unraveling toward waiting longshoremen who pulled the ferry tight to the wharf and tied her off.

SuLin helped her father gather their burlap bags, one filled with herbs, the other with their clothing, and followed him across the boarding ramp onto the wharf.

Fine thing! She did not see her count.

A Chinese man dressed in traditional, colorful Chinese costume, approached and bowed at the waist. "Doctor Chiang? SuLin?"

SuLin set their bags on the wood planks of the wharf. "Where is my count?"

The man snapped upright and sneered, a demonstration of his traditional superiority as a man. "Mr. Zabel has asked me to meet you and escort you to the White Chapel Saloon."

"Saloon?"

"He is in meetings with civic leaders, trying to convince them to improve the septic system here in the city. I am Han Wok."

"Saloon?"

MOLLY HAD ARRIVED AT the White Chapel early that morning, making sure her old bedroom had fresh linen, making sure it had been properly cleaned. Martha Scott and Sally Portman knew what to do, having worked for Molly for many years, too many years to count. They'd both stayed when Molly married Michael. Molly could never show them enough gratitude.

Sally lifted her wash bucket and backed toward the bedroom door. "Are they both sleeping in the same bed?"

"How could I know?" Molly knew nothing of Chinese family practices. "Did you put together a fish stew with some rice?"

Sally nodded. They had.

Molly led the ladies into the kitchen, hoping beyond hope her husband's guests would eat fish stew. It smelled pretty good.

Thoughts of bedroom preparations lingered. "We should probably put extra blankets in there, just in case. The girl might want to sleep on the floor or something. Do we have an extra mattress?" She knew they had extra bedding up in the attic.

"Ah." The kitchen table had been set for three. "Good. They can eat in here. Did you make a fresh pot of tea?"

"The kettle's on." Martha stirred a pot of steaming rice. "We wouldn't want their tea to get cold, now would we?"

None of them liked having Chinese guests under the roof of the White Chapel Saloon. At least the kitchen would be better than the dining room.

Molly would definitely not want them staying in her home. It had been hard enough writing to them every Christmas, a favor for that man.

She smiled. Keeping that man and their son happy filled her life. She loved them so.

Raul entered through the back gate, leading them into the yard from the alley after meeting their taxi. He knew better than to bring them in by the front door. Feeding them in the kitchen and keeping them in her old bedroom would keep them away from their regular tenants.

Martha filled the teapot with boiling water as their Chinese guests entered through the back door into the kitchen.

Raul set their burlap bags on the floor and fanned toward their three Chinese guests. "Miss Molly, you already know Han Wok." The well dressed, always polite Chinaman bowed at the waist, stood, and presented an older Chinaman dressed in a simple, American made wool suit. "I present Doctor Chiang Po."

The older Chinaman bowed and looked up with a humble twitch and smile. "I delight to meet you."

His daughter didn't wait to be introduced. "My father is learning English, for many long years, since we arrive with my count. Where is he?" Her eyes widened, her head spun, and her jaw jutted toward Raul. "Huh?"

Rude little . . . "You mean my husband?" Molly thought she might grow to like this one, even if it killed her.

Raul smiled into the daughter's boldness. "Mister Mike asked me to bring you here first, get you settled, then take you to the Palace for chowder."

"We've prepared a lunch here." Molly looked for a face to slap but that man was not there. She, Sally, and Martha had gone to a lot of trouble.

Raul smiled sheepishly. What could he do?

Oh, that wicked man.

MIKE ENTERED THE PUMPING station office of the Bensley Water Company on Van Ness, at the bottom of Russian Hill, keeping his appointment with Alexei Waldemar von Schmidt at 11:00 a.m. Alexei was the chief engineer. It was only a short walk from the

Palace. They shook hands over Alexei's desk. They'd been friends for a few years.

"So, Mike, what brings you?"

"We have water problems."

They both sat and Alexei spread his hands, questioning. "Why don't you go see George Enseign? He's got the city charter."

Mike smiled. "Alex, you deliver more than promises. Come, let's take a walk. Let me buy you lunch."

Both men stood, and Alexei nodded to his young assistant at the chart table.

His assistant nodded and smiled at Mike.

They left Alexei's office and strolled along the bay toward Meigg's Wharf on a beautiful June day. Mike said, "I didn't want to say this in front of your assistant. I'd hate to see a reaction like we had a few years back." He touched Alexei's arm and held his eyes. "There's cholera in Chinatown."

They stopped walking and faced each other. Alexei asked, "How bad?"

"It's not spreading to the city's general population, if that's what you're asking."

Resuming their walk, Alexei said, "Yeah, they burned all of Chinatown back in the fifties."

Two blocks away, a taxi stopped at the head of Meigg's wharf. Dr. Richard Beverly Cole, the King Family doctor, climbed down. He looked their way, turned abruptly, and paid the driver. The taxi pulled away.

Cole smiled at their approach. Everybody shook hands, all brothers in the same Masonic Lodge on California Street.

Another taxi approached and stopped. Billy Cahill climbed out. He paid the driver then shook hands with everybody, Mike last. "I caught a sense of urgency in your note."

Mike had sent around a courier the day before.

"We'll talk inside." Mike ushered them down two steps onto Meigg's Wharf and through the open double doors into the Palace.

Abe Warner's two monkeys tugged at their leashes, stretching to grab their passing trouser legs.

The strong, mouth-watering aroma of Abe Warner's famous chowder filled the interior.

Count Vladimir Preslova, Mike's former commanding officer in the Army of the Czar, sat at the long table set up near the bar. He stood and shook hands with everybody, saving Mike for last. He held Mike's hand, looking into him. "We need to talk. After our meeting here, of course."

Mike pulled him slightly away from the others, speaking softly. "Something is wrong?"

Vlad looked out the door then spun back. "We need to talk."

Bowls, spoons, platters of cheese and crackers, wine glasses, and four bottles of wine had already been placed around the table with more than enough chairs.

Abe delivered a large serving-bowl and ladled himself a bowl of steaming chowder. "Gentlemen!" He sat at the head of the table and crumbled crackers into his chowder. The others grabbed bowls, took turns filling them, and found chairs.

In the middle of slurping, a shadow filled the open doorway to Mike's right.

"Ah." Mike stood to usher Han Wok, Po, SuLin and Raul to the long table. "Gentlemen, this is Han Wok, a local businessman. And these are my very good friends, Chiang Po and his daughter, SuLin. You all know Raul."

Raul led the two Chinamen to the stacked bowls and helped them dish up chowder.

Little SuLin punched Mike in the gut, threw her arms around his waist and hugged him. Her head reached his chest. She pushed away, glaring. "Why do you never write me, huh? I write to you. Why make your woman write to me?" She slapped his chest, smiled, hugged him again, and found her place at the table. She had become a beautiful young woman.

Mike remained standing and looked around the table. Everybody's eyes were on him. He looked around the Palace. Nobody else was in the room. He addressed the group. "What I'm about to say needs to be held in confidence. We don't want to repeat the destructive panic that occurred a few years ago." He made eye contact with Dr. Cole, Billy, and Abe. "Han Wok has informed me that cholera has broken out in Chinatown."

SuLin whispered in Po's ear.

"Dr. Cole has set up an isolation ward at St. Mary's Hospital on Stockton, but he's worried it might spread because of our inability to talk with the Chinese. For this reason, I've asked for help from Chiang Po and his daughter."

Han Wok gazed adoringly at SuLin. His attention had been diverted.

Mike nudged Han's shoulder.

Han returned to their meeting.

Mike put a hand on Po's shoulder. "Po is a Chinese doctor. I'm sure he can help isolate the cause, and limit the potential spread. Most importantly, our Chinese community will understand him, with the help of Han Wok, of course."

Dr. Cole stood. "The cause is dirty drinking water. The question is, how do we get clean water in there, and who's going to pay for it?"

Po spoke softly with SuLin and Han Wok.

SuLin stood. "Po needs to go there and see what can be done." Her English had greatly improved since their previous time together.

Abe Warner wiped chowder from his wide mustache and stared at Mike. "Why call the group?" He looked at Vlad.

Mike fanned toward Han Wok. "As I said previously, Han and I have negotiated a deal to provide labor for the Central Pacific

73

Railroad project. I've since submitted our bid. We're in final discussions, but we need to provide a clean environment for new labor arriving from China."

He turned to Alexei Waldemar von Schmidt, the chief engineer of the Bensley Water Company. "Most of you already know Alex. He knows more about San Francisco's water supply than anybody." Mike sat and ate some chowder.

Alexei cleared his throat, wiped his whiskers, and remained seated. "The problem, as I see it, is that the Chinese get their water from Mission Creek. The whole city uses capped over cesspools for waste and it seeps into the underground aquifer. Mission Creek is seriously fowled and not potable. I filed official complaints with the city commission but that bunch of politicians is never eager for anything but collecting taxes.

"I've invented a water meter we could use to charge for usage and bring in revenue for new piping and distribution points, but they won't even approve that. We've already surveyed the area all the way down to China Basin, but we can't afford to lay pipe without being paid." He apologetically shook his head, frustrated.

"Give us some numbers, man." Abe sounded angry. The burn of losing his silver Comstock Watch in the train robbery had not yet cooled.

"A six-inch main could supply the needs for now, but growth is expected." Alex held Mike's attention.

Mike nodded his agreement.

"I'm therefore recommending a twelve-inch supply with a branch and faucets at every possible entrance into the Chinese community. It's too complex for direct piping, and it's always changing."

"How much? That's twice I've asked." Abe leaned over the table, ready to jump to his feet.

Mike pressed him back into his chair, calming him.

"Well . . ." Abe glared into his empty chowder bowl.

Alexei spread his hands, head wagging. "I haven't yet calculated the cost."

Mike asked, "Can you give us any idea?"

"Look . . ." Alexei stood and straightened his vest. "Let's get three or four water wagons down there for immediate water supply, and let me get some numbers together. I was going to recommend that anyway." He looked into Abe's stare. "Whatever we do regarding a more permanent solution is not our immediate task. They need clean water now."

Abe nodded, temporarily satisfied.

Dr. Cole nodded.

Billy Cahill said, "Once the threat of cholera has ended, the Bulletin will run some articles about the need for a more permanent water supply system. We'll pressure the city to act upon it."

This inspired Alexei. "While you're at it, we need to clean up the city's wastewater system. I know the city engineer is pushing to build brick septic tanks, but the necessary drain fields will still percolate wastewater into the aquifer. China Basin will become a stinking, mosquito-infested swamp. If that happens, we're looking at yellow fever, malaria, or dengue."

Mike stood. "Okay, we've found a way forward. Has anybody anything to add?"

Everybody but Preslova seemed good with the plan. Something else bothered him.

Billy stood and took Mike's hand. "When are you and Molly planning to visit the Kings?"

"Yeah. We need to do that. How are they?"

"They're good. They just finished painting the building, and they've found some new tenants downstairs."

He pulled Mike closer, speaking privately. "Have you heard anything about missing boys in Chinatown?"

"I have. Han said something about this. Why don't you go down there with Po and Han? Poke around. I'll come down as soon as I can." He turned toward the door. "Doctor Cole?"

Cole turned back.

"Can you and Billy go down there with Han and Doctor Po?"

Cole pulled out and looked at his silver pocket watch. He nodded, *Okay.*

Mike shook hands with Cole, Han, and Po, all on their way out the door. Last, he hugged SuLin. "Thank you for coming."

"Exciting, heh? For now?"

"Have you settled in at the White Chapel?"

"Yes. Is fine. Your wife is very pretty woman."

"Thank you." Deep respect and friendship passed between them; a nearness too long ignored. "I'll meet you in Chinatown as soon as I can."

She smiled and spun out the door.

Mike returned to the table and sat between Abe and Preslova. Abe always sensed when something was amiss.

Mike turned to Preslova. "My colonel, something is bothering you."

Preslova stared at Abe, not wanting to speak in front of him.

"It's okay. Whatever it is, Abe Warner can be trusted."

Preslova adjusted his chair, looking back and forth at both of them. "My two longtime comrades have gone missing."

"When?"

"Three days ago."

Abe jumped in. "You think they've been Shanghaied?"

"No. They know better than to visit the Barbary Coast at night."

Mike said, "Have you had any troubles with them?"

"You know them both. They are good men, and loyal. They don't drink much vodka, and they stay close."

"How can we help?"

"You know why I am worried. You should worry too. You have a wife and son."

Chapter Nine

BY THE TIME MIKE CLIMBED down from the taxi below Portsmouth Plaza, two water wagons had already been delivered and Chinese residents had formed lines with buckets. Po, SuLin, and Han were directing them in Chinese.

Billy Cahill and Dr. Cole climbed a short distance uphill to meet Mike. Cole said, "That Chinese doctor took control. No stopping him. He's already got water pots boiling. They're washing everything touched by human hands. We've got a wagon of lye coming down to cover the open waste pits." He chuckled. "I'm not worried about cholera anymore. I think Cahill might write a scare article about the threat of cholera, if you know what I mean."

Billy nodded. "I'll write the truth about what's happening here." He smiled and tapped Cole's shoulder. "I'll quote Doctor Cole. 'I'm not worried about Cholera anymore.' And, the Bulletin will thank him. We will especially thank Chiang Po and his daughter for coming all the way down from . . ." He looked at Mike. "Weaverville, is it?"

Mike said, "Yes. You should also thank Alexei Waldemar von Schmidt and the Bensley Water Company for their rapid and unselfish response to the threat."

Billy laughed softly and shook his head. "Alexei who? I should be taking notes. It's almost as bad as your name."

Mike smiled and said, "You might also mention the rapid growth of Chinatown. We must try and get in front of our incoming labor force."

Billy said, "I'll also lay into the city for not providing water pipe. Why should Bensley bring in water wagons?" He stopped and looked down at the cluster of Chinese families surrounding the wagons. He turned back. "I'd like to start with an article about the missing kids, as a feed-in to the water and sewage problems."

Mike said, "Great idea. What, exactly, is the situation with missing kids? Time has passed since Han first told me about it."

Billy said, "Eight boys have gone missing in the past ten days, ages five to nine. One of them was orphaned by cholera. That's my connecting link to the water and sewer problems."

Raul walked around one of the water wagons and climbed uphill to join the group.

Mike asked, "What did you find out?"

Raul said, "A man's been seen in the area around the same time as the disappearances, always in the twilight hour."

"Any descriptions?"

"He's a big man. He always wears a heavy black coat and black, broad-brimmed hat."

Mike nudged Cole. "You want to stay here, or come with us to police headquarters?"

"I should stay here."

"Meet us later at the White Chapel for dinner?"

Dr. Cole nodded, *Sure.*

Mike hooked Raul's shoulder. "Can you find Molly and let her know to bring our son down there for dinner and let the ladies know we'll have a crowd?"

"She's gonna be mad."

Mike smiled. "Yeah." He'd grown to love her seesaw temper. She always let it out so she could reel it back in.

SERGEANT ANGUS MCFEE sat at his desk among a dozen other desks, one of only three officers not out on city streets. He'd been following articles in the Daily Evening Bulletin about the investigations, pursuit, and arrests of eight alleged conspirators involved with the assassination of President Abraham Lincoln. William Cahill, the article's writer, had become a clever and popular journalist for the Bulletin.

Hearing approaching footsteps, Sgt. McFee folded the newspaper onto his desk and winced. "Mike Zabel and Billy Cahill." He stood and shook hands with two men he'd grown to respect and dread. He dragged two nearby chairs around his desk and motioned for them to sit.

All three men sat and McFee smiled at Billy. "Nice article." He patted his newspaper.

Billy glanced down at the newspaper. "Which one?"

"The Lincoln conspiracy. I mean, I'm amazed how fast they ran these conspirators down."

Billy leaned closer, getting into McFee's face. "Amazing what good law enforcement can do when they want to."

McFee ignored the gibe. "You think they'll hang that Surratt woman?"

"We'll be following the trial and reporting every evening, as soon as reports come across the wire."

McFee settled back in his chair, bracing for the coming wind in his face. "What brings our state detective and his news hound?"

Mike said, "Always nice to find officers at work, holding down their desks." He smiled big, teasing McFee about almost never leaving his office, always relying on reports back from subordinates.

"What's going on, Mike?"

"Two of my Russian friends have gone missing."

"How long?"

"A week." It had only been three days but Mike needed for McFee to get out of his chair.

"They like their vodka, do they?"

"You've met Vladimir Preslova. He and these two attended our New Year's party at the Palace. I've never seen any of them drunk."

"What are you thinking, Shanghai Kelly?"

Mike said, "Maybe." He shook his head and leaned into McFee. "But, probably not. They never go down to the Barbary. They keep pretty much to themselves." Mike leaned back and stared at McFee.

McFee spread his hands. "What?"

"You've met these men. They're trained soldiers of the Czar. Do you really think anybody could . . ."

McFee said, "Yeah, yeah." He looked at his wrestling thumbs. "I don't know. Maybe not. But, Kelly's been a thorn in our side for a long time. Every time we think we're closing in, we come up empty. Our current thinking is that he's spread his net and working up and down the coast. It's getting difficult to man the old sailing ships. They're paying top dollar for able-bodied deepwater sailors."

Mike's jaw locked. He didn't seem to like McFee's response. McFee knew not why.

Cahill scribbled notes.

McFee knew not what. He didn't look forward to any embarrassing quotes Cahill might print in the Bulletin. McFee knew not what.

Mike's jaw stayed locked, leaning across McFee's desk. "We also have missing children; eight so far, ages five to nine."

"What?" McFee grabbed the edge of his desk but stopped himself from standing. "Why hasn't anybody reported this before? Why haven't I heard about this?" He met Mike's stare. "When did this all start? Who's kids are they?"

"They're Chinese."

"Oh." McFee settled back in his chair and relaxed. "Young Chinese girls are often kidnapped and taken out of state to smalltown brothels."

Cahill scribbled notes.

Mike said, "These abductees were all boys."

"Well, they're still Chinese. That's why we never heard anything."

Cahill scribbled.

Mike stood and leaned over McFee's desk. His eyes pierced to the back of McFee's skull. "These are citizens of this city and this state. If I need to go to the governor, I will."

"Easy, Mike. Take it easy." Sweat slicked McFee's underarms, very uncomfortable looking up into Mike Zabel's aggravation. "What do you want me to do?"

THAT MAN . . . Molly waited with Jimmy in front of their home on Russian Hill, both watching Raul flag a taxi.

A taxi driver saw them from the crossing street below and turned uphill. The taxi stopped across the street.

Raul pointed downhill.

The taxi turned around and stopped in front of their house.

Raul helped Molly and Jimmy board and asked the driver, "You know the White Chapel Saloon?"

"Yessir."

Raul climbed in and the taxi rolled downhill.

Molly said, "I don't know why that man needs me to run back and forth like this. It takes Jimmy away from his schooling."

"He got Doctor Cole and maybe Sergeant McFee. Them and Billy Cahill gonna eat with us, and Mister Mike's Chinese friends. I think he don't want to show up in your home with all those people."

"What about our regular tenants?"

"I think you gonna feed them first before Mister Mike's guests."

"Well . . ." *That man.* "We need to stop at the market."

Raul nodded and leaned out to shout at the driver, "Make a stop on Market Street first."

The taxi turned right at the next corner and rolled downhill toward the Mission District. Raul leaned out and looked behind them. He settled back, looking from Molly to Jimmy. He looked uneasy about something.

"What is it?"

"I think somebody following us."

"Really?" Jimmy jumped up, excited, looking through the oval rear window. "You mean that taxi way behind us?"

"Sit down, Jimmy." Molly pulled her seven-year-old son back onto the seat and leaned forward. She had to tell somebody. "Raul, don't say anything. Mike has enough on his mind right now."

Raul nodded, never one to argue with Molly.

"I'm pregnant."

"I thought you meant about that wagon back there." Raul smiled. "A new baby. About time. Mister Mike gonna love this."

"Don't you say a word."

Raul nodded with a toothy smile. He couldn't wait to tell Michael.

"Don't you dare."

Raul chomped down on his smile and looked out at the street.

The taxi slowed to a crawl, easing through the crowd on Market Street.

Raul stepped out onto the running board. "Pull up here."

With no curb space, the taxi stopped in the middle of the road.

Raul climbed down and helped Molly and Jimmy onto the brick paved street. He told the driver, "Wait here."

The taxi driver nodded.

Up the street, behind them, the other taxi pulled to the curb and stopped.

Raul led Molly and Jimmy into the open-air meat market and stopped. "I'm gonna go check that other taxi."

That dread feeling tugged her stomach. "No, no, Raul. You stay close."

Raul thought about it and nodded, never one to argue with Molly.

Molly said, "Now, why would anybody want to follow us?"

Chapter Ten

WHAT NOW? Tommy Chandler put his edition of the Sunday Times aside and dropped both elbows onto his bar.

Three uniformed policemen pushed through the front door and crossed toward the bar. Tommy had seen one of them before, back in the days of the Law-and-Order Party. He seemed to be in charge. "Tommy Chandler." He smiled slightly and showed Tommy his search warrant. "We've got orders to check all the houses down here on the coast." The other two officers marched upstairs.

"What for?"

"Some Chinese boys and two Russian gents have gone missing." He shook his head and smiled, not expecting to find anything.

"Missing Russians in my house? Chinese? By all means, be my guest."

"Orders are orders." The officer leaned against the bar and looked at the beer taps.

"Sure thing, officer." Tommy pulled down a mug and filled it with frothy beer. He raked the foam off, filled the mug again, and set it on the bar.

The officer took a long pull and turned slowly, inspecting Tommy's boarding-house.

Four of his boarders played stud poker at the corner table, Tommy's Chinese coolie swept out under empty tables, and two other boarders played cribbage; a quiet time of day.

The other two officers strolled back downstairs. One shook his head. "There's a little girl up there with the whores, but she's white."

Tommy drew two more beers, raked off foam, refilled, and set them on the bar. He signaled for the officers to help themselves.

The officer in charge asked the others, "You see any Russians?"

Both shook their heads, sidled up to the bar, and grabbed their beers.

The officer in charge asked, "How old is the girl?"

One of his officers said, "Seven or eight."

The officer in charge turned to Tommy. "What's a seven-year-old doing with whores?"

Tommy nodded toward the card game in the corner. "Ask her uncle. He's wearing the red beard."

FRANKLIN MOSBY AND Moses Broadback climbed onto Pacific Street Wharf and carried their luggage to the customs desk at 4:52 p.m., on Monday, June 26, 1865.

The customs officer said, "You coming into the country together?"

Franklin nodded. "We're coming from Savannah, Georgia, by way of Panama."

The customs officer looked Moses up and down. "I need to ask; are you free or slave?"

Moses stood erect and squared his shoulders, proud. "I am a free citizen."

Franklin said, "Sir, the war is over. How could he possibly be a slave?"

The customs officer smiled and wagged his head. "I need to ask."

Franklin looked at the line, only four people behind them. *They can wait.* He motioned to Moses.

Moses pulled out the portfolio and handed it to Franklin.

"I need to ask." Franklin smiled, opened the portfolio, and showed the officer the portraits of Melanie and the bearded man.

"Have you seen either of these? This is my daughter." He indicated her portrait.

The customs officer barely glanced at the portraits. "How long ago?"

"Probably late January or early February. The man has red hair. My daughter's hair is yellow gold."

The officer looked again and shook his head. "I rarely look at faces."

"Thank you for your time." Franklin returned the portraits to the portfolio and Moses put it away. They collected their luggage and hurried up the crowded wharf toward Tommy Chandler's Boardinghouse. They'd seen the barker aboard a speedy sloop with a banner advertising the establishment.

Three uniformed police officers stepped out from inside, looking up and down the wharf. When one of them stared suspiciously at Franklin and Moses, Franklin decided to bypass Tommy Chandler's. He wanted no confrontation with Yankee police officers.

They walked farther up the wharf and hailed a taxi. While Moses loaded their bags onto the rear platform, Franklin asked the driver, "You know of any reasonably priced rooms for rent?"

The driver looked closely at Franklin, the cut of his clothing, the suit worn by Moses. "Might know of one or two."

NOW NEARING DARK, FRANKLIN climbed back into the taxi. They'd just been rejected by the fifth establishment they'd visited. Two had refused rooms because of Moses, whites only. Three others had claimed to be full. The last two had been serving the evening meal, reminding Franklin of his own hunger. Moses must have been hungry too. Both establishments had asked them to come back the following day.

He asked the driver, "What about Chandler's Boardinghouse?" The police must have gone by then.

"No, no. You don't want to stay at Tommy Chandler's unless you want to be put out to sea as a common sailor. You'll surely wind up in Shanghai." He slapped reins and the taxi lurched forward. "I've got one last place to try before we head into the city."

After their first stop, they'd shown the driver the portraits and discussed possibilities. He'd said the bearded man and Melanie were more than likely boarded on the Barbary Coast.

The driver turned his taxi left, staying close to the bay. "This last place is where I'd bring a young girl. It's the most reputable house down here."

"Why didn't we go there first?"

"They're probably full."

Along their rout, lamplighters carried oil-lit torches on long sticks, reaching up to ignite gas streetlights, adjusting them with chest-high knobs. This city-of-lights had earned its name. Gas streetlights stepping steeply uphill, disappearing into settling fog.

Beautiful.

Moses said, "Master Franklin, sir, you suppose we can afford a new book of canvas and some charcoal?"

Franklin smiled. "Of course." He spoke softly. "Moses, I'm no longer your master. You might get us into trouble."

RAUL HELPED MARTHA and Sally clear away dinner dishes.

Mr. Mike and his guests talked business.

Raul would find out later, what's going on.

Mr. Mike stood and addressed his guests. "Here is my understanding; we will press forward with the water supply for the Chinese community. The Bulletin will strike up a news campaign demanding that the city council improve the waste water system and repay the costs of the new water supply."

Little Jimmy, Mike's son, jumped up and grabbed Mr. Mike's coattail, happy for his father's nearness.

Mr. Mike pulled him close and held on, not looking down and not letting go.

Jimmy smiled and squirmed closer. He liked it.

Raul stacked dishes on the center table in the kitchen, watching the women at their work. A knock at the front door took him into the entry and he opened the door.

A well-dressed gentleman stood under the porch light. A well-dressed Negro stood just behind.

Raul asked, "Help you?"

The white gentleman said, "We're looking for a room."

"Come in."

The white gentleman looked back at the Negro. "Go ask the taxi to wait." He smiled at Raul, stepped inside, and Raul closed the door.

Raul said, "Wait here." He entered the dining room and signaled Miss Molly.

She stood and rounded the table toward him.

"Two gents looking for boarding."

Molly followed Raul around the corner to where the white gentleman waited. She said, "One of our rooms just came open. It's small but it has bunk beds and a small table with two chairs. It has a window facing the bay." She looked at Raul. "You said two."

The white gent said, "My associate is holding our taxi. Do you board by the month?"

"Certainly. Fifty dollars each, includes two meals a day."

Raul said, "Miss Molly, the other one's a Negro."

Molly turned back to the white gentleman. "Is he your slave?"

"No, Ma'am. Not anymore." The white gent turned and opened the door.

His Negro waited between the house and the street. "Moses, these folks would like to meet you."

The Negro stepped into the light wearing a healthy smile. "Evening, Ma'am, sir."

Miss Molly said, "Well, what'll it be?" She didn't mind the Negro.

The white gent asked, "Can we see the room?"

Miss Molly smiled and nodded at Raul.

"Come on. I show you."

The white gent turned to his companion. "Go ask the taxi to wait a minute longer. I'll take a look and come outside."

The Negro turned out toward the street.

The white gent followed Raul up the main stair and down the hall. Raul opened the last door on the left side. The window faced the street. "Miss Molly get confused. The window face the street. She don't live here no more."

The white gent stepped into the room for a look, no linen on the beds.

"You take the room, the ladies gonna come up and make the beds. They gonna bring towels and water pail with soap."

"Is it too late to eat? The food smells lovely."

"I'm sure they gonna whip something up." Raul liked this gent. As for the Negro; he'd sailed with some in the past. They'd usually been okay sailors.

"We'll take it."

MIKE SHOOK HANDS WITH Dr. Cole and Alexei Waldemar von Schmidt, saying goodnight. He ushered them onto the thick redwood planks outside the White Chapel, stepped back inside, closed the door, and turned back into the dining room.

Raul came downstairs with the well-dressed gentleman. They brushed past Mike and went outside.

In the dining room, Han Wok had stayed behind, speaking softly with Chiang Po and SuLin; a private conversation at the far end of the table. Han had definitely taken an interest in SuLin. She'd become a fine looking young lady.

Raul ushered the white gentleman and a colored man upstairs, all carrying luggage.

Molly sat at the dining table and pulled Mike into a chair next to her. "We've just rented our open room. The girls will fix them something to eat."

Their new tenants came downstairs and sat in the center of the long table, between the Chiangs and Han.

Sally and Martha cleared away the remaining supper dishes.

Mike looked across at Molly's new boarders. He had some questions. Molly always trusted everyone.

The white gentleman sensed Mike's curiosity. He motioned and his companion stood, left the table, and trotted upstairs.

Martha brought out a pot of fresh hot tea and cups.

Billy Cahill came in from the back porch and joined them.

Their new tenant smiled, not shy. "I'm Franklin Mosby. My home is near Savannah, in Georgia."

The colored gentleman returned from upstairs with a worn canvas portfolio.

Mr. Mosby took the portfolio and his companion sat. Mosby said, "This is Moses Broadback, a free American citizen who volunteered to join me in my quest."

Billy perked up, suddenly interested. "Excuse me? Did you say your name was Moseby?"

"Yes. Franklin Adam Mosby. Why?"

A loud knock sounded at the door. Mike started to stand but Raul hurried out from the kitchen, rounded the corner, and opened the front door.

"We're here to search the premises," a man said loudly.

Mike stood and rounded the corner.

Three policemen stood outside the door.

Mike asked, "To what purpose?"

"There's kids missing from Chinatown. We've got orders to search all the boardinghouses on the Coast." He waved a warrant at Mike.

"Let them in, Raul." Mike stepped aside and the three uniformed officers brushed past. One headed upstairs. The other two separated, searching the downstairs.

Mike returned to his chair with a smile and nod at Billy. "Sergeant McFee has finally decided to get involved."

One officer returned from the back porch and another came from inside Molly's bedroom, where SuLin and Po were staying. They joined each other near the middle of the table, both looking suspiciously at Moses.

Mike asked, "What about the missing Russians?"

The officers both looked surprised. One asked, "Have you seen any Russians."

Raul puffed out a short laugh.

Mike held his breath.

The third officer hurried down the rear stairs and tugged the other two toward the door. "Thank you for your cooperation."

Mike smiled and nodded, "Any time, officers. Please thank Sergeant McFee for me."

The one with the warrant turned back. "You're him. You're Count Mike."

"Please thank Sergeant McFee for me."

The officer tipped his hat and smiled.

Raul ushered them out the door and stood near the main stairs. He wanted to hear this.

Mike looked at Billy. "Where were we?"

"Yes. He was asking me why I asked about his name." Billy turned to Franklin Mosby. "Do you know a man named John Surratt?"

Franklin smiled, a little surprised by the question. "I am originally from Virginia. There's a town, Surrattsville, outside the capitol city. It was founded by the Surratts of Virginia. Funny you should ask." He stared into Billy.

"Ah." Billy smiled with a nod. "I work for the Daily Evening Bulletin. I'm covering the conspiracy trial over the Lincoln assassination. John Surratt is the son of Mary Surratt, one of the alleged conspirators on trial. He used an alias. Moseby. They're still searching for him."

"How's that spelled?"

"M-O-S-E-B-Y."

Franklin smiled, maybe a little relieved. "My name is M-O-S-B-Y. And, no, I don't personally know any Surratts."

Molly said, "You said you're on a quest."

"Yes, Ma'am." He opened the portfolio and spread charcoal sketches across the table. A couple of them were very well drawn portraits.

Molly took a breath and gripped her lower neck. "Did you draw these? They're wonderful."

Franklin motioned toward his companion. "Moses Broadback is the artist."

Mike lifted a close-up portrait of a little girl.

Mosby said, "That's my daughter, Melanie. She's seven years old." He picked up a portrait of a mean looking, bearded man. "This is the man who took her, after he murdered my wife."

Billy stood and spread the drawings across the table. Several were of this man and the little girl. Six drawings were aboard boats or ships, and three were mountainous landscapes, all of excellent quality. Billy said, "Is this what your daughter actually looks like?"

"Very much so, yes. Why . . ." Franklin stood and leaned over the table, anxious. "Have you seen her?"

"No, no. But I've got an idea." Billy picked up two detailed portraits. "Can I borrow these for a few days? I'd like to show them to my publisher. I'd like to front page these, and I'll need some background story."

Franklin snapped around to look at his companion.

Moses waved a hand across his drawings. "Take what you want. Keep them as long as it takes."

Mike said, "These are very nice drawings. Are any for sale? I know of a restaurant that would love some of these on the walls."

Moses's eyes popped wide, surprised by the question. "I never thought . . ." He looked at Franklin.

Franklin sat, slapped Moses's shoulder, and nodded.

There was a deal to be made. Mike liked very much making deals. He lifted a wary brow toward Moses. "Tell you what, we'll negotiate with Mister Mosby. Would that be okay?"

Moses smiled and leaned closer to Franklin. They both liked the idea.

Mike said, "Han, come down here."

Han broke away from his ogling of SuLin and stood. He took two steps and noticed the drawings spread across the table. "Very nice." He nodded. "What you want?"

"You think we might use this man . . ." Mike turned and looked at Moses. "Mister Broadback might agree to talk to some witnesses. They might be able to work up a drawing or two of the kidnapper." He turned to Franklin and Moses. "We'll pay for the drawings, of course."

Chapter Eleven

THE SHRIEK PIERCED General Krestyanov's ears, as Duncan Frack sliced and peeled skin from the small child's back and side. Krestyanov turned away and stared at the grand duchess. How could she associate herself with such evil as this?

Grigori Balakirev and Luka Varvarinski had been assigned to follow Count Zabalkansky's family, and Sacha had gone outside, unable to watch this butchery.

Sweat sheeted down the general's back and sides, so hot was the interior of this old blacksmith shop known as the Forge.

The small child's screams of pain sickened him and weakened his knees. He could no longer watch the exposure of raw, pink flesh. Very little blood. Such was the practiced skill of this demon, Duncan Frack.

The wood planks under the general's feet jolted sharply downward and moved from side to side. *God help us.* God must have been angry with this demon.

The grand duchess gripped her throat and gawked at the general, a wild-eyed fear he'd never before witnessed.

Frack stepped back from the hearth as a crack opened and separated bricks. The bricks quickly returned and the shaking stopped.

Frack chuckled, seeing the fear in the duchess. "Nothing to be afraid of, Duchess. That was just one of our frequent earthquakes. They never do much damage. Most of the time, I don't even notice. Not anymore."

Sacha rushed in to check on the duchess, saw she was okay, and returned outside.

"I've heard back from Bundy," said Frack, demanding Krestyanov's attention.

Krestyanov stared into Frack.

Frack backed away from the small boy.

The child had either fainted or died.

Frack carefully stretched the peeled skin across the hearth of the open fire pit, probably planning to join it with other pieces of peeled skin. A patchwork of dried, stretched skins resembling a tattered flag hung on the wall above the hearth. He reached overhead and pulled the rope. Pulleys squeaked and the rope opened large billows, feeding the coals with fresh air. They glowed red with heat.

Krestyanov coughed, chasing his urge to vomit. "What is that?" He looked at the flag-shaped collection of skins.

Frack looked up. "That? Not sure yet." He smiled, proud of his work. "It's not strong enough for a purse or hat. Maybe I'll have Juanita paint something colorful on it. I think we might hang it over our bed."

Disgusting.

The child whined, waking up.

Frack moved quickly with his knife, slicing open the child's lower back. He reached inside with his knife, and the child went limp. Not a sound. Frack pulled out what looked like the liver, cut it free from vessels, and carefully laid it into a greasy skillet. He slid the skillet over the glowing coals and pumped the billows twice. The liver quickly sizzled.

Frack added salt and pepper and turned toward Krestyanov. "I was talking about Bundy. He's my informant up at police headquarters. I figured they'd bring your count in on this but they couldn't care less about Chinese. Then, like magic, Count Mike went to Sergeant McFee and demanded the police take action." He smiled, proud of his cleverness. "Whenever you're ready, I can lead him wherever you want. Right here, would be fine."

The Grand Duchess Catherine Mikhailovna showed no emotion over the torture of little boys. She smiled a little, enjoying this. She said, "Your plan is to make a trail of bodies that he will follow?"

Frack cocked his head sideways and waved his knife like a wand. "Not exactly. We'll let Bundy, my informant . . . We'll let him find the bodies where I've been stashing them. Your count will see them and get the coroner's reports. Count Mike's a big hat with the state police."

Grigori led Luka in and stopped, their eyes adjusting in the darker interior. They both stepped back at the sight of the butchered child.

"Well?" The grand duchess had been waiting for their report.

Grigori stepped forward, looking at the floor. "They spent the day in Chinatown and at the White Chapel Saloon, and then they returned to their home on Russian Hill."

"And?"

"That little Portuguese was with them. We've heard bad things on this one."

Duncan Frack chuckled, turning the sizzling liver over in the skillet. "His name's Raul. I watched him take down two guys big as me like they was kids. He's the one trained your count. Together, they'll be near impossible to best without bullets. That's why we need to bring him to us, without Raul."

The grand duchess needed more. "What did my brother's bodyguards tell you?"

Grigori glanced at Luka, then he looked back at the floor. He would not look at the duchess. "They said the grand duke exposed himself to danger against the advice of their colonel, the Count Vladimir Preslova."

Luka nodded his agreement, glanced at the butchered child, nervously glanced at the duchess, and stared down at his shifting feet.

Grigori squared with General Krestyanov, shoulders hunched, hands spread, pleading. "The grand duke could not be stopped. His passions were always so high. Count Zabalkansky was not armed. The grand duke shot at him once and missed. When he stepped forward to shoot again, three other men shot him down. One was the governor of California. Another was a state legislator at that time. He later became governor." His head shrank between his shoulders.

The duchess said, "Where are these peasants now?"

Niet! Grigory did not want to search for these men.

MIKE ZABEL STEPPED down from the police carriage a little past 10:00 p.m., not sure exactly. His gold watch had been stolen by train robbers.

He followed Sergeant McFee into the center of a group of men gathered around handheld lanterns on a grassy, vacant lot just above Portsmouth Plaza.

Dr. Thaddeus Pearson, the coroner, knelt under two lamps, examining the left hand of one of two dirt covered bodies in a hollowed out, shallow grave.

The coroner looked up. "Mike Zabel. Haven't seen you since the assassination riots down on the Coast."

"Yes. This seems like a long time ago." Only two months had passed since the Barbary Coast riots following President Lincoln's assassination.

Mike worked his way around the grave, gently pressing policemen and onlookers aside. "Doctor Pearson, I know these men."

Pearson stood and faced Mike. "Sergeant McFee said you might." He pulled Mike away from the crowd, speaking only to Mike and Sergeant McFee. "All of their teeth were pulled. Not bashed. Pulled. All their fingers and toes were cut off. From the blood evidence, it looks like one at a time."

Mike said, "Torture."

Pearson nodded. "Looks that way to me. I've not yet found any other signs of trauma. I think they both slowly bled to death." He turned into the lamplight.

Mike stood shoulder to shoulder. "This was often the practice of their former sovereign, the Grand Duke Nikolai Nikolaievich." Preslova's worry now made perfect sense.

McFee said, "Is this Grand Duke . . . what's his name, currently in the city?"

Mike smiled. "He was shot dead at the Palace eight years ago. These two men were his bodyguards."

"Shot by who?" McFee pulled his pad and pencil, ready to take notes.

"Governor J. Neely Johnson, state legislator John Downey, and Abe Warner. Hard to say who shot him first. They all shot him before he could try again to shoot me. He'd already taken one shot and missed. I was unarmed at the time."

"Oh." McFee grinned and returned his pad and pencil to his breast pocket, next to his standard issue Bowie knife.

Mike grabbed the coroner's shoulder. "You need anything from us?"

Pearson shook his head. "We'll get them over to the morgue. If I find anything of interest, I'll get word to you." He rejoined those at the shallow grave.

Mike led McFee toward the police carriage. "You know the Saint Francis Hotel?"

"At the bottom of Russian Hill? Sure."

"Let's go talk to my colonel."

They climbed into the police carriage behind the driver and McFee said, "Take us to the Saint Francis Hotel."

The driver snapped reins and turned the carriage around, heading uphill.

Mike said, "You come up with anything on our stolen watches?"

McFee shook his head. "God, I've been meaning to talk to you about that. Chief said, 'No!' The robbery occurred outside the city. We don't have the manpower to chase down every crime in the state. He mentioned your name, not too nice about it."

"Yes." Mike smiled. He'd known the chief since his election. A good man, strictly by the book. Since the train robbery happened down the line, outside both San Francisco and San Jose, it actually was a state matter. "Okay, I'll look into it. Do you keep a list of pawnshops or jewelry stores suspected of being involved with stolen goods?"

"Any of those on upper Market Street. I recommend you look at what's on display first. You'll know what to do."

Yes. Mike knew what to do. He'd simply been too busy.

The police carriage stopped across the street from the St. Francis Hotel, an unpainted, redwood, four-story building.

Mike led McFee across the street and into the small lobby, with nobody at the desk. Mike leaned across the desk to look behind it. The clerk lay face-down on the floor, unconscious or dead.

Mike dragged McFee closer, motioned for him to be quiet, and showed him the clerk. "Check on him."

Mike reached for his shoulder holstered Colt but it wasn't there. He never wore it in the city. A stupid promise he'd made to Molly.

He vaulted up the carpeted stairs two at a time, turned left on the second floor, and rushed toward the third door on the left side. He slowed to a silent walk and approached the door, open a crack. He held his breath to listen.

Inside, men spoke softly in Russian, too soft to understand. He squared to the opening and pushed the door inward. The hinge squeaked. The voices from the inner room abruptly stopped.

Mike crept quietly into the entry foyer of Colonel Preslova's three room suite. He neared the corner, backed against the wall, and listened.

A large man in a gray wool coat stepped around the corner.

Mike grabbed his coat lapel, kicked his shin, pushed him to the floor, and stomped the back of his neck. He rounded the corner and faced another man, dressed similarly to the first.

Behind the man, Preslova had been tied to a chair. Blood trickled from his swollen nose. His dazed eyes did not see Mike.

The second man circled near the window and pulled a gun from the back of his belt, keeping his distance. He jerked sideways then darted around Mike, grabbed, and dragged his semiconscious companion off the floor. Moving fast, they lurched out into the hallway and disappeared.

McFee would stop them.

Mike hurried to untie Preslova.

The colonel looked up, blinked twice, and recognized Mike. As soon as his hands were freed, he swiped his shirtsleeve across his face, smearing blood. "Mikhail."

"My colonel." Mike smiled and stepped back. "Who were those men?"

"Lady Catherine is here."

"We always knew she would come."

Preslova stood, shaky, and moved to the table by the window. He poured himself a short vodka and turned up another glass for Mike.

Mike shook his head. "Thank you, no." He braced the colonel and looked into him. "I have bad news. The grand duke's bodyguards are dead. They died badly, in the style of the grand duke himself. I

101

think it best if we move you to the White Chapel. It's full, so we'll need to make some kind of arrangement."

Chapter Twelve

WHEN SERGEANT MCFEE arrived at his desk at 10:00 the next morning, a gang of Chinese men and women had gathered around a well-dressed gentleman and a large, well-dressed Negro. The Negro sat at McFee's desk, sketching on parchment with charcoal.

The white gentleman stepped forward and offered to shake hands. "Sergeant McFee? My name is Franklin Mosby."

McFee shook hands and shoved into his crowded workspace.

Mr. Mosby dragged a Chinaman in a gray suit from the group and guided him closer to McFee. "This is Han Wok. He's here to interpret descriptions from these witnesses. Mister Zabel asked us to do this here, as an assist to your important work." He pointed to the Negro artist. "This is our very excellent artist and my close friend, Moses Broadback."

"Witnesses to what?"

Mr. Mosby's brow popped up, evidently surprised by the question. "There have been at least eight small boys abducted in recent days."

"Oh, yeah. That Chinese thing." McFee wanted to sit down and read the previous night's edition of the Bulletin, but there the Negro sat. McFee stiffened and squared to Mr. Mosby. "And, just exactly, who are you in all of this?"

Mr. Mosby stepped closer, eyes narrow, speaking evenly, softly. "My wife was murdered and my seven-year-old daughter was taken. The man who did this is believed to be in this city, hopefully with my daughter." He slid a canvas portfolio from McFee's desk and opened it, displaying a high-quality sketch of a bearded man and a little girl on a wagon. "You might have seen them."

McFee took a closer look and shook his head. "Sorry."

The well-dressed Mr. Mosby leaned close, ready to fight or something. "Are you an officer of the law or not?"

McFee blinked, relaxed, and sat on the edge of his desk. "Look, if you want to leave a couple of those drawings, I'll post them here and our patrol officers will keep a sharp eye."

"Today's Bulletin will have more detailed portraits and an article about this man and my daughter. We're from Savannah."

"Where's that?"

"In Georgia."

"Ah, a rebel. I thought so." McFee bobbed toward the gentleman. "Your accent."

The gentleman's lips pursed tight. He blinked, controlling his anger. He stepped back and organized his sketch filled portfolio. He closed and placed the portfolio at his Negro's elbow. He then turned back with a polite smile. "Not anymore. That war is over."

"Okay." McFee stood and turned toward the large bulletin board against the far wall. "Who you working with at the Bulletin, Billy Cahill?"

Mosby relaxed, immediately more friendly. "Yes, that's right."

"Ask him to drop off a couple of extra copies of the Bulletin and take copies to all of our telegraph stations." Passing his indifference toward Chinese off on Mr. Mosby hadn't been fair. McFee liked better going toe to toe with Mike.

McFee had often lain awake most of the night, imagining chats with Mike Zabel, like the way he'd scolded McFee the night before, accusing him of allowing those two Russians to *sashay* right past him and *stroll* out of the St. Francis Hotel. McFee smiled inside. None of his imagined chats had ended well. McFee had to admit, those two Russians had walked right past him and his patrolman. No getting around it. Hence, no defensive chats with Mike, except when he was trying to sleep.

McFee and his patrolman had been behind the front desk, attending to the hotel clerk, who'd just then been regaining consciousness. He should have stationed the patrolman at the bottom of the stairs, an afterthought from his earlier sleepless night.

Mike's circle of friends seemed always to be expanding. "How long you known Mike?"

"Mike Zabel?"

McFee waited.

"We arrived in this city yesterday and found lodging at the White Chapel Saloon."

"Well, Mr. Mosby, you keep falling into good fortune like that, you'll have your daughter back in short order." Mike Zabel had earned McFee's respect a hundred times over; as grudging a respect as it was. Squaring off with him always piqued McFee's confidence. He'd grown a little with each incident.

"Right off, he and his wife made us feel welcome. I feel more hopeful of finding my daughter, having met this man."

"Make sure Billy gets those copies of the Bulletin out to our telegraph posts and we'll do all we can." McFee leaned over the Negro's back to watch.

Several small sketches had been created on one sheet of parchment, of a man wearing a long overcoat and broad-brimmed hat. The Negro's charcoal swept across another sheet of parchment in quick, sure strokes, creating a face under the hat.

Several Chinamen yakked in Chinese, shoving at the well-dressed Chinaman called Han.

Han said, "Chin bigger, cheekbone higher."

The artist filled in with charcoal, and the face took shape.

The Chinese yakity-yak sounded affirmative.

McFee couldn't stand listening to Chinese yakity-yak. He pulled Mosby aside. "I need to get over to the Saint Francis Hotel to interview the desk clerk. What's the plan for these sketches?"

"Mister Zabel said we should leave them with you. Moses can do another sheet or two from memory. We'll take those over to Billy Cahill as soon as possible."

"Count Mike. The one and only." McFee had to admit, nobody worked as hard as Mike Zabel.

MIKE HAD TAKEN JASMINE that morning. Horses needed exercise and contact, being good friends for life.

After his meeting with Alexei Waldemar von Schmidt and the mayor over how to get water piped into the Chinese community, a complete waste of time, he trotted Jasmine down to Market Street and hitched her to a post in front of the first of several pawn shops and jewelry stores.

Two hours and seven shops later, under the jingle of another overhead doorbell, he entered Simon's Distinctive Timepieces and Fine Jewelry, a small shop with glass display cases on three sides. The center display case contained a variety of men's pocket watches and women's purses, brooches, and a variety of watches suspended on necklaces and bracelets.

Mike spotted his gold watch and chain immediately, between Abe Warner's and John Downey's Comstock Watches. Their cases, chains, and fobs had been made of pure silver from Comstock Mining.

A hunched over, bespectacled man with a gray fringe surrounding his shiny dome slid through a black curtain on the back wall and limped up to the back of the display case. He gazed down at his watch collection adoringly, waiting for his only customer to speak.

"That gold watch in the center."

"Yes, sir. A very fine used watch. Still in excellent condition. Keeps perfect time." He unlocked and opened the front hinging case from the back and lifted it out, deliberately allowing the gold chain and carved-jade, ornamental fob to dangle. He eyed the tooled gold cover of a man on horseback and wound the watch. He started to open the cover.

"The engraving inside the cover reads, 'Matthew O'Brian – from your loving wife, Molly.' You are Simon?"

He blinked across the top of his spectacles, worried beyond words. His hand dropped away from the gold cover.

"Inside the covers of those two silver watches you'll find 'Comstock Load.' One belongs to Abe Warner, the other to John Downey, our former governor." Mike opened his coat and displayed his California State police badge. "Who sold these to you?"

Simon shook his head and frowned, feigning innocence.

Mike suspected this man might be part of a gang. He'd find out. "These items and others were stolen from passengers on the San Jose train, which is state jurisdiction. Lock your shop. You're under arrest for receiving stolen property."

Simon gaped and stepped back. His head dropped between his shoulders, hands waving, projecting total innocence. "I had no idea these were stolen. He said he won them at faro."

"Who?"

Simon opened the black curtain wide, exposing a small room with a desk, no doors or windows. He looked at Mike for permission.

Mike nodded.

Simon stepped into the back and dragged a ledger from his desk. He set the ledger on his display case and opened it, hands trembling. He quickly perused the pages, working from back to front. "I keep a record of all purchases and sales. Yes, here it is. He said his name is Jack Wick."

"You have an address?"

"No sir."

"How often did this man sell you such valuables?"

Simon's shaking finger slid up the pages, back to front, counting, ". . . four, five, six, seven." He turned the page and continued his count. He finally closed his book. "Sixteen times over the past thirteen months. I never saw him before that. It's a total of thirty-seven items."

"I'll need his description."

Simon shrank back, blankly staring at his ledger. "He's a big man, not fat. He wears a heavy black coat and black, broad-brimmed hat."

"Yes, this is the man. I need you to collect everything you've purchased from this man and come with me to the Evening Bulletin. We'll place an article in the newspaper with descriptions, maybe sketches or photos of these items." Billy's publisher needed to make those decisions.

Simon's head sank between his shoulders. "Many of them have been sold."

"You have a list of the buyers?"

Simon squirmed, knowing he'd already said he did, obviously not wanting to give them up. Refunds could end his business. False claims would certainly be a problem. Mike would need to think on this one.

"Give me the watches. I'll see these get back to their owners. The gold one actually belongs to me."

"You're Mathew?"

"No. I married his widow."

After examining all three watches, making sure of the engravings, Simon handed them to Mike. "Let me check my stock against the ledger. It'll only take me a few minutes."

SERGEANT MCFEE ENTERED the St. Francis Hotel at 11:30 a.m.

The desk clerk was an older man, wide at the hip.

McFee showed his badge. "I'm Sergeant McFee. I was in here last night. How's the night clerk doing?"

"He's off for a few days. He'll be okay." He craned forward, eager for another question.

"You familiar with Colonel Vladimir Preslova?"

"Of course. He and two other men share rooms on the second floor. For five years, now."

"When did you last see any of them?"

"Colonel Preslova left here early this morning, with a large trunk. He didn't check out, so we assume he'll be coming back. He's paid until the end of the year. He pays on January first, every year. Maybe he's traveling."

"The other two?"

"I haven't seen them for about a week. They left on a rainy afternoon with two other gentlemen." He thought about it, remembering. "They seemed very uncomfortable. They didn't say anything. They didn't even look my way."

"Can you describe these other two men?"

"I remember they were bigger than average and wore heavy wool coats, gray in color, with black fur collars. In fact, they looked a lot like Colonel Preslova's companions. I thought they might work together."

This matched the men McFee had seen the night before. He'd only caught a glance from behind the front desk. "Thank you for your cooperation. I might be back with more questions."

"Happy to help, any way we can."

"Where can I check on the night clerk?"

MIKE AND SIMON ARRIVED at the Bulletin shortly after noon. Billy Cahill sat behind his desk. Franklin Mosby sat opposite. Both watched Moses Broadback scratch charcoal onto parchment. Strong facial features under a broad -brimmed hat had already taken shape.

Simon leaned across Billy's desk. "That's Jack Wick. That's him."

Billy leaned back, surprised by Simon. He looked up at Mike and nodded toward the sketch. "Look at this, Mike. Isn't this the same man who robbed the train?"

"Count Mike?" Simon's eyes popped wide. His spectacles dropped and hung from a slender silver chain. His mouth hung open.

Billy smiled. "Major, the Count Mikhail Diebitsch-Zabalkansky. Count Mike. Mike Zabel. You didn't know?"

Mike placed a hand on Simon's shoulder. "This man is Simon Pettibone. He has been buying stolen goods from this man, Jack Wick. This is probably not his real name."

Simon opened his black leather bag and drew out women's brooches, watches, rings, and a few more men's pocket watches, spreading them across Billy's desk. "These are all the items I have left. I've sold several items and . . ." He stopped himself, stepped back, and shook his head. "I never knew. He always claimed to be a faro bank at the Palace."

Billy and Mike both said, "The Palace?"

Simon took another step back, blinking, fearful.

Billy smiled. "Mike is part owner of the Palace."

Simon looked at Mike and slumped, needlessly overwhelmed. He'd been cooperating fully.

Mike saw no need to arrest the man; a difficult case to prove anyway. "Mister Pettibone has been cooperative. Let's leave his name out of this. He's already suffered financially." He stared at Simon. "He will contact us if he sees this man again."

"Yes, yes." Simon nodded vigorously. "Of course."

Mike said, "If he returns to your shop, act like today never happened. Just do your business as usual. He's dangerous, so try to act normal."

Simon looked around, like he needed to relieve himself.

Billy placed a hand on Franklin Mosby's shoulder. "This is a big story. This man has apparently kidnapped no less than eight small boys from Chinatown, and is also responsible for several robberies. He's an ongoing menace to this city. I can't possibly squeeze your situation onto today's front page. With my publisher's approval, we'll miniaturize your two portraits at the bottom of the front page, with a blurb for tomorrow's edition. You'll probably get more readers by doing it that way."

Mike said, "We'll hold off on the jewelry descriptions until after we catch this man." He looked at Simon. "We will catch him."

Franklin and Moses looked up at Mike.

Mike cocked his head at Franklin. "Is Billy's schedule okay with you?"

Franklin smiled shyly. "I am delighted and surprised by your support for our quest. I'm happy, sir, to follow your lead." He nudged Billy. "Sergeant McFee asked that extra copies of your paper, with our pictures, be provided to his desk, and to the telegraph stations throughout the city. That might be a good idea for today's edition, as well."

Billy slapped his desk. "Absolutely! Now I need to get to work or this won't get out at all."

Mike thanked Simon and escorted him back to the waiting taxi. He untied Jasmine from the back of the taxi and tied her to a hitching post. He reached up and paid the driver, a little more than enough. "Take this man back to his shop."

The taxi driver snapped reins and the coach lurched forward.

Mike walked back inside and pulled Franklin toward the door. "We get a crowd at the Palace at night. We've got faro and poker.

I'd like to invite you and Moses to join us for chowder this evening. We'll talk to my partner about setting Moses up with a space to do charcoal portraits for some of our customers. Who knows, your man just might come in."

Chapter Thirteen

THE SUCHOI WAREHOUSE on California Street Wharf always chilled Han Wok's bones, especially after ten o'clock at night. He'd never cared for these late meetings, but this meeting had special importance. The Chinese Council of Elders needed the information that had been printed in the current edition of the Evening Bulletin.

Han Wok knew them all. He still held his position as a Tong boss, though not so high in standing as these three council elders, who, on nights like this, sat as judges over community disputes.

At the top of the outside stair stood two large men dressed in traditional black. He knew them both and they knew him. They knew his name but he'd never bothered to learn theirs. They stepped aside, opened the door, and Han entered the second-floor chamber.

A woman stood before the seated, three-member council, complaining that her seven-year-old son had vanished. She said he'd never before strayed from home.

The council boss spoke Cantonese. "We can do nothing unless we know the person or persons responsible."

She spoke Cantonese, tears streaking down her angry face. "Why do I come here? Why do any of us come here?" The woman scowled and bumped past Han on her way out.

Behind the three elders, all Tong bosses, sat a man in a traditional black quilted coat, black pants, black slippers, and black bowler hat, the traditional attire of a Tong hatchet man, a highly respected dispenser of justice. His hat had been pulled down to his ears, making it hard to see his face.

Han hadn't seen him before. Their previous hatchet man had been much older. He'd gone back to Hong Kong on a mission of reprisal. This one had probably just arrived from Hong Kong.

The council boss, Han's uncle, smiled and bowed from his seat, speaking in Cantonese. "Han Wok. This council is honored by your presence."

"I have a report on our missing boys. Eight, now, have disappeared during the past month, maybe nine with this last woman's boy." He pointed toward the door through which she had left.

He stepped forward and placed the Evening Bulletin in front of his uncle. Two sketches by Count Mike's new black friend topped the front page, one full-figured, and the other of the suspect's face. The headline read, "HAVE YOU SEEN THIS MAN?"

Han's uncle, the Tong boss, did not like to admit his inadequate understanding of English. He leaned forward and studied the drawings. He glanced both ways at the other two council members, then looked at Han for interpretation.

"This man was seen in Chinatown on days these boys went missing. One witness watched him give a blanket to a boy on a rainy day. He gave him food and took him away in a closed carriage. She thought nothing of it at the time. Then they found the boy's mother had died from cholera. The boy has not come back."

Han's uncle handed the paper to the hatchet man and turned back. "What about cholera?"

"Count Mike brought his friend down from Weaverville. He is an excellent Chinese doctor. Count Mike is also working with a city water engineer to import clean water for drinking and cooking. They brought clean water wagons already."

"Yes, we have seen these wagons. We already knew some were sick. You know how many?"

"Only very few for now. No epidemic."

114

"Your Count Mike saves our face. Please extend our humble gratitude."

Han bowed at the waist. He would gladly thank Count Mike. "He has bid for Chinese labor on a new railroad over the mountains."

"Same as San Jose line?"

"No. He will buy tents, cooking pots, and food. He will provide the doctor and nurse, supply two hunters for meat, and maybe to trap fish in mountain streams. We supply rice and cooks. He seeks your approval."

His uncle pretended not to understand, making sure the others would be properly informed.

"He will not take advantage. Okay? We will not take advantage. Okay?"

All three council members smiled. They would always try to take advantage.

Han Chow, Han's uncle, said, "Wok, when will you marry, huh? You are old man already. What, thirty-two years old already?"

Han Wok hesitated, shy to speak of it too early. "Count Mike's Weaverville doctor has a daughter. Maybe you will meet with him and negotiate?"

THE BASTARD CHILD OF a Romanov duchess who'd become queen of the Netherlands could never be considered part of the House of Romanov. There'd been many such bastards. Most of them knew who they were, and knew their place. From what General, the Count Boris Romochka-Krestyanov knew, Major, the Count Mikhail Diebitsch-Zabalkansky, had not known of his Romanov mother. He'd been a victim of his own ignorance, daring to be familiar with the grand duchess.

It had taken place at an event in Vladivostok, on Christmas Eve, January 6, 1855. The grand duke had taken offense and had attempted to kill the count. In self defense, as a reflex, the count had chopped off the right hand of the grand duke. There had been many witnesses, including the grand duchess.

Now, the grand duchess and her party had arrived in San Francisco, seeking revenge for her brother's death.

Noblesse oblige. Her nobility should oblige responsibilities toward those less fortunate. The duchess had no understanding of this long-held French philosophy. Neither had her brother. The duke had been an abusive, arrogant fool. She was too much like him.

That day, standing on the mezzanine floor of the Cosmopolitan Hotel, the general hated to even knock on her door. He had no choice.

He held his breath and knocked softly, three times.

Sacha Varvarinski, longtime handmade to Lady Catherine, cracked open the door and peeked out. Relieved to see the general, she smiled and pulled the door slightly wider. Her smile faded quickly and she looked at the floor. "Madam, the general is here."

"Bring him."

Sacha swung the door wide and stepped aside.

The general entered, bowed at the waist, and stood to attention.

The duchess sat at the small table near the east facing bay window, sipping her morning tea, not seeming to enjoy the morning sun, or the magnificent view. She glanced at the general, her signal for him to speak.

He laid the newspaper on the table where she could clearly see the sketches, should she choose to do so. "Your Highness has been in the presence of this man. He is now being hunted for the disappearance of Chinese boys, and for armed train and stagecoach robberies."

She glanced at the sketches and stared at Krestyanov, her signal for him to continue. Commanding her personal space, she turned to stare out the window. She would listen.

"Your Highness might choose not to be seen with this man. Should Your Highness choose, I will send Luka and Grigori to communicate with this man in the future."

She sipped tea and nodded, still staring out the window, still seeing nothing, still commanding her space. After a measured moment, she set her teacup on the table and glared at him, demanding more.

He dreaded saying more but he had no choice. "After the bodies of the grand duke's former bodyguards were discovered in a shallow grave, Major, the Count Mikhail Diebitsch-Zabalkansky, hurried to the Saint Francis Hotel and interrupted our interrogation of Colonel, the Count Vladimir Schardakava-Preslova. Grigori and Luka walked past police Sergeant Angus McFee and another police officer attending the wounded clerk in the hotel lobby. They left the hotel successfully, without being questioned."

Her eyes widened. Her mouth turned down. She wanted more.

He had no choice. "We have lost Colonel Preslova. We do not know where he went. He is in hiding, Your Highness."

She stood, straightened her gown, and turned toward the window. She would not again look at him. Her voice shook with rage. "In future, general, I suggest you be more directly involved."

He snapped his boot heels together and bowed at the waist. "Yes, Your Highness."

"I need for you to speak with this man, personally." She tapped the newspaper, indicating Duncan Frack.

"What must I say to him?"

TOMMY CHANDLER FILLED a flagon with a quart of cool beer and carried it to the corner table, making sure nobody sat near enough to hear. He set the beer in front of Jethro Townsend and sat opposite. From there he could watch the room.

Jethro gulped several swallows, licked his upper lip, and burped. He glanced around the room and leaned over the table. "Wells Fargo's got a pick-up at seven o'clock Friday morning. There'll be two guards, one up, and one inside. Two chests will be loaded into the boot, one with new minted gold coin, and the other with silver. A total value of sixty-thousand-dollars is bound for Union Bank in Sacramento. They'll need to catch it between the ferry landing and the riverboat landing. That's only a five-mile stretch, so there's almost no traffic." His eyes narrowed, asking if Tommy could handle this one.

"Yeah. Sorry about that. One of my guys got shot dead, before they got to the safe. The other two escaped. I've got another guy in mind to replace the one who got shot."

Townsend relaxed a little. "Okay. Trains are tough. I'll give you that. I read about it in the Sunday Times. I'd like to stab Mike Zabel's eyes."

"Yeah. I'd like that too. He's been a blister on my butt for years. He used to board here, you know. He's a Russian count of some kind." Tommy rubbed the scar in the center of his left hand, where he'd shot himself while fighting Mike Zabel. Tommy had never returned to boxing. "I was middleweight champ."

"Have you seen last night's Bulletin?"

Tommy shook his head. "I don't read that rag."

Townsend produced the paper from inside his coat. He spread the sheets on the table and pointed at the sketches. "Does this man look familiar?"

Duncan Frack. Tommy shook his head and stared at Townsend. "Who is he?"

Townsend said, "It says here he's wanted for questioning about a train robbery and some missing Chinese kids. If this is your man, and it sounds like it is, you're not in any position to do another job."

Tommy's right hand unconsciously balled into a tight fist, ready to punch Townsend's smug face. "Don't worry about me. We'll get it done."

"I'm taking a huge risk here. We're stealing from the U.S. Treasury. That's where I work."

Tommy said, "Don't worry. You'll get your twenty-five percent." He stared hard at Townsend. Tommy, Duncan, and Juanita were the ones taking all the chances. One of Tommy's team had already paid the ultimate price.

Townsend said, "I like the Andy Johnson quote, 'The goal to strive for is a poor government but a rich people.' He's a better president than Abe Lincoln ever could have been. I like making this government poorer, as long as I'm getting richer. That's why I'm here in your stinking, slap-sided boardinghouse."

Tommy stood and left the table, afraid of knocking Townsend's well-groomed head into the bay.

DONALD THORNE WAS RUNNING out of money. He'd been unable to win consistently at faro or poker, and paying for food and lodging for himself and little Melanie had drained most of it.

Paulette Blanco, Donald's live-in lady, worked nights as one of Tommy's prostitutes, and she paid her own way. She'd fallen in love with little Melanie. They all had, including Donald.

Tommy Chandler had kept his distance. Maybe he just didn't like kids. Maybe he didn't like women. Donald had never seen him do more than talk business with his whores.

Melanie had a good sense for people. She liked keeping her distance from Tommy. Whatever the cause, Donald favored that distance.

Paulette and the working ladies in Tommy Chandler's Boardinghouse had pooled funds and purchased three new dresses for Melanie, all with colorful lace and frills.

Melanie loved them all. She even loved sleeping behind a curtain in their long, narrow room.

Paulette and Donald shared a bed near the table and window. Her hostess room was down the hall, shared with one of the other six working girls. Paulette was the youngest and prettiest.

Paulette brought in two cups of coffee and a cup of hot cocoa, set the tray on the table, and spread the curtain in back. "Come on, little bit." She dragged Melanie from her small bed against the back wall; cute, in her long underwear. They all sat at the small table to sip coffee and cocoa. Paulette smiled nice at Donald. "Tommy needs to speak with you. He said to hurry you up."

Donald had already brushed out his hair and beard, already wearing his pants and boots. "Finish my coffee first." He sipped, stood, and strapped on his Navy Colt and knife. He sat and finished his coffee quickly, kissed Melanie's forehead, stood again, and tugged a cotton shirt over his head. No need to tuck it in.

He hurried downstairs and found Tommy in his usual place behind the bar. Donald said, "What's going on?"

"You interested in easy money?"

DUNKAN FRACK HAD BEEN carefully peeling the skin from this Chinese boy's back all morning. The kid squirming and crying the way he did made the task more time consuming. *Okay*. Dunkan enjoyed that too. "You have very nice skin. You should be proud I got a use for it. You Chinese got to be good for something."

He'd already taken his pleasure in the boy, the surprise in his little face while taking a bath together. Duncan most enjoyed introducing young boys to erotic pain.

The boy stopped squirming. He'd fainted from the pain, not from any blood loss. Duncan's skill with a sharp blade never drew much blood, only slow oozing after the skinning.

He peeled the remainder of the boy's skin from his back and carefully spread it over the hearth for curing. He'd take it up to Juanita later, let her stitch it to the others. A couple more, they could paint her tribal mosaic on it and frame it. He'd hang it on the wall with his other creations.

She liked it fine.

The outside door squeaked, somebody coming in.

Silhouetted by daylight, a square, powerfully build man stood inside the open doorway.

Without looking, Duncan reached back and grabbed the handle of his knife. "What do you want?"

"You Duncan Frack?"

Duncan said nothing.

"Tommy Chandler said you might need a man like me. He's got a job." The man's eyes had adjusted, scanning the brick hearth behind Duncan. He saw the half skinned Chinese kid.

Duncan said, "Never you mind that."

"I'm Don Thorne. Tommy asked me to bring you this." He pulled a folded newspaper from inside his coat and stretched it toward Duncan. "He suggested you stay inside during the day and buy some new clothes, maybe grow a beard." He waved at his own face, his bushy red beard.

Duncan let go of his knife, grabbed the newspaper, and turned toward the door for better light. "Joseph weeps. Who drew these?"

"Can't you read?"

Duncan didn't want to say. He glared at Thorne. "Light's not so good in here." He handed the paper back. "What's it say?"

Thorne took the paper and leaned toward the light. "The article was written by William Cahill, yesterday. This here's the Daily

Evening Bulletin. '$500.00 reward offered for information leading to the arrest of this man. Moses Broadback, a recently freed slave from Georgia, created these likenesses from eyewitness interviews with residents in Chinatown, where nine boys, ages five to eight, have been abducted during the past month.

"'State police lieutenant, Mike Zabel, Count Mike, has identified him as the man who, with two others, robbed the southbound train to San Jose.'

"Tommy said to buy some new clothes, maybe grow . . ." He waved at his bushy red beard. He smiled then frowned, looking past Duncan at the kid.

"Never you mind that. I got business with some big shots from Europe." He poked a thumb over his shoulder. "I need these kids to set a trap for that Count Mike. He's the only white man I know of cares about Chinese."

"Big shots?"

"Never you mind about that, neither. What's Tommy got?"

Chapter Fourteen

COIRA MACAULEY STOOD six inches taller, only one of the ways she could look down on Molly. She'd finally put Jimmy to bed and wasted no time coming downstairs to pin Molly into the corner next to the kitchen stairs. As if her natural height were not enough, Coira stood on the first stairstep, looking even farther downhill at Molly. Her voice shook, so angry she was. "Your little angel told me to shut up today."

Molly pushed under Coira's hip propped elbow, crossed to their gas stove, and poured two cups of coffee. She set the cups on the kitchen table and sat, motioning for Coira to join her.

Coira cocked her head, thought about it, climbed down to the kitchen floor, and sat across the table from Molly. She sat erect and hoisted her head, making sure she could look down her long nose at Molly.

Molly took a sip of coffee. After sitting on the stove all day, it tasted bitter. She spooned in two mounds of sugar and stirred. "What happened, Coira?"

Coira dumped two heaping spoonfuls of sugar into her coffee and stirred. "It was during his geometry lesson. We were studying the relationships between axioms, postulates, and theorems."

Molly shuddered, unable to stop herself. She knew nothing of Geometry.

Coira knew she was talking above Molly's level of education. She always loved that aspect of their relationship. "Your little angel heard your husband come in and leapt for the door. When I tried to stop him, he told me to shut up."

Molly laughed, unable to stop herself, and looked away.

"You think this is funny?" Coira's indignation bounced off the walls, so intense it was.

Molly turned back and sipped coffee. "Trying to stop Jimmy from greeting his father is ridiculous. Yes, and laughable." Molly stared evenly at Coira, reminding her who was the employer, and who was the employee. "My husband works very long hours. When he arrives home, he wants to be greeted by his wife and son. It's up to me to make sure his supper is ready."

Coira said nothing.

"Jimmy starts his schooling early in the morning and works all day with only one hour for lunch. He's seven years old. When is enough enough? I'd like to know." Molly shook her head and stirred her coffee. "I've never studied geometry. What purpose does it serve?"

Coira stiffened, shocked, or pretending to be shocked. "Geometry is the only true science. By geometry, we are able to measure all things and calculate relationships between shapes, and within those shapes, like triangles, spheres, circles, squares, rectangles, and the like. By geometry, we establish boundaries and define our relationship to the universe."

Molly's eyes rolled up. No stopping them. "Good grief!"

Coira said, "When your husband first interviewed me, he was most specific about the importance of teaching your son geometry."

The clock in the entry hall chimed, 10:00 p.m. "My husband needs to get up now and go to work." Molly stood and cleared the coffee cups. "We usually visit North Beach amusements on Sunday afternoons, after church. You should join us and share your concerns with him?"

MIKE'S PLACE OF EMPLOYMENT had become known as the Cobweb Palace. Spider webs could no longer be distinguished from cobwebs. Together, they had completely occupied the spaces between the second-floor joists.

Mike took his usual barstool at the end of the long, crowded bar. Abe delivered a bowl of chowder with crackers. "Need a beer?"

Mike shook his head, chewing down tender clams from the bay, tasty as always. Nobody had ever gotten sick from Abe's fresh chowders.

"Your new friends are in back." Abe nodded toward the gambling parlor. "That Negro's quite the artist, ain't he?"

Mike smiled and nodded, wiped his mouth with a white cotton towel, and stood. "What about his gentleman friend?"

"He's banking a game of faro."

Mike turned toward the double doors leading to the other room. He remembered, turned back, and reached into his breast pocket. He dug up Abe's silver watch and chain and laid it on the bar.

"You've caught the bastard?"

"Not yet. I finally found time to check the pawnshops and jewelry stores down on Market Street. I found our property at one of those shops. The owner said he bought our stuff from a man named Jack Wick. His description matches the man who robbed the train. Moses Broadback, that Negro artist, did a sketch from eyewitnesses to the kidnappings in Chinatown. When I took the shop owner up to the bulletin, he recognized the man in the sketch as Jack Wick. I'm sure that's not his real name."

Abe grimaced. "Gad! What's become of this city? How many boys now?"

"Nine. Another one disappeared yesterday."

Abe shook his head and wiped the bar. "You and me hardly ever talk anymore."

"Oh. I never realized." He elbowed up to the bar. "I've got all the time you need, my very good friend."

Abe smiled and leaned closer. "I've been meaning to ask, when are you and Molly going to give me another Godchild?"

Mike said, "I'd like that. Jimmy being seven without siblings seems irresponsible. It's not from lack of trying. Molly and her first husband, Matthew, never got pregnant. What a miracle; children, I mean." Mike smiled, humbled by the wonders in his life. "I'm sure Molly and Jimmy want this too. Pray for us." He smiled. "Who knows. It might help."

Abe grinned, dragged off Mike's empty bowl and spoon, and maintained eye contact. "What about the railroad deal?"

"Ah. I planned to discuss this at the Olympic Gym in the morning." Mike smiled. "Our labor bid is in place. I've worked through the details with Han Wok. He's taken our proposal up to his uncle and the other Tong bosses. As for Union Pacific, both houses of congress are quibbling and debating legislation for funding. They've already approved the eastern stretch from Saint Louis into the Rocky Mountains. I'm told the legislation for Union Pacific funding should pass later this year. We are well positioned on this one."

"Thanks, Mike. Ask Molly to give us a daughter this time."

Mike smiled. "Pray for that . . ." He'd like a little girl. "I'll pass your request up to the boss."

Abe smiled and moved away, surveying customers at the bar.

Mike turned through the double doors into the gambling parlor, picked up his pail, and made his rounds, collecting house fees from each table. He saved Franklin Mosby's table for last. "Did Abe explain the house rules?"

"Mister Warner? Yes, he did." Franklin put money into the pail, no hesitation. "You've got a nice parlor here. Clear away the spiders, it would be a palace."

"Abe's superstitious about the spiders. Besides, they control the flies."

Franklin dealt a king of clubs and paid the winner. He raked in his winnings from the other players, counted, and tossed the house percentage into the pail.

Mike reached through the double doors and set the money pot on the bar.

Abe dragged it off the bar and nodded.

Mike returned to the parlor and found Moses Broadback. He'd set up a well-lit corner space behind the stairs.

Amy, one of the upstairs ladies, sat on a stool, posing for a flattering charcoal portrait. "Hi Mike." She wiggled slightly and smiled, maintaining her pose.

Moses stopped and stood to face Mike. "Good evening, sir. How much I owe you to work here?"

"I thought you understood. You're an attraction. Eat all the chowder you want, drink some beer, as long as you don't get drunk, and draw portraits for our customers. Negotiate your own prices and keep the money."

Moses sat, stiff with surprise. "How do I know what to charge?"

"Ask Mister Mosby. Talk to your customers. Work it out."

Moses relaxed a little.

Mike said, "I do ask two things. Tack some of your portraits on the walls. Advertise yourself. And, give us a fair price on those from aboard ship, or any you might do around the city. We will buy some of these for framing and hang them as part of our décor."

Moses said, "I'd like to draw you and Mr. Warner, if that's okay. No charge, of course."

"On one condition. Allow me to pay you for a portrait of me and my family."

Moses smiled wide. He liked it.

While weaving back through the gambling tables, Franklin stopped him. "I'd like to post a reward notice for information about my daughter and the man who took her."

Mike said, "The Evening Bulletin will print the pictures in tomorrow's edition. You should be able to pick up the original portraits sometime after noon. While you're there, ask Billy to post the reward notice."

Franklin said, "Thank you. You have all been very helpful." He turned back to his game of faro. All five players looked familiar to Mike, regular customers who had never caused any trouble.

Chapter Fifteen

VERY EARLY FRIDAY MORNING, Duncan Frack waited outside the Forge.

Juanita, Duncan's attractive Mexican lady, led three saddled horses from the neighboring stable in near total darkness. With no moon, their only light came from a distant streetlamp.

Juanita tucked tight under his arm and shivered in the chill night air. "He is already late?"

Duncan pulled up his silver pocket watch, one he'd kept from an Overland Stage robbery a year earlier. He couldn't see it in the dark. "We need to wait. There's gonna be two armed guards."

"You waiting for me?"

Duncan spun toward the husky voice.

Donald Thorn blossomed out of blackness, barely visible up close.

Duncan said, "You're late. What time is it?"

"It's around two. You said . . ."

"Okay, okay."

Horse hooves thudded across the thick wood planks of the wharf, Juanita lining up the horses. "Here." She handed leaders to Duncan and Thorne.

Duncan mounted and prodded his horse toward the streetlight. "We'll take the early ferry."

Thorne and Juanita mounted and followed. Thorne said, "I don't need to travel by night. My face ain't in no newspapers. I can come back early."

Duncan said, "We'll be all day getting down to Oakland."

"Oakland?"

Duncan said, "Idiot! We can't return on the same ferry. Don't want nobody seeing our coming and going in the same day, now do we?"

HEAVY HAZE STILL BLOCKED the sun, having already travelled about three miles up the wagon road from the ferry landing. Rocks stood shoulder high on the land side of the road. On the Sacramento River side, sawgrass stood tall.

Duncan pulled up his silver chain and flipped open his silver watch. "Ten minutes past nine. They won't reach here for another couple of hours." He motioned toward the rocks and looked at Juanita. "Build a small cook fire, start some coffee, and fry up that bacon. Me and Thorne need to go up ahead and pick our spots."

Juanita stood down from her horse, snapped the leader rope over a low tree branch, and unpacked. She nodded for Duncan to go ahead. She never spoke unless necessity convinced her otherwise.

Duncan kicked his mount uphill toward a curve and Thorne followed. Just across a high point, the wagon road veered to the right, away from the Sacramento River, and ran sharply downhill for about a hundred yards. At the bottom, the road turned back toward the river. A giant Douglas fir stood next to the turn, surrounded on three sides by two giant boulders. Two mature pine trees rose above tall sawgrass on the river side of the road.

Duncan pointed. "Tie your horse behind that big fir."

"Fir?"

"Yeah, that fat tree on the right. Get out of sight. I'll wait behind them two trees on the left. I'll step out first. Soon as you hear my voice, you step out with that there scattergun.

"What about Juanita?"

"You never mind about her. She knows what to do."

Thorne said, "I need to know exactly who's doing what." He showed no fear of Duncan's superior size. He was built powerful but so was Duncan. He figured he'd be a mite quicker, should it come to that. He said, "I'll tie my horse over here." Ignoring Thorne's need to know everything somehow pleased Duncan, stepping down to lead his horse off the wagon road, and behind the pine trees on the left.

Thorne still sat on his horse in the middle of the road.

Duncan crossed the road and found plenty of room behind the Douglas fir. He stepped back onto the road. "Lead your horse over here. There's plenty of room."

Thorne climbed down and joined Duncan. He looked behind the tree, led the horse around it, and tied her to a low-hanging branch. He asked, "She bringing her horse down here? I mean, I just want to understand the layout."

"She'll stay up there. Drivers see a pretty lady drinking coffee makes a nice distraction." He squared to Thorne. "Get this straight in your know-it-all head. I'm in charge here. You don't like that, you can walk on back to Chandler's."

Thorne took a step back, maybe listening for once.

Duncan said, "There's a feedbag behind your saddle. We'll let the horses eat and go have some breakfast for ourselves."

Juanita had already loaded feedbags with grain and tied them behind their saddles. Both men put them on their horses.

Duncan nudged Thorne and his scattergun back up the hill, following close behind. He instinctively did not trust this man. "Stage driver will ride his footbrake down this grade, and hold the horses back. I'll step out first, and you step out after. I'll hold the lead horse and you walk up your side with that there scattergun. Let me do all the talking."

Juanita sat on a fallen tree near a small fire. She poured coffee and pointed across the fire at a good size rock for Thorne to squat on.

Duncan sat next to Juanita and sipped coffee.

Thorne grabbed his coffee, squatted, and watched Juanita stir bacon.

She stopped stirring long enough to toss each of them an empty flour sack.

Duncan took off his hat, pulled the sack over his head, found his left eye with his left hand, pinched the sack, pulled it away from his face, and used his knife to slice an eyehole. He carefully positioned the sack and eyehole, found his other eye, pinched, pulled, and cut the other eyehole.

Thorne sipped coffee and watched.

Duncan pulled the sack off of his head and tossed it to Thorne. "See if that works for you. I'll cut another one for me."

Thorne pulled the flour sack over his head, positioned the eye holes, and nodded. "What about her? She got a sack?"

Duncan had had just about enough. "You ought to walk back to Chandler's."

"I just . . ."

"I already told you, don't you worry about her. Don't ask again."

GRIGORI BALAKIREV AND Luka Varvarinski sat in a covered carriage a block from the Olympic Club Gym, waiting for Count Mikhail Diebitsch-Zabalkansky to exit.

Grigori cared nothing for this mission. If not for the fanatically obsessed duchess, he might be in Moscow. Against her rage, he dared not state his discomfort with being forced to watch the torture and murder of young boys.

The duchess seemed to enjoy their suffering, perhaps delighting in the thought of what they might do to the count's young son.

"Why must we play these games?" Luka didn't like it either. "Why can we not shoot him down and go home?"

Grigori said, "I do not like this American butcher, Duncan Frack. The grand duchess is . . ." He dared not say more.

"Da, da. I don't like killing of the children. Not even the Chinese children. I kill a man, is okay."

Grigori nudged Luka. "Look at that."

A block away, Count Mikhail Diebitsch-Zabalkansky exited the Olympic Club Gym with Colonel, the Count Vladimir Schardakava-Preslova, and a tall, thin man wearing a plug hat.

"Abe Warner," said Grigori. "One of those who shot the grand duke." Why the duchess did not want this man, and the two others who had actually killed her brother, remained a mystery.

Luka picked up the reins and waited.

Abe Warner flagged a taxi. The taxi turned wide and stopped in front of the Olympic Gym. All three climbed aboard and the taxi turned downhill toward the bay.

Luka slapped reins and followed.

Three blocks downhill, the taxi turned right.

Luka said, "Mikhail is going to his home, like always."

"We will follow Colonel Preslova."

Luka rounded the corner and followed the taxi.

A HALF MILE DOWNHILL from their position, the Wells Fargo stage rounded a wide curve on the wagon road, climbing uphill from San Francisco Bay. Six horses pulled the stage at a trot.

Duncan stood and gulped his lukewarm coffee. "Okay. Let's get down there."

Thorne tossed his coffee into the fire, causing a burst of white smoke and steam.

Idiot. Duncan said, "Juanita, you know what to do."

She looked down the wagon road and took her position, making sure they'd see her from two hundred yards downhill. She unbuttoned the top two buttons of her blouse and spread the lapels, sure to invite stares. She had very nice, firm bosoms.

Thorne ogled her cleavage and smiled.

"Come on." Duncan strolled down the wagon road.

Thorne grunted and followed, close enough.

They reached the bottom of the hill, separated, and took their positions. They could see each other without being seen from the road. Duncan had picked a good spot. He pulled on his flour sack and adjusted the eyeholes.

Across the road, Thorne pulled on his flour sack and nodded.

"Whoa," barked the coachman, slowing the thunder of hooves to a plod.

Duncan waited. When the plodding hooves neared the bottom of the hill, he stepped out onto the road, blocked the path of the horses, and aimed his pistol at the top guard's face. "Stand and deliver." He grabbed the lead horse's rein with his left hand, skidded backward until the team stopped, and used the horse's bobbing head as a shield.

Thorne hurried out, shotgun held high, and worked his way along the edge of the road to the passenger compartment.

Wearing her flour sack mask, Juanita silently climbed onto the roof from the rear.

Duncan said, "No need for anybody to get shot. Pass that scattergun and rifle back."

The top guard turned with a jerk and froze, surprised by Juanita. He slowly passed his scattergun back.

She tossed it behind the coach onto the dirt road. She leveled her pistol at the guard and motioned for the rifle.

The guard moved slowly, picked up the rifle, and handed it back. She tossed it back onto the road and motioned again.

Duncan said, "Give up them sidearms."

The driver and top guard passed them back, and Juanita tossed them to the road.

Duncan said, "You, inside, toss out them weapons or take a closeup, scattergun pelting to your faces."

The stock of a scattergun poked out from the right side and a rifle butt from the left.

"Drop them weapons to the ground and toss out your sidearms."

Those inside complied, and Thorne opened the passenger door. "Climb down out of there."

The inside guard climbed down first, hands held high, showed Thorne he had no weapons, and turned to help an elderly lady down.

An older gentleman followed her down onto the road.

Thorne poked his scattergun into the older man's stomach. "Don't make me use this."

The man pulled out and handed a gold watch to Thorne.

Thorne looked at the watch and dropped it into his side pocket. He pressed the scattergun barrel to the gentleman's chest.

The old gent reluctantly pulled his diamond stickpin and handed it over.

Thorne looked at the diamond and dropped it into his pocket. "That there ring, too."

The man stuck his finger into his mouth for lubrication, pulled the ring off, and handed it over.

Thorne turned the weapon on the woman.

She pulled off a gold framed, white cameo brooch and handed it over.

Thorne dropped the ring and brooch into his pocket.

"Enough!" Duncan had previously told this idiot to let him do the talking. He held his pistol on the top guard. "I want to see two strong boxes come up from under that seat, or I will blow your head clean off."

The guard struggled with the heavy boxes, lifting and lowering them one at a time.

"Get them passengers back inside."

They didn't need orders from Thorne, nearly scrambling over each other to climb back aboard. No ladies first. None of that.

Juanita climbed off the back, picked up weapons, and cradled them in her skirt.

Duncan stepped to the side, let go the rein, and pointed his gun at the driver. "Let off that footbrake and slap them horses."

The coach lurched forward, followed the road around the turn to the left, and picked up speed.

Across the road, Thorne leveled the scattergun at Duncan's belly. "Why don't I keep those cash boxes for myself?"

BY EARLY AFTERNOON, misty rain drizzled onto the waxed-canvas lid over their carriage, waiting a half block uphill from the home of Count Mikhail Diebitsch-Zabalkansky. Grigori Balakirev and Luka Varvarinski had been waiting for nearly two hours.

Grigori's stomach rumbled from hunger. They'd had no breakfast that morning.

Luka's boot impatiently tapped at the footboard. "How long does it take them to eat the lunch?"

"Maybe we should knock and see if they can feed us."

Luka laughed and nodded. "Da, da. Yes, this would be a good one."

Grigori said, "They are maybe discussing business. They invest together."

"Yes, with whose money?"

"Yes. We were interrupted before the colonel could inform us, with whose money he is investing. We both know he uses the grand duke's gold."

Downhill, Count Zabalkansky and Colonel Preslova exited the front door and stood on the small porch, not seeming to be bothered by the drizzling rain.

Coming from uphill, behind them, a closed taxi passed their carriage and stopped in front of Count Zabalkansky's house. The two counts shook hands, saying goodbye.

Colonel Preslova trotted down the front steps and climbed into the waiting taxi.

Luka let off the footbrake, softly slapped rein, and they slowly followed the taxi downhill at a safe distance.

Count Zabalkansky reentered his house as they passed.

Luka sighed in relief. "He did not see us."

Preslova's taxi turned right near the bottom of the hill and Luka let off the reins. Their horse sped up, and they rounded the corner at a lope. He slapped rein twice, and their horse trotted faster. He skillfully guided the horse to the left, passed the closed taxi, and yanked right, blocking the colonel's taxi. He reined in sharply and set the foot brake.

The taxi driver pulled hard on his reins and stomped his footbrake. His horse skidded on wet bricks and reared, barely stopping the taxi in time.

Luka jumped down, and Grigori leapt out after him. They ran to the left of the taxi and yanked open the passenger door.

A booted foot rushed toward Grigori's face, painfully kicking his nose.

Grigori flew back, landed on his shoulder, rolled, and sat on wet bricks, stunned. He wiped his nose and looked at the blood.

Count Zabalkansky's small Portuguese friend jumped down and rushed around the back of the taxi.

A moment later, Luka rushed toward their carriage, holding the side of his bleeding face.

Colonel Preslova stepped out of the taxi holding a pistol.

Grigori jumped to his feet, dodged left, and rushed toward their carriage.

Luka had already slapped reins, and their carriage lurching forward, away from Grigori. He scrambled onto the boot and clutched the luggage bar with both hands.

Behind them, Count Zabalkansky's little Portuguese friend stood in the middle of the road, shaking both fists at the sky, begging them to come back.

Chapter Sixteen

MIKE RODE JASMINE DOWN the alley from his horse barn in time to see one of the Russian guards jump onto the boot of the passing carriage and grasp the luggage bar as it sped past. Mike and his colonel had been aware of their following from the Olympic Club Gym, both wary since Mike had interrupted their interrogation of Colonel Preslova.

After Mike arrived home from the Olympic Club Gym, he'd asked Raul to saddle Jasmine and make his way up the alley to find an enclosed taxi, where he could hide in case the Russian guards chose to follow Colonel Preslova.

After Preslova left, Mike had gone back inside, strapped on his shoulder and hip holsters, checked his Colt revolvers, holstered them, pulled on his rain slicker, and stepped into Molly's questioning stare. "If we don't want trouble, we need to be prepared to handle it."

"Trouble?"

"I'm in a hurry." He'd kissed her on the forehead. "I'll explain later." He'd pushed past her and gone out through the alley door.

Less than a minute after leaving Molly, Mike had ridden Jasmine out of the alley and rounded the corner onto the brick-paved road. He held Jasmine back at a safe distance and followed the Russian carriage downhill.

The Russian carriage stopped a block ahead, and Mike reined in Jasmine to a slow walk. The guard on the back climbed down and stared at Mike for a minute, maybe trying to identify him through drizzling rain. Maybe he had.

Mike doubted this, too far away, but he maintained Jasmine's slow pace.

The guard climbed into the carriage and the carriage moved off at a canter.

Mike slowly increased Jasmine's pace, allowing his distance from the taxi to widen until they were moving at about the same speed, now two full blocks apart. The carriage turned uphill toward the Cosmopolitan Hotel.

Of Course. Mike turned up the nearest street and kicked Jasmine uphill at a trot. After two blocks, he turned her left and trotted down to the north side of the Cosmo. He reined in, dismounted, and tied Jasmine's leader to a hitching post. He walked to the corner of the building, from where he could see both entrances.

The Russian carriage turned into the hotel's stable entrance.

Mike strolled into the entry foyer, grabbed a copy of the Police Gazette, and sat in a chair near the window. He had a clear view of all three entrances, and of the grand staircase.

He read an article about Shanghai Kelly, remembering his previous troubles with Tommy Chandler, having been nearly shanghaied himself. While reading, he frequently glanced over the top of his Gazette, watching for the Russian guards.

A newspaper column later, the two Russian guards entered through the stable door and hurried up the grand staircase.

Mike set the paper down and strolled to the front desk.

The middle-aged clerk looked familiar, smiling like a friend. "Count Mike. It's been a long time." He offered his hand.

Mike shook and held his hand, remembering the voice, the face. "Patrick! It has been a long time. Empire, wasn't it?"

"That's right. I've missed our lunches."

When Mike, then Major, the Count Mikhail Diebitsch-Zabalkansky, had first arrived in San Francisco, he'd frequented the free lunches availed at the glittering casinos of

Portsmouth Plaza. Patrick had been a bartender at the Empire, and had offered to help him find work. This had been a time in Mike's life when he'd desperately needed help, those days when he'd nearly been shanghaied.

Patrick leaned across the counter, more private. "Say, whatever happened? I mean, I often read about you in the Evening Bulletin, but I never knew what happened with that longshoreman job. Last time I saw you, you were at the powder end of a cannon."

"That same day, after your job offer, Tommy Chandler knocked me out, took me for dead, and dumped me into the slime under Pacific Street Wharf. I woke up and found Molly O'Brian's Boardinghouse. She saved my life, in more ways than one."

"Yeah. I read how you and her got married." He smiled, always friendly. "You've come a long way, like I knew you would." His brows shot up. "What brings you to the Cosmopolitan Hotel?"

"Those two men who just came in."

"Those Russians? Yeah. There's five, all together; two women and three men. One of the women seems to be the boss. They've got three rooms at the east end of the mezzanine floor. Those two who just came in are gone a lot."

"You have a work schedule?"

"You mean me? For myself?"

Mike smiled.

"I start after lunch and get off around midnight."

"Do me a favor?"

"Sure. Anything."

"Hand me a sheet of paper and a quill."

Patrick reached under the counter and pulled up a quill pen and ink well. He reached again and slid a sheet of hotel stationary next to the pen.

Mike dipped ink and wrote his address. "Here's my address. You know Raul?"

141

"That little Portuguese bouncer?"

"The very same. He works for us now. If you see those ladies go out, send a runner up, and let us know where they've gone."

"I never know where they're going."

"Tell us what you know. Tell us what you think."

"What's this about?" He thought for a second. "Say, what should I call you?"

Mike smiled. "Please, call me Mike."

"What's this about, Mike?"

"I think I might know this lady." His colonel had already told him. "I'd like to make sure." He slid a twenty-dollar gold piece across the desk. "This is for the runner."

Patrick reached then hesitated. "That's more than enough."

"Keep whatever's left and I'll still owe you."

Patrick took the money.

"Do me another favor? Stop in at the Palace after work. Let me buy you some chowder and hot buttered rum."

"The Cobweb Palace on Meigg's Wharf?"

GENERAL KRESTYANOV had been raised under the boot of the Romanov Dynasty. He'd grown indifferent about their arrogance and willful barbarism, but this current Czar, Alexander II Nikolayevich, seemed nothing like his father.

Czar Nikolay I Pavlovich had been a determined and often brutal emperor.

Grand Duke Nikolay Nikolayevich, younger brother of Nikolay Pavlovich, had been the cruelest person Krestyanov had ever known. Krestyanov had always been fearful in his presence. He hated being afraid.

The grand duke's sister, the duchess, was much like her brother. She enjoyed the suffering of peasants. To her, anybody not born of royal blood was a peasant, Krestyanov included. To her, Major, the Count Mikhail Diebitsch-Zabalkansky was worse than any peasant. He was the bastard son of her reckless cousin. She'd often said that he should have been killed in her womb.

When Alexander lifted the warrant on Count Mikhail Diebitsch-Zabalkansky, she'd been so infuriated as to shoot one of her guards, for simply greeting her with a smile. That guard had survived and had been reassigned to Alexander's staff.

Lucky man. Krestyanov sometimes wished he'd been the one to smile and be shot.

Alexander II Nikolayevich was known as Alexander the Liberator, for freeing the serf class of all Russia. His current objective was to sell Alaska to America, a frozen wasteland out of reach. This money would pay war debts and allow for the development of Siberia.

Alexander exuded nobility, unlike his aunt, Lady Catherine.

Krestyanov poured his second glass of vodka and turned toward the window overlooking San Francisco Bay, a soothing view in drizzling rain. The horizon-line had vanished. Gray sky had fused with the chill-gray water of the bay, an infinite reach into distant, unknown places. He absently sipped vodka and watched three gulls fly from the hotel rooftop toward the bay. This tranquility pacified him.

Four sharp knocks broke his serenity. He crossed in three paces and threw open the door.

Grigori and Luka snapped their heels in unison and stood to attention.

Grigori's face had been smeared with blood from his bleeding nose. He wiped with his shirtsleeve and smeared it more.

The side of Luka's face evidenced a swollen-purple boot print. Bleeding at the side of the boot mark had stopped but the cut remained.

Krestyanov stepped aside. "Get in here."

They marched into his room and he closed the door. "What is this?"

Grigori blinked several times, afraid to say.

"Well?"

"My general, there is much to report."

Krestyanov backed toward the window and fanned the table. "Take some vodka. Relax." He stared at Grigori and nodded toward the wash table. "Go wash your face."

Grigori stepped to the corner and splashed into the washbasin.

Luka crossed to the table and half filled two glasses with vodka. He took a sip and held the second glass out for Grigori.

Grigori held a wet towel to his nose and took the glass. He sipped, stiff and nervous. "Sir, we followed Count Zabalkansky as you directed. He went early to his gymnasium and stayed there three hours. He came out with Count Preslova, and we followed them down to Count Zabalkansky's house. Two hours later, both men came out, and Count Preslova got into a taxi by himself. We thought it better to follow him, since we already know where Count Zabalkansky lives."

"Da, da. Of course. We need Preslova."

Both men gulped the remainder of their vodkas and looked to the table, asking for more.

"Go ahead." Krestyanov folded his arms and waited.

They filled their glasses nearly full and turned to face Krestyanov. Both bolted their vodkas and set their empty glasses on the table.

Grigori looked at Luka and waited.

Luka shook his head. He would say nothing.

Frustrated, Krestyanov threw his glass at the fireplace. It shattered against the carved marble surround, and he spun back, glaring at Grigori.

Grigori and Luka stood to attention.

Grigori said, "Sir, we chased the taxi downhill, rounded the corner, and sped to block the road. We both jumped out and ran back to seize the colonel. When I opened the door, a boot met my face with such force that I tumbled backward onto the road. I have never been kicked so hard. Not even by a horse." He touched his bruised nose and cheekbone. "It stunned me. I fear he may have broken my face, it is still so painful.

"Luka opened the other door, and a small man booted his face, then climbed onto him, striking his face with blows faster than I could see."

Luka touched his bruised cheek and blinked past his bruised and swollen left eye. "My eyes so flooded with tears, I could not see, but yet the blows continued. Such hard blows, I thought it must be a much bigger man."

Grigori said, "It was this little Portuguese friend of Count Zabalkansky. We are certain. You have already heard what Duncan Frack said about him, how he trained Count Zabalkansky."

Krestyanov almost laughed. He wished he could have been there to watch this little man fight. "What about Colonel Preslova?"

Grigori said, "He stood over me with a gun, while Luka fled for his very life."

"How did you get away?"

"The colonel did not shoot when I ran to catch the speeding coach." Grigori glared angrily at Luka.

Krestyanov said, "So, they must have followed you here."

"No, sir. We stopped to check. Their taxi was not in sight."

"This is not good. Count Zabalkansky knows somebody from Russia is in this city, and looking for him. Perhaps he knows not who, but he will suspect the duchess." Krestyanov turned to Luka. "Go to her rooms. Send Sacha over to clean this up." He motioned to the broken glass, stepped to the table, poured more vodka, and handed them both refills. He poured himself another and sipped.

"Sir," said Gregori. "Do we need to report this to . . ." Both men looked more scared than worried.

"Nyet. This is for me. She insists on a daily report."

Grigori gulped his vodka. "But, sir . . . do you need to tell her about this little Portuguese, about what happened?"

Luka sank into himself with shame. "He is too much smaller."

TWENTY MINUTES LATER, after the duchess had listened patiently while Krestyanov reported the events of the day, she stood, stiff like a stone, and stared out her north facing window. "So, he knows we are here."

"He cannot be sure that you are here, but he will suspect this. Yes."

She turned to face him, red with rage, voice shaking. "Must we find another residence?"

"Grigori and Luca both assured me they were not followed." He forced himself to calm. Perhaps she would calm, too. "Madam, a bigger problem for me is this Duncan Frack. He is wanted for armed robbery, and for the abduction of children."

Her shrill voice rang. "Nobody cares for Chinese. Nobody cares what happens to these stinking, yellow peasants."

"Madam, they care enough to put it into their newspaper. It is on the front page."

She thought about this and returned to her chair. "What do you recommend?"

Krestyanov had been thinking about this for a long time. He wished he could convince her to return to Moscow. "With your indulgence, Duchess, I served under Mikhail's father in Crimea. I know Colonel Preslova as a brother at arms. He is an honorable man. I also served under your brother, the Grand Duke. He was an unstoppable force. No person could withstand his ferocity."

She grew more rigid with every word, her patience disappearing.

Krestyanov said, "Of course, whatever your decision, we are here to serve you."

"General, what is your recommendation?"

Krestyanov said, "Colonel Preslova and his men certainly would have served your brother as best they could. We've both read the newspaper reports. Your brother entered a private party and shot at Major Zabalkansky, who was unarmed. Three powerful Americans shot your brother, defending the unarmed major's life. He is well liked here. He is a man of substance."

She pushed against the arms of her chair, ready to jump, eyes burning with rage.

"He is the son of the queen of the Netherlands. Illegitimate? Yes. But, he is her son, just the same. He is the son of your aunt. Informants tell us she knows of his presence here. I have no doubt, she will plan to visit him. She is his mother. Would you want to explain to your nephew, Czar Alexander, how he died?"

Her glowing red eyes and flushed face seemed to fly toward him with an ear-splitting shriek, "I don't care!" Her shrill cry surprised even her. She stepped close, voice shaking, and spoke softly. "That bastard dared to ask me for a dance. My brother had no choice but to defend my honor. That bastard cut off the right hand of my brother, right in front of me. Now my brother is dead. Tell me, how is this not his fault?" Her decision had been made. No turning back.

"Very well, Your Highness. We are here to serve you."

She spun and returned to her chair, stiff as if on a throne.

Krestyanov said, "We must arm ourselves. We must wait until Mikhail is away from his family to take his wife and son. Duncan Frack must then immediately see that the bodies of these Chinese boys are found, and that Mikhail sees them. If his Portuguese friend gets in the way, I will shoot him myself."

She allowed a slight smile. She liked this plan.

Chapter Seventeen

FRANKLIN MOSBY AND Moses Broadback sat across the desk from Billy Cahill in the press office of the San Francisco Daily Evening Bulletin, studying the front page of that evening's newspaper.

Moses's sketches of Melany and the bearded man had been sharply reproduced in an easily recognizable size. The bold print headline read, "REWARD OFFERED FOR INFORMATION." The brief article invited any individuals who might have seen either of these persons to immediately contact the Bulletin.

"Perfect." Franklin hadn't wanted information of his wife's death or the abduction of his daughter made public for fear this villain might take flight or worse, that he might end Melanie's life to conceal his guilt.

Billy Cahill nodded at his typesetter.

The typesetter hurried out. It was time to run the presses.

Billy looked back and forth between Franklin and Moses. "You want print screens of these portraits? They'd be on canvas, mountable for framing."

Franklin liked the idea. "Of my daughter? Yes. How much?"

Billy showed Franklin the flat of his hand. "No charge. The Bulletin is grateful for your help. The least we can do."

"Mike asked us to put some drawings up in the Palace. Can we give you some sketches for screening? Moses could hang them in his workspace and Mike could hang them around the Palace. Moses will bring you the charcoal sketches. We will pay for those, of course."

"Get the sketches to me and I'll get some prices worked up for screening and framing. If you and Mike approve, I'll bring them to the Palace and chew some chowder. Pay for them when I deliver them." His eyebrows shot up and down with a smile. "We can screen as many prints of each sketch as you want. We can even number them."

Franklin said, "You are too kind, sir."

"Nonsense. We'll take care of it. Because of you, our circulation has nearly doubled. Our readers appreciate pictures. And, the news is compelling."

Franklin turned to Moses. "You need anything?"

"No, sir. I cannot clear this man from my memory." He pointed at his sketch of the murderer.

Billy said, "Okay. As soon as I get all the sketches, I'll get over to our art department. It should only take a day or two to determine the cost."

Franklin and Moses stood, and Franklin shook Billy's hand.

Billy gestured toward Moses.

Moses bent slightly at the waist and extended his trembling hand. Billy took and shook it. Moses stiffened, awkward, and pulled his hand back. It was a very new thing for him to shake hands with a white man.

Franklin resolved to change that.

Billy said, "The Bulletin will get the paper out and make sure it gets to all of the police stations, as well as to the hotels and boardinghouses."

THE FERRY RIDE BACK from Oakland took longer than Donald Thorne could ever have imagined, thinking on another terrible decision in his life. He'd never be asked to work with Duncan Frack again.

Juanita's gun barrel had pressed hard on his ear, even before he'd been able to pull back the shotgun hammers.

Stupid.

He'd apologized. He'd sworn to them, he'd just been playing around. He'd admitted it had been a stupid stunt. He'd even shown them the still seated hammers, trying to convince them, he'd had no intention of actually shooting anybody or of taking any of their loot.

His cowing hadn't worked. They'd disarmed him. They'd even taken his knife. They'd even debated whether to kill him or just to leave him on that wagon road by the river, without a horse.

The San Francisco mint had bagged the gold and silver coin in separate canvas bags before loading it into the strongboxes and onto the Wells Fargo stage.

Juanita and Duncan had loaded the confiscated weapons and coin sacks into two tent canvases and tied those onto their two horses. Duncan had even talked about shooting Donald and leaving him on the roadside leading to Oakland, disconnecting his body from the site of the robbery, and then to use his horse as a packhorse.

Cold fog on the bay chilled Donald's emptiness. He yearned for his room at Tommy Chandler's Boardinghouse. He yearned to see little Melanie's smile. He yearned for the warmth of Paulette.

Finally! City lights winked through fog, not far away.

Duncan Frack adjusted the loads on their horses, with only a glance at Donald. "You stay in front of us."

Donald stood close to Duncan. "Look, I was just playing around. It was stupid. I shouldn't have done it. I'm sorry about . . ."

Gears clanked loudly and sideboard paddlewheels reversed. They braced against the lurch, as the boarding ramp nosed onto the slope of the ferry landing.

Duncan handed Donald the leader for the horse he'd used. "Go to the stable next to the Forge. We'll be right behind."

They led their horses off the ferry and well up the landing before Duncan said, "Get up, now."

Donald mounted and rode slowly toward the first of many streetlights, spaced a block apart at street corners. Horse hooves plodded slowly over the thick wooden planks of the Barbary Coast.

Behind him, Duncan and Juanita spoke in Spanish. Donald didn't understand much. They sounded like they were arguing whether or not to shoot Donald in the back.

Such shootings had been common on the Barbary Coast since Donald's arrival. Dead bodies turned up every day, and nobody cared. Some died of too much drink, some from one disease or another, especially after coming in from foreign ports. Only a few got murdered with a gun or a knife.

Nobody cared.

How many more victims must be rotting under these wood-plank streets? How many had been feeding the crabs for how many years?

Juanita shouted something in Spanish.

Duncan's soft voice quieted her.

Thinking about it, in the short time he'd known him, he'd never heard Duncan raise his voice. Even robbing the Wells Fargo, his voice had barely been loud enough for the coachman to hear. That quiet might have signaled weakness to Donald. Maybe that's why he'd pulled such a stupid stunt. *Senseless!*

Donald had managed to burn the best opportunity of his life. He'd been invited into something nice. An easy income had been placed at his feet, and he'd kicked it into the dirt. His whole life, he'd never before known such an opportunity. He'd always been forced to accept a fistful of hard knocks.

His father had put him to work in a cotton mill in upstate New York on his tenth birthday, to help pay for his food and keep. He'd worked twelve hours a day with no food until he got home, after which his mother had taught him to read.

His first bad decision, at age 28, had been to join the Union Army, a sure escape from the factory. Hard, cold marches into battle had caused him to wish he'd remained in New York. Seeing comrades torn apart by cannon fire, and watching friends drop from swarms of enemy rifle fire had driven him face down into the cold, wet dirt.

He'd never before known that kind of fear. He'd nearly always been controlled by fear, and fear gripped him right then.

Now, with this darling child to look after, a dry bed to sleep in, a pretty woman to keep him warm, and a chance at easy money, look what he'd gone and done.

Fool!

Duncan said, "Turn into this here stable."

A death chill ran up Donald's back, riding into the small, lamp-lit stable. He pulled rein and waited for a bullet or a blade to pierce the back of his goose-bump neck.

Juanita rode slowly past, guided her horse into a stall, and climbed down.

"This'll do." Duncan climbed down close behind Donald. "Let Juanita take care of the horses. You help carry this stuff into the Forge. Stay in front of me."

Donald climbed down and untied the heavy tent canvas from Juanita's horse. He set it on the wood-plank floor to shift the weight, then lifted and swung it over his shoulder.

Duncan walked a few steps behind Donald into the warmth of the Forge. "Set that over near the fire, and step away where I can watch you."

Donald set the heavy load on the raised brick hearth and backed toward the wall, bracing to receive whatever might be coming, listening to the rapid beat of his heart.

Duncan set the second canvas bundle on the hearth. "Near forgot. Set them watches and such you took off the Wells Fargo right there." He pointed his shotgun at a spot between the bundles.

Donald pulled watches, coin purses, and the broach from his coat pockets, and set them on the hearth.

"Divvy that stuff into three shares."

Donald divided the jewelry and cash the best he could. "Listen . . ." He stood to face Duncan. "That there shotgun wasn't even cocked. I got no idea why I did what I did. You been real fair with me. I aught not to have done it." He backed against the raised hearth. "I sometimes get the compulsions."

Duncan twitched with the shotgun and sneered. Maybe he had the compulsions too. Like Donald's compulsions in Savannah. What he'd done to that woman had never bothered him till he'd gotten to know Melanie. Now, what he'd done to Melanie's mother bothered him near every day. He'd taken that little angel's mommy. He'd hurt her and killed her. He'd even enjoyed it, at the time.

Duncan pulled both hammers back on the shotgun. "Open them two canvas satchels."

Donald untied the rope from the first bundle and spread the canvas. The shotgun, rifle, and sidearms from the Wells Fargo had been stashed inside.

"Shovel some of that coal onto the fire." Duncan motioned toward a coalbin and a shovel.

Donald dumped two shovelfuls of coal into the center of waning embers.

"That'll do." Duncan slowly backed away. "Now, pull that chain and pump that billows." He pointed his shotgun over Donald's head.

Donald reached up and pulled the chain. Up and down, the billows pushed air under the fire. The new coals ignited quickly.

"Now, step back against the wall."

Donald backed against the wall and returned the shovel.

Juanita came in from the stable and stood next to Duncan.

Duncan nodded toward the weapons. "Nita, drag them weapons over by the stairs." He nodded toward the far side of the room.

Keeping the weapons between herself and Donald, she wrestled and dragged the canvas across the wood plank floor to the stairs.

"Okay." Duncan waved the shotgun at Donald. "Now, open that other satchel. Open them bags inside and stack them coins into ten-coin stacks. Keep the gold and silver separate."

The task took fifteen to twenty minutes. It looked okay to Donald.

"Put half of them gold coins into sack, and half thar silver into t'other."

It took about a minute.

"Split what's left into three separate piles."

This took a little longer.

Duncan nodded at Donald. "Sack up your share, including that jewelry, then step back against the wall."

Donald followed orders.

Duncan leveled the shotgun on Donald's belly. "This is how we do business. We don't cheat nobody. Juanita wanted to shoot you dead, and shove you under the docks, but we need a third man for future jobs." His eyes narrowed, hard to see in the reflection of flickering light from the fire. "You understand me?"

"I do."

"You try and cheat Tommy, he will find you, and he will end your life. He won't need me for that."

"I've learnt my lesson. I'm real glad to be working with you. No more joking around."

"He's not with us." Juanita spit into the fire.

"Nita, never you mind." He lowered the hammers slowly and cradled the shotgun in the crook of his arm. "Collect your weapons and take them two sacks to Tommy."

"Can I bundle everything into one canvas? It'll be easier to carry over my shoulder and look normal."

"Sure." Duncan twitched toward the door, *Get going.*

Making sure Duncan could see both hands, Donald slowly holstered his revolver and sheathed his knife. He dropped Tommy Chandler's two sacks into the center of a canvas tent and tossed his smaller sack next to them. He tied the bundle with rope, slung it over his shoulder, and squared to Duncan. "You been real straight with me. I'm in your debt."

"Don't try and cheat Tommy. He'll kill you dead."

"I won't."

He walked out of the Forge and turned toward Pacific Street Wharf, toward Tommy Chandler's, toward Melanie, toward home.

Fifteen minutes later, he entered Tommy Chandler's Boardinghouse.

Friday nights had always been full with sailors, drunk or getting that way. That night seemed fuller than most. Accompanied by a small accordion, men in their cups sang *Paddy Get Back,* an old-world sea song. He'd heard it many times since coming west.

Tommy set mugs of beer on his bar and collected money, the same as most nights. Always attentive, he motioned for Donald to follow him into the back room.

They entered Tommy's office, and Tommy closed the door. "How'd it go?"

"Good. Duncan knows how. He's a good man."

"He is."

Donald slung the heavy bundle onto Tommy's desk and untied it. He slid his smaller sack aside, and nodded at the others. "Juanita and Duncan shared everything out, and I come straight here."

Tommy stared at Donald's sack. "You owe me rent?"

"No, Tommy. I'm paid up."

Tommy folded the tent over his two sacks and unfolded a newspaper in front of Donald.

It took a few seconds for Donald to focus. He bent close, studying sketches of himself and Melanie. He read the descriptions of his red hair, of her blonde hair, and of her age.

Tommy leaned close. "You know who that is?"

Donald said nothing. He could barely keep his balance.

"You need to get your whore to shave that beard and cut your hair. Then you need to get some sun. I still haven't decided if you need to find another place to live." Tommy's eyes narrowed. "The whore stays here. She works for me."

BY 12:15 A.M., THE bar side of the Palace had thinned to a few drunk sailors, one of whom chased a monkey around a post. The monkey was winning, dragging his looped leash close behind.

Mike finished his cup of tea and set it on the bar.

Abe Warner dodged around his floor-scrubbing Chinese coolie, shelving clean bowls, mugs, and steins.

Mike turned through the double doors into the gambling parlor. Behind the stair, Moses Broadback sketched one of the New Orleans ladies from upstairs. She sat on the lap of an elegantly-dressed Mexican patron, hard to know if he might be drunk.

Mike grabbed his bucket from the small table near the double doors and moved slowly between the tables, collecting house percentages.

One of the players at Franklin's table stared hard into Franklin, waiting for the next card to turn up, a three of clubs. He slammed a fist onto the table when Franklin took his money.

Mike grabbed the man's shoulder with a friendly grip.

The man looked at Mike and grumbled, grudgingly calming himself.

Franklin counted out and deposited the house percentage into the bucket.

Several screened canvas sketches of ships, a railroad locomotive, mountains, and interesting trees had been properly mounted and framed behind glass. Other sketches had been scattered around the room between artifacts from San Francisco's ever-growing sea trade. The drawings added nicely to the rustic décor of the Palace.

He pushed back through the double doors and set the bucket on the bar.

Abe set it under the bar and nodded toward the far end.

Patrick from the Cosmopolitan sat near the front door. He waved.

Mike said, "Got any more chowder?"

Abe said, "Coming right up."

"Give us a couple of bowls and give Patrick a mug of hot rum?"

"Yes, sir." Abe smiled and turned toward the stove.

Mike strolled along the bar, shook hands with Patrick, and pulled him to a clean table with a fresh tablecloth. "I hope you don't mind if I join you. I'm hungry."

Patrick smiled. "It smells good." He looked around at the sea trade décor, then looked up at the mix of cobwebs and spider webs. "I see why it's called the Cobweb Palace."

Mike sat and slid back in his chair. He looked up. "You get used to it."

Abe delivered a tray with three bowls of chowder, a platter of crackers, two mugs of beer, and a hot buttered rum. "Mind if I join you?" He sat.

Mike grabbed a bowl of chowder, crumbled crackers into it, and snagged a mug of beer. He motioned to Patrick. "Abe Warner, meet Patrick. He used to work at the Empire, when I first arrived here. I didn't care for Tommy Chandler's cooking, and Patrick kept me from starving. He even had a job lined up for me." Mike slurped chowder, well cooked and always tasty.

Patrick and Abe shook hands and dipped spoons into chowder, both hungry.

When their spoons scraped the bottoms of their bowls, Abe said, "Anybody want a refill?"

Mike put up the palm of his hand and shook his head.

Patrick said, "Maybe half as much?"

Abe put their empty bowls on the tray, stood, and placed the tray on the bar. He hurried around the bar to his steaming kettle.

Patrick glanced over his shoulder and leaned close. "About those ladies staying at the Cosmo. They almost never leave their rooms. One of the men pays every week with gold coin from Russia."

"Can you describe these ladies?"

"The one dresses very elegant. I think she employs the rest."

"Pretty?"

"Oh, yes. They're both beautiful. The one's got dark hair, ruby red lips, green eyes, and looks around thirty. The other's got blondish hair, dark blue eyes, and looks maybe twenty, maybe younger."

"Does the young one sound Ukrainian, with a nice figure?"

Patrick said, "I wouldn't know Russian from . . . what?"

"Ukraine is south of Russia, on the Black Sea."

"Wherever she's from, she makes me want to go home and throw rocks at my misses." His eyes opened wide. "Both can cause a man to stare."

Chapter Eighteen

COIRA MACAULEY SHOWED no sign of enjoying herself at mass on Sunday morning. She stood and knelt at all the appropriate utterances, knowing the Latin probably better than Michael. She stood in line for the holy sacrament of communion. She'd obviously been to confession at some point. She was certainly Catholic, but not one to regularly attend church.

Her church visit that Sunday morning did nothing to improve Molly's appreciation for Miss Coira Macauley. She'd somehow managed to flaunt her superior education and refinement, even during the mass.

Look at that! Raul appreciated Miss Coira Macauley's presence.

Plain enough to see. When Coira looped Raul's arm, he strutted like a peacock, maximizing his height, as they paraded down the church steps toward their waiting coach. Paddy had the top down on a fine, warm, rare, sunny day.

Raul gently nudged Coira aside to help Molly into the carriage. He then helped Coira onto the opposite bench and climbed in beside her.

Michael hoisted Jimmy onto the bench next to Molly and climbed in beside him. He tapped Paddy's back. "North Beach."

Jimmy hugged himself and giggled, anticipating a North Beach excursion on such a fine day.

The carriage lurched forward, and Coira immediately leaned across toward Michael. "I've been wanting to speak with you, sir."

Michael leaned forward to listen.

Coira threw an irritated glance at Molly, at Jimmy, and leveled her eyes on Michael. "The other night, we were in the middle of geometry exercises regarding right angles. Little Jimmy slid his worksheet onto the floor, jumped up, and rushed to the door. I told him to pick up his work and sit back down." She glanced angrily at Jimmy.

Jimmy leaned into Molly and looked down at his suddenly combating thumbs.

Coira said, "Well, he shouted for me to 'Shut up,' and dashed out of the room." She leaned back with a smug nod.

Michael looked at Jimmy, waiting for a response.

Jimmy leaned tighter into Molly. He dared not to look up.

Michael said, "Well, young man, what about this?"

Jimmy slowly looked up at his father, tears welling in his eyes, lips puffed out, stubbornly biting down in an effort not to cry. "Daddy . . ." He choked, afraid to say more.

"Yes?"

Molly wanted to jump in and defend her son, but she'd learned not to interfere. Michael had his ways, and he was always fair.

"You came home." He looked down at his battling thumbs.

Michael smiled and leaned back. He cradled Jimmy's head and pulled him close.

You wonderful man.

Michael said, "Jimmy, look at me."

Jimmy slowly looked up at his father.

"Don't ever be rude to your elders, especially Miss Macauley. She's your teacher. Okay?"

"Yes, Daddy." Jimmy hugged into his father.

Michael turned to Coira, speaking softly in what sounded like French.

Coira nodded several times as the smugness drained from her face.

AFTER THE MISHAP WITH Grigori and Luka, General Boris Krestyanov hired new coaches and drivers. Mikhail would not recognize these. Both open sided coaches had fixed tops for better concealment. Mikhail and his Portuguese thug could not possibly know they were still being followed.

Mikhail's coach stopped at an arcade near the bay.

Boris Krestyanov told his hired driver, "Turn uphill here and park." This street had a clean escape route. He climbed down and flagged their second coach.

Grigori and Luka turned uphill, drove past, and parked near the front of Boris's coach.

Boris walked uphill and leaned into the second coach. "Where is the duchess?"

Grigori said, "She and Sacha took a taxi down to California Street Wharf."

"She's gone to see Duncan Frack?" *Why does she not tell me?*

"She makes sure he is ready. She says, we must now hurry."

"You both know what to do?"

Grigori climbed out. "Yes, sir."

Luka walked around and stood next to Grigori. They both paid attention.

Boris said, "We need to be sure of our moves from here on. Count Zabalkansky is no fool. Now that he knows we are here, he certainly deduces we are here with the duchess."

Gregori briskly shook his head. "He cannot possibly be sure."

"Is possible." Boris turned toward the arcade. "Wait for me to get into position. You know what to do."

MIKE LOVED MOLLY'S nearness, walking arm-in-arm through the arcade, following Jimmy's rush from one attraction to the next.

Raul and Coira stopped at a caramel apple booth.

Jimmy jumped in line for his favorite attraction, a steam driven carousel with brightly painted wooden horses.

Mike gave Jimmy a nickel and sat with Molly on a nearby bench.

Molly asked, "What did you say to Coira? French, was it?"

"Yes, French." He smiled and squeezed Molly's hand. "I thanked her for bringing this to my attention. Then I told her I enjoy being greeted when I get home from work."

"And?"

"She understands."

Molly put her head on Mikhail's shoulder. "I don't like her."

"I know." He held back a laugh.

Jimmy scrambled onto the giant carousel with a dozen other kids and a few adults, found his painted horse, and climbed onto the wooden saddle. The shrill whistle blew, rotation began, and the carousel slowly built speed.

Michael said, "Coira's a good teacher. She's confident, which I think is what bothers you." He gazed into Molly, so beautiful. "Is she ever rude to you, or disrespectful?"

Molly stared up at blue sky. She wanted to say yes. "I know she doesn't respect me, but she tries to hide it."

"She's told me, more than once, of the respect she has for you."

"What?"

"She thinks it improper to become too friendly with her employer." He took and caressed Molly's hand. "Maybe you could help with that."

The carousel slowed.

Mike pulled Molly off the bench and stuck her hand into the crook of his arm. They strolled toward the carousel's rear gate. When they reached the gate, Molly hugged his arm. She pressed her head into his shoulder. "I love you."

He squeezed her hand. "You and Jimmy are my whole life."

"You need to move beyond that, if it's true."

His head jerked sideways. "What?"

She hugged his arm. "I'm with another."

He pushed away and looked into her. "What?" *What do you mean* . . . "Another man?"

She laughed. "You silly man." She slapped his chest. "I'm with child."

He threw both arms around her and hugged her tight.

"Easy. You might . . ."

"Oh." He let go and held her shoulders, smiling into the wonder of this woman.

Jimmy pressed between them. "Can I have one of those?" He pointed.

Raul took a bite from a caramel apple on a stick and handed it to Coira.

Molly said, "That looks delicious."

"I get one for each of you." Raul turned and hurried toward the apple stand.

A gunshot rang and echoed across the arcade.

Silence followed, as people ducked and looked in all directions.

Raul stopped, looked down, grabbed his belly, and dropped to his knees. He threw a surprised glance at Mike and fell facedown.

Mike pushed through spectators, knelt next to Raul, and slowly rolled him onto his back.

Raul's eyes flashed side to side, struggling to breathe, bewildered over what had happened.

Mike said, "Raul, where . . ." Blood oozed through a small hole in his jacked, below his left ribcage.

Twenty meters away, outside the arcade, a man holstered his revolver. He looked familiar.

"Go," said Coira, pulling at Michael's shoulder.

Molly and Jimmy stood behind Coira.

Mike jumped up and charged through the stunned crowd. Men pulled women and children out of his way.

The shooter climbed into a carriage and it lurched forward. The horse trotted brusquely up the slight hill and turned downhill toward the Barbary Coast.

Mike ran after the coach until the distance grew too wide to follow. Out of breath, he braced both hands on his knees, breathing hard. Sweat gushed from his face and dripped onto the brick pavement.

Still breathing deeply, more slowly, he straightened and walked back toward the arcade.

From a block away, a gathering crowd shouted and waved, "Mike!" . . . "Count Mike!" . . . "Hurry!"

He jogged back to the arcade.

A uniformed officer said, "Mike, they're gone."

"What? Who?"

"Your wife and son. That other woman, too."

"What?"

"Two well-dressed men grabbed and threw them into a carriage." He pointed. "The carriage rushed up toward Russian Hill."

"What?" Mike looked through the crowd.

A man knelt over Raul, still flat on his back.

Mike turned to the policeman, trying to understand. "What do you mean, 'They're gone?'"

"Molly and Jimmy were taken, and that other woman."

Mike stepped back. The information had finally registered.

Of course. He knew, now, he would soon hear from Lady Catherine. His wife and son had been taken to get to him. This obvious probability only momentarily eased his anxiety.

He pushed through the crowd and knelt next to Raul.

Raul's eyes searched, unfocused, dazed.

Mike stood. "Can somebody find a taxi."

A man waved and ran toward the street.

"Can somebody help me carry him."

Several men stepped forward, volunteering to help.

Mike grabbed two of them. "You each grab a leg." Mike and the others knelt over Raul. "Try to keep him level." Mike took Raul's shoulders. "Ready?"

They lifted Raul and slowly carried him toward the street.

A man on the street waved both arms.

One of the waiting taxies turned toward the arcade at a gallop, but Paddy pulled into position first. Mike thought he'd returned to the Palace.

They carefully loaded Raul onto the rear bench seat. Mike asked, "Can you men come with us?"

Both volunteers climbed onto the back rail.

Mike climbed up and sat across from Raul. He looked at Paddy. "Saint Mary's Hospital on Stockton. And, Paddy, keep it smooth."

Chapter Nineteen

MIKE BACKED THROUGH the main entry to St. Mary's Hospital carrying Raul's upper body. His two volunteers each carried a leg, shouldering through the double doors behind Mike.

A white frocked nun approached from a side office and blocked their path. "Who is this, might I ask?"

"He is shot!" Mike pushed past her. "Who are you?"

"Sister Elena."

"Where do we take him?"

"Follow me." Sister Elena led them into the surgery.

Two nurses guided them to a clean, sheet covered table and helped them slide Raul onto it.

Sister Elena said, "I'll send a runner for Doctor Murphy."

Mike said, "How about Doctor Cole?"

"I don't think he'll come. He's not on call today."

"I am Mike Zabel. This is Raul. Tell him. He will come."

"I'll dispatch two runners, sir, in the event we can't locate Dr. Cole."

"Thank you."

Sister Elena hurried down the long corridor toward her office.

The nurses carefully cut away clothing and exposed the bullet wound in Raul's stomach. They rolled him slightly, side to side, cutting away his shirt, exposing a small and clean exit wound. His dark red bleeding looked minimal. The flesh surrounding the entry and exit wounds had swollen purple.

Raul had been unconscious since Mike's return to the arcade. His breathing had become slow and steady.

Mike leaned over Raul's shoulder. "You need to fight, my friend." He turned and shook hands with both volunteers. "Thank you. He would not live without your help. If there is ever anything I can do . . ."

The second man held onto Mike's hand. "You're Count Mike, right?"

"Some people call me by this name. Yes."

"I'm real proud to meet you. I'm Danny Watson." He nodded toward his friend. "This here's Andrew Peterson. We saw what happened. If we can help . . ."

Mike hadn't yet considered his next move. *One thing . . .* "Did you see the men who took my wife and son?"

Danny let go, put his hands on his hips and looked down, thinking. His head popped up, wide eyed. "Sure. I saw the man who grabbed the boy and dragged one of the women away by her hair. The other guy dragged the second woman by her arm. Both of the men had bruised faces. Both ladies tried to get away, but I think the one was more worried for the boy. Your wife?"

"Yes. My wife and son. The other woman is my son's governess."

Andrew said, "They loaded them into a waiting carriage at gunpoint and sped off. You were chasing the one who shot your friend, here."

"Can you describe them?"

They looked at each other, blinking, heads bobbing. Danny finally said, "They was well-dressed gents, but bruised, like I said." He fanned his face.

"Can you get up to police headquarters at City Hall, and ask for Sergeant Angus McFee?"

Danny took a step back. "Well . . ." He looked at his friend.

Andrew said, "Sure. We can do that."

"Report what you saw. Get it on record before your memories have time to paint inaccurate pictures."

They both nodded and turned toward the door.

"Wait. You like chowder?"

They turned back, looked at each other, smiled, and nodded.

"You know the Palace?"

They didn't.

"It's at the foot of Meigg's Wharf."

Andrew's eyes popped wide. "Oh, the Cobweb Palace? Yeah, we've heard of that."

"After you leave City Hall, go down there and tell Abe Warner everything. Tell him I said to take good care of you. Also, please let McFee and Warner know where we can find you, if need be."

"We're at German House, down on Front Street."

"That three-story boardinghouse?"

They both nodded.

"Please, tell Abe I may not see him for a while."

They nodded and turned toward the corridor.

Raul lay on his side, still breathing slow and steady.

Both nurses gently washed his stomach and back with clean rags and water. Their actions did not wake him.

Footsteps echoed from the long corridor.

Sister Elena and Dr. Cole marched toward the surgery.

Dr. Cole reached out and shook Mike's hand.

"Thank you for coming."

"Of course." Cole let go and turned toward Raul and the nurses. He examined both wounds and placed a hand on Raul's forehead, feeling his temperature.

Raul's eyes opened, rolled upward and focused on Cole.

"Just take it easy, Raul." Cole turned to the nurses. "Any blood from the mouth or nose?"

The older nurse shook her head. "No, doctor."

"Have you checked his anus and penis for signs of bleeding?"

The nurses blinked, looked at each other, and slumped. They had not.

Cole said, "Okay. You did a good job cleaning him up. Let's get his wounds dressed and bandaged. Then get his pants off and check for signs of bleeding." He examined both bullet holes in Raul's shirt, fitting the torn fabric into place.

He took Mike's arm and led him a few feet away, speaking softly. "If they don't find blood, Raul's probably going to be okay. I'll double-check his clothing to see if any fabric might have entered his body. If it did, there's a good chance it passed straight through." He shook his head. "I think the wounds are probably clean. His fever's not very high. Where did this happen?"

"At the arcade on North Beach."

"You think you can find the ball?"

"That would require a miracle, and I do not have the time."

"What? Why not?"

"They took my wife and son."

"What?"

"And Coira." Raul's whisper barely reached them.

Mike and Cole turned back to Raul.

"Two men." Raul grabbed Mike's hand. His eyes and voice strained against the pain. "The same two followed you. The ones I chased off."

"We'll find them. Don't worry."

God help me.

Cole said, "He'll stay the night here. We need to keep an eye."

Mike squeezed Raul's hand. "Doctor Cole says you'll be fine. Don't worry. I'll come back tomorrow to take you home."

The nurses had finished cutting away Raul's pants and long johns. They displayed them to Dr. Cole and Mike, no signs of blood.

Cole pulled Mike aside, again. "Raul's got an angel on his shoulder. I sometimes think that angel might be you."

"Not me, to be certain."

Cole said, "About that other thing..."

"What other thing?"

"They've got clean water in Chinatown. The cholera is not spreading. Your friend, Han Wok, says he needs to talk to you about something. I think it's about your young Chinese lady-friend. The Chinese doctor's daughter, is she?"

"She is. I'll find them when I have time." Mike gripped Raul's arm, saying goodbye, then he hurried toward the exit.

IT TOOK FIFTEEN MINUTES for Paddy to reach the Cosmopolitan Hotel. Mike hurried into the lobby and found Patrick at the front desk.

Patrick said, "Mike, that was quick."

"What do you mean?"

"I came on a half hour ago. Soon as I read the registry, I sent the runner."

"He never reached me. What happened?"

"Your Russian friends checked out early this morning, men, women, and luggage."

"Where'd they go?"

"I asked the other clerk but they didn't tell him anything. They paid with Russian coin and left."

THE TWENTY METER, TWO-mast schooner procured by Grigori pleased General Boris Krestyanov, but it wasn't good enough for her. The nicely-appointed private yacht offended Lady Catherine. It had been thoroughly cleaned and provisioned by Luka and Sacha the day before. Not good enough. Nothing seemed good enough for the duchess, not even the Cosmopolitan, the most luxurious hotel in San Francisco.

Her entire staff now understood the truth. Her brother, the grand duke, had caused his own death. Colonel Preslova and the two bodyguards had been unable to stop him. Plotting revenge against Mikhail was madness, but stopping her was as impossible as stopping her brother had been. Mikhail had acted in self defense, probably a reflex, when he'd taken the grand duke's right hand in Vladivostok.

He is a Romanov. Why . . .

According to reports, earlier that same day, Mikhail had saved the lives of the grand duke and his entire infantry regiment. He'd positioned his skilled cannon company on higher ground, able to watch the vastly superior Chinese force encircle the grand duke's regiment. Mikhail's skillfully launched cannon volleys had turned back the Chinese force, and the Chinese commander had subsequently surrendered.

After their interrogation of colonel Preslova, Grigori reported that Mikhail had not known, back then, of his illegitimate link to the Romanov Dynasty. He could not have known of the insult and revulsion his approach would be to the duchess, or to her brother, the grand duke.

The situation had become impossible. She had become insane with hate.

Only the general's loyalty denied him the possibility of marshalling support from Grigori, Luka, and Sacha to restrain her and return her to Russia. It would be impossible to convince her to return to Russia voluntarily.

If done without her consent, her nephew, Czar Alexander II Nikolayevich, would remove their heads for disloyalty.

What was this thing with the Romanovs, this taking of heads.

She would never consider leaving without Mikhail's head on a plate. It did not matter that the czar had rescinded the warrant on Mikhail. It did not matter that she'd brought them halfway around the world without her nephew's knowledge or consent. If Alexander's family loyalty did not demand their heads, she would pester him relentlessly until she exacted her vengeance on all of them.

Now, under her authority, Boris had shot a man. The man would certainly die in this primitive frontier.

The general had killed before, of course. Those deaths had been in combat. This shooting had been murder. There was nothing noble about this.

At her command, they had abducted Mikhail's wife and son, along with another woman. Those three had been tied and hooded inside the coach. They had been roughly treated. Their abductors had been given strict orders to remain silent. These three hostages could not possibly know where they had been taken.

Their hooded prisoners had been dragged and carried onto the boat, wrestled down the narrow ladder, and forced onto the hardwood bench in the galley. The slight motion from bay swells and the odors of the bay would certainly inform them of being on a boat.

The little boy sat stiff and upright, either afraid, or, possibly, determined to be brave.

Both women sat with their heads lowered, possibly praying.

The general stood near the ladder between Grigori and Luka, all bracing for Lady Catherine's next command.

As if summoned by his thoughts, the duchess burst from the master's cabin in the stern of the boat and marched into the galley.

Sacha followed close behind.

The duchess smiled a little, a rare event, perhaps recognizing their success in capturing Mikhail's wife and son. She asked, "Why are there two women?"

The general looked to Grigori.

172

Grigori dipped at the waist and snapped to attention. "They are all together. We are not sure which is his wife."

The general said, "The woman in the blue dress is his wife. Her name is Molly. This other might be her sister."

The little boy said, "She's Coira Macauley. She's my teacher."

Everybody, even the duchess, admired his boldness.

The duchess said, "Take this other woman back. She is to remain hooded until she is let out of the carriage."

Luka yanked the teacher from the bench and dragged her up the ladder onto the upper deck. The boat rocked slightly. They had climbed up to the wharf.

The duchess motioned.

Grigori lifted the hoods from Mikhail's wife and son.

The duchess said, "I am the Grand Duchess, Catherine Mikhailovna, a Romanov of the ruling order of all Russia. You are here because of the death of my brother, the Grand Duke Nikolai Nikolayevich. I hold the Count Mikhail Diebitsch-Zabalkansky personally responsible for his death. He will suffer as I have suffered. Then he will die."

The wife said, "He didn't kill your brother. I was there."

"You have not the permission to speak, you peasant whore." Her shriek might be heard two blocks away.

"You can't talk to my mommy like that." The boy's shout could be heard one block away.

None of them could help but smile at his courage.

He is a Romanov, like his father before him.

The duchess stiffened, replacing her smile with a frown. "Be quiet. You will respect me, and your father will fear me."

"My daddy's not afraid of anything. You'll find out."

The duchess said, "He will fear me, and you will respect me."

Chapter Twenty

MIKE WALKED INTO POLICE headquarters at 5:17 p.m., Sunday.

Sergeant Burt Carpenter had the front desk. "Mike, there's a telegram here for you." He sifted through his paperwork and delivered a Western Union envelope.

Mike tore it open and read.

"U.S. Treasury shipment robbed STOP Wells Fargo stage held up on route to Sacramento between ferry landing and riverboat landing STOP Three well armed and hooded robbers involved STOP One very tall man and one woman STOP Please consult Wells Fargo office your location END"

It had been sent from the U.S. Marshal's office on California Street, already two days old.

"Thank you." Mike folded the telegram into his vest pocket. "Is Angus McFee in today?"

"I think he's back there. He doesn't usually work Sundays, but there's been some Chinese here to see him, every day."

Mike wound his way between offices and into the squad room.

Angus stood at his desk, looking tired. He bent and blew out his oil lamp, getting ready to leave. Seeing Mike, he shook his head and looked down at his lamp, probably wishing he'd already gone.

Mike asked, "Did two men come in and report what happened?"

"Yes, they did. Have you found your wife and son? Who's that other . . ."

"Not yet." Mike sat on the edge of a nearby desk, feeling that emptiness that drains the spirit. "I don't know where to look. The Russians have checked out of the Cosmopolitan Hotel."

"Russians?"

"I'm sure it was the Grand Duchess Catherine Mikhailovna. Her men, anyway."

Angus said, "That's the sister of that grand duke who got himself shot in the Palace a while back?"

"The very same."

"Anything we can do to help?"

"I wish I knew." Mike thought for a minute and stood. "There are two Russian ladies, my wife, Molly, my seven-year-old son, his governess, and at least three Russian men. They used two carriages to abduct my wife and son. They will need more than one carriage to move around the city. Both Russian ladies are beautiful and one will be very elegantly dressed." Mike waited for a response.

Angus scribbled some notes and looked up. "Two Russian women, three Russian men, your wife and son, and the governess. How old is she?"

"She's around thirty or thirty-five." He'd never asked.

Angus said, "Okay. I'll get the word out." He tapped his pencil on his notepad. "How's Raul?"

"I think he will be okay. He is very strong and very lucky. Doctor Cole thinks he will recover quickly." Mike remembered. "What about those two men who were here?"

"They already went down to the Palace. Wish I could join them." Angus relaxed a little.

Mike remembered again. "Raul recognized the men who shot him. These are the same Russians who walked right past you at the Saint Francis Hotel."

Angus scratched the back of his neck, looking as tired as Mike felt. "Another Chinese boy got taken last night." He hesitated to say more, his face drawing down into a scowl. "They've found some of the missing boys. You should go down to the coroner's office. Maybe it's all connected." He winced and shook his head. "I don't know how. It's just a hunch."

MIKE DRAGGED HIMSELF into the coroner's office under growing darkness.

Two uniformed officers guarded the doors. They both recognized Mike, nodded, and opened an exterior door.

Several Chinese waited outside, all watching him enter.

Han Wok, Chiang SuLin, and Chiang Po waited inside the vestibule. Chiang SuLin jumped in front of Mike. "Ah, you finally come."

Mike scrubbed his scalp with both hands, hoping to get fresh blood into his brain. He looked down at SuLin. "I just heard."

Han said, "They won't let us in. These families want Po to examine their children. Do they not have this right?"

SuLin's lip twisted derisively, wagging her head. "My count is too busy. He plays with his family all day."

Mike flushed, struggling for self-control. He took a deep breath. "Molly and Jimmy were kidnapped this afternoon. Raul was shot. He's in the hospital."

SuLin sank back in shame, speechless, for once.

Mike grabbed Po's arm and pulled him through the doors into the morgue. The pungent odor of human decay hung heavy, burning his nostrils and throat. He pulled his handkerchief and covered his nose and mouth. Tears flooded his eyes, soothing the burning irritation from the bitter air.

At the far end of the room, Dr. Thaddeus Pearson sat at his desk, not outwardly bothered by the horrific stench.

A line of nine small, toe-tagged victims lay on the floor to Mike's right. Two adult size, sheet covered victims had been placed upon benches to his left.

Po knelt to examine the first in the line of naked, dead children.

Mike stood in front of Pearson's desk. "Have you identified these children?"

Pearson removed his glasses and stood. "Count Mike!" He rounded his desk and shook Mike's hand. He pulled away, frowned, and shook his head. "No. A couple are puffed purple, beyond recognition. Three might be identified. We should be able to identify the most recent four." He pulled Mike to the end of the line and nodded at two of his attendants.

The attendants positioned two lanterns for better light.

Mike reached down and pulled Po forward. "Doctor Pearson, this is Chiang Po, a Chinese doctor. He's been helping with the cholera situation."

Po bowed respectfully.

"There is a crowd of Chinese outside." Mike thumbed toward the doors. "They want Po to examine these children."

"Sure. Of course." Pearson nodded at his attendants.

They rolled the newest child onto his left side, exposing a large, ragged, blood crusted opening below his right ribs.

Pearson said, "They were all cut open in a violent manner and their livers have been removed. I think they were conscious at the time. We're dealing with one perpetrator."

Po knelt beside the body to look more closely.

"Lord, Jesus!" Mike couldn't block his mental image of Jimmy as the victim. "My son and wife were kidnapped today."

Pearson sucked air. He understood the implication. "How old is your son?"

"Seven."

Pearson shook his head with something to say, but not wanting to say more.

"What?"

"There are signs of sexual abuse on those we could still examine. Their anuses have been penetrated and traumatically torn."

Mike's legs gave way and he sat on the floor. "Jesus! Lord!" *What can I do?*

THE 8:00 P.M. MASS at Mission Dolores had ended, and the church had already emptied. Mike shuffled through the open main doors, dipped his fingers into holy water, and crossed himself in the Orthodox manner, right to left. He walked up the center aisle and knelt near the altar, subconsciously heaping his desperation onto the Lord. No words or prayers rose through his emotional fog. Simple words would not do.

"Michael?" Father Amadeo Gallo placed a hand on Mike's shoulder. "Tell me what's wrong."

Tears burst from Mike's eyes. No stopping them. "I don't know what to do. I don't know where to go."

"Tell me what happened."

Mike took a deep breath and organized his thoughts. He had no time to dive back into his history with Grand Duke Nikolai Nikolayevich or Lady Catherine. *No need to . . .*

He only suspected her involvement. He had no hard evidence. He had not even seen her since fleeing Vladivostok. He said, "Earlier today, after the morning mass, Raul was shot. While I chased the man who shot him, my wife and son were kidnapped."

Father Amadeo turned toward the altar and crossed himself, left to right. His head shrank between his shoulders and he turned back. "I remember seeing you this morning. How old is Jimmy now, five?"

"Seven."

Father Amadeo sat next to Mike. "How quickly they grow." He caressed his gold crucifix. "It seems like only a year ago that I christened him." He placed a hand on Mike's knee. "Do you know what they want? The kidnappers, I mean."

"No."

"Have you received a note or been contacted?"

"No. I've been on the move since it happened. Nobody is at my home to receive a note. Coira, Jimmy's governess, was also kidnapped."

He thought about this and stood. "I should go home and check, or maybe get down to the Palace."

Father Amadeo stood. "You look tired, Mike. You should get some rest. You'll think more clearly. I will light candles for Molly and Jimmy. And, I will pray, of course."

Mike said, "Light four candles, father; one for Raul, and one for Coira Macauley. Raul is in care at Saint Mary's Hospital on Stockton."

"Jimmy's governess was with you in the mass this morning?"

"Yes."

"I will light five candles, including one for you, and I will pray for all of you. Now, go. Get some rest. God often informs and inspires while we sleep."

"I can't sleep." Mike stared at the statue of Jesus behind the pulpit and crossed himself again, right to left. He said softly, "Please, Lord . . ."

THE MOMENT HE STEPPED back onto the street, he thought of Colonel Preslova. They'd never talked at length about that night in the colonel's rooms. He waved at Paddy's taxi, parked across the street.

Paddy snapped reins, turned the taxi around, and stopped in front of the church.

Mike climbed in. "Let's get down to the White Chapel."

Paddy slapped reins on the horse's back and turned down toward the coast. Paddy turned back and shouted, "Are they going to be all night?"

Mike had no answer for Paddy.

A few minutes later, the taxi stopped at the White Chapel Saloon.

Mike climbed down. "Go on home, Paddy. Your day has been very long."

"Not as long as yours." Paddy held fast. "I'll feed and water my horse."

"Come inside after that. The girls will fix you something to eat."

Paddy smiled and climbed down with his horse's feedbag.

Mike crossed the redwood planks and entered Molly's boardinghouse through the front door. The lamps had been turned low. Everybody had retired for the night.

Sally came from the kitchen area in a robe, holding her lamp high, squinting into the darker entry. "Who's there?"

"Sally, it's me."

"Mister Mike? What brings you at this hour?"

Mike took her lamp and led her into the kitchen. "Please, sit down." He worried she might faint and hurt herself.

She sat.

Mike set the lamp on the table and sat opposite, staring evenly into her blank face. "Raul was shot today."

She gasped and grabbed her throat.

"He'll be okay." Mike leaned across and took her hand. "Molly and Jimmy were taken. Coira too."

Sally's eyes popped wide, mouth agape. "Taken?" She shut her mouth and held her throat. "What?"

"I didn't want you to hear this from anybody else. They were kidnapped by the men who shot Raul. Don't worry. I'll find them."

The front door opened and closed.

Mike said, "That's Paddy. Can you fix him something to eat?"

"That's your coachman?"

"It is. He's had a long day."

"I'll be happy to." Sally stood, opened the stove door, and stoked the fire.

Paddy entered the kitchen and Mike stood, waving at his chair. "I'm going upstairs to speak with Colonel Preslova." He looked at Sally. "He is here?"

Sally said, "Yes, Mike. He rarely leaves."

"We'll come down so we don't wake anybody else. Can you make some tea?"

She smiled and nodded, went out back, and returned with some firewood. She opened the stove door again and fed the wood into the fire.

"Thank you, Sally." Mike turned and hurried up the kitchen stairs to the second floor, hurried down the hall, and knocked softly on the last door on the left. He entered without waiting.

Preslova stood near the window in his long johns. He looked ready to dive through the glass if need be. "Mikhail." He relaxed.

"My colonel, can you pull on some trousers and follow me downstairs? We need to talk. I don't want to wake anybody else."

Preslova nodded, dragged his trousers from the back of his chair, pulled them on, buttoned them, pulled the suspenders over his shoulders, sat, and tugged on his boots. He stood, pressed his feet to the souls of his boots, and opened the door. He led Mike down the corridor, down the kitchen stairs, and into the kitchen.

Sally poured hot water into a teapot and set it on the table. Two clean cups already sat there.

Paddy chewed a beef sandwich on shepherd bread and started to pick up his plate to make room.

"Stay put, Paddy. Is okay for you to hear." Mike sat nearest the stair and motioned to one of the remaining chairs. "Thank you, Sally. We can let ourselves out."

"Nothing to eat? Maybe a sandwich?"

Mike shook his head. "I might eat some chowder at the Palace." He looked across the table at his colonel. "You?"

Preslova sat near the stove and waved off Mike's offer.

"Good night, then." Sally went into her room and closed the door.

Mike looked at Preslova and said, "Thank you for coming down."

Preslova nodded and pointed at the teapot.

"Give it a few minutes." Mike liked his tea properly steeped. "We haven't had a chance to talk about what happened at your hotel."

Preslova nodded, waiting for Mike.

"What can you tell me about those two men?"

"What do you mean? I do not know them."

"You said they are from Russia."

"Da, da. Yes. They spoke to me in Russian. They want to know what happened that night at the Palace. I tell them you are not armed that night. I tell them I try to stop the grand duke. They punched and slapped me for no reason. I have nothing to hide."

"Did you hear a name?"

Preslova thought about this and pointed to the teapot.

Mike poured them both a cup of tea. It smelled of jasmine.

Paddy stood, crossed to the cupboard, grabbed a cup, sat, and poured himself a cup of tea.

Preslova picked up the cup and blew across the top. "I ask them many times, who are they. One called the other Grigori. I think he made a mistake to do this."

Mike asked, "Do you know who they work for?"

"We both know they work for the grand duchess. She wants to avenge her brother. They were very close. We both know this."

"Two men took my wife and son this afternoon, after a third man shot Raul."

"What?" Preslova set his teacup on the table and stood. He paced back and forth in front of the stove, looking around the kitchen like a caged bear.

Mike said, "They stayed at the Cosmopolitan Hotel, on the mezzanine floor. Three men and two women. My friend said the women are very attractive."

Preslova sat and drummed the table with his fingernails. "Da, da. This is the grand duchess. How can I help?"

"You need to stay put. They might shoot you on sight. If they knew of this place, they would have already come here."

Preslova shook his head and stared into Mike. "I want to help. I tire of this feeling, that I am in prison."

MIKE AND PRESLOVA ENTERED the Palace a little after midnight. The saloon crowd had thinned to a few hot rum drinkers, singing in a Scandinavian tongue, maybe Swedish. Danny Watson and Andrew Peterson were nowhere to be seen.

Abe leaned over the bar, forehead furrowed, jaws set tight. "Your two friends just left. They told me what happened. How's Raul?"

"Doctor Cole thinks he will recover."

"Raul's hard as week old biscuits. How about Molly and Jimmy?"

"I have heard nothing."

Abe reached under the bar. "This note came for you." He handed Mike a wax sealed envelope, stamped with a Romanov imprint.

Mike tore it open and unfolded a single sheet of paper. The note was in her hand. "Be in front of Bella Union tomorrow at noon. Be alone. Be unarmed."

He handed the note to Abe. "Who brought this?"

"A young runner from Bella Union." Abe read the note and handed it back. "The kidnappers?"

"This is Lady Catherine's handwriting." Mike twitched with a slight smile and handed the note to Preslova.

Abe said, "You hungry?"

"Yes. Bring us two bowls and a bottle of white wine." He smiled at Warner. "Please."

Mike and Preslova sat at a clean table with no tablecloth. Mike said, "Can you stay at my house tonight?"

MIKE OPENED HIS FRONT door and held his watch under the gaslight. 1:15 a.m.

"What is this?" Exhaustion had dulled his senses. His front door had been unlocked. He reached for his Colt but it wasn't there, that promise he'd made to Molly.

Preslova noticed Mike's disquiet and pulled his Starr revolver from a shoulder holster.

Mike opened the front door wide.

Light came from the kitchen at the far end of the hall.

They crept halfway down the hall and stopped. Mike reached back without looking.

Preslova handed Mike his revolver.

Mike cocked the weapon and stepped boldly into the kitchen.

Raul and Coira sat at the kitchen table. Raul was eating scrambled eggs and bacon. Coira's puffed face looked red from crying, something Mike had never imagined her doing.

Raul said, "I got hungry. I can't stay in that hospital another minute. They never give me rest, always poking and turning me. Never give me anything to eat. Said it was doctor's orders."

Coira slugged Raul's arm.

Raul smiled at her. "Doctor said my intestinals might be tore or something."

Coira smiled at Raul and wiped her nose with a handkerchief. "Oh, sir, I'm so sorry with what's happened."

Mike asked, "Why would you be sorry? Do you know these men?"

"Certainly not!" She started to stand, so surprised by his question.

Mike showed her the palm of his hand and smiled. "Calm down, Coira." He sat in one of the two empty chairs at the small table and motioned for Preslova to take the other. He lowered the hammer on Preslova's revolver and slid it across the table. "Why should you be sorry?"

She said, "Your misses, sir, and little Jimmy."

"Were they hurt?"

"No, sir. They're fine, as far as I know. They tied our hands behind and put sacks over our heads as soon as they dragged us into their carriage, but I believe them to be unharmed."

"I need to ask you some questions."

She nodded and leaned forward, eyes dry, eager to help.

"Do you know where they took you?"

"They never removed the hood until they brought me here. But, I'm sure it was a boat. It moved underfoot, and I could smell the waterfront."

"Were any other women there?"

"Oh, yes. She was in charge." Worry creased her face. "I'm frightened for them. She said she wants you to suffer the way she suffered. I think she intends to harm our Jimmy." Her shoulders shook and tears pooled in her eyes. "She scares me."

Preslova said, "The grand duchess."

"Yes," said Coira. "They called her gertsoginya. They didn't know I understand Russian."

Mike said, "This is Grand Duchess Catherine Mikhailovna, sister of Grand Duke Nikolai Nikolaievich. She blames me for her brother's death."

Preslova said, "She is a vicious woman. In Russia, she does whatever she wants. All Romanovs are above any law, including God's law. My two colleagues were tortured to death. The Romanovs honor only their own law."

"They are the law. Russia has no constitution." Mike turned back to Coira. "Do you have any idea what kind of boat, or where it's docked?"

Coira stared at Raul, thinking. "I don't think it was a big boat. I could smell fresh varnish." She shook her head. "That's all I remember." She leaned back and pointed at Raul. "Oh, we walked on wooden boards, then went down a narrow stair onto the boat, and inside what felt like a large room. I didn't need to stoop over, like on most boats. The ladies, I think there were two, they came from another room. I could hear them walking for . . . maybe five seconds."

"Do you know where was this?"

"Like I said, they put a sack over my head from when they first took us, until they brought me back here."

Mike asked, "They said nothing to . . ."

"Wait." Coira's eyes grew wide. She smiled, remembering. "They won't be on that boat. She told them to take your missus and Jimmy to the Forge, tomorrow morning, wherever that is."

Mike pulled the note from his vest pocket and unfolded it onto the table. "This was delivered to the Palace, earlier today. It says I need to be outside Bella Union at noon. It's in her hand."

Raul said, "I can't move fast, and I can't take a punch to the gut, but I can carry a gun."

"No." Mike tapped the note. "This says I must be alone and unarmed. They already know who you are. They are certain to watch for you." Mike leaned close, smiling at his good friend. "Is this not why they shot you, to keep you out of their way?"

Raul smiled, proud to be known by the pain he'd inflicted.

Mike said, "Besides, you need to rest. We can't afford to lose you. Molly and Jimmy would never forgive me."

Chapter Twenty-One

BEATRICE, ONE OF TOMMY Chandler's working girls, almost had to carry Jackson Patterson upstairs. He'd had too much to drink and she'd be putting him to bed. Tommy said, "He'll be shipping out next week, and good riddance." He stood across the bar from Donald Thorne.

Thorne had shaved his head and beard, making it difficult for Tommy to recognize him. Only his bushy-red eyebrows reminded Tommy of the man's previous appearance.

Tommy said, "I like the earring."

Thorn touched the gold ring pierced through his left earlobe. "I got that before the war. You just never saw it before. With my hair and beard, I couldn't see it my-own-self."

"It makes you look like a deep-water sailor. Get out and get some sun." Tommy drew a beer and set it in front of Thorne.

Thorne looked at the beer, hesitated, then picked it up and swallowed a mouthful. He set the beer back on the bar. "It's late and I'm tired. You said you needed to talk to me." He looked at Tommy's boxing billboards. "Say, do you ever sleep?"

Tommy smiled and glanced at his billboards. "I sleep about four hours every night, even when I was in training. I can't sleep more than that. There's always too much to get done."

Thorne smiled and drank some beer. "What did you want to talk about?"

Tommy said, "After that picture in the Bulletin, I worried about you staying here, not to mention using you again. Now, I'd never be expected to recognize you from that picture in the Bulletin." He drew himself a beer, took a slug, and set it on the bar. "What's that about, anyway?"

Thorne looked into his beer and shifted his weight. He didn't want to answer.

Tommy didn't need an answer, but he was too curious not to press. "I have a right to know who's staying in my house."

"They think I done some things during the war."

"Who thinks what?"

Thorne blinked and looked away. He looked back. "Does it matter?"

Tommy needed Thorne. He didn't want the man to move out. "Not really." Tommy sipped beer and toweled his bar. "I need you to go see Duncan, early in the afternoon, tomorrow." Jethro Townsend had another job lined up.

Thorne looked upstairs. "You know if she's with a customer?"

Tommy shook his head. "Her last beau left an hour ago. She already took a bath. Go get some sleep."

DINK WATKINS HAD BEEN ordered to leave San Francisco twice, both times by Committees of Vigilance. Both times, he'd been deemed an undesirable alien, simply for running with the wrong people. *Wrong people?* He'd never felt a need to abide by orders coming from illegal committees of illegal vigilantes.

Back in 1851, he'd been seen with The Dogs, a bunch of Australian ex-convicts, like himself, who'd sailed to San Francisco in search of gold. Most of The Dogs never went to the gold fields, or, if they had, they'd failed to find gold and had returned to the city. Desperate to survive, many had resorted to thievery, using schemes Dink had never before imagined. The bottle and stopper had been his favorite, luring unsuspecting fools into a dark place to steal their valuables.

Little Dink could still work the bottle and stopper, if need be. His quick little hands had successfully picked many pockets.

Back in those early days, what had riled so-called law-abiding citizens most were the extortion rings and the fires. If a store or business owner refused to pay The Dogs for protection, the store or business got burned to the ground. A lack of city water had made firefighting nearly impossible, and some of their fires had spread. People had been killed.

Little Dink had never personally set a fire. He had never been an extortionist. He was too small to extort anybody. But he'd always stood behind his mates. His guilt had been by association only. His being an ex-convict from Australia, and witnesses who'd seen him running with The Dogs, had been his undoing.

He'd never been caught picking a pocket. He'd never been caught in the bottle and stopper. He'd never been caught for rendering his victims unconscious. But he'd still been put on *Sunrise* and told never to return.

Was me who was a victim.

After four long years aboard *Sunrise,* suffering under the cruel whip of Captain Boggs, Dink had returned to the city and had gone to work for Tommy Chandler. He got free room and board for helping to fill Tommy's boardinghouse with lodgers, often using the bottle and stopper to impoverish incoming travelers and lure them into the first boardinghouse on Pacific Street Wharf, that being Tommy's house. He got free room and board for helping Tommy fill crews on outbound ships, including *Sunrise.*

One they'd worked the bottle and stopper on was that Russian count. They'd done the deed at night, when he'd just landed on Pacific Street Wharf. When the Russian woke up, he'd staggered into Tommy's, stupefied and broke.

Later, in 1855, during the second Committee of Vigilance, with the takedown of the Law-and-Order Party, Dink had been deported again, this time just for being recognized from his first deportation.

After seven long years at sea, this time under both sail and steam, Dink and his sea bag hit the redwood planks of the Barbary Coast at a jog, somewhere after midnight. He rushed through the crew gate on Pacific Street Wharf, turned the corner, and headed for Tommy Chandler's, eager to see his old mate.

After seven long years, Dink had surely been forgotten by them coppers, or so he hoped. Not forgotten by Tommy, he hoped.

The light inside Tommy's window went dark, and Dink broke into a run. He reached the front door quickly, and tried to enter. Locked.

Why would Tommy be locking his doors?

He raised a fist to pound on the door, but the noisy latch stopped him.

The door swung inward, and there stood Tommy Chandler. "Dink. Dink Watkins." He stepped back and motioned for Dink to enter.

Dink lunged in and tossed his sea bag onto the center of the empty saloon floor. He almost dropped to his knees to kiss it.

Tommy closed and barred the door. "Where have you been?"

"All around, you Tommy. All around. That last Committee of Vigilance put me on a steamship and shipped me out. Told me again to never come back."

"You villain, you." Tommy smiled and walked toward the bar, where the only lamp still lit had been turned low. He stepped in back, filled a mug with beer, and set it on the bar. "Good to have you back, Dink. And, just at the right time."

Dink chugged down half a mug and wiped his mouth with his sleeve. "Thank you, you Tommy. It's thirsty, I was."

"You can use that little bunk under the stair. No rooms are open right now."

"Anything, Tommy. Anything."

"I was just thinking about you, Dink. You were always reliable for errands and such."

Dink sipped beer. "Anything."

Chapter Twenty-Two

AT 10:00 A.M., ON MONDAY, Dink Watkins stepped down from a taxi at the corner of Washington and Montgomery, directly across from the Daily Evening Bulletin. He paid the driver, crossed Montgomery, and entered the Bulletin office. A long front counter, it was.

A gray haired, chubby man sat nearest.

Dink stood on tiptoe and leaned across the counter. "Is there a William Cahill works here?"

Gray hair pointed toward the back of the large room behind the counter, where many desks were occupied by just a few people. "He's the one nearest the press." His voice grew louder. "Billy!"

A much younger man stood, looked at Dink, picked up his notepad and pen, and wound his way between the desks to the near end of the long front counter. He motioned to Dink, set his notepad on the counter, raised his brows, and waited.

Dink hurried to the end of the counter with the edition of the Bulletin Tommy had given him the night before. He opened it, private as he could, and showed the front page. "You're the one looking for these two? You wrote this?"

"Uh, no, and yes. I wrote this but somebody else is looking. Why? Have you seen them?"

"Maybe I have, maybe I ain't. How much is this here reward?"

"The man who's looking is holding back information on that. He wants no action taken for fear something bad might happen to the little girl."

"I wouldn't take no actions. I'd just report where they might be, should I might see them."

"The reward offered is five-hundred-dollars for information about both. Information on only one might be of interest but they really want both."

Dink smiled. Clever was this Billy Cahill. "Thank you, sir. If I might see them, I might come on a rush and say so."

JIMMY FINISHED HIS morning poop and Molly hand pumped it into the bay.

The flour sacks had been removed from their heads the night before, but they'd been kept tied most of the time, only freed to eat, and to use the toilet.

Jimmy motioned, and she bent so he could whisper in her ear. "I can do it. I'm really fast. I know I can."

She stood and shook her head, speaking softly, "No. It's too dangerous. Where would you go? I'd like to know. Do you even know where we are? Because I don't." Molly opened the louvered toilet door.

That duchess stood in the passage, eyebrows pinched over her nose, scowling. "You have finally finished with the toilet?"

Molly said nothing, leading Jimmy back into the salon. Only the duchess, the general, and the hand maid remained. The other two men had gone.

The duchess spoke through clenched teeth. "Remember, my men have orders to kill your child if either of you make trouble."

Molly could find not one reason to respond.

The general stood at the bottom of the narrow ladder, impossible to get past him.

Molly held Jimmy close to her legs.

One of the other two men, the one they called Grigori, climbed halfway down the ladder. "We are ready, madam."

The general stepped away from the ladder and motioned.

Molly let go and Jimmy rushed up the ladder.

"Jimmy! No!"

The general blocked Molly and bolted to the upper deck in front of her.

Molly rushed up the ladder after the general.

On deck, Jimmy squirmed against Grigori's grip.

With the tide out, the wharf stood at least ten feet above the upper deck. The man they called Luka waited at the top of the ladder.

The duchess pushed past Molly onto the deck. Her handmaid followed close behind. The duchess said, "Teach him."

Grigori hesitated, saw her rage, spun Jimmy around, and backhanded him across his face.

Jimmy slammed hard onto the deck and rolled onto his hands and knees. He looked up at Molly, tight lipped. His nose dripped blood and tears flooded is angry eyes. He quickly wiped them away. He never allowed himself to cry. *You sweet little brat.* She'd told him not to do that.

The duchess strutted around Molly and hovered over Jimmy with her fists propped upon her hips. "If you do not stop with your foolishness, we will be forced to punish your mother."

Jimmy wiped his bloody nose, looked at his bloodied hand, and stood.

The duchess shook her finger at Jimmy. "Do you understand me?"

Jimmy's teeth clinched, defiant. "You better not hurt my mommy."

The duchess spun and slapped Molly's face with her gloved hand.

Molly spun and grabbed her stinging cheek. She blinked away a tear and showed the duchess her most indifferent smile.

The duchess motioned, and Grigori hoisted Jimmy onto the ladder.

Jimmy stopped midway up the ladder to look back at Molly.

She nodded, *Go ahead.*

Jimmy climbed up to the wharf and Luka grabbed his arms, not trying to hurt him.

Grigori climbed to the wharf and looked back at Molly. Her turn.

Molly climbed to the wharf and Grigori took her arm, firm but not painful.

The duchess climbed to the wharf and her handmaid followed.

Down on deck, the general secured the boat then followed up the ladder.

Luka dragged Jimmy into one of two coaches, and Grigori led Molly into the other. The duchess and her handmaid climbed into the coach with Molly, and Grigori climbed onto the driver's bench.

The General took charge of Jimmy in the second coach, and Luka climbed up to drive.

Grigori slapped reins and Molly's coach led the way. They turned along Front Street for several blocks, then turned back into the Barbary. After a long block, they stopped in front of a free standing, isolated, two story, unpainted, wood building.

RAUL HAD BEEN SLEEPING off and on for most of 24 hours. He'd had enough rest. His bleeding had stopped, not a drop for 16 hours. He'd scabbed over, back and front. He still had gut pain, but so what? He'd had worse, plenty of times.

Sitting across from Colonel Preslova, eating flapjacks and bacon cooked up by Coira, he could think of no reason to sit this one out.

Mike entered the kitchen from the entry hall. He'd spent the whole night in his office with the door closed. They all knew not to disturb him when his door was closed. He sat between Raul and the colonel. "Good morning."

"Mister Mike . . ." Raul spread his hands, pleading.

Mike smiled and shook his head. "I can't risk it. They know both of you on sight. They will hide someone in the shadows. Russians are well trained at this."

The colonel nodded his sad agreement.

Raul pushed his plate aside and leaned over the table. "I been in the shadows all my life. You know that."

Coira hovered over the table with a breakfast plate, inviting Mike to eat.

"No thank you, Coira. I have no appetite."

She set the plate on the table, two flapjacks and some bacon. She picked up a fork and sat. She always ate in small bites, and in a most proper style.

Raul liked it.

She looked at Raul. "You'll stay put, right here. You start bleeding, I'll slap your ear with a wooden spoon. I'll slap it hard as can be." She liked Raul. Anybody could see it.

Raul liked her, too. Funny, their eyes had rarely met before the previous day. He hid his smile and said, "Mister Mike, Miss Coira mentioned where she thinks they gonna take them. You remember that place down on the coast, a few blocks west of the steel mill, kind of a blacksmith shop and stable?"

Mr. Mike thought a moment and shook his head.

"It closed after they gonna open the steel mill in the Mission District."

Mike shook his head. "The mill opened shortly after I arrived here."

Oh, yeah. Raul remembered. He said, "Well, they used to call that place the Forge, more like a blacksmith shop. She say someone on the boat mentioned the Forge."

Mike stared at Raul, wanting to hear more.

"Yes, that's right." Coira softly thumped Raul's knuckles with her wooden spoon. "You'll be needing your rest, now. Doctor's orders."

MIKE REACHED PORTSMOUTH Plaza at 10:52 a.m., with plenty of time to spare. He tapped the taxi driver's shoulder in front of California Exchange, the casino most distant from Bella Union, waited for the taxi to stop, got out, and paid the driver.

He entered the Exchange, not yet time for the free daily buffet, and took a quick turn around the tables. Nobody wore Russian suits, and nobody resembled the two men he'd wrestled with in Preslova's hotel room, nor the man who'd shot Raul.

He exited the front doors of the California Exchange and walked across the plaza into the Empire. He took a quick turn through the tables with the same results.

He crisscrossed the plaza, entering and touring Verandah, Parker House, and El Dorado, all with the same results; no sign of any Russians.

The crowd grew steadily larger on the plaza, with the casinos filling up for the free buffet lunches.

He still had no appetite.

GENERAL KRESTYANOV had no stomach for this, but he'd been ordered to stay.

After tying the American woman and her son to chairs, Grigori and Luka had gone to Portsmouth Plaza for their rendezvous with Mikhail.

Lady Catherine and her handmaid stood just behind their prisoners' chairs, closer to the open door, and closer to fresh air.

Inside the Forge always felt like a sauna, especially considering the outside cold.

Duncan Frack carried a Chinese boy down the stairs, freshly bathed and fed, and wearing no clothes. "Ah, the ladies have arrived." He looked closer. "And, Count Mike's kid." He crossed to the hearth and set the Chinese boy near the coal fed fire pit, where it must be very hot.

"You want me to show what's going to happen to them?"

Lady Catherine marched around their prisoners and stood close to Duncan Frack. "Yes! I want them to tremble with fear. We will bring Mikhail here. I want his wife and son screaming with fear when he arrives."

Duncan Frack smiled. "I don't mind. You might want to try this yourself. Chinese livers always swell me up with a most splendid power. 'Specially when it's so young."

The young Chinese boy squirmed, when Frack pressed his back onto the hearth.

He whimpered, "What you do? What you do?"

Frack positioned himself and the boy, making sure Mikhail's wife and son could watch. He held the child down with his right hand and thrust his left thumb into the boy's anus.

A shrill cry filled the Forge, and the boy stiffened, still as death.

Frack pulled a knife sheathed at the center of his back and waved it at his audience. "I press my thumb down on the center of the spine from the inside. It hits a nerve and freezes his body. That makes what comes next easier." He slit into the boy's side and the boy went limp, probably having fainted from the pain.

Frack removed his thumb, rolled the boy onto his side, and flayed the skin like skinning an elk. He carefully spread the skin to one side, cut deeper into the boy's back, and spread open a bleeding gash. "I could just hang him by his heels, slit his throat, and let him bleed out, but I like the liver better with fresh blood inside. Tastes best just after they eat a meal of fish and greens."

Sacha rushed outside but the duchess remained, fascinated by Frack's torturous procedure.

Mikhail's wife groaned and turned to her boy. "Close your eyes, Jimmy. Don't look at this."

Her son's eyes and mouth could not be more open. He shook his head and turned to Mikhail's wife. His face quivered down in a frown and his tears gushed. "I want my daddy."

Mikhail's wife looked at the floor and closed her eyes.

The duchess said, "Your father will be here shortly, little one. This will happen to your mother next. You and your father will both watch this. Then, your father will watch when this happens to you."

Tears dripped to the floor from Mikhail's wife. She looked up and said, "Why?"

"Your husband . . ."

A heavy, iron skillet clattered onto hot coals. Frack scooped a spoonful of lard into the skillet and laid a blood-dripping liver, the size of his hand, into it. "You'll like this. It's delicious." He sprinkled the liver with salt and shoved the boy's lifeless body off of the hearth. It made no noise, settling onto the floor. Frack slid the liver around the skillet, turned it over, and added more salt. It smelled like sheep liver.

AT 11:55 A.M., MIKE stood in front of Bella Union. He'd seen no sign of anything Russian.

Across the plaza, in front of the Empire, a wiry little man moved in and out of the crowd, mostly men going into casinos for a free lunch. The little man's quick hands slid in and out of pockets, many of which produced a small purse, a watch, or some other trinket. He deftly deposited his pickings somewhere inside his long duster.

Dink Watkins. Mike had first met Dink aboard *Silent Mistress*, the Yankee clipper his uncle had put him aboard, after his being badly wounded by the grand duke in Vladivostok. *So long ago.*

Dink had been put on a ship by the last Committee of Vigilance and told never to return. He was probably boarding down at Tommy Chandler's.

Mike had no need to go down to Pacific Street Wharf.

A closed carriage stopped in front of Bella Union. One of the Russians he'd met in Colonel Preslova's hotel room sat up on the bench, holding the reins. The side door opened and a pistol waved hello from the dark interior.

Chapter Twenty-Three

DONALD THORNE SAT AT the small table in his room at Tommy Chandler's Boardinghouse, quickly peeling and dividing fresh orange wedges between little Melanie and Paulette Blanco, Thorne's live-in lady.

Thorne enjoyed the early morning hours. He felt like part of a real family at breakfast. He'd never thought it possible, but he'd grown to love this very sweet child. "Do you like that orange, Melanie?"

Melanie sucked the juices from an orange wedge, chewed the pulp, and swallowed. "I like Georgia peaches better." She would not look at Donald. "I miss my mommy and daddy."

"Melanie, I'm real tired of this. How many times do I need to tell you?"

Melanie jumped from her chair, threw both arms around Donald's neck, and hugged him. "I love you, Uncle Donald." She looked at him, tears building in her wide-open eyes. "But I still miss my mommy and daddy."

"I love you too, honey. So does Paulette." He hugged her and let her go. "I'm sorry your mommy and daddy ain't never coming back, but they ain't. I'm tired of saying so, 'cause I miss 'em too." He kissed the top of her head. "You like your new dress?"

She nodded and rubbed his recently shaved face. A little stubble had grown back. She giggled. "It tickles." She rubbed his shaved head and laughed.

Somebody knocked softly on their door. Paulette stood, took one step, and opened it.

Angel, one of Chandler's older prostitutes, leaned in. "Good morning, Donald. He needs to talk to you." She smiled at Melanie. "Good morning, sweetheart."

Melanie rushed to the doorway and hugged Angel. She loved everybody, and everybody loved her.

Donald said, "I'll be right down."

Angel turned down the hall and left the door open.

Donald tugged on his boots, stood, and stomped them snug, pulled on his coat, and trotted downstairs.

Tommy Chandler stood behind his bar, same as always. He handed Donald a folded sheet of paper. "Take this over to Duncan. Tell him not to come around here for a while."

Donald opened the note without looking.

"You don't need to read that." Tommy's eyes narrowed, hard as stone.

Donald folded and tucked the note into a vest pocket, and left. He didn't need to tell Tommy how Duncan Frack couldn't read a word.

The waiting taxi took him down Front Street and turned to a stop in front of Duncan Frack's shop. No payment was necessary.

Donald stepped into the doorway, walked toward the inner room, and waited a minute for his eyes to adjust before entering the Forge.

Duncan stood near the brick hearth with another man. Seeing Donald, the other man pulled a gun and pointed it at Donald.

Duncan slid something dark from a cast iron skillet onto a tin plate. "Don't shoot him, general. We sometimes work together." He waved his tin plate at three women and a kid. One woman and the kid had been tied to chairs.

The other two women stood near the hearth. One wore an elegant purple dress with white fluff sleeves and collar.

Duncan said, "Anybody want a taste?" He extended the tin plate toward the elegantly dressed lady. His move exposed a naked child, crumpled on the floor near the hearth.

The heat of the place exceeded comfort.

The well-dressed lady nodded and smiled at Duncan.

"Ah." Duncan set the tin plate on the hearth, stuck a fork into the browned meat, cut it into small pieces with a knife, and held it out to the lady.

She took the fork with meat on it, smelled the meat, peeled her teeth back, and slowly fed it between her teeth. She chewed, smiled, and turned to the tied-up lady. "Chinese liver is very tasty. You want to try?"

The tied-up lady looked away.

The elegantly-dressed lady took another bite and chewed. She swallowed and said, "I think American liver will taste better."

Tears twinkled in the eyes of the chair bound lady. Rage pushed from behind her tears. "Who are you people? How can any civilized person do such a thing?"

Duncan Frack chuckled and took a bite. "He's Chinese. Nobody cares about him. Better to find something they're good for. Besides, he tastes good." He dipped his fingers into a cotton sack on the hearth and sprinkled salt over the meat. He took anther bite. "Needed more salt."

The elegantly-dressed lady smiled down at the boy tied in the chair. "You want some?"

The child sat frozen, eyes wild with fright. His mouth quivered down, into a frown.

Donald said, "Look, I got a note here from Tommy Chandler." He reached inside his coat and produced the note.

Duncan took the note but did not open it. "Did you read this?"

"No. Tommy told me not to bother reading it." Donald backed toward the door. "Look, whatever's going on here has nothing to do with me." His urge to leave drove him toward the outside door. He'd never been so mean as these fiends.

MIKE'S HANDS HAD BEEN tied behind his back, making it uncomfortable to sit in the back of the coach. It stopped in front of a lonely, two-story wood building on one of the lesser used wharfs of the Barbary Coast.

His Russian captors dragged Mike from the coach, close to the building's entry.

A burly, scowling, freckled, bald-headed man rushed out of the building and bumped past Mike. He hurried toward Front Street without looking back.

One of Mike's captors strolled into an open stable near the end of the building.

The other man shoved Mike through the same doorway from which the bald-headed man had exited. The narrow hallway was dark. At the end, wooden stairs led to the second floor. Being pushed from behind, Mike stepped into a hot, dark room. His eyes adjusted quickly.

The Russian lifted Mike's arms from behind, pushed down on his shoulder, and forced him into a chair. He quickly tied him to the chair from behind.

"Daddy!" Jimmy's screech mixed joy with desperation. He'd been crying.

Molly had been tied to a chair between Mike and Jimmy. She'd been crying too.

Grand Duchess Catherine Mikhailovna stood near a brick hearth, exuding her usual presence and power, both glowing and glaring at Mike.

"Colonel Krestyanov?" Mike laughed softly, surprised to find Krestyanov with the duchess.

"He is general." The duchess stepped up and slapped Mike's face.

Mike ignored her slap and looked at Krestyanov. "You served with my father in the Crimean War. Why are you . . ."

The duchess screamed, "Here?" She slapped Mike again.

Krestyanov frowned. "Da. I remember you, Mikhail. You were just a boy."

A large man stood behind the duchess, nearer the hearth, very familiar.

Jack Wick. He'd started growing a beard. A small, naked, bloody body lay crumpled on the floor. He could not possibly be alive.

Mike reflexively jerked back. "Is that another Chinese boy?"

The big man took a bite of something from a tin plate. "Who gives a pickle about Chinese?"

"You're the one who calls himself Jack Wick."

The big man stepped closer, staring thoughtfully down at Mike. He swallowed. "Never heard of him."

"Yes. I know you. I recognize your voice. You robbed the San Jose train a month ago." Mike smiled. "Sorry about your partner." Mike had killed the man with the shotgun.

"What train? What partner?"

The duchess pushed between them in a rage. "Enough of this." Her once beautiful face had grown a deeply-creased forehead and thin ridges around her mouth, marks from her anger and hate. She stepped close and stood over Mike. "My brother was next in line. You took that from me."

"Had I only known." He wanted to laugh at her outrage.

The irises in both of her eyes stood out, completely surrounded by her eye whites. Her shrill shriek hurt his ears. "Known what, you bastard son of a common soldier?"

"Had I known of your self infatuation, to the point of being offended by the mere presence of others, I never would have approached you at the duke's ball."

"You . . ." She stretched back and swung with all of her strength. Her painful slap might have been heard outside.

Mike forced a smile through his burning cheek. "I am deeply saddened by what you have become. Look at you." Mike's smile disappeared, looking her up and down. "You are repulsive."

"You peasant's brood." She slapped him with the back of her hand.

Now the opposite side of his face stung.

Molly's soft voice embraced Mike. "He is your cousin. How can you . . ."

"Enough," howled the duchess. "Bring the boy up here. I am still hungry."

Jack Wick smiled and helped the Russian who'd shackled Mike lift Jimmy's chair and carry it next to the hearth.

The duchess sneered down at Mike. "Now, you will know what it is to suffer."

"Put that chair down." Raul stood in the hallway, silhouetted by light from the outside doorway, holding one of Mike's Navy Colts. "The police are on their way."

A loud thump from behind sent Raul to the floor, having been clubbed from behind.

The Russian who'd gone into the stable stepped across Raul's unconscious body.

Krestyanov looked at Raul and shook his head.

Mike smiled. "That's right. Your ball went right through. By now, Colonel Preslova has been to the local police station and telegraphed Sergeant Angus McFee. He's already on his way here with a squad of well-armed police officers."

Jack Wick tossed the tin plate into the fire pit, shoved past the duchess, and charged upstairs.

"Bring the brat." The duchess stepped over Raul on her way out the door.

The two Russians cut Jimmy's bindings and the younger man hoisted him under his arm.

Jimmy kicked and fought, screaming, "Mommy! Daddy! Mommy!"

He carried Jimmy out the door.

"I am sorry for this." Krestyanov nodded at Mike on his way past.

"Ugh . . ." Raul struggled to lift his bleeding head off the floor.

Mike jockeyed his chair nearer the stairs, better to see his old friend. "I told you to stay home."

Outside, horse hooves plodded over the wooden wharf, rushing away.

Raul's eyes darted side to side, struggling to focus. "Am I . . ." His head dropped to the floor.

"Come on. Wake up." Mike jockeyed his chair closer to Molly.

Molly sobbed softly, red faced, wet with tears. Her eyes begged Mike.

"We'll get him back." *Dear God . . .* "Raul! Wake up."

Raul struggled to his hands and knees, looked at Molly, and crawled behind Mike's chair. He tugged at Mike's bindings, weak and slow.

Once freed, Mike yanked the Bowie knife from the sheath under his left arm and cut Molly's binding.

She spun around, threw her arms around Mike's neck, and sobbed into his chest.

Mike hugger her with his left arm, sheathed his knife, and pulled Raul to his feet. "Are you okay?"

"I been worse."

Mike picked up his Colt and led them out the door. He squinted against bright sunlight and stepped back.

Two horses rushed from the stable pulling a flatbed wagon, Jack Wick at the reins. A woman on the back sat on bundles of their portable property.

Mike asked, "Are the police coming?"

Raul bent and braced off his knees. "Vlad went up Front Street toward the telegraph station." He looked at Mike and Molly. "I hope so."

Molly said, "I know where they went. They have a boat."

They hurried up to Front Street and flagged a taxi.

LUCA AND GRIGORI ROWED the skiff, towing the sailboat into San Francisco Bay, where they hoped for wind. Luca said, "We are lucky for you, Grigori. You are sailor."

"My father owned three fishing boats in Caspian Sea. I learned to sail at an early age, I think nine or ten."

"How did you come to serve the Czar?"

"We fish for sturgeon and harvest roe. We perfectly salt the roe for the finest Caspian caviar. Czar Nicholas heard of our caviar and ordered us to bring a shipment to Moscow. He liked the caviar, and liked to see me." Grigori smiled, humble. "I was handsome boy, and I had a quick mind for the riddles of his courtesans. After this, he put me into training for police work, and I was selected for the service of the Romanov family. Worst day of my life, was to be assigned to the grand duchess. We have bad trouble here in America, I think."

"Da, da. She is bitter woman with bad temper, and bad judgments. My family has served her from her first breath. She is always for the trouble."

Grigori stopped rowing and looked back at the schooner he'd purchased for the duchess.

The schooner had cleared the docks and most of the ships at anchor. The water had become choppy from a steadily building breeze. "Is time to get our sails up."

They back paddled the skiff to the stern of the schooner, where Grigori quickly tied to a stern cleat. They climbed aboard the schooner and hurried forward.

Grigori loosened the ties and the jib sucked into the wind. He pointed to the centerboard mast. "That rope on the front, pull it to raise the jib." He hurried back to help. They quickly raised the jib and tied it off. The jib billowed in the wind and turned the schooner back toward the docks.

Grigori stepped to the starboard rail and trimmed the jib into a broad reach, turning the small schooner away from the docks. "Now we raise the main."

MIKE CLIMBED FROM THE taxi to the dock. "Wait here." This was their fourth stop. He was losing hope of finding Jimmy in time.

Ignoring Mike's order, Molly and Raul followed to the end of the short pier. Molly said, "Yes, this is the place." She pointed. "Look, I think that's the boat."

Two hundred meters into the bay, a black main sail went up on a twenty-meter schooner with a black hull.

Mike said, "It looks like a smuggler's boat."

The boat sailed south and quickly disappeared behind large ships at anchor.

"We know what to look for. Come on."

They returned to the waiting taxi, climbed in, and Michael said, "Take us up to city hall."

The driver slapped reins and the horse broke into a gallop.

Fifteen minutes later, the taxi stopped in front of city hall.

Mike jumped out and helped Raul climb down, slowed by his injuries.

Raul turned to help Molly.

Mike paid the driver.

Molly took Mike's arm.

Raul led them to the end of the building and into police headquarters. Mike nodded at the desk sergeant and led them into the squad room, past several desks, and stopped at Sergeant McFee's desk.

Angus McFee pushed back in his chair, surprised. "What the heck?"

"Did Preslova not contact you?"

"He did. I sent a squad of seven men with him."

"They still have Jimmy."

"Who?"

"Grand Duchess Catherine Mikhailovna and General, the Count Boris Romochka-Krestyanov, along with three of their subordinates. They have Jimmy on a black schooner, maybe sixty feet in length."

"Russians?"

"Yes, of course."

McFee stood, looked at Molly and Raul, and spread both hands. What could he do? His normally placid face creased with what looked like genuine concern.

Molly shouted, "Find my Jimmy!"

"You said they're on a schooner?"

"Yes," said Molly. "A black one."

"This department has six rowboats." McFee stared at Mike. "I can ask to send them out, but we both know what the chief will say."

"Yes." Mike turned and cupped Molly's cheek. "He's right. Can you remember anything that might help?"

Molly retreated into her memory, staring blankly at Mike. "They fried and ate a little boy's liver." Her tears flowed.

Mike turned back to McFee. "There's a young boy's body still there, at the Forge, I think they call it. There was an American there, the one who calls himself Jack Wick. It's that old stable and blacksmith shop down on the Barbary."

"The man who's been kidnapping Chinese kids?"

"I'm sure of it."

Molly put her handkerchief to work, soaking up tears. "He's a cannibal. Him and the woman who took Jimmy. They both ate that little boy's liver."

"What?" Mike had no previous knowledge of this. Neither had he ever seen such fear in his wife.

Molly grabbed Mike's coat and pulled him close. "She said, Jimmy's American liver would taste better than Chinese. She said that you would know her pain, and that you would fear her."

Chapter Twenty-Four

FRANKLIN MOSBY SPENT long hours every day, searching for a burly, red-bearded man and his beautiful daughter, Melany. After searching the streets, docks, wharfs, and boardinghouses of the Barbary Coast, starting at Molly Zabel's White Chapel Saloon, he'd finally reached Pacific Street Wharf, his first landfall in San Francisco.

He walked down the wide wharf and stopped outside Tommy Chandler's Boardinghouse. The front doors stood wide open. He stepped inside.

Six tables in the large, downstairs parlor hosted no more than ten men, total, many of them drinking mugs of beer. Four played cards at a corner table. A large man stood at the bar, talking quietly with the bartender. The bartender bore a likeness to several boxing posters over and around the bar.

The big man talking to the bartender had not shaved for at least a week. His stature looked like the man Mike Zabel wanted in connection with a train robbery, and with the abductions of Chinese children. Franklin would tell Mike later.

"Help you mister?" The bartender leaned past the big man's frame to look at Franklin.

"Maybe." Franklin walked up to the bar and nodded at the big man. He nodded at the bartender. "Are you Tommy Chandler?" He looked at one of the posters.

"What do you want?"

"Do you have any rooms?"

The bartender wiped the bar with a towel, glancing up and down at Franklin. "Not right now, I don't. Come back in a week or two. Some of my boarders are due to ship out. One ship sails Tuesday, next week. Another sails on Monday, week after next."

Franklin smiled and nodded, "Thank you." He poked a thumb toward the corner table. "Might I possibly sit in?"

"Okay with me. Want a beer?"

"Is it properly chilled?" Franklin instantly regretted having said that.

"Well, it ain't hot, if that's what you mean."

Franklin smiled and nodded. He pulled his coin purse from a vest pocket and dropped a nickel onto the bar. "Is that enough?"

"Perfect." Chandler drew a draft from the barrel, set the mug on the bar, and raked off foam with a wooden blade. He added more beer, raked foam again, and slid the mug to Franklin.

Franklin picked up the beer and wove between tables to the card players. A burly, bald headed man dealt cards to a wiry little man and two bare-footed sailors. They'd all anteed one dollar for five-card draw.

The players picked up and shielded their cards, spreading, studying, and arranging.

The little guy said, "Pass."

Both sailors passed.

The bald, stocky man tossed a twenty-dollar-gold-piece into the pot. The other three players tossed their cards.

"My turn. Give them cards over." The little man had a British accent. "Maybe I can deal some of the rest of us a good hand."

His quick hands shuffled the deck like a professional, cut it several times, and set it on the table.

The bald man cut the deck. His bushy red eyebrows seized Franklin's attention.

The little man tossed a silver dollar into the pot. "Ante up."

The others tossed in.

The little guy dealt quickly and set the deck on the table.

After looking at their cards, the first sailor knocked on the table, a pass.

The second sailor tossed in a silver dollar.

The big man called.

The little dealer tossed in six dollars. "Bump it five."

The first sailor shook his head and tossed his cards.

The second sailor called.

The bald man called and looked up at Franklin. "You need something, mister?"

"I'd like to sit in?"

"Sure. Drag up a chair."

Franklin dragged a chair from a nearby table and positioned it between the two sailors, a good place from which to watch the bald man and the nimble-fingered, current dealer.

Both sailors shifted their chairs, making room.

"Thank you, gentlemen. I'm Franklin." He sat and set his coin purse on the table.

The little dealer said, "Cards?"

The sailor on Franklin's left tossed three cards. "Three."

The dealer dealt him three cards.

The sailor to Franklin's right leaned back to watch. He'd already folded.

The bald man tossed three cards. "Three."

The dealer dealt him three cards. After a glance, he tossed three cards and dealt himself four more. He shielded his hand, looking closely at his cards. He deftly slipped a card up his shirtsleeve and looked around.

Franklin pretended not to notice.

AT 8:07 P.M., MIKE kissed Molly goodnight and left their house on Russian Hill. He climbed into Paddy's taxi and waved him forward.

"The colonel's house, Mike?"

"Yes, Paddy. Please."

Paddy slapped reins and his horse tugged up the steep hill. They turned left, hurried two level blocks, turned uphill, and stopped at the second house.

"Wait again, Paddy?"

"Sure, Mike. Whatever it takes."

"Thanks. I will not be long." Mike jumped out and hurried up to Colonel William Tell Coleman's front door. He yanked the silver chain and the interior bell chimed.

Jong Chi, Coleman's long-time servant, answered the door, smiled, and bowed. "Count Mike. Come in, please."

Mike entered and stepped into Coleman's parlor. "Please tell him, it is important."

"Take your coat?"

"No, Chi. I am in a hurry."

Chi bowed and hurried down the hall toward the kitchen.

Moments later, with his coat unbuttoned, Coleman strolled past the main stairs and turned into the parlor. He looked at Mike, his head shot back, and he closed the door. "What's wrong, Mike?"

"Molly and Jimmy were kidnapped, yesterday."

"What?"

"Molly is home now, but they still have Jimmy."

"Who would do such a thing?"

"Grand Duchess Catherine Mikhailovna, General Krestyanov, and two other men. It is only the duchess who is responsible. The rest follow her orders."

"Has this anything to do with that Russian duke we shot at the Palace?"

"She is his sister."

"Have you notified the police?"

"Of course. Listen, they are on a small schooner. They sailed south, this afternoon. The police only have row boats."

"Ah." Coleman nodded. He understood why Mike had come to him. "Would you know the boat if you saw it?"

"Yes. It was a black, rake-masted schooner. Two masts, maybe sixty feet in length, with black sails. It sailed south, this afternoon."

Coleman sat behind his desk, thinking dark thoughts. "That sounds like *Black Swan*. I sold it last month to a Russian named Grigori. He paid with gold coin from Russia." He shook his head. "I had no idea."

"Of course. How could you know?" Mike spread his hands. "Bill, I need your help."

Coleman stood, animated. "My pleasure. My new yacht, *Sister Sal*, is a steam driven, center-screw, cabin cruiser. She does sixteen to eighteen knots, and she's sea worthy. I'll send Chi to find the skipper. His name's Thomas Yates. You should be well outside before morning."

"Outside?" Mike hadn't thought about this. "You think they left?"

Coleman blinked, surprised. "Don't you?"

Mike said, "They sailed toward south bay."

"Could be just a tack to get deeper into the bay. If I were you, I'd get out past where they can reach overnight, and start searching deep water in the morning. If they're out there, they'll either be bound for Vladivostok, or heading south along the coast. I'd bet on Vladivostok, but that's a rough sail."

"What if they are still here? What if they are gathering provisions and have not yet left?" Mike's thoughts tumbled together. "I do not think the duchess would cross the Pacific Ocean in a small sailing vessel."

"Good points. Look, *Sister Sal* is tied at the end of Meigg's Wharf. We'll come get you at the Palace when we're ready to set sail."

"We?"

"You think I could sleep with this going on? I'm one of Jimmy's godfathers. We'll set up watch at the end of Meigg's Wharf. There's a navy vessel anchored out there. If they try to leave the bay before we get back, I'll make sure the navy stops them. I've known her captain since before the war."

Mike stood, ready to go.

"Give me a minute. No need to send Chi."

BY 9:30 P.M., ONLY Franklin and the stocky, baldheaded man remained in Tommy Chandler's parlor, still playing five-card draw. Franklin had emptied the purses of the little man and both sailors. Not hard to do. The bald man called himself Donald and possessed an unpredictability which had fueled moments of fear in the other players.

Franklin had unbuttoned his coat to expose the handle of his Navy Colt. This seemed to have levelled the bigger man's threatening manner. Franklin dealt them each five cards and took a peek; three fours, a jack, and a nine. He'd been riding a lucky streak all evening.

"Twenty dollars." Donald tossed in a new gold coin, probably bluffing again.

"I'll call and raise twenty." Franklin set two gold coins in the pot.

Donald studied Franklin's face, looked at his cards, glanced at Franklin, and tossed in another new gold coin.

The big man who'd been talking with Tommy Chandler had gone out two hours earlier. Franklin was sure this was the man half of San Francisco wanted for robbery, kidnapping, and murder. Bracing anybody in this place might prove fatal, or, more likely, get him Shanghaied.

Sailors had been coming in and going out, climbing upstairs and coming down. Some drank beer at the bar. Three sat at a middle table with lace-dressed ladies.

Franklin wanted to ask all of them about Melanie, but he didn't dare. He couldn't be sure this burly card player was the man who'd killed Allison and taken Melanie. This presented a tricky situation, any way he looked at it. He hoped Moses would know him by his angry, green eyes.

Donald arranged his cards and tossed three.

Franklin dealt him three cards and set the deck aside. "I'll keep these." He set his cards face down on the table.

Donald picked up his new cards and arranged his hand. He smiled with a hint of confidence. He tossed in two more new gold coins.

Franklin hesitated for show, looked at his cards, then picked up four coins. He dropped two into the pot. "Call." He dropped two more. "And raise."

"Mister, you're bluffing. You ain't got no straight or flush." He tossed four gold coins into the pot. "I'll raise you right back."

Franklin stacked coins, pretending to worry, picked up two, and set them in the pot. "Guess I'd better call."

Donald slapped his hand onto the table; two tens, two deuces, and a queen. He chuckled and moved to rake in the pot.

"Uh . . ." Franklin turned his cards up and spread them. "Three fours beats two pair."

"Mister, you're just too lucky."

Franklin turned slightly, reminding Donald of his holstered Colt, and raked in the pot. "I have had a good run of luck, with your help along the way."

"What's that supposed to mean?"

Franklin stacked coins into his coin purse and filled it. "Maybe poker isn't your game." He put the purse into his left breast pocket.

The remainder, about half his winnings, he fed into his right vest pocket. Counting his winnings in front of Donald would be impolite.

Donald's face turned red with rage, staring at Franklin's Colt.

Franklin stood and took a step back, clear of any lunges from Donald. "You seem like a nice fellow, Donald. You aught not to play, if you can't afford to lose."

"What do you know about it?"

"I deal faro up at the Palace. I've watched a lot of men lose at cards, men who couldn't afford it. I don't like seeing that happen, but I deal an honest game. Maybe faro's a better game for you."

Donald calmed some, unwinding. "I like faro okay. What you doing down here, anyway?"

"I live down here on the coast. I've been looking for a boardinghouse better situated for getting up to Meigg's Wharf. I might check in here in a week or two. When I saw your game, I decided to sit in. Now, I need to get up to the Palace. You should come up and try your luck."

Donald looked at his losing hand. "Not tonight. I need to work early tomorrow." He stood and smiled at Franklin, more like a sneer. "We will meet again."

"Good enough. I look forward to it. Maybe we can share some chowder."

Donald moved to shake hands, but Franklin acted like he didn't see it. Letting this bulky man get a hold on him would be stupid.

Franklin wove his way through crowded tables, smiled at Tommy Chandler, and walked out onto Pacific Street Wharf.

That little man, Dink, stood nearby. He bent at the waist, saying goodnight, and smiled like a man with a plan.

A chill crossed Franklin's back, the kind he'd felt during the war, usually before a Yankee raid. He hurried up to Front Street to hail a taxi.

HAN WOK TAPPED THE coachman's shoulder, a signal to stop in front of the White Chapel Saloon. His uncle signaled for Han to go inside. He'd wait in the coach with his honorable hatchet man.

Han trotted quickly across the heavy wooden planks of the Barbary Coast and hesitated at the front door of the White Chapel Saloon. It was too late for callers, but he must. He knocked and waited a minute. He knocked again.

Sally, one of the housekeepers, opened the door, wearing her dark night coat and white sleeping cap. She frowned, not happy to see Han.

"Most sorry to disturb, ma'am Sally."

"Han! What do you want at this hour?"

"We need Dr. Chiang. Is urgent."

Sally studied Han for a moment and closed the door.

Han turned and bowed to his uncle, signaling a delay.

He rocked back and forth, trying to get warm. This city was always cold under dense fog, hanging down to the tops of gas streetlamps.

SuLin opened the door, fully dressed in her dark wool coat. "Han, what you want?" She smiled, maybe happy to see Han.

"Another Chinese boy has been found. Can Po come with us?"

Po opened the door wide, already carrying his canvas medical bag. He pushed his daughter out the door, followed her out, and Sally closed the door.

Han led them to the waiting coach and spoke in Cantonese. "Uncle, this is honorable Chiang Po and his daughter, Chiang SuLin." He spread his hand toward his uncle. "This is my uncle, Honorable Han Chow. Big business here. This is honorable hatchet man." He fanned toward the black clad man. He always stayed in the shadows.

Po stiffened and peered inside the wagon. He touched SuLin's shoulder and both bowed at the waist, showing respect.

"Come." Han helped Po into the coach first, then SuLin. Han climbed in last and sat next to SuLin.

His uncle nodded and smiled approvingly at SuLin, then at Po.

The coachman clicked his tongue and the horse broke into a canter. They turned out to Front Street, drove two blocks down, and turned onto a short, dark pier. A police wagon had parked in front of a two-story wooden building. Light showed through the open doorway.

Han Wok led his uncle and the others into the large room called the Forge, where many lanterns had been set in place by Police Sergeant Angus McFee.

The city coroner, Dr. Thaddeus Pearson, had already arrived.

Two uniformed police officers trotted downstairs from the second floor. The first reported to Sergeant McFee. "There's nothing upstairs but some old clothes, including a dark wool coat and a black, broad-brimmed hat. Looks like those pictured in the Bulletin."

Dr. Pearson stepped out from the raised brick hearth and shook hands with Po. "Thanks for coming, Dr. Chiang. I thought you should examine the remains, and be the one to report to the Chinese community."

SuLin quickly interpreted in Cantonese.

Han stepped around the conversation to look.

A small boy lay on the floor, his body twisted around the curve of the brick hearth. Flies swarmed over a crust of dried blood.

Han spun away, dizzy. He bent and gripped his knees, swallowing back his urge to vomit fried rice. His throat burned with acid.

The honorable hatchet man placed a hand of Han's shoulder. Both watched Chiang Po stoop to examine the body.

Han stood and breathed deeply. Sweat burned his eyes. He pulled a handkerchief and wiped his face.

The hatchet man tipped his hat to Han and his uncle. He'd seen enough.

Han's uncle nodded, and the hatchet man walked out the door into the night.

Chapter Twenty-Five

GENERAL, THE COUNT Boris Romochka-Krestyanov stood on the steeply pitched deck of the schooner with Grigory, a surprisingly good sailor, and Luka, the lifetime servant to the grand duchess. None of them appreciated the situation into which the duchess had plunged them.

Still, the general needed to demand their loyalty. He dared not bring her authority into question. "It is our job to serve and protect her, even at the cost of our lives, if need be."

Grigory and Luka bit down on any complaints. They still did not like it.

Boris said, "Da, da. Yes, I know she has put us in a dangerous position. I am at my wits end, trying to reason with her. She is much like her brother. He is dead, because his guards could not control his rage. We must not allow that to happen here. We must find a way to control her actions." He looked from one to the other. "Have you any suggestions?"

Grigori said, "Colonel Preslova made this clear, as did the two guards we interrogated."

Hopeless. Krestyanov didn't need further confirmation of their seemingly irreversible, headlong plunge into the darkness wrought through the Romanov Dynasty's pomposity.

Luka looked away. He had no clue. He, too, seemed stuck in the previous day's dilemma. He turned back and said, "What can we do? Both guards took this story to their death. I am sure they were telling the truth."

Krestyanov said, "We are all trapped by what has happened during the past week. We have committed serious crimes in a foreign country. We have no royal protections here." He thrust his fists to the star-filled sky, frustrated by his own lack of direction.

Grigori seemed to fully understand Krestyanov's anxiety. "We can put into a spot in the south bay. I've anchored there before." Gregori sounded matter of fact. He must have been planning forward all along. "There is an estuary that can carry us near the railroad station in San Jose. We can row in there in the morning. I sailed down here before you and the duchess arrived. Sacha and Luka can take the boy back to his home and let him out, without being seen."

Boris said, "Da, da. A sensible solution, except for her. How can we convince her? You both heard her shouting. Her hatred for Mikhail places her beyond reason."

Grigori said, "General, Mikhail is very well connected here. He has very powerful friends. There is an American Navy ship in the bay, near Meigg's Wharf. Sailors from this ship surely visit the Palace, Mikhail's restaurant and gambling house. They will certainly move to block the channel out to the Pacific Ocean. We are trapped here on a boat that can easily be recognized during the day. I bought this boat from Colonel William Tell Coleman, a close friend of Mikhail."

"Why would you buy a boat from Mikhail's friend?"

Grigori shook his head. "The boat was for sale. I did not know of their friendship, at that time. You ordered me to purchase a boat before I left Moscow, '. . . in case we might need it,' you said. I lived on this boat until the arrival of your ship was announced in the Daily Evening Bulletin. Then I rented our rooms at the Cosmopolitan Hotel. I did not learn of Mikhail's friendship with Colonel Coleman until we interrogated Preslova's men. Only then did I learn of Coleman's friendship with Mikhail. They are close friends."

"Okay." Krestyanov put a hand on Grigori's shoulder, calming him. "I understand. Is alright. And, you are correct. We cannot sail safely at night. We need to anchor before we run aground and are trapped like dogs. In the morning, we will again try to convince her highness. Tell her nothing about this . . . Colonel Coleman."

"You see those lights?" Grigori pointed to a flicker of lights about two kilometers off the starboard.

FRANKLIN ENTERED THE casino side of the Palace at 10:04 p.m., four minutes late. Three regular players at his assigned table nodded and smiled, ready for him to set up a game of faro. He smiled on his way past. "Gentlemen, I'll be right with you."

He waved at Moses, stationed in his usual place under the stair, sketching a nice-looking Chinese prostitute on a Yankee sailor's knee.

Franklin looked over the top of the saloon doors.

Mike stood at the bar, eating chowder and talking with Abe Warner.

Franklin pushed through the doors into the saloon, where Yankee sailors drank hot buttered rum, swilled beers, or slurped chowder. A smattering of civilian sailors mingled with the navy, telling and listening to sea stories.

"Evening Franklin." Abe Warner smiled. "Cup or bowl?"

"I'm hungry tonight." He pulled a coin from his heavy vest pocket and set it on the bar.

"Your money's no good here. You already know that." Abe smiled and strolled toward the stove, scanning the bar for possible refills.

Franklin grabbed Mike's elbow and stepped closer. "As you know, I've been spending my afternoons and evenings patrolling the Barbary Coast. Today, I visited Tommy Chandler's Boardinghouse."

Mike shifted to face Franklin. He nodded, only mildly interested.

Franklin said, "You look very tired."

Mike grinned and slumped.

Franklin said, "I'm reasonably certain, the man calls himself Jack Wick was in there talking to Mister Chandler."

Mike stiffened and leaned close, suddenly very interested. "Was anybody else with him?"

"No, not that I could see. He's growing a beard and wearing light colored clothing. He left alone."

"I saw him this morning."

"What's wrong, Mike. What happened?"

Warner heard the question, returning with a platter of Chowder and crackers. He said, "Some Russians shot Raul and Kidnapped Molly and Jimmy. That's what happened." He reached over the bar and scrubbed Mike's back, reassuring and comforting him.

Mike flinched away. "I got Molly back this morning, but they still have Jimmy."

"Who?"

Warner said, "Some Russians with an old score to settle."

Franklin knew the feeling. He'd returned from the war to an empty house. And, earlier, he'd spent several hours with the man who'd probably killed his wife and kidnapped his daughter. He had found new hope. "Don't give up hope."

Mike's eyes flared at the thought. He'd never give up.

Franklin asked, "What can I do to help? What can we do to help?" Moses Broadback would be proud to join them.

Abe said, "They're on a schooner. Starting at dawn, we'll be posting volunteers to watch for a black, rake-masted schooner with black sails."

"Her name's *Black Swan*," said a well-dressed gentleman. He removed his bowler hat and nodded at Abe and Mike.

Mike stood back, shook the man's hand, and turned to Franklin. "Franklin Mosby, meet Colonel William Tell Coleman." Mike waved his hand with a slight grin. "Don't worry. He wasn't with the Union Army."

Coleman said, "You served with the Confederacy?" He extended his hand.

"I did." Franklin shook Coleman's hand. "It seems a long time ago. I've read about you in the Bulletin. A sincere pleasure to meet you, sir."

Coleman held his grip. "Any relation to Colonel John Mosby, from Virginia?"

"My older brother, sir. I was honored to serve in his regiment."

"My, my, what a small world in which we live. I've read about your exploits during the war."

"We were busy."

"Indeed, you were. It is my pleasure to meet you. We'll need to get together sometime and share stories."

"I'd like that."

Coleman let go of Franklin's hand and threw an arm over Mike's shoulder. "*Sister Sal* is ready to shove off, and I've spoken with Captain Patterson. He skippers the U.S.S. Thomas Jefferson, that navy ship out yonder."

The saloon doors blew open and four uniformed, Yankee sailors marched inside, as if summoned by Coleman. A chief petty officer strutted in after them and shouted, "Shore leaves are cancelled. All U.S.S. Thomas Jefferson personnel are ordered to report to the ship immediately."

Coleman nodded and smiled.

The four uniformed sailors moved quickly through the tables, tapping shoulders with nightsticks, herding sailors toward the doors.

One of the sailors stood and said, "Paxton's either in the other room or upstairs."

"Go get him," said the chief.

Coleman said, "The Jefferson will patrol just outside. They'll block any black schooners trying to get out."

Franklin asked, "Who's setting the watch schedule at the end of the wharf?"

Chapter Twenty-Six

SISTER SAL steamed south under the purple glow of dawn, the sun rising beyond California's Coastal Mountains.

Coleman stood behind his captain, Thomas Yates. "What's the plan, Tom?"

Standing at the wheel, Yates turned to Mike, knowing who needed to hear the answer. "We'll steam south to Monterey. No way they could sail that far since yesterday. Not on *Black Swan*. If we don't see her, we'll steam out a few miles and head north until we're off the bay. Then we'll steam in a few miles and continue up the coast until mid-afternoon. Then we'll turn out and steam for Vladivostok until morning. We'll chase the windvane all the way out and then circle back."

Mike asked, "What if we miss them?"

"Not possible. I know these winds and I know these waters. And, I know *Black Swan*."

Coleman squeezed Mike's shoulder. "Mike, you're exhausted. Take the captain's quarters and get some rest."

Mike's bones ached from weariness. "I can't sleep."

Captain Yates said, "Go ahead, Mike. I've got two lookouts on top. They both know *Black Swan*."

GENERAL KRESTYANOV had not slept. With first light finally creeping across the bay, he shook Grigori's shoulder. He slept in a fold of the main sail. "Is this light enough to move the boat?"

Grigori rolled out, stretched, and scanned their position in the early light. "Da, da." He pointed toward a barely visible, wide expanse of tall grass. "We can't see from here. To the right is a channel where we can tow the schooner. There is a small landing there, for local fishing boats. The village with a rail station is just beyond."

"I will get Luka to help you." Krestyanov went below.

The duchess sat with Sacha and the boy at the table, splitting bread and eating. It was very early for her to be up. Maybe she had not slept either.

"You made a bad mistake," said the boy, pointing a finger at the duchess. "Mom says, I need to always eat fruit first." He shook his head and chewed off a mouthful of bread. "Yummy. Sourdough shepherd bread."

"Da, is very tasty." Sacha sliced yellow cheese onto a plate and set it in front of the boy. She'd obviously come to like him in a very short time.

The duchess restrained a smile, but she could not disguise her affection for the boy.

He is a Romanov. The boy's grandmother was Queen of the Netherlands. His boldness displayed his royal blood, whether or not he was aware of it.

His father is the same.

The duchess said, "We are on a boat. No fruit trees here."

The boy said, "I like fresh strawberries. They don't need trees to grow on."

Luka smiled and handed Krestyanov a two-day-old loaf of shepherd bread.

Krestyanov broke off a chunk and handed the loaf back. "Take this up with some cheese and help Grigori. Is time to move the boat."

Luka grabbed a brick of cheese from the small galley and climbed to the upper deck.

The duchess stood, brushed crumbs from her travel dress, and turned to face Krestyanov. Her eyes pierced, speaking softly in Russian. "Who do you think you are talking to? How dare you tell me what to do? I am not one of your stupid soldiers. I do not like to raise my voice, especially in front of my young cousin, here." She glanced at the boy. Her brow hooked upward, leaning toward Krestyaniv, daring him to respond.

Krestyanov had not spoken to her since the previous day. He lowered his head in a bow and straightened slowly, thinking how to say what needed to be said. "Your brother, the grand duke, is dead because Colonel Preslova and his men could not control his irrational behavior."

"How dare you?"

"Your Highness, please understand. All of us want only to serve you and your family. Our lives are bound to this, as were those of Preslova and his men. As was this boy's father, your first-degree cousin."

"How dare you presume to . . ."

"Highness, allow me to remind you. We are not in Mother Russia. We are in America. The people, here, neither fear you nor feel any compulsion to obey you. They choose to rule themselves. They choose to elect those who will represent their interests."

"What nonsense! This is doomed to fail. How can a mob choose to rule itself? Corruption of the masses is inevitable." She had convinced herself of this, long before ever leaving Russia.

"Your Highness, we are discussing, here and now, this present moment. You . . ." *No, no, no.* "We have placed ourselves on a dangerous path. We have jeopardized your safety."

The boat dipped slightly and chain ground against a brass grommet. The anchor was coming up.

She stepped back a little, allowing Sacha and the boy to climb to the main deck.

"Your Highness, Czar Alexander, your nephew, has withdrawn the warrant on Count Mikhail Diebitsch-Zabalkansky."

"Of course! Had this son of a soldier not killed my brother, Nikolai would now be Czar." She crossed her arms, her most stubborn stance. "Idiot!"

"Your Highness, Mikhail did not kill your brother. Since our arrival, I have visited the archives of three reputable newspapers. All three report this incident with an identical chain of events. Colonel Preslova first entered the Palace with his warrant. He was told his warrant would need to first go to the United States Department of State before any extradition could be enforced. This is American law."

"What nonsense. Mikhail deserted his post and fled prosecution. He chopped off the right hand of the grand duke, an assault on the royal branch. Russia has every right to seek justice, anywhere in the world. How dare this disorganized mob stop us, just because they call themselves a republic?"

"Your Highness, do you want to be at the mercy of this mob?"

Her mouth clamped shut, thinking about this one, perhaps for the first time.

Krestyanov said, "The count was unarmed, on the night your brother was shot. Your brother shot at the count in a room filled with important citizens. He missed. He pulled back the second hammer on his twin barrel pistol and marched between the tables to get closer. When he, again, took aim at the count, three other men shot him. One was the elected Governor of California. One was an elected legislator. The third was a respected local businessman, the owner of the very establishment where your brother lost his life.

"Now, in front of at least one hundred witnesses, I shot the counts companion, while Grigori and Luka kidnapped his wife, his son, and another woman.

"We then brought Mikhail, a duly sworn officer of the state police, to the location of our American colleague, this . . ." Krestyanov waved a hand, remembering. "Duncan Frack, where he had just killed an innocent young boy and cannibalized his liver. I could not believe a Romanov would ever turn to cannibalism. What would Alexander say about this?"

The duchess stood stiff, finally listening.

"If this mob would put us in jail, we would rot there, or be executed."

The duchess turned and sat at the table. She took a bite of cheese and sipped red wine.

"Your Highness, do you have a plan?"

"We will sail this boat to Vladivostok, and we will take the boy. This will bring Count Zabalkansky to where our authority will never be in question."

Krestyanov flinched, impossible to stop himself.

"What now?"

"Your Highness, Grigori had no way of knowing this when he purchased this boat. It belonged to Colonel William Tell Coleman, a very close friend with Mikhail. Mikhail will certainly go to him for help."

"Of what importance is this? Nobody can see us at night. We will hide here until the sun goes down. Sacha and Luka can go ashore for provisions. We will depart here after sunset."

"But, Your Highness, there is an American naval vessel in the bay. She is anchored between us and the open sea. They have certainly been alerted and will be watching."

"How can they see this boat at night?"

Krestyanov said, "To navigate this crowded bay at night will not only require a bright, full moon, but extraordinary good luck. Do you want to risk our capture? This boat is known."

AT 7:45 A.M., DONALD Thorne met Duncan Frack at Mission Station, waiting to board the southbound train to San Jose.

Duncan studied Donald, apprehensive about something.

"What?"

Duncan looked toward the station, then back to Front Street, nobody else around. "Last time, when we took the Wells Fargo, you robbed the passengers before we secured the strongbox. I can't blame you. We did the same thing, trying to rob a train. There was a state policeman aboard. He shot my partner in his face, when I wasn't looking, and we never got the strongbox. Tommy says, that happens again, and he'll find somebody else."

"Sure. I'll do whatever you say." Donald needed the money. Bad luck and a rebel card shark had cleaned him out.

"We're getting on that there train." Duncan poked a thumb over his shoulder, toward the waiting train. "We'll take seats in the second car from the end and wait for speed. We'll get between the last two passenger cars and climb onto the roof. We'll cover our heads, up on top."

The train whistle blew.

Donald stepped toward the train but Duncan stopped him. "I ain't finished. We'll move quietly to the caboose. Won't be no shadows with this here fog."

A gray haze lay across the city and bay as far as Donald could see. "Okay." Donald moved toward the train, again.

Duncan stopped him, again. "They most always keep the side door open when the trains up to speed, rain or shine. "I'll swing down inside first. I'm quick for my size. You wait a minute, up on top, then climb down the rear ladder to the back platform." He grabbed Donald's arm and pulled him toward the train.

The whistle blew twice.

Duncan handed him his ticket.

LITTLE JIMMY'S FACE twisted with fear. "Daddy!"

Mike bolted up from this nightmare, scrubbed his face, and rolled out of the captain's bunk aboard *Sister Sal*.

He opened the cabin door and entered the wheelhouse. The sun shined hazy above the coastal mountains, framed through a porthole.

Captain Yates stood at the wheel with his back to Mike.

Bill Coleman slept in a hammock near the portside door.

Mike placed a hand of the captain's shoulder.

The captain glanced back. "You sleep okay?"

"Yes. As much as possible. Maybe too long."

"There's nothing for you to do, anyway."

Coleman grumbled and moved from inside his hammock. They'd been speaking softly, but they'd wakened him. He rolled out and stretched his legs to the deck. He stood and stepped out the portside door to urinate into the ocean. A steady wind pushed from the starboard side.

The 24-hour chronometer above the forward window read 09:17. The sky was clear over the ocean. Clouds hung over the mountains.

Captain Yates picked up the haling hose and blew into the mouthpiece.

A moment later, a voice came back, "Yes, sir."

The captain spoke into the mouthpiece. "Get some breakfast up here. There's three of us."

"Aye-aye, captain."

Coleman came back inside, buttoning his britches. "Breakfast, Tom?"

"Should be about fifteen minutes."

Coleman said, "Seen anything yet?"

"There's a few sails running up the coast for San Francisco, Eureka or Seattle. Nothing black. We passed a few boats headed out. No sighting of *Black Swan*."

Mike said, "Do you think they are still in the bay?"

Chapter Twenty-Seven

GRIGORY AND LUKA PULLED *Black Swan* tight to the small fishing pier and tied her off to waist-high pilings. She was the largest boat in the area.

Grigori followed Luka back onto the boat and helped raise the skiff onto the stern sheet, turned it upside-down, and tied it off. "I will retie the schooner for the tides after you are gone." Grigori led Luka below.

The duchess sat at the small table with the boy. She could not help herself. She liked him.

The general stood, folded his hands behind his back, and rocked up and down on the balls of his feet. "The duchess has decided; Sacha will take the boy with her on the train. She will take a taxi up near the boy's house and drop him off."

The duchess looked at the boy. "You can find your house, yes?"

"Of course, I can." The boy's confidence never failed to shine.

"Luka, you will take them to the train station and give her this." The general handed Luka a coin purse.

The duchess said, "Once Sacha has deposited the boy, she will buy ocean passage for four of us to Panama City, then she will meet us at the train station." She handed Mikhail's address to Sacha.

Sacha looked at the address and nodded. She understood.

The duchess said, "Grigori, you will stay here with the boat. If they should question you, you are to deny any knowledge of any of what we've done here. You have never worked for the Russian government. You do not, nor have you ever known any of us."

"Da, da." Grigori understood this. He had been thinking about this since the general's first mention of his staying behind. He could earn a living. He had always been a good fisherman. He already had enough money to buy the nets. He had already made contacts at the fish markets in the city.

Sacha dragged a heavy travel case forward from the stern cabin and looked at Luka.

Luka transferred the case to the upper deck and waited.

Sacha cupped the boy's face and smiled. "Are you ready to go to the home?"

"Am I ready to go home?" The boy jumped to his feet and raced up the ladder.

The duchess stood and faced Sacha. "We will take the last train tonight and meet you at the station."

The general said, "You will find sailing schedules in the Daily Evening Bulletin, with instructions on where to buy tickets." He pulled and looked at his pocket watch. "If you miss the early train, come back here." He put his watch away. "If necessity demands, we will revise our schedule."

"Da, da." Sacha hurried to the upper deck. Everybody seemed eager to get home.

Gregory could only hope.

The boy rushed back down the ladder, ran head first into the duchess, buried his head in her dress, and hugged her waist.

She stroked his hair. "Yes, yes. You grow up big and strong. Always remember, you are a Romanov. Nothing will stop you."

He looked up at her, smiled, let go of her waist, and scrambled back up the ladder.

The general said, "He is a fine, strong boy."

The duchess stiffened and straightened her dress. "As soon as we reach Moscow, you will engage three assassins to work independently of one another. They must not know each other. They will individually return to San Francisco to do what must be done; first, the boy's mother, then his father. Do not forget Preslova."

The general flinched and shook his head. He did not understand.

She said, "Colonel Preslova and Major Zabalkansky are both deserters from the imperial forces of Mother Russia. They must die. As for the major's wife; the major must be made to suffer, as I have suffered. Only then, he must die a painful death."

Gregori swelled with gratitude. She had not added any such tasks to his responsibilities.

DONALD THORNE AND DUNCAN Frack sat near the forward door in the third of five passenger cars on the southbound train. They were ten minutes out of the Mission District Station, and already up to speed.

Duncan nudged Donald, *Time to go*. They'd come this far forward on the train because these doors had curtained windows for better concealment. They stepped out onto the platform and Duncan closed the door. He pointed up.

Donald climbed the ladder onto the roof and dropped to his hands and knees, surprised by how much more the roof of the railcar swayed than did the floor below.

Duncan reached the roof, pulled Donald off his knees, and both men spread their feet for better balance. Duncan crouched and tapped Donald's shoulder. "Keep low. Makes it easier."

Fog and cloud cover had thickened, making it impossible to cast shadows, as Duncan had predicted. Nobody inside the train would see their shadows. They moved toward the caboose.

Duncan stopped at the rear of the middle car and pulled Donald close. "You pull any stunts this time, I'll shoot you in your neck."

Donald waved him off. "How many times I got to tell you, I'm sorry for what I done. It won't happen again. I need this work."

Duncan nodded, turned, and jumped to the next car. That, and one more passenger car to go.

Donald took a deep breath, jumped, and fell to his hands and knees, sliding sideways.

Duncan grabbed his arm and pulled him to his feet.

Donald said, "You said, '. . . the second car from the end.'" Donald feared falling off the train.

Duncan ignored him.

Donald had always been confident around other men. He wasn't tall but he was strong and quick. Duncan was also powerfully built. He was quick and agile, and much bigger than Donald. Donald didn't like being the lesser man.

Duncan turned and swayed, staggering, crouching, with his feet spread wide. He lurched toward the caboose, still two cars back. He jumped to the last passenger car and turned back.

Donald jumped easily, finally getting used to the motion.

They shuffled to the rear of the last passenger car and Duncan pulled out their flour-sack masks. He took off his new white hat, handed it to Donald, and pulled the sack over his head. He adjusted the eye holes, tucked the tails into his coat collar, and took back his hat. He pulled his hat tightly over his head and grabbed Donald's hat.

Donald put on the mask, adjusted it, took his hat back, and pulled it down tight, lest it should fly away. He followed Duncan onto the caboose and they shuffled to the middle of the car.

Duncan crouched and bellied onto the roof, grabbed the bar-rail at the edge, and slid out where he could look below. He pushed back to his hands and knees. "Damn door's closed."

He crawled to the other side, grabbed the rail, and leaned out. He motioned and Donald knelt next to him. Duncan leaned close to Donald's ear. "Wait for me to take charge down there, maybe half a minute." Duncan pointed to the rear of the caboose. "Then climb down that there ladder and come inside."

"Sure." *Easy.* The hand rails to the ladder looped high and fixed onto the rooftop. Donald pushed to his feet and shuffled to the back of the caboose.

Duncan crossed his arms and gripped the rail with his knuckles facing downward. He looked forward, took a deep breath, kicked out, and swung down, disappearing from Donald's view.

Donald figured he must be inside. He would otherwise be laying on the ground.

Donald stood into the center of the ladder and gripped the high, looped handrails. He counted to thirty and climbed down to the rear platform.

The rear-door window had no curtain. He stepped to one side, leaned against the wall, craned his neck, and peered into the window.

Inside, Duncan sprawled on the floor, hands held up.

A man in a conductor's uniform stood over him with a gun.

A smaller man stood near the rear door, his back facing Donald. He couldn't hear what they might be saying.

Duncan slowly removed his hat, getting ready to pull off his mask.

Donald pulled his knife and slammed through the rear door.

The smaller man turned, surprised.

Donald stabbed his throat and slashed hard.

Blood pulsed from the little man's neck. His eyes filled with questions.

Donald shoved him to the floor and pulled back his knife.

The man with the gun swung toward Donald.

Duncan deftly grabbed the gun, jammed the hammer with his little finger, and spun the gun hand about. His free hand yanked the man's foot, bringing him down to the floor. Still controlling the gun, Duncan lifted the smaller man off the floor and slammed his face with a hard right. Still in control of the gun, he grabbed the man's neck, slammed him into the wall, wrenched the gun out of the other man's hand, and tossed him to the floor.

The man rolled side-to-side on the floor. Both his hands flew to his bleeding nose. His eyes filled with tears.

Donald bent and used the dead man's coat to clean his knife before putting it away. "You want his liver?"

"Shut up with that. I'll shoot you dead." Duncan stepped over the dead man on the floor and stood in front of an *E.R. Morse & Co.* safe. It had been bolted to the floor. It had a brass key slot to the left, hinged on the right. He reached down and dragged the bloody-nosed man to the front of the safe. Leaning close to his bleeding face, he said, "You want to wind up like your dead friend?" He pointed at the dead man.

"No, sir."

"You the conductor?"

The man shook his head. He wasn't.

"Who's got the key to that there safe?"

Bloody-nose glanced at the dead man.

Donald turned the man face up and rifled through his pockets. He shook his head. "Not here."

Duncan backhanded bloody-nose hard, slamming the back of his head against the floor.

The fool whined like a baby, holding his face with both hands, blood oozing through his fingers. Both his eyes had already swollen bright blue, a broken nose for sure. "He keeps it around his neck." He rolled onto his side and curled into a ball, desperate to protect his face.

Donald stepped back and ripped open the dead man's shirt. A large brass key on a heavy silver chain lay on his gray-haired chest. Donald grabbed the key and yanked, but the chain didn't break. He yanked harder, lifting the man off the floor, but the chain held.

Duncan said, "Lift it over his stupid head, you . . ."

Donald pulled the man's head up by the hair and lifted off the key.

Duncan stomped on the head of the man on the floor and kicked him again.

Donald said, "He's out. Here's the key." He handed the key to Duncan. "You know how to open that?" He pointed at the safe.

"Usually need to turn the key in one direction then back in the other." He examined the key and looked at the safe. "Hope I didn't kill this one, in case I don't know how." Duncan inserted the key, turned it left a half turn, then back to the right until it stopped. "Turn that center knob wherever it's willing to go."

Donald grabbed the knob and twisted clockwise. It clicked and stopped.

Duncan grabbed the lever and pushed down. It clicked heavy, and they pulled the thick, steel door open.

Four canvas bags filled the safe's floor.

Duncan picked up two of them, straining from the weight, and nodded.

Donald picked up the other two. "Heavy as gold, ain't they?"

"Follow me." Duncan stood to the center of the open side door, looked forward, and jumped out. He let go of both bags, hit the ground, and bounced. His butt flew high as a hitching post, his head slid into gravel, and he stopped.

Donald tossed both bags and jumped. He hit the ground, stiff-legged, bounced up, and barely missed a tree limb. It knocked his hat off.

The train rushed south, moving quickly away.

On the other side of the tracks, five hundred yards to the south, Juanita kicked her horse into a trot, with two others in tow.

Chapter Twenty-Eight

SISTER SAL steamed back through the Golden Gate channel at 12:21, according to the ship's 24-hour chronometer. The marine layer stood high enough to see clearly. The red brick Presidio stacked up near the shoreline to their right, bringing memories of a very special period in Mike's life.

Mike and Bill Coleman stood behind Capt. Yates, while Yates piloted Coleman's steam-driven yacht through the ships and boats anchored in San Francisco Bay. Yates pointed out the portside window, toward an iron clad ship at anchor. "That's the *U.S.S. Thomas Jefferson*." A thin line of black smoke rose from her centerboard stack. "If they see black sails, they're prepared to stoke up, pull anchor, and move to stop her. *Black Swan's* the only boat I know with black sails."

15 minutes later, nearing Meigg's Wharf, Coleman said, "Thomas, have we enough coal to cruise the bay? I think we've got plenty of daylight."

Both men looked at Michael, asking.

"Please. You read my mind." Mike had been thinking of asking Coleman to do exactly that.

They cruised at half-throttle around the curve at North Point and steamed south, as close-in as possible to the Barbary Coast. Mike saw no place among the many wharfs and docks for the tall masts of *Black Swan* to hide. Neither had she anchored outside.

Slightly south of the shipping wharfs of the Barbary, Yates pushed the command bar forward and pulled back to three-quarter throttle.

Sister Sal built speed, cruised past Mission Bay, and turned east to cruise around Point Avisadero. They then turned down toward South Bay. No sighting of *Black Swan.*

An hour later, Yates said, "Bottom here gets tricky." Trees and tall grass covered the shoreline, only a couple of small fishing boats with their nets down could be seen. "I don't want to go in there. I might run us aground. There are a dozen or more creeks and estuaries down here. Some flow with seasonal rain. Others flow year-round. If *Black Swan's* down there, she's got a thousand places to hide. We'd need a massive load of luck to find her down here. But, don't worry. Sooner or later, she'll come out and we'll be waiting."

Yates spun the wheel and ran east, putting the grassy shoreline off to their starboard.

They steamed east for twenty minutes and turned north, where several small streams flowed into the bay, one big enough for a dock and small boats at anchor. Yates said, "That's Coyote Creek. She flows pretty shallow year-round. I don't think they could get very far up there. The only sure way east is the Sacramento River. We can steam up there tomorrow, if you want."

Coleman said. "It's getting late. We should head back to the city."

Yates said, "Let's stay over here till we reach Oakland, then we'll shoot straight across for Meigg's Wharf."

Mike, Bill Coleman, and Yates talked about fish in San Francisco Bay, about the gold rush days, now long past, and about city politics, but never about their families. Both Coleman and the captain exhibited a welcome sensitivity toward Mike's missing son, and the shooting of Raul.

Mike and the others, including at least two crewmen aloft, kept watch for *Black Swan,* all the way past Oakland harbor. The captain spun the wheel to a heading of west-northwest, toward the city. The sun had already gone.

Somebody lit the tall lighthouse atop a stone hump island in the middle of the bay which Mike had never before noticed. "That's Alcatraz Island," said Yates. "The Mexican alcalde built a military prison there, around forty years back. It's not used anymore, but we still need the lighthouse, especially when there's fog. We'll cruise around it, just in case. There's a small dock on the far side."

The east side of Alcatraz Island lay barren. They cruised to the west side, where a ten-foot fishing skiff had been pulled onto the rocky shore near a small dock. No *Black Swan*.

A growing display of gaslights twinkled across San Francisco, just then being lit. Their flickering light reflected across the water.

Mike said, "This is a beautiful city. Coming from here, it's hypnotic."

"It is," said Coleman.

Crewmembers lit lanterns aboard Coleman's yacht and darkness swallowed *Sister Sal*. Time rolled with the motion of the yacht and the thump of steam engines.

Hypnotic.

Yates pulled a chain. The whistle blew.

Above, footsteps scrambled across the deck, nearing the end of Meigg's Wharf.

Yates cranked the command lever all the way back then shoved it slightly forward.

Gears clanked, the props reversed, and *Sister Sal* slowed quickly, as Yates skillfully guided her port side into the dock.

Four crewmen jumped to the wharf, others tossed heavy rope, and Yates pushed the command levers all the way forward, all the way back, and returned them to the center position. The thump of the drive pistons stopped and steam hissed, depressurizing the boiler.

With the ship tightly secured to the wharf, the boarding ramp went down, and Coleman said, "I'm hungry and it's cold out. Allow me to buy chowder and hot buttered rum."

"No, Bill. It is for me to pay." Mike owed more than chowder.

They crossed onto the wharf, but Mike wasn't in the mood for food.

Franklin Mosby and Moses Broadback stepped out of the shadows and hurried up to Mike. Franklin asked, "Did you find anything?"

Mike shook his head, thrust his hands into his coat pockets, and walked toward the Palace. "We might as well bring it in. They are hiding up some creek or have gone up the Sacramento River." He didn't want to say it. "We can only hope they are still in California."

The thought of losing his son brought him to a dizzy stop. He braced both hands against his knees and wavered, trying to stop the wood planks of Meigg's Wharf from spinning away. He whispered, "Oh, God, help us find him alive."

Coleman grabbed and braced him. "No need for that. We'll find Jimmy." Coleman had never met the duchess.

Mike said, "You don't know . . ." He could not know what they had done to little boys.

DONALD THORNE FOLLOWED Duncan Frack and Juanita, leading their horses into a small hay barn in the swampy, bad-smelling China Basin.

Duncan lit a lantern and took the reins from Donald. He handed the reins to Juanita and lifted two heavy sacks from Donald's horse. He handed those to Donald and lifted the other two from his own horse. "Follow me."

Donald followed him out into darkness, crossed a dirt road, and entered a small house. Duncan turned up a lamp in a large room with a dirt floor. A bed of hay and blankets had been set up against the far wall, near a cast iron stove. Duncan said, "Them Russians cost me a good home." He dropped his bags onto the dirt floor and nodded at Donald.

Donald dropped his bags and stepped back, waiting on Duncan.

Duncan pointed at his two bags. "We'll divide this here three ways." He crossed to an open trunk near the doorway and pulled out two empty sea bags. He tossed one to Donald and spread the other on the floor. "Put those two into that bag. Them's for Tommy."

Donald opened the sea bag, fed both heavy coin bags into it, and dragged it nearer to the door.

Duncan dumped new silver coins onto the spread sea bag and started separating them into three equal piles. "Supposed to be five thousand in silver and ten thousand in gold."

Donald's heart thumped faster. His breathing quickened. Five thousand dollars would go far.

Duncan separated the gold, took a leather bag from his trunk, and dumped Donald's shares into it.

Donald tied the leather bag tight and dropped it into the sea bag. He tied the sea bag with the connected rope, and turned back. "Got another job lined up yet?"

Juanita squeezed past Donald, knelt, and fed wood into the cast-iron stove. She looked up at her man. "Donald will stay for the dinner?"

Duncan asked, "We got enough?"

Donald smiled and waved off. "Thanks, but I need to get back to my niece and tuck her in for the night." He looked out at the darkness. "How do I get back to Pacific Street?"

MIKE LED THE OTHERS into the saloon side of the Palace. The regular crowd ate, drank, and chatted. Abe's two monkeys, chained to center posts, begged food and ate well, like always.

Abe worked behind the bar, with his ever-present plug hat seemingly glued to the top of his head.

Mike held up four fingers and Abe turned to his chowder pot.

Some regulars near the end of the bar saw Mike and willingly vacated three stools. Two stools at the end had already been vacated.

The Chinese coolie cleaned the area on the bar and Mike sat on the end stool. He pulled Franklin Mosby onto the next stool. Moses sat next to Franklin. Bill Coleman and Capt. Yates sat nearest the center of the long bar.

Abe brought chowders to Coleman and Yates, the coolie brought a community platter of crackers, and Abe returned with two more bowls of chowder, for Franklin and Moses. Abe leaned close. "Any luck?" He somehow knew Mike wasn't hungry.

Mike shook his head. "I don't know what to do." He nudged Franklin. "I now know exactly how Franklin feels."

Franklin swallowed chowder. "Never give up." He gripped Mike's shoulder. "I think I might have found the man who murdered my wife and took our daughter."

Mike said, "Molly watched the man who calls himself Jack Wick skin a young boy's back and carve out his liver. He fried the liver in lard and shared it with a Russian duchess."

Franklin clamped shut, shook his head, and blinked, not looking at Mike.

Abe delivered a tray of five buttered rums.

Mike needed to shift his focus, clear his mind, and move forward, wherever he could. Momentum had a way of growing. "Tell us what you found. Maybe we can help."

"I've been scouring the Barbary Coast, looking for signs of the man sketched by Moses. Maybe I could get lucky and find Melanie."

He sipped rum. "Yesterday, I stopped into Tommy Chandler's Boardinghouse, down on Pacific."

Abe chuckled. "Mike knows that place. Chandler used to claim title to be the American middleweight boxing champ."

Franklin nodded. "I saw the posters."

Abe put a hand on Franklin's shoulder, stopping his interruptions. Abe was telling a story, in his saloon. "Mike stayed awhile at Tommy's when he first arrived here from Russia. Tommy knocked him out, thought he'd killed him, and dumped him into the saltwater sludge under the wharf.

"Mike survived and found his way to Molly O'Brian's White Chapel Saloon. About a year later, after Mike started working here, Tommy came in wearing Mike's mink coat and cap. Mike owed him money from when he stayed at Tommy's boardinghouse. Mike paid his debt, plus interest, but Tommy claimed he'd won the coat and cap in a boxing match."

Mike waved Abe off. "Come on, Abe. Let the man tell us about what's going on with his daughter."

Abe stood erect, not to be denied. "Just wanted to say, Mike here's the one took Tommy's championship away from him. He soundly beat Tommy Chandler, right here at the Palace. Tommy shot himself in his hand that night." Abe patted Mike's shoulder and smiled like a proud papa.

Mike shook his head and turned to Franklin. "Go ahead."

"I can't be sure if it's the same man. He's shaved his head and beard, but his eyebrows are red as any I've seen. He's a thick man, like Moses described. He calls himself Donald Thorne. I've invited him up here to try his luck at faro. Moses thinks he can make a positive identification, if he comes."

Mike turned and looked over the double doors into the gaming room. "You should probably take down the drawings of him and your daughter. You would not want to scare him away."

Franklin nodded and nudged Moses.

Moses stood, scooped out his last bite of chowder, and hurried into the gaming room.

Abe said, "This man's staying at Chandler's?"

Franklin stared at Abe, slack mouthed. "I don't really know. I assumed . . ."

Mike said, "Stay strong. If he comes in here, and if Moses identifies him, we will find a way to follow him. We will find your daughter." He turned to Abe. "Can you bring me a bowl of chowder?" His appetite had awakened.

Abe hurried to his chowder pot.

Mike spun on his stool and faced Franklin. "What was that name again?"

"He calls himself Donald Thorne. If he's the man I'm looking for, he's most likely a Yankee deserter."

"We will send this name with Moses's sketch to the Department of the Army." Mike wagged his head and smiled. "Who knows?"

Franklin relaxed. "Thank you, Mike. I suddenly feel lighter, like some invisible weight has just been lifted."

"If he comes in here, we will see what we can do. The main thing is what Moses says. He was the one who looked into the eyes of this man."

Chapter Twenty-Nine

DONALD THORNE LUGGED the heavy sea bag out of China Basin on foot and finally caught a taxi below Chinatown. He reached Tommy Chandler's at 10:12 p.m., according to his new silver pocket watch, an item he'd kept after the Wells Fargo stage robbery.

The usual gathering of sailors and prostitutes populated the saloon. His live-in partner, Paulette Blanco, sat at the corner table between two sailors. He didn't see Melanie. *Who's watching . . .*

Ah. Melanie sat halfway up the second rise of stairs with her head poking through the balusters. She smiled and waved. He waved back and quietly set the heavy bag on the floor near the bar.

His catch of fresh money broadened Thorne's outlook. He and Melanie needed to find another place to live. A saloon with prostitutes was no place to raise a little girl. He no longer planned for her to become a prostitute to earn him money. He'd found a better way to earn a living. She could grow up to be a proper lady.

He would need to prove himself loyal to Tommy Chandler and Dunken Frack. He'd never before known this level of financial success.

Tommy moved from behind the bar and motioned for Donald to follow.

Donald picked up the bag and followed Tommy into the office in back.

Tommy closed the door. "How'd it go?"

"You tell me." Donald hoisted the heavy bag onto Tommy's desk, opened the top, and removed the leather bag. "This here's my share."

Tommy spread the sea bag, looked inside, hefted the weight, and nodded. "Any problems?"

"One of the guards got the drop on Duncan. I had to kill him."

"One of the guards?"

Donald grinned. "The other one gave up the key to the safe. Duncan worked the lock and got it open, then he clubbed and kicked the second guard bad. He might be dead too. But we got away clean."

"If that guard lives, can he identify you?"

"Not likely. We wore masks."

"What about Juanita?"

"She never came aboard. She brung the horses."

"Did the guard see her?"

"Like I said, Duncan clubbed and kicked the second guard. Might have killed him." He shook his head. "No, he couldn't have seen her."

Tommy nodded, satisfied. He synched the sea bag, dropped it under his desk, led Donald out, and locking his office. "Want a beer?"

"Better not. I need some time with my little girl."

Donald waved at Paulette, looking his way.

She smiled, being careful not to interrupt her work.

Donald ran up the stairs, two treads at a time.

Melanie stood and held out both arms. "Uncle Donald, where have you been?"

"THANK YOU, PADDY." What would Mike do without their longtime coachman, hired by the Palace several years earlier to serve both Abe Warner and Mike Zabel. Warner rarely used him. Mike used him all the time. Paddy rarely needed to be told where to go. Late at night, he always took Mike to his home on Russian Hill, giving Mike time for uninterrupted thought. That night, with Jimmy still missing, a flood of past images mingled with future possibilities, creating a very cloudy perspective.

The coach stopped across the brick paved street from Mike's house.

"Get a good night's sleep, Mike. Things always seem brighter in the morning."

"Thank you, Paddy." Mike crossed the street slowly, not eager to face Molly. She'd be expecting him to return with Jimmy. He had no defense for his failure.

He stopped at the bottom of the front steps to survey his house. Curtains had been drawn and the interior lights had been turned low. The porch light had been turned up for his eventual arrival.

Okay.

He took a deep breath, climbed the steps, and inserted his key. The latch tripped loud. He waited a moment and entered as quietly as he could.

At the far end of the hall, the kitchen lamp glowed bright, lighting his way. He shed his coat, hung it on the coat rack, and crept toward the kitchen.

Molly sat at the kitchen table with Raul and Coira. A tea set had been arranged between them. Molly jumped up. "It's not enough to be worried about Jimmy. We've worried about you all the long day and into this night. Where have you been?"

"Sorry. Bill Coleman took us out to look for that schooner. Turns out, it is his old yacht, *Black Swan.*" He gave Molly a quick hug, sat, and poured a cup of tea. He shook his head. "We found nothing and I do not know what to do."

Raul smiled at Mike but said nothing.

Molly sat next to Mike, leaned face-to-face and used her most reproachful tone. "You might send someone to let a woman know. For all any of us knew, you'd been shot and dumped under the docks of the Barbary." Her head bobbed up and down, lips tightly pursed, red-faced as ever he'd seen her. "Do you not remember how we first met?" She straightened and crossed her arms. "I certainly remember. Half dead, you were. Half eaten by the crabs, you were."

Raul gasped a short laugh, put his hand over his mouth, and faked a cough, trying not to break Molly's beratement.

Mike slumped. "I remember." After Tommy Chandler had nearly killed him, they'd dumped him under Pacific Street Wharf. Down in that sludge and brine, he'd lost the end of a third finger and a little toe to crabs. "I am sorry. I have been so anxious to find Jimmy before . . ." He dared not say the rest, worried about cannibals who liked little boys, who skinned them and ate their livers. All this, and still worrying about his son being taken to Russia. He worried about things his brain could not yet clearly form. Coming home, exhausted, he'd worried about Molly's wrath. She had certainly justified that worry.

"Well . . ." She leaned back and looked at Raul. They shared some kind of secret communication. They always had, for as long as Mike had known them.

Mike sipped tea. "I have no excuses. I have failed."

She glared into his anguish. "There's someone here waiting to see you."

Raul smiled at Coira.

Molly pointed down the hall. "He's waiting in your office and you've walked right past. He's been waiting for hours. He's probably fallen asleep by now, I'd be thinking."

"Who is it?" *Han Wok?*

Raul nodded toward the hallway, "Go and see."

Mike stood, looked at the others, took a deep breath, and turned into the hallway. He entered his office and turned up the gas wall sconce.

"Jimmy!"

His son had curled into a stuffed chair across from his desk, asleep.

Mike dropped to his knees in front of the chair. "Thank you, God." He laid a hand on his son's forehead and kissed his cheek.

Jimmy groaned, opened his eyes, and sat up. "Daddy!" He threw both arms around Mike's neck and hugged him.

Mike stood with Jimmy, holding him tight. He patted Jimmy's back and stood him on his desk to examine his face. "Did they hurt you?"

"No, not very much."

"Not very much?" Mike forced himself to calm. "Where did they hurt you?"

"In that hot place, when they tied our hands. They hurt Mommy, too."

Mike took and looked at his son's wrists, still red, but no broken skin.

"I cried when they killed that little boy." Jimmy's mouth turned down. "They . . . I . . ." His face quivered. He could not stop his tears.

"That's over now." Mike needed to change the subject. "So, how did you get home?" Mike felt a presence and turned.

Molly and Raul stood in his office doorway, eyes filled with love.

Mike lifted Jimmy into the crook of his left arm, turned into the doorway, and hugged his wife.

Molly kissed Jimmy's cheek, wiped his tears, and combed her fingers through his hair.

"You're safe at home, now," said Mike. "We need for you to be strong. Can you be strong for us?"

Jimmy leaned back against Mike's arm and nodded. "That's what she said, that I need to be strong because I'm a Romanov."

Mike asked, "Who said that?"

"They called her a highness. Aren't you a Romanov, too?"

"I guess I am. I am her illegitimate cousin."

Jimmy said, "Her ill . . ."

He shook his head and smiled. "Never mind. Can you remember how you got home?"

"Sure. We took a train, but I slept."

"Who brought you?"

"Sacha. She's very nice."

"Did you see any water?" Mike immediately realized how stupid this question had been. There was only one train in and out of the city, and they'd been on a boat.

"Sure." Jimmy looked to his right and pointed. "It was over there."

Mike turned toward the others. "The San Jose line, of course. It's still the only train into the city."

He looked at Jimmy. "How did you get here from the train?"

"She brought me in a taxi and let me out down the hill."

Raul smiled at Jimmy. "He kicked the front door to get in. I was sure it was trouble."

Mike asked, "What time?"

Molly said, "Around noon."

"Raul, I need for you to stay here and guard this place. I will get a police officer over here if I can." Mike handed Jimmy to Molly and opened a cabinet. He took off his jacket, hung it on the cabinet door, and looped his shoulder harness over his left arm. He buckled the strap, pulled the Colt, and checked it. All six cylinders carried fresh loads. He holstered the Colt, slid his hip holster onto his belt, buckled his belt, and checked his second Colt. He pulled on his jacket and kissed Molly's and Jimmy's cheeks.

He stepped into the hall and lifted down his coat. "Raul, keep your gun handy. They have already committed murder, and they tried to kill you. They know where we live." He locked the front door and turned toward the kitchen. "It is already too late for a taxi. I will take Jasmine."

Raul hustled past him into the kitchen, limping only slightly from his belly wound. He opened the back door for Mike and turned back. "Jasmine's been fed and watered." He smiled. "She likes having you on her back."

Mike needed to ride her more often to maintain their friendship.

MIKE TIED JASMINE TO the hitching post in front of the city hall police station and went inside at 2:26 a.m., according to the Regulator clock over the front desk. Behind the desk, a sergeant two sizes larger than his already large uniform snored softly, with his head back against the wall. Mike couldn't see a chair behind the fat filled uniform.

A telegraph pad lay on the desk with a graphite pencil. Mike picked up the pad and pencil and wrote out his message.

"To all stations in the Mission and waterfront districts STOP Be on the lookout for five Russians seeking passage to Panama City or to ports in Canada or Alaska or Vladivostok or China STOP Hold 2 women and 3 men wanted for questioning regarding kidnapping and murder END"

He tore off the page and wrote another message.

"To all waterfront stations STOP Be on the lookout for Black Swan a two masted black schooner with black sails STOP Hold all parties for questioning END"

He tore off the second note and wrote another.

"To Mission District Station STOP Be on the lookout for 2 Russian women and 3 Russian men possibly departing San Jose train STOP Hold for questioning END"

He knew these messages would be nearly impossible to enforce. How could they determine who might be Russian?

He pulled his hip Colt, gripped the barrel, and thumped the handle onto the desk.

The sergeant snorted.

"Sergeant!"

The fat sergeant rolled his eyes in Mike's direction and sat upright. He scrubbed his face and stared angrily at the Colt.

Mike holstered the Colt and displayed his state police badge.

"Oh." The sergeant stood and stretched. "You're Count Mike, right?"

Mike nodded and put his badge away.

"Find your kid yet?"

"We have. Thank you."

"He's okay?"

"He is." Mike smiled.

"What do you want, then?"

Mike handed him the telegraph messages. "I want you to get these out right away. These people are responsible for multiple crimes committed against citizens of this city."

"Okay, as soon as we can." He set them on his desk and sat. "Our operator comes in around eight."

"Is there no way to get him here sooner?"

"Only the chief can order that."

"Should I go and wake him?"

"That's your business. Don't ask me to do it."

"Do you have a tide chart?" Steam driven boats still used outgoing tides. The Golden Gate Channel flowed like a river, in or out.

"We've got one around here somewhere." The sergeant opened his top drawer and shuffled papers around. "Oh, yeah." He closed the top drawer and opened the second. "Here it is."

San Francisco's tide charts were printed by the month. That morning was December 6, 1865, the day before Thanksgiving Day.

Mike had so much for which to be thankful. "Low tide is in about one hour. High tide is at nine-fourteen a.m. That will not give them much time." The bay had about a one-hour delay. Ships would start out to sea at around 10:00 a.m. He asked, "What time does McFee get in?"

The desk sergeant sneered his disrespect for McFee. "He comes and goes when-ever he pleases."

"Let him see those telegrams, and ask him to contact me if anything turns up."

"Yes, sir."

The sergeant's caustic tone stabbed Mike's normally calm nature. He leaned across the desk, close to the sergeant's fat face. "There have been serious crimes committed."

The sergeant leaned back and blinked, something in Mike's eyes.

Mike asked, "Do I need to speak with somebody else?"

There were always reasons why sergeants got the night desk, usually attitude, stupidity, or laziness. He said, "No. I'll see to it, even if I've got to stay late."

MIKE STEPPED DOWN FROM Jasmine, closed the alley door to his barn, set the crossbar in place, and unsaddled Jasmine. He brushed her down, put grain in her feed bin, checked her fodder and water, gave her an apple, and crossed his back yard in darkness. He used his key and entered the kitchen.

Raul's head bolted up from the kitchen table. His revolver lay on the table in front of him. "Sorry, boss."

"I do not worry about you, Raul. You have always been a light sleeper." Mike shucked his coat and strode toward his office.

Raul followed close behind.

Mike hung his coat, removed his weapons, put them in his office cabinet, closed the door, and stared at the closed cabinet door. "I have done what I can. The rest is up to the local police."

"We got Jimmy back, and everybody's okay. We been plenty lucky. Not like that Franklin Mosby." He shook his head, worried over someone who had become a friend.

Mike smiled and nodded. "I have this feeling, he will be fine." Mike took a step toward the front stairs and stopped, looking back at Raul. "We need to start teaching Jimmy how to work."

Raul had no idea what Mike meant.

"Let's give him some chores. Teach him to clean and stock the stable. Teach him to clean the back yard and to sweep the front porch. I will speak with Molly. He should make his bed when he gets up in the morning."

"Sure, boss. We can do that."

Mike said, "At the same time, I want you to start training him to defend himself."

"Sure, boss. We can do that." Raul smiled.

Mike chuckled. "Can you lock up? Then get some rest. If you are up early, make sure I am awake."

Chapter Thirty

GENERAL KRESTYANOV had ordered Gregori to accompany them on the early train, helping to protect the duchess. He would also help with their luggage.

The early train reached the San Francisco station at 8:45 a.m.

Sacha waited on the platform with two coachmen.

Luka and Gregori handed down six cases of luggage, four belonging to the duchess, one to the general, and one to Luka and Sacha.

Grigori helped Luka and the coachmen carry the cases to waiting carriages. They loaded the luggage onto the tops in cold, dense fog.

A nod from the duchess expressed her wishes. They'd previously discussed possibilities.

Krestyanov pulled Grigori aside. "Take the train back to the boat. Check every week with the Western Union. We will send instructions and money over time. Be ready to house three separate appointees in three separate locations. They will receive instruction and funds directly from the duchess, or from me. Whatever they will do must remain a mystery to you."

Gregori clicked his heels and bowed at the waist. He shook hands with Luka and snapped to attention for the duchess. He bowed and abruptly turned back toward the train.

Sacha said, "The carriages will take us to California Street Wharf, where we will board SS Fremont, a three masted steamship owned by Flint and Holladay, a company of good reputation. They take passengers to Los Angeles, San Diego, and Panama City."

The duchess stiffened, her usual posture, whenever events displeased her. "There are no ships sailing directly to Panama City?"

"Golden Age sails directly to Panama City, you highness. She departs in three days. Fremont departs later this morning, with the outgoing tide."

"Very well."

Krestyanov helped Lady Catherine into the forward carriage and climbed in next to her.

She touched his hand but did not hold it, nervously patting up and down, staring straight forward as the coach moved away from the station.

Krestyanov turned to look back.

The second coach followed at forty meters.

The duchess frowned. Her eyebrows bunched over her nose. "What will happen if Major Zabalkansky finds us?" Her hand quivered. She might be finally realizing the severity of their situation.

"He will very likely arrest us." A simple matter of fact.

Water filled her eyes and her lips pinched tight. She grudgingly wiped away her tears. "What will they do to us?"

"Is difficult to say, Highness." How could he know? "We are Russian officials who came here in a non-official capacity." He needed more time to think. "One good thing, Your Highness. We have killed no one. The man I shot looks healthy enough. He is the durable one."

"What about the Chinese boys?"

"We did not harm them. We were not involved in their abductions."

The duchess sniffed, pulled a handkerchief, wiped her nose, and blinked back tears. "I ate some of his liver. Am I cannibal?"

"No, no." Krestyanov would lie under oath, if need be. "I never saw you do such a thing. This will be vigorously denied."

"We abducted his wife and son." Her eyes searched his.

"He is your cousin. He is a Romanov. You simply wanted to meet with them." He looked out the window. He looked back. "Is not your fault if we acted too aggressively. You never authorized such aggressions." He looked out the window.

"You would do this for me?"

"My lady . . ." He turned to face her. "That, and more. Whatever can be done, we will do."

As the marine layer thinned, the carriage turned onto the wharf at California Street and noisily thumped over heavy wood planks. More than 100 meters later, the carriage stopped near a side-wheel sloop with three masts.

The coachman climbed down, climbed onto the back, and lifted down two cases. Luka hurried from the second coach, took, and carried the cases up the ship's boarding ramp.

Krestyanov helped the duchess down from the coach and followed her and Sacha onto the top deck of the ship.

The boarding officer took and examined their boarding documents. He waved to a steward.

The steward opened the wheelhouse door, where a man wearing a fine sable coat and cap stepped out into incipient sunlight. He waved toward the wharf.

Krestyanov sucked breath and froze. "Mikhail." He looped Lady Catherine's arm and yanked her toward the wharf.

Several uniformed police officers had already gathered on the wharf, all staring at Krestyanov and the duchess.

Krestyanov spun around with the duchess and faced Mikhail, elegant and powerful in his sable mink coat and cap.

Mikhail approached to arm's length and reached inside his coat.

The duchess flinched and squeezed Krestyanov's arm.

Mikhail produced several stamped and wax sealed documents. "Grand Duchess Catherine Mikhailovna, I have warrants for your arrest, and for the arrest of General, the Count Boris

Romochka-Krestyanov." He looked sadly at Krestyanov, not outwardly taking pleasure in this duty. "I also carry at-large warrants for three unnamed members of your party. All warrants are signed by Judge Christopher Simms of the San Francisco County Superior Court."

The duchess dropped Krestyanov's arm and slapped Mikhail's face. "How dare you do this to me?"

Mikhail did not flinch or blink. Her slap had neither surprised nor daunted him. He turned toward the wharf and nodded. He stepped in front of Krestyanov and motioned over his shoulder. "This is Detective Sergeant Angus McFee, of the San Francisco Police Department. He and his men will take you into custody and transport you to the city jail, where you will remain until your arraignment at ten a.m., on Thursday morning."

Sergeant McFee politely gripped the left hand of the duchess, locked the brass bracelet around her wrist, took her right hand, faced her, and completed her shackling.

Another plain clothes officer spun Krestyanov and cuffed his wrists from behind. He was not gentle.

Two uniformed officers climbed the boarding plank and cuffed Sacha's hands in front, and Luka's from behind.

Several uniformed officers collected their luggage, while others led them, single file, down the boarding ramp.

A two horse, iron-clad police wagon took a wide turn on the wharf and stopped near the ship. An officer climbed down, marched to the back, and opened the iron door.

Police officers helped the duchess into the back of the wagon first, then Sacha.

Krestyanov stiffened against their grip and turned.

Mikhail stood on the deck of the ship, frowning down at Krestyanov. He shook his head and looked away, possibly saddened by this situation.

Two officers lifted Krestyanov, fed him feet first into the wagon, and turned to Luka.

Luka stepped to the wagon's rear opening and spun, positioning his butt on the edge of the wagon bed. The officers lifted and pushed him in. A third officer closed the door and darkness surrounded them.

Krestyanov's eyes quickly adjusted. A thin sliver of light at the top of the door led him onto the bench, sitting across from Sacha and the duchess.

Luka scooted backward, braced his back against the bench, and stood, sliding onto the bench next to Krestyanov.

The locking bar outside the door slammed into place, and the wagon lurched forward.

Iron rimmed wheels hummed over wood planks.

Nobody spoke.

MIKE STOOD ON THE MAIN deck of *S.S. Fremont* with Sgt. Angus McFee, both watching three police officers load luggage onto a flatbed wagon.

The prisoners had been secured in the police wagon, which turned left onto Front St.

McFee locked his hands behind his back and rocked onto the balls of his feet. "What now?"

Mike squeezed McFee's shoulder from behind and nudged him down the boarding ramp. "Do you have enough cages to keep them separated?"

McFee stopped at mid-span and faced Mike. "You want to put a Russian duchess in a cage?"

"She kidnapped my wife and son. She is an accessory to kidnap and murder of at least one child. She forced my wife and son to watch her, and this man known as Jack Wick, eat human flesh. She is complicit in the kidnapping and murder of Preslova's two associates. What do you suggest, that we put her in the Presidential Suite of the Cosmopolitan Hotel?"

McFee blinked, thinking about this. "Were there any witnesses with Preslova's men?"

Mike said, "Me. You already know this."

"You were there when they were taken?" McFee squared to Mike. He already knew the answer. "I mean, the dead kid is Chinese. Nobody cares, especially not the chief."

Frustrated, Mike brushed past McFee, hurried down the boarding plank, and walked onto the wharf. He turned back.

McFee followed Mike onto the wharf, bewildered, blinking questions he did not dare to ask.

"What would you suggest?" Mike had no proof of her involvement with the deaths of Preslova's men. He had plenty of evidence for kidnapping, attempted murder, and cannibalism.

McFee said, "I don't know. Maybe we can put her into a hotel room with a female guard."

"No!" Mike stared into McFee's blinking face. "I personally witnessed the shooting of Raul. That was attempted murder. I watched Krestyanov leave the scene. I was abducted and taken to the house of Jack Wick, as he calls himself. My kidnapped wife and son had been tied to chairs in this man's house."

McFee turned away, took two steps, and turned back. He didn't like the situation into which Mike had thrust him. "The chief won't like it."

"I can contact the governor, if he wants."

McFee shook off Mike's suggestion. "There's really no need to tell the chief."

"You will isolate the duchess and the general?"

McFee looked down at his polished shoes. "Okay. I can do that."

"They are to speak to no one before I interrogate them."

McFee blinked and folded his hands behind his back. "They'll have my job."

Mike stepped closer, with a reminder. "They are Russian. I am Russian. If I need more heat, I will wire the governor about this."

McFee shook his head and shifted his weight. He hated saying this. "They'll need to be booked in. The chief checks the book at least twice a week."

"Of course." Mike relaxed a little and grinned. "Look, Angus, just use their names; Catherine Mikhailovna and Boris Krestyanov."

McFee nodded and smiled. "I can do that. They'll stay in the wagon until I arrive. I've already given that order."

"The dirtier her cell, the better. Whoever takes them food, water, or the waste bucket, is not to speak with them. The dirtier the bucket, the better."

McFee blinked, shook his head, and grinned. He finally understood.

Mike slapped McFee's back. "I will try to meet with Judge Heydenfeldt this afternoon. I will be in to talk to the prisoners tomorrow morning."

"Heydenfeldt's in town?"

"He is now here most of the time. He likes me to keep him informed about local problems. We meet twice every month."

FIFTEEN MINUTES LATER, Paddy's taxi stopped in front of the Daily Evening Bulletin. Montgomery St. bustled with traffic. "Wait here." Mike stepped down and hurried inside the Bulletin office, around the front desk, where they knew him, and found Billy Cahill handwriting an article at his desk. He stood next to Billy's chair and cleared his throat.

Billy finished a sentence and turned. "Mike." He smiled, stood, and shook hands. "Any news? What brings you?"

Mike said, "Jimmy is safely at home. We have just arrested The Grand Duchess Catherine Mikhailovna, her chief of security, General, the Count Boris Romochka-Krestyanov, and two others. I thought you might want the story.

Billy nearly jumped. "Do I?" He looked at the wall clock, 10:42 a.m. "We have time."

"Not in today's Bulletin. I need to talk to Judge Heydenfeldt first. I thought you might like to come along."

Billy pulled on his jacket, grabbed his notepad and pencil, and followed Mike out the door.

Mike ushered Billy into the taxi, climbed in, and told Paddy, "Take us to the top of Knob Hill, on the south side of the reservoir."

Paddy slapped reins and looked back. "That Jew judge's house?"

"Quick as you can." Mike slapped Billy's knee. "I will be going in to talk to the duchess at nine o'clock tomorrow morning. Maybe you can run your story tomorrow and follow-up the day after."

Billy smiled. "Thanks, Mike." He eyed Mike's mink coat and cap. "I haven't seen you wear that mink coat and cap in years. I nearly forgot how nice it looks."

"It seemed appropriate."

The front gate to Heydenfeldt's estate stood open, meaning he was probably in the city.

The taxi followed the tree-lined, gravel road and stopped near the front steps of the judge's mansion, one of the finest in the city. Mike tapped Paddy's shoulder. "We might be awhile. Does Abe need you?" Mike climbed out and Billy followed.

Paddy smiled. "Not that I know of. I'll just take a wee nap." He set the foot brake and climbed into the back.

Mike led Billy up the steps and onto the front porch. He pulled the chain and the inside bell rang.

The judge's man servant answered the door and smiled. "Count Mike. Please, come in."

Mike led Billy into the front parlor.

The servant closed the entry door and stepped into the parlor doorway. "I'll tell the judge you're here."

Bookshelves in the study held four rows of law books and a couple of thick, leather bound books with gold-embossed Jewish lettering.

Billy said, "He's still a judge?"

"Not anymore." Solomon Heydenfeldt stood in the doorway to his study, smiled, and extended a hand to Mike.

Mike smiled and shook hands. "Your honor . . ." He turned toward Billy. "I am happy to introduce William Cahill."

Heydenfeldt shook Billy's hand. "Are you that journalist with the Evening Bulletin?"

"I am." Billy smiled, shy in the presence of the still powerful Solomon Heydenfeldt.

Mike had met very few men who commanded a room the way Solomon Heydenfeldt could. He was powerfully built, always well dressed, and always impeccably groomed. His determined, piercing blue eyes held Billy's. "I read your articles nearly everyday. You're an honest reporter. You look for who, what, when, where, and how. I'm very pleased to finally meet you. Michael talks about you in glowing terms." He dropped Billy's hand and motioned to two stuffed chairs near the bay window.

Mike and Billy sat.

Heydenfeldt dragged a third chair into the warm sunlight, having finally burned through the fog. He sat and studied Mike. "I haven't seen you wear that mink since . . ." He shrugged and smiled.

"That time I went up to Weaverville."

"Yes, yes. That corrupt sheriff who was enslaving Chinese, wasn't it?"

"Your memory is as good as ever."

Billy said, "I read how you left the bench. What, exactly, was that about?"

"Ah. I'm from Charleston, South Carolina. When they asked me to take an oath to support the Union, should hostilities erupt, I refused." His eyes pierced into Billy. "Is that why you're here?" His question was friendly, but intense.

"No, sir."

Heydenfeldt smiled at Mike, stood, and gazed out the window. "For the record, my family never owned slaves, and we were against secession." He looked at Billy and sat, with a slight smile. "It was a matter of legal principle, not taking the oath. Had any cases come before the court regarding the issue, I would have had to recuse myself." He leaned back in his chair and stared at the wall above the window, as if reading text. "As a point of history, the Jewish race was enslaved twice, once in Egypt, and again in Babylon. Because of that, very few Jews have ever owned slaves."

Billy scribbled notes.

"So, Mike, what brings you?"

"I need some legal advice."

"Your business dealings?"

"No. This one is criminal. We arrested the Grand Duchess Catherine Mikhailovna this morning, her chief of security, General, the Count Boris Romochka-Krestyanov, and two others."

"Russians?"

"Yes."

"You had warrants?"

"Yes. Of course. Signed by Judge Christopher Simms of the San Francisco County Superior Court."

"On what charges?"

"Abduction, unlawful imprisonment, attempted murder, accessory to murder, and cannibalism."

Heydenfeldt flinched and shook his head, unbelieving. "Cannibalism?"

"The grand duchess knowingly shared the fried liver of a tortured Chinese boy."

"One of those missing boys they found?"

"No. This one was new. Skinned alive and sliced open for his liver. The man known as Jack Wick, the very man who robbed the train to San Jose, is also the man who has been kidnapping Chinese boys."

"The Russians are involved with this man?"

"Yes, definitely so."

"How in the world do Russian nobles get mixed up with such a man?"

"Does it matter?" Mike did not care to relive what had happened eight years earlier, with the grand duke.

"No. Not really. You catch him, too?"

"Not yet. He is still at large. I have seen his face. It is only a matter of time."

"Who was abducted, the Chinese boys?"

"I do not believe the Russians were involved with that. They kidnapped my wife, my son, and my son's governess. The general shot Raul during the abduction. They later abducted me."

"They shot Raul?"

"Da, da. Yes. He is fine. He is a very sturdy fellow."

"And your family?"

"They are safely back home."

"Thank God. Are the Russians okay?"

"Da, da. Yes. They are being booked into city jail, as we speak."

"I see." Heydenfeldt stood, clasped his hands behind his back, and paced the room, staring down at his shoes, out the window, up at the ceiling, and back at his shoes. "I hope you realize, there'll be outside influences." He sat and propped his hands on his knees, leaning toward Mike. "Our Secretary of State, William H. Seward, is in negotiations with Russia to purchase Alaska."

"So . . ." Billy pointed his pencil at Heydenfeldt. "We just let them go?"

"No, no. Of course not. We can't allow people to come into our country and commit serious crimes with immunity. This just presents an interesting wrinkle. We need to be sure the Russian Government is informed." He stood, clasped his hands behind his back, and paced. "Do you plan to run the story tonight?"

"Maybe." Billy leaned back, looked at Mike, and clicked his pencil between his teeth.

"Go ahead. Send it out over the wire where other papers will pick it up." He turned and pointed at Mike. "Get down to police headquarters and tell them to wire the Russian Consulate over on California Street. Don't you go over there. You might not get back out. When's the arraignment?"

"Day after tomorrow."

Heydenfeldt sat and slapped his knees, both curious and excited. "Who is she, anyway? I mean, why you? Why your wife and son?"

Mike had no choice but to relive the past. "Her brother was the Grand Duke Nikolai Nikolaievich."

"The man who got shot at the Cobweb Palace, what, eight years ago?"

"Yes."

Heydenfeldt leaned back and relaxed. "Why you? You didn't shoot him."

"He tried to kill me in Vladivostok. As a defensive reflex, I accidentally chopped off his right hand. He later followed me here and tried to kill me again. I am only alive because others shot him to defend me."

Heydenfeldt shook his head and frowned, with a bewildered gaze. "Yes, of course. I was there." His eyes opened wide. "Is she crazy?"

Chapter Thirty-One

MIKE MET BILLY CAHILL in front of city hall at 8:55 the following morning. Billy handed him two copies of the Daily Evening Bulletin from the night before. "You might want the duchess and the general to read this."

Mike folded the newspapers under the arm of his wool-tweed coat. "Thank you. Good idea." Mike led Billy into the police station, wove his way through the desks, and stopped at the desk of Sgt. Angus McFee.

A slender, pale, bespectacled, too young to be a nearly bald-headed man sat across from McFee. Both men stood and McFee said, "Mike Zabel, this is Percy Bickford, an agent with the U.S. Treasury Department back in Washington."

Mike shook the treasury agent's clammy, limp hand and handed the newspapers to McFee.

McFee glanced at the folded newspapers. "I've already read this." He nodded at Billy. "Nice work."

Mike said, "Billy thought the duchess and the general might want to read them."

"Oh. Sure." McFee grinned and turned toward the cellblock.

"Angus."

McFee turned back.

"Did you wire the Russian Consulate?"

"First thing this morning."

Mike asked, "Have they responded?"

"Not that I know of."

"Do they know the arraignments are scheduled for ten o'clock tomorrow morning?"

"They do." McFee's head bobbed, organizing his thoughts. "What, exactly, are the charges?"

"The warrants have been executed and filed with the superior court. The exact charges should be in the arrest booking. Do you not have that?"

McFee blinked. "It's out at the front desk."

Mike said, "I'll need that. You have anybody who can copy the page from the book?"

McFee turned and scanned the squad room. "Johnston."

Two desks down, a young, plain-clothed man stood and faced his superior.

"Go copy the arrest log on those four Russians we brought in yesterday morning."

Johnston turned and hurried through the door leading to the front desk.

McFee said, "I'll bring it into the interrogation room."

Mike smiled and nodded. "Perfect. After I interview the prisoners, I will draw up a formal list of charges and deliver it to the district attorney's office."

McFee's face turned down, thinking. "Can I look at it first?"

"Of course." Mike pointed at the newspapers in McFee's hand and waved toward the cellblock.

McFee turned and hurried in that direction.

Mike turned to the treasury agent. "What can we do for you, Mr. Bickford?"

"You're a busy man. I've been trying to get with you since last week."

"I apologize. I hope it is not urgent." Mike locked in on Bickford's eyes.

Bickford said, "There have been a rash of robberies against the United States Treasury. You were recommended by the governor's office to help."

Mike dragged an empty chair from a nearby desk and motioned for Billy to sit.

Billy sat and positioned his notepad on McFee's desk.

Mike walked around the desk and sat in McFee's chair. He looked into Bickford, ready to listen.

Bickford looked at Billy, questioning his presence.

"Ah. Agent Percy Bickford, this is William Cahill, star reporter for the Daily Evening Bulletin, our city's leading newspaper."

They shook hands but Bickford still seemed reluctant.

Mike said, "Mister Cahill has my trust. He would never print or say anything without your authorization."

Bickford looked at Billy, asking for confirmation.

Billy nodded.

"Okay, then." Bickford looked around the squad room.

Those few officers still in the squad room were too far from McFee's desk to eavesdrop.

Bickford turned back. "We have reason to believe that one of our agents is working with the outlaws. We've developed a short list of suspects."

Mike waited.

"We intend to give false information of a large shipment to these suspected agents, one at a time, for the purpose of setting a trap."

"This sounds like a good plan."

"Thank you."

"I would be the one to gather the prize?"

Bickford bristled with excitement. "Exactly!"

"There has been a recent train robbery."

Bickford's eyes pinched into his glasses. "How did you know?"

Being at the front of his investor group, Mike had received the information from the railroad. "I know some railroad detectives."

Bickford backed into his chair and waited for more.

Mike said, "There are three operatives, two men, and one woman."

"I only know about two men. Where . . . How . . ."

Mike propped his elbows onto McFee's desk and leaned toward Bickford. "The one I believe to be their leader sometimes goes by the name of Jack Wick. I have encountered him twice. He is a particularly bad individual. He is also involved with kidnapping, murder, the torture of children, and cannibalism."

Bickford pulled out a handkerchief and removed his glasses. He buffed the lenses, put the glasses back on, returned the handkerchief to his vest pocket, and looked at Mike. "Oh, my . . ."

"Sergeant McFee should still have composite sketches of this man. If not, it has been published in the Bulletin. Billy can get you a copy."

Billy asked, "Do you know where the Bulletin office is located?"

Bickford said, "I'm sure I can find it."

"So . . ." Mike spread his hands, asking.

"Oh, yes. Why you?" Bickford squirmed to the front of his chair and thrust an open hand toward Mike. "We need your help to trap our inside man. If you arrest your man too early, our man will just find somebody else to work with."

Mike said, "This man is a brutal murderer. We are not about to pull back from this one."

Bickford said, "If this is the same man who is involved with robbery from the United States Treasury Department, our plan will serve both of our causes."

Mike leaned back in his chair and looked at Bickford. "What, exactly, is your plan? Give me some details."

"Our short list consists of three agents. If we give each a shipping invoice for one-hundred-thousand-dollars in newly minted gold coin, we can get this done quickly. Say. . ." He shrugged. "Over a one-week period. "We'll ship one strongbox of worthless rocks on a ferry to Oakland, one to San Jose by train, and one to Sacramento through Wells Fargo Stage Lines."

"If I can find enough men, why not do it all in one day?"

"These men all work on different shifts. Each controls different shipping routs. They'll each need to witness the packing of the gold, sign it off, then schedule the shipment. After that, we'll swap the strongbox with the substitute."

"It sounds like you are already certain."

Bickford's head dropped between his shoulders. "Yes, but . . ." He stared at Mike. "We want to be sure that the guilty party is not somehow gleaning information from one or both of the other two."

"That would be the smart move."

Bickford smiled and leaned forward. "I can tell you this. One of these men was a known confederate sympathizer. The other two . . ." He pushed back into his chair and spread both hands with a shrug. "There is no evidence that either of the others ever held political views. Those who work with them have made that clear."

Mike said, "So, you have been holding an investigation at the mint and everybody knows this."

"Of course."

"Maybe we should delay this plan for a while." Mike waved his hand toward Bickford. "No. Never mind that. We need to get this murderer behind bars."

Bickford said. "I discontinued the investigation before the last train robbery. Everybody thinks I'm already back in Washington."

"Everybody?"

"Well, no, actually. There are four men who I trust completely. They'll be responsible for switching the strongboxes."

A tap on Mike's shoulder caused him to turn. "Angus." Mike stood and stepped away from the chair. "Did either one of them want to read the paper?"

"Yeah. The general. The duchess wouldn't even look at it. She just sat, staring at the wall."

"Okay. My turn." Mike motioned to Billy and leaned near McFee. "Agent Bickford will need some police volunteers. He will explain." He turned to Bickford. "We cannot do this tomorrow. We will be in court. Sergeant McFee will give me your scheduling information, as soon as he gets it from you."

Bickford stood and looked at McFee. They both agreed.

A SQUARE TABLE AND four chairs sat in the center of the freshly cleaned, twenty-foot by twenty-foot interrogation room. Maybe the current guest list had something to do with getting lazy jailers to sweep and mop. With no windows, it took an overhead gas lantern and two wall sconces to provide ample light.

Mike dimmed the gas lights down to create an unnerving atmosphere. Satisfied, he stepped out into the corridor and stood at the jailer's desk.

Billy Cahill leaned against the opposite wall.

The tightly uniformed police officer overlapped the small chair behind the desk, cleaning his fingernails with his police issued Bowie knife. He deliberately ignored Mike.

Mike kicked a table leg.

The overstuffed officer blew across his freshly cleaned fingernails before looking up.

Mike said, "Bring in General Krestyanov."

"Do you have an interrogation order from the desk sergeant?"

Mike dropped both hands onto the small desk and leaned close. "Hasn't Sergeant McFee spoken with you yet?"

The officer leaned back a little, holding his knife defensively. "You Mike Zabel?"

"I am. This is William Cahill, from the Bulletin."

The chunky officer set his knife down, pushed back from the table, and struggled to his feet. His uniform fit so tightly that it threatened to pop buttons from his chest to his belt. "Why didn't you just say so?" He turned and took two steps toward the cellblock door.

Mike grabbed a ring of keys from a wall hook. "Don't you need these?"

Chunky turned back and Mike tossed him the keys. The keys hit his fat, outstretched hand and fell to the floor. Chunky scowled, spread his legs, bent, and scooped them off the floor. "Thanks."

"The general first."

Chunky turned, inserted and cranked the key, opened the door, and entered the cellblock.

Billy grinned and shook his head.

"We need to get ready." Mike led Billy into the square room and Billy pulled out a chair. He dropped his notepad onto the table and sat, pencil in hand.

Mike sat diagonally to Billy, facing the door. A moment later, Chunky led General Krestyanov in, hands and feet in connected shackles. Mike stood, pulled out the chair nearest the door, and motioned for the general to sit.

The general sat and stared at his shackled hands.

Mike followed Chunky into the corridor and closed the door. "When you bring the duchess, be sure she is shackled, hand and foot."

"What? Why would I do that to a pretty little lady like her?"

Mike forced calm, leaned close, and spoke softly. "I need to dampen her arrogance."

"But, she's a fine lady, and . . ." Chunky shook his head. "She won't try to escape."

"Do I need to have you replaced?"

"Okay. Take it easy."

"Put a chair over here." Mike pointed at the wall across from the interrogation room. "Bring her out in shackles and put her in that chair. I want her sitting here, shackled, when I bring Krestyanov out. And, don't bring her servants."

Chunky crossed his arms, clamped his mouth shut, and shook his head.

Mike leaned close. "Her frame of mind is important."

"This ain't normal." He blinked into Mike's stare. "Okay, okay. Take it easy."

Mike pointed at the interrogation room door. "Keep this door closed, until McFee gets here. Knock once, let him in, and close the door."

Chunky unwound and surrendered. "Okay, okay."

"Bring her out here now." Mike opened the door, stepped into the interrogation room, closed the door, walked around the table, and sat, looking at the top of the general's head. "General Krestyanov, I am very sad to find you here. You have been a friend to my family for my entire life."

The general might have been deaf, the way he reacted, head still down, still staring at his shackled wrists.

"This is William Cahill, a journalist with the Daily Evening Bulletin. His newspaper publishes sailing schedules on a daily basis, in case you were wondering how we came to be waiting for you."

Not a twitch from the general.

"There were two additional men with you at the Forge; an American, and another Russian. We are still looking for them. If you can help with this, I will mention your cooperation to the district attorney. He will prosecute your cases. If you like, I can recommend a good attorney to defend you."

Not a twitch.

Mike could only speculate why. Perhaps the duchess had ordered him to remain silent and not to cooperate. It was impossible to know what had been said in the police wagon. Perhaps he was simply stunned into silence by his legal jeopardy. Impossible to know.

A knock at the door preceded the door opening. McFee entered and handed Mike a single, handwritten sheet of paper. Mike leaned and stretched sideways to look past McFee.

The duchess sat opposite the door, shackled hand and foot, glaring at Mike.

Mike grinned and nodded. "Thank you, Sergeant McFee. Please close the door when you leave."

McFee shook his head, stepped out, and closed the door. Nobody liked seeing the duchess in chains, not even Mike.

Mike studied the handwritten copy of the arrest sheet. There were no names. "I know both you and the duchess. I will enter your names into the official charge sheets. Who are the other two, the man and the woman?"

Not a twitch.

"The Russian Consulate was notified early this morning, but we have not heard back." Mike snapped the single sheet of paper noisily and set it on the table. "Does Czar Alexander know you are here?"

The general's head twitched upward, then slumped back down.

"It does not matter. I'm sure your consulate will inform him." Mike put his hands flat on the table where the general could see them. "This is America. You have committed serious crimes, here. Our justice system will treat you with the same indifference as everyone else. I wish there was some way to help you, but there is not. Not unless you help us find this man known as Jack Wick, and the other Russian operative."

The general's head lifted slowly. His grim face and sad eyes looked to have surrendered. "The American man's name is Duncan Frack. He is a monster. The duchess . . ." He shook his head and bit down. He would not speak about her.

Mike asked, "How did the duchess come to involve herself with this man, Duncan Frack?"

The general flinched, shook his head, and returned his stare to his shackles.

Mike said, "Okay. We will not ask about her. I can appreciate your loyalty. I do want you to fully understand something." Mike waited for the general to look up.

He did not.

"This is important."

The general lifted his head far enough to see Mike's face.

"You will have your arraignment tomorrow morning on charges of kidnapping, unlawful imprisonment, attempted murder, and accessory to murder. The duchess will be similarly charged. She will also be charged with cannibalism. Your trial will be speedy, as required by the Constitution of the United States of America, unless you wish otherwise. Only you can choose to delay, for legal cause, or to go forward with a speedy trial."

The general sat erect, very deliberately looking at Mike. "Cannibalism? The duchess would never do such a thing as this. I was there. This never happened."

Billy scribbled notes.

The general leaned toward Mike. "Who would say such a wicked thing?" He leaned close to Billy. "This is propaganda."

"Of course." Mike could not suppress a grin. He knew this would be the general's position, and hers.

The General leaned back in his chair and contemplated his shackles.

Being as conciliatory as he could manage, Mike said, "I am very sorry to see you like this. She has placed you, and the others, in a very bad situation." Mike stood, walked around the table, took the general's arm, and helped him to his feet. He positioned himself between the general and the door, making it impossible for the general to see the duchess, and opened the door. He led the general out, keeping himself between the general and the duchess. He nodded at Chunky, "Take him back to his cell and give him something to eat."

Mike faced the general, still not allowing him to see the duchess. "Thank you for your cooperation, General. I will see if we can intervene with the district attorney, on your behalf."

The general's head remained down, totally unaware of the duchess.

Mike handed him off to Chunky and Chunky guided him into the cellblock.

Mike turned back into the interrogation room, deliberately not looking in her direction. He picked up the handwritten booking sheet, turned, and approached her. Reading from the sheet, he asked, "You are the Grand Duchess Catherine Mikhailovna?" He looked at her.

She glared into him.

He leaned over her, demanding she answer.

She refused to respond.

"Please, Lady Catherine." He motioned toward the interrogation room and helped her to her feet.

Chunky returned from the cellblock as Mike led her into the interrogation room. He sat her down and stepped back into the doorway. "I will leave this door open." Chunky would witness her treatment. No telling what she might claim.

He sat across from her. "This is William Cahill, top journalist with the Daily Evening Bulletin. He will be following and reporting what happens with you and your operatives. This interview will be conducted in English. Is this acceptable, Lady Catherine?"

If her eyes were Navy Colts, Mike would be dead. Hard to believe that he'd once thought her beautiful.

"Your arraignment will be tomorrow morning. You are, at least, complicit with many serious crimes, among them kidnapping, accessory to the murders of Colonel Preslova's comrades, accessory to the murder of at least one child, attempted murder of Raul Perez, unlawful imprisonment of my wife and son, and cannibalism." His mouth turned down in disgust.

"How dare you look down on me, you bastard son of a common soldier?"

Here we go.

Mike could not hide his slight smile. She would open up, and Billy was taking notes. Mike said, "My father was a general. He served your family his whole life, as did my uncle. Yet, you tortured my uncle to death. This was not an act of nobility."

She fumed, "He would not tell us where you are."

Mike said, "He had no way of knowing where I was. He probably thought me dead. Your brother did nearly kill me."

Her eyes narrowed. "You will die. You deserted from the Army of the Czar."

Mike smiled and nodded. "Da! Yes, I did. It does not matter that I was unconscious."

His open admission pleased her.

He said, "You may not know this. I grew up believing my mother died giving me birth. When I dared to ask you for a dance at the grand duke's ball, given partly, at least, in my honor, I did not know I was your illegitimate cousin."

"Bastard!"

"Da. Yes. I am the illegitimate son of the Queen of the Netherlands, and a Romanov."

Her rage filled eyes pierced to the back of his brain.

He said, "When you and your brother reacted the way you did, I had no idea why. When he tried to kill me, I reacted by instinct."

"You chopped off his right hand."

"I had excellent training from my Russian commanders. It did not matter that your brother's bullet had passed through my body. It did not matter that I had been blinded by my own blood." He pointed to the scar over his left eye. "My excellent Russian training took control and I reacted. Otherwise, out of loyalty, I would certainly have let him take my life, when he tried to shoot me a second time."

"Loyalty? How dare you? You are deserter. You should be shot, beheaded, and fed to the dogs."

"Your brother tried, twice."

Her face twitched, a slap of reality.

Mike said, "His death was not by my hand."

"You are the cause, just the same."

"I stood perfectly still, resolved to receive the second shot from his double-barrel pistol. I was loyal to the Romanov crown."

She blinked repeatedly. Her face twitched to the right, like turning a page in her mental book.

Mike said, "So, now we know why you are here. You seek revenge."

She leaned forward, still shackled hand and foot, and shrieked her response. "I want justice!"

Mike remained calm, getting everything he wanted. "Lady Catherine, we are in the United States of America, a constitutional republic."

"Ha!" She leaned back in her chair, more relaxed. She'd gotten something off her chest. "How can unwashed peasants hope to govern themselves? Is impossible."

"Da. Yes. It is an amazing experiment. I like this experiment, very much."

She said, "Of course you would like this. Any bastard and deserter would like this."

Mike nodded. "We also seek justice. American justice is based on laws. Our laws evolved from the British common law and are inspired by the Holy Bible. Those laws bring us to you. Tomorrow morning, at your arraignment, the presiding judge will hear the evidence against you and will decide whether to hold you over for trial. Even though you are not American citizens, you will be treated with the same judicial indifference as if you were. Our laws have no regard for birth rights or wealth."

"How dare you? I will never submit to the judgment of peasants."

"Yes, I already know this." He stared into her rage-filled eyes. "If you are held over for trial, it will be difficult to find a jury of your peers. You will be given the option of being tried before a jury of twelve men, or before the judge, without a jury."

"I have choice?"

"Yes. This is America. Which reminds me; does the czar know you are here?"

Her jaw tightened. She looked away. The Czar did not know.

Mike said, "Your consulate will inform him. In case you do not know, Czar Alexander is trying to sell Alaska to the United States. Russia needs money after their last war. Russia is always at war. Your criminal actions may make that sale more difficult."

She blinked twice and looked through him. Perhaps she knew nothing of this sale.

Czar Alexander was her nephew, but he still might go hard on her. The fact that Krestyanov had not presented a warrant for Mike's arrest must mean that the czar had revoked the warrant assigned by his father, Czar Nicholas.

Mike said, "The Russian Consulate has been notified of your arrest. We have not yet heard back."

She looked at Billy.

Billy wrote into his notepad.

Mike said, "From this point forward, I will not be involved with this case. I will be a witness for the prosecution. However, if you can help us find this man, Duncan Frack, I will speak of your help with the district attorney. While I cannot deter him from your full prosecution, I might convince him to recommend leniency with your sentencing. Otherwise, if found guilty, you could be hung on the gallows." Mike did not want this, but he did want her to imagine what that would be like.

Her eyes widened, surprised, maybe afraid for the first time in her life.

Mike said, "Why you would associate with such a man as this is a mystery. Duncan Frack is wanted for multiple robberies and murder." Mike frowned and shuddered. "How could you eat human flesh?"

"What? I never . . . Who tells you this?"

"My wife and son were there. Remember? You forced them to watch."

She said, "They are liars. I would never do such a horrible thing."

Mike scanned the handwritten booking sheet. "General Krestyanov was also there. As were your personal servants."

She stiffened. She would not speak again.

Mike would not give up. "Why would you want to protect such a man as Duncan Frack?"

She shook her head, as if she'd never heard of the man.

Mike stood, moved around the table, and stood behind her. "I was also there. Remember?"

Mike stepped through the open doorway, into the corridor.

Chunky sat at his desk.

"We're finished here. You can take her back to her cell." He reentered the interrogation room, slid her chair back, and pulled her to her feet. "If you decide to remember anything, tell Sergeant McFee. I might forget to mention the cannibalism to the district attorney."

She tossed her head back, proud as a peacock, and strutted through the open door.

Mike stepped into the corridor.

She and Chunky disappeared through the cellblock doorway.

Billy finished writing, closed his notepad, and looked up.

Mike checked his gold pocket watch, 12:14. "Feel like some chowder? I'm buying."

Chapter Thirty-Two

STEPPING FROM THE COLD on Meigg's Wharf into the warmth of the Cobweb Palace pushed quickly into the marrow of the bone. The saloon side held the aroma of chowder. After all the years, Mike still loved it.

Banjo and mandolin music pealed from two sailors near the front, as Mike dragged Billy through crowded tables to the far end of the bar, nearest the gaming room.

Abe waited by the chowder pot, ready for Mike's signal.

Mike held up two fingers and spread his hands. *Large.*

Abe nodded, ladled chowder into three large bowls, set them on a tray with spoons, napkins, and a platter of cheese and crackers. He slid it onto the bar for the coolie and pointed to the front corner of the dining room, near the entry. He drew a beer and hurried down the bar toward Mike. He elbowed onto the end of the bar with a nod. "Some guy calls himself a U.S. Treasury Agent said he wanted to wait and eat with you. He's over at that corner table."

Mike and Billy started back around the bar and Abe caught Mike's arm. "You've not been to the Olympic Club, and you've not been to work for a week. Are you okay?"

Mike smiled. "I have been running like a six-legged goat. I guess you have not heard."

"What?"

"Jimmy is home, and we have arrested four of the Russians responsible."

"Those royalty Russians?"

Mike smiled. "I will tell you about it later." Being one of the men who'd shot the grand duke, Abe would love hearing about the duchess. Mike said, "Bring us some beers, if you please."

"I might do it later." Abe tossed down his beer, winked, and hurried toward the beer barrel. He didn't want to miss anything.

Mike dragged Billy through tables toward the front corner. Twanging, happy music filled the air. Mike's spirit soared.

Agent Percy Bickford waited while the coolie delivered three chowders and a platter of cheese and crackers to the round table in the corner. He smiled and nodded.

Mike and Billy sat across the table from Bickford.

Mike grabbed a bowl of chowder and crumpled crackers into it.

Agent Bickford spooned chowder into his face, chewed, swallowed, and smiled. His eyes flared with surprise. "This is good." He looked around. "Nice place. Makes me feel at home."

"Of course. Abe Warner is from New York." Mike slurped chowder, *good*, as always.

Bickford looked puzzled by Mike's comment.

Billy said, "Mike and Abe Warner own this place."

Abe set four beers on the table, dragged up a chair, and sat between Billy and Bickford. "Will any one of you tell me what's happened?"

Mike chewed a tasty, tender clam and looked into Abe. "It will probably be easier to read about this in the Bulletin."

Billy slurped and chewed, held up a hand, and nodded.

Mike said, "Right now, we need to talk to Agent Bickford, here. He is building a trap." Mike sipped beer.

Billy stood, dragged a napkin across his face, and slugged down half a beer. "I need to get to my desk." He burped. "See you in the morning." He hurried out the door.

Mike looked across at Bickford and hooked a thumb toward Abe. "This is Abe Warner. He is the owner here. I trust him with my life."

Bickford looked at Abe, nodded, and sipped his beer. "That chowder was amazing. It reminds me of Boston."

"We do our best." Abe stared hard at Bickford, waiting for more information.

Bickford pulled a sealed envelope from his breast pocket and slid it across the table toward Mike.

Mike picked it up and handed it to Abe.

Abe opened it, read it, and handed it back to Mike, apparently still clueless after his reading.

HAN WOK AND HIS UNCLE sat at the end of the dining room table of the White Chapel Saloon. His uncle spoke in Cantonese with Chiang SuLin's father. Han only half listened.

SuLin sat across the table, totally disinterested in Han.

Not good.

Han's uncle had entered into negotiations with Chiang Po for SuLin's hand.

SuLin had directed her total attention to that negotiation. "No, no. This is America. Not Canton. My father will not pay you to take me. I will stay with Po. You can keep your nephew." She glared angrily at Han Wok, back-and-forth, while saying these things to Han's uncle in Cantonese.

Not good.

Han could not hide his deep attraction for SuLin. Whenever in her presence, his manhood testified to this fact, very difficult sometimes to hide, and very embarrassing.

Han's uncle cleared his throat and frowned. "No pay, no wedding."

They all spoke in Cantonese.

"Uncle, I don't need Po's money to care for his daughter. I have my own business. She can help me with my work." His impatience crowded his senses. "This is America!"

She offered a slight smile. She seemed okay with Han's suggestion.

Po smiled, proud of his daughter.

The kitchen door slammed shut, somebody coming in from the back, not visible from where Han sat.

Count Mike entered the dining room, hands spread wide. "Sorry to be so late. I have been tied up all morning at police headquarters." He dipped his head and shook hands with Chiang Po, showing him first respect. He kissed SuLin's upturned forehead then turned to Han, waiting for introductions.

Han stood.

His uncle remained seated.

Count Mike walked around the table, shook hands with Han as an equal, and turned to face Han's seated uncle.

Han pulled Mike one step closer to his uncle and spoke in English. "Uncle, this is Michael Zabel, Count Mike. He heads an investor group. They need labor for a railroad over high mountains to the east. I already tell you. Count Mike, this is my uncle, Han Chow."

Mike bowed at the waist, showing polite respect. "I am happy to finally meet you, sir. Let us hope we can do some business together."

Han Chow stood and dipped his head, a rare show of respect from a Chinese Tong boss. He spoke Cantonese. "I have viewed your proposal and taken it to the council."

Han Wok interpreted.

In Cantonese, Han Chow said, "We can satisfy your requirements." He smiled and dipped his head again, very rare.

Han Wok interpreted.

Still in Cantonese, Han Chow said, "I will leave negotiations to my nephew, Han Wok." His uncle sat.

Han Wok interpreted, mentioning how rare it was for a Chinese boss to show so much respect. He could not read Count Mike's thoughts.

Molly hurried down the main stairs and stood across the table from Mike. "Well, you've found some time for us, and at long last."

Mike smiled. "I have." He marched around the table and hugged his wife.

Molly squirmed free and straightened her dress. "You . . ." She fought against a smile. "There's Franklin Mosby . . ." She pointed upstairs. "He and Mister Broadback have been waiting to speak with you all the long morning."

Mike leaped up the stairs two treads at a time, turned the corner on the second floor, and found Franklin's door wide open.

Moses worked at the table, sketching with colored chalks, looking back and forth out the open window, on a rare, clear, beautiful day on the bay.

Franklin lay on his bunk, propped up on pillows, reading Anne S. Stephens's well-worn paperback novel, *Malaeska: The Indian Wife of the White Hunter*. It had taken Molly nearly a year to read it after Mike had consumed it in about a week. He was still fascinated by the diversity of the American culture.

Mike knocked softly on the open door.

Franklin spun off the bed to his bare feet and Moses turned, both happy to see Mike.

"Sorry to keep you waiting." Mike shook hands with Moses, then with Franklin. "Molly said you wanted to see me."

Franklin sat on his bunk and looked at the floor. He shook his head and stood. "The man I met at Tommy Chandler's Boardinghouse hasn't yet visited the Palace." He looked at Mike, desperate. "I don't know what to do. I'm worried he might move away and take Melanie with him."

"I understand. You cannot risk going in there again. Your southern manner and speech are easily identifiable."

"I'm not the only southerner to come west."

"No, you are not. However, I've seen sketches of your daughter. If those sketches are near accurate, which I suspect they are, you and your daughter bear a quite remarkable resemblance. He might already be suspicious. That might be why he has not yet visited the Palace."

Franklin shrank back onto his pillows, crossed his arms, and stared at the ceiling.

"What about me?" Moses stood to face Mike, clear-eyed, resolute. "He never saw me. I could ask about a room and keep my eyes pealed for this man, and for Melanie."

"Does she know you? Would she recognize you?"

Moses blinked and glanced at Franklin. "She come into the store a few times during the war. I don't think she'd recognize me. White folk don't much look at coloreds."

Franklin stood. "No." He placed a hand on Moses's shoulder. "We can't take that risk, my friend. Neither of us could do anything inside Chandler's, anyway. If she did recognize you, it might get you killed."

Mike said, "It might be better to keep a watch from outside Chandler's. It is a busy wharf. This should afford sufficient concealment. We can post Raul across the wharf to watch for your Melanie. He can disappear in plain sight." He looked at Franklin. "Raul and Moses could take shifts. Across the wharf is a warehouse with a deep, overhanging roof."

Franklin relaxed a little, happy to be forming a plan.

Mike looked at Moses. "If either of you sees anything, we will get a warrant and make a search."

Franklin shook his head and grinned. "If either of them sees anything?"

"You cannot just run in there. Somebody might get himself shot. If Moses sees this man, or your daughter, we have cause to get a search warrant and go in."

Franklin stepped back and nodded. He'd live with it.

"Look, I need to be in court tomorrow morning. Then, early Saturday morning, I need someone to be on the Wells Fargo stage to Sacramento. I could use some deputies."

Both Moses and Franklin nodded, eager to help.

"Moses, can you ride?"

Moses hesitated, then nodded.

"Somebody will need to follow behind with the horses. We will need two men in the coach."

Franklin said, "Who's watching Tommy Chandler's?"

Mike had no argument. "You are correct. We still have a couple of days to think this through. I will ask around. We will finalize our plans tomorrow night at the Palace."

"What if it was your son?"

"You are again correct. Your daughter has priority. We will work it through."

Franklin said, "We want to help with these robberies, of course."

"We will get your daughter back. I need to get home and get some sleep. Raul is at the house. I will give him that sketch and ask him to go down to Chandler's. Moses can relieve him at eight o'clock tonight. He will be under the warehouse roof, directly across from Chandler's. I will be at the Palace later tonight. Maybe your man will show up. Who knows?"

Franklin nodded, slapped Moses's back, and returned to his bunk.

"Okay. Good." Mike turned out into the hallway and crossed, two doors down, to Colonel Preslova's room. He knocked on the closed door.

"Come." Preslova's voice could barely be heard.

Mike opened the door and faced Preslova's raised pistol.

Seeing Mike, Preslova lowered his pistol and set it on the table. "Mikhail." He smiled, relieved.

Mike said, "The duchess and General Krestyanov have been arrested, along with another man and a young woman. They are in the city jail. Their arraignment is scheduled for ten o'clock, tomorrow morning. We will need for you to testify."

Preslova leaned toward Mike and blinked twice. "Was the other man tall and thin, or closer to your size?"

"Tall and thin. I think he is a little older than the woman."

"These are Luka and Sacha Varvarinski. They have served the duchess, almost from their birth. Grigori Balakirev is still at large?"

"We do not have him."

"Grigori and Luka were the men in my room that night."

"Da. Yes. This Grigori did not board the ship with the others. He is still at liberty. I suspect he is on *Black Swan*. It is easy to see a black schooner with black sails. It used to belong to Bill Coleman."

"Grigori remains under orders from the duchess. Of this I am certain. She will order our executions. We are both deserters from the Army of the Czar."

"Do you think this Grigori will be at tomorrow's arraignment?"

Preslova puffed a brief laugh and shook his head. "Ridiculous. He probably knows nothing of their arrest."

"So, you will testify?"

"Da, da. Yes, of course."

"Will you move back into your rooms at the Saint Francis Hotel?"

"Do you think it is safe?"

Mike asked, "Does it matter?"

Preslova crossed his arms and stared at the pistol on the table. "No. I am tired of hiding."

"Are you free Saturday morning?"

Chapter Thirty-Three

AFTER THE SUN WENT down, Duncan Frack's hunger for Chinese liver always spiked. Without it, his sense of invincible power faded. His new residence in China Basin had immediately become a cage he needed to escape.

Sure, Juanita had fixed the place up, using a heavy blanket as a door, some oil lamps, a potbellied stove, a table, a couple of chairs, their bed over in the corner, but the foul odors of China Basin still hung heavy.

"Where you going now?" Juanita always recognized his hunger.

"Chinatown."

"Why? The Russians have gone. No need for small boys anymore."

"Woman, what are you talking about? We never did this for anybody but us. You know the power that comes into me . . ." He spread his hands above his head, summoning spiritual forces. "When I eat their livers. Maybe it's the blood."

She frowned and looked at the dirt floor. "We never did this thing. You did this thing."

"You saying you don't like what it does for me?"

She looked up, teary eyed and frowning.

"Juanita, nothing can stop us. You know that. We've been protected. We've got money and plenty of it. You go wild, when I take you. You crave it, much as me."

She smiled slightly, her eyes a little brighter. "I know you before you kill little boys. I like you before. I maybe like you better, before"

Duncan said, "I don't think as much as you like me now." She became more passionate. She enjoyed painting their skins and hanging them on the wall.

She stepped closer. "Those little boys . . . They all seemed so precious. I feed them. I clean them. Their mothers must love them very much."

"They're Chinese. Nobody cares about these stupid Chinese."

"Chinese care for Chinese, especially boy Chinese."

"Okay. I might not take a boy, this time. We haven't tried little girls yet." He pulled on his tan slicker and donned his new white hat, a completely different look than his picture in the papers. Sure, his size hadn't changed. Not too many his size in this city. But, hey, his hunger needed to be fed. Finally, the growth of hair on his face had grown enough to hide his winning smile. Nobody would know him now.

"Why we don't leave this place? We have plenty money, now."

"Not quite enough, my pet." There never was enough. He backed toward the doorway and nudged into the heavy blanket drawn across to keep the cold out. "I'll bring her back here. You get some nice hot soup and hot tea on. It'll clean out her liver."

"Take me with you?" She'd never asked that before.

"Stay put. We should be hearing from Tommy. It's high time for another job."

"And after that?"

He needed to say it. He needed to keep the peace between them. "After this job, we might have enough to move down to Puerto Vallarta. We'll buy that rancho you like. We'll grow corn, horses, and kids of our own."

She smiled, relaxed, and slid her arms around his waist. She always liked that promise. She always believed it, too.

Duncan grabbed the folded blanket by the door and walked out into a biting-cold wind, perfect weather for finding a kid.

Good thing, actually, Count Mike's kid escaping and all. Duncan felt uncomfortable killing a white kid. If the fancy Russian lady hadn't promised to pay such good money to torture the kid, Duncan would never have agreed.

She never paid a penny. Having believed her promises made him feel stupid.

He took a three block walk up and out of China Basin and flagged a taxi. "Take me to Portsmouth Plaza."

A few minutes later, the taxi stopped near the back of Bella Union. Ducan climbed down and paid the driver. The taxi pulled away and Duncan strolled toward the wafting odors of Chinese cooking.

The wind wasn't so bad below Portsmouth Plaza, walking between straw huts. He stopped. Two huts downhill on his right, a little girl huddled in the glow of a single candle, gripping her legs against the cold, shivering violently, alone, and crying.

Perfect.

He reached into his coat pocket, pulled out and unfolded the handkerchief, stepped close to the child, and knelt. He extended a chunk of bread. "Here. Don't cry."

The child's dark eyes rolled up to meet his and she stopped crying.

"Here." He pushed the bread closer.

She looked at the bread, looked at him, and hesitated.

He spread his nicest smile.

She looked into her empty hut, looked up at him again, took the bread, turned away, and ate it quickly. Maybe she feared he might take it back.

"You look cold." He hugged himself and shivered.

She understood.

He pulled the folded blanket from under his coat, unfolded it, and pulled it over her shivering shoulders. "I know a very warm place with lots of hot food. Are you hungry?"

Her eyes widened.

"Come along. My woman will feed you."

JETHRO TOWNSEND ARRIVED at Tommy Chandler's sometime after 9:00 p.m., not exactly sure.

Tommy stood in his usual place behind the bar, filling a pewter flagon with beer. He dropped the hinged lid and handed the flagon to one of his girls. She delivered the flagon to a table with four sailors in the center of the room.

Tommy cocked his head toward the back office and turned away from the bar.

Jethro crossed the room quickly, stepped behind the bar, and followed Tommy into his office.

Tommy closed the door and slid a chair from the wall to his desk. Jethro sat.

Tommy rounded his desk. "I've been waiting to see you." He bent, pulled up a floor board behind his desk, and lifted out a heavy looking strongbox with iron straps and a lock. He yanked up a chain from around his neck, showed Jethro a key, and opened the box. "Fifteen thousand." He used both hands to lift a canvas bag from the box and set it on his desk.

Jethro stood, opened the bag, and stacked gold coins onto Tommy's desk, counting it as he stacked. Not that he didn't trust Tommy. He did. "Any trouble?"

"Not for me." Tommy twitched a slight smile. "One of the guards got his throat cut. The other one will live."

"So I heard." Jethro put half of the money in his left coat pocket and half in the right. "Can you manage a shipment on Saturday? Same time and route as the last Wells Fargo stage you took."

Tommy smiled and nodded. "That's what I was hoping to talk about."

"This is a big one." Jethro instinctively hesitated. Trust had always been difficult but this was Tommy Chandler. He'd never yet let Jethro down. "We're shipping one-hundred-thousand dollars in gold coin. My share's twenty-five-thousand, then I'm out for a while." Jethro turned for the door.

"Out?" It sounded like Tommy didn't like that.

Jethro turned back.

"What's that supposed to mean?"

"Treasury sent an agent out here to investigate. He didn't find anything and he's gone back to Washington. He'll file his report and be finished. After Saturday, they'll probably send somebody else. We need to lay low for a while. Maybe a year or more."

"Listen, you." Tommy's eyes speared cold ice into chills already crawling up Jethro's back. "Anything happens and you find yourself in the stocks . . ."

"It won't. This isn't even my consignment. This came across another desk, some new guy out from the treasury department. I just happened to see the paperwork. They don't even know I know. More likely for your men to make a mistake and get caught."

Tommy stiffened, thinking about it. He shook his head and relaxed. "No. They know better. If I go behind the bars, they're dead, and they know it. The same goes for you."

Jethro didn't appreciate the threat. There would be no next time with Tommy Chandler.

DUNCAN FRACK AND THE little Chinese girl reached his new place in China Basin, where the bitter-cold wind drove hard. He pulled the heavy blanket aside and they entered a well lit, warm home.

Juanita had already prepared a fine smelling menudo and a platter of corn tortillas.

Duncan carried the little girl to the pot-bellied stove, close to Juanita. "Juanita, this is Susan Han. Her parents named her to be American."

Duncan leaned over the stove with the girl and they both inhaled fumes from Juanita's slowly bubbling stew. He looked at little Susan. "You hungry?"

She smiled and nodded, wide-eyed. This little bit didn't seem afraid of anything.

Juanita cupped the girl's cheek. "You're a pretty one."

"Hello, the house," called a man from outside.

"Watch her." Duncan handed little Susan to Juanita, pulled his knife, and stepped to the blanket draped doorway. He looked back.

Juanita and the little China doll stared wide-eyed at Duncan.

He yanked the heavy blanket aside. "Donald Thorne." Duncan put his knife away. "Tommy send you?" Duncan pulled him into the warmth and dropped the blanket back into place.

"Yes." Donald looked at Juanita and Duncan's new China doll. "Say, something smells good." He smiled at Duncan. "I'm tired of Tommy's cooking." His bushy red eyebrows shot up and twitched.

"Sure."

RAUL STOOD IN THE COLD, dark wind blowing across China Basin. He'd been following a stocky-built man from Tommy Chandler's Boardinghouse who matched Franklin Moseby's description.

When the blanket got pulled open on the small, stone-built cottage, Raul immediately recognized the man standing in the well-lit interior, the same man who'd held Mr. Mike, Miss Molly, and little Jimmy. No doubt about him.

Seeing the man he'd just followed enter this man's house raised Raul's doubts. Maybe this wasn't the man Franklin Mosby wanted. No way of knowing, based on Moses Broadback's charcoal sketches. How could these two men be together?

He'd let Mr. Mike and Mr. Mosby work this out. He needed to let them know.

Raul hurried back up the dirt road and walked to the nearest paved street, already late at night. After two more blocks, he rounded a corner and stopped.

A gentleman in a plug hat staggered out of a taxi and slumped under the streetlight, fingering through a palm full of coins.

Raul walked to the front of the horse and motioned to the driver. "Are you city bound?"

The driver nodded and leaned out to take coins from the tottering gent. He counted the money under the streetlight, dumped the coins into his coat pocket, and motioned for Raul to climb aboard.

"Take me to Meigg's Wharf."

"Cobweb Palace?"

MIKE WORKED TABLE-TO-table with his bucket, collecting the house share. He stopped at the faro table where Franklin raked in winnings, no black king.

One of the players, a stocky, well-dressed man, said, "There are no black kings in that whole deck."

Franklin set the deck in front of the man.

The man thought for a moment, scooped up the deck, and spread it on the table. The second card from the top was the king of clubs. The king of spades was a few cards from the bottom. He shook his head, scooped up the deck, and handed it back to Franklin. "Sorry, Franklin." He smiled, apologetic. "It is Franklin, isn't it?"

"It is." Franklin picked up the rest of the cards and edge-tapped the deck on the table, ready to shuffle. "No need to apologize. You can check the deck, anytime." He looked up at Mike.

"Did he come in yet?"

Franklin took a slow breath and glanced around at the other tables. "No."

"Do not worry, Franklin. We will get her back."

"I pray so."

The double doors from the saloon burst inward and Raul flagged Mike.

"Isn't he supposed to be . . ." Franklin turned in his chair, ready to stand.

Mike placed a hand on Franklin's shoulder. "I will report to you, whatever has happened." He walked through the double doors and joined Raul at the end of the bar. "Are you hungry?"

Raul shook his head.

"Do you want something to drink?"

"No. I'm okay." Raul glanced quickly around and grabbed Mike's arms. "Listen, I follow this heavy guy, not fat, like Moses and Franklin say. Too dark outside to see his face, but he got no beard and no long hair."

"Did you see my daughter?" Franklin had abandoned the faro table to join them.

Raul stared at Franklin for a moment, then looked at the floor. "No."

Frustration and fear boosted Franklin's voice. "Raul, why are you here?"

Raul settled a dark stare on Franklin. "I need to see Mister Mike."

Franklin blinked and stepped back. Any man looking into Raul's stare would step away.

Raul turned back to Mike. "I follow this man down to China Basin. He going to see that big guy, the one who had you and Molly and Jimmy tied up. The man you call Jack Wick."

"Well done."

"We gonna go grab him?"

"No. Not tonight. We need to spring our trap, and try to work it all the way to the top."

"What about Melanie?" Poor Franklin could think of nothing else.

Mike couldn't blame him. "Look, if we try and grab these guys tonight, we might never find your daughter. If we can capture them on Saturday, we'll have just cause to get a search warrant on Tommy Chandler's."

Chapter Thirty-Four

FRIDAY MORNING, AFTER Colonel Preslova joined them at Mike's house for breakfast, Paddy drove them down to the courthouse on California Street.

Nearing the courthouse, Molly squeezed Mike's arm and leaned close. "I don't want Jimmy to be questioned about this."

"Of course not." Mike smiled across at his son, squeezed between Raul and Coira. "Nobody will testify today. This is why we have all written statements about what happened. Jimmy did not write a statement, and neither will he testify. His memories do not seem to trouble him, and I do not wish for anything bad to squirrel back into his mind."

Paddy's taxi stopped on California Street, uphill from a line of taxis and other carriages parked in front of the San Francisco County Courthouse. Preslova climbed down from the driver's bench and opened the double doors to the passenger compartment.

Jimmy jumped down to the brick sidewalk, spun, and waited. The others climbed out and filed down the crowded sidewalk, up the steps, and into the courthouse.

Sergeant McFee stood in the wide foyer with a uniformed officer. He held up a hand, stopping Mike and the others. "We drew Judge Edward G. Maxwell. He's already convened the grand jury. The D. A. is in with them now."

Mike pulled and looked at his watch, 9:57 a.m. "Are we to go in?"

"Take a seat in back and keep quiet." He smiled down at Jimmy. "Can you keep still through this?"

Molly pulled Jimmy into her legs. "We'll do our best."

McFee said, "The accused are waiting in a holding room. Is Jimmy okay, seeing them again?"

Mike smiled. "Jimmy actually liked them. The duchess is his cousin."

Jimmy puffed with pride. "I'm a Romanov."

McFee smiled, straightened, and led them into the courtroom. They remained standing, as Judge Maxwell was just coming in.

The bailiff said, "All rise."

The spectators stood, Billy Cahill among them. Billy looked back and smiled at Mike and his group.

Maxwell took his seat and gaveled.

Billy waved and motioned for Mike and his group to sit in seats he'd previously reserved. After everybody was seated, the judge nodded at the bailiff.

The bailiff opened a side door and Clive Nielson, the assistant district attorney, led the twenty-nine-man grand jury into the courtroom. The jurors took their seats on the oversized jury platform.

Clive Nielson moved behind his desk, pulled a notepad from his valise, and sat.

Judge Maxwell studied the jurors head-to-head, nodding at the many regulars he already knew. "Gentlemen, you've been called to hear evidence regarding felonies allegedly committed in the County of San Francisco, by foreign persons." He nodded at the bailiff.

The bailiff opened another side door.

A uniformed police officer led Lady Catherine, Sacha Varvarisnski, General Krestyanov, and Luka Varvarinski into the courtroom. They'd all been shackled, hand and foot. Six-foot lengths of chain connected their shackled feet, left ankle to left ankle.

The bailiff positioned them along a wooden bench and helped them sit, one by one.

Judge Maxwell looked down at the prisoners, one at a time. "Do you all understand why you are here?"

The four accused Russians sat, motionless.

"Do you speak English?"

No response from the four Russians.

A tall, heavyset man in his fifties, pinched spectacles over his nose, and stood. "Your honor, I am Count Ivan Stropova-Mikhailovna, Russian consul in this great city. I wish to speak in defense of Grand Duchess Catherine Mikhailovna, General, the Count Boris Romochka-Krestyanov, and Sacha and Luka Varvarinski." His Russian accent carried a diplomat's refinement.

Judge Maxwell grinned. "Count Mikhailovna, is it?"

"Da. Yes."

"Are you related to the duchess?"

"I am her cousin, in the second-degree. We have never before met."

"Well, Russian Consul Mikhailovna, this is a hearing before a grand jury. There is nothing yet to defend. If these four are held over for trial, they may present a defense such as they see fit."

"But, Your Honor . . ."

Judge Maxwell gaveled once. "Take your seat. If you disrupt this hearing again, I will have you removed."

"How dare you?" His voice rang shrill, surprising for a man his size. "This is the Grand Duchess of all Russia, aunt to . . ."

Maxwell slammed the gavel onto the bench and waved at the bailiff.

The bailiff and a uniformed police officer took the arms of the Russian consul and led him out of the courtroom.

The consul glared at Mike on his way out.

Mike had never seen him before.

Once the consul had been forcibly removed, Maxwell nodded to the assistant district attorney. "Mister Nielson, what've you got?"

Nielson stood and shuffled papers. He glanced back at Mike. "Your honor, I'd like to call State Special Officer, Mike Zabel."

Mike stood with his handwritten papers and carried them up one step, past the court recorder, and set them on the judge's bench.

Maxwell said, "You are Mike Zabel, otherwise known as Count Mike?"

"I am. My full name and title is Count Mikhail Diebitsch-Zabalkansky. I am a special deputy of the state police."

"Yeah, I've heard of you. Glad we can finally meet." Maxwell nodded at the bailiff.

The bailiff led Mike to the witness chair, where Mike remained standing.

The bailiff said, "Raise your right hand."

Mike raised his hand.

"You swear to tell the truth?"

"I do."

"You can sit."

Mike sat.

Maxwell leafed through the handwritten sheets. "What's this?"

"These are written statements taken from witnesses shortly after the incidents in question here today."

"Just tell us about it, Mike."

Mike looked at the four Russians in front of him, all shackled, their clothing wrinkled and their hair in disarray. "The duchess employs the other three. Sacha and Luka Varvarinski are her personal servants, and General Krestyanov is in charge of her security.

"About a month ago, Colonel Preslova's two associates disappeared. They were later found in a shallow grave, in the south city district."

"Colonel Preslova?"

Preslova stood and nodded.

Maxwell found his statement. "Ah, yes." He read it quickly and motioned for Preslova to sit.

Preslova sat.

Maxwell said, "Go ahead, Mike."

"I was summoned to the south city location by Police Sergeant Angus McFee for possible identification."

McFee stood and nodded.

Maxwell massaged his furrowed forehead. "And?"

Mike said, "Yes, I knew them both."

McFee sat.

Maxwell tapped his right temple with his index finger, remembering. "Wait. Is there any connection with the death of that Russian duke a few years back?"

Mike said, "Yes. Colonel Preslova and his associates were in charge of security for Grand Duke Nicholai Nicholaiavich. He was shot dead at the Palace by Governor J. Neely Johnson, State Assemblyman John Downey, and Abe Warner, proprietor of the Palace."

"Are there any relationships we should understand?" Maxwell waved his gavel at the defendants.

"The Grand Duke and Duchess were siblings. I am an illegitimate cousin to them both."

Lady Catherine's jaw muscles bulged. Her eyes grew so wide that the whites of her eyes surrounded her green irises.

"I see." Maxwell leaned back in his chair and relaxed. "Continue."

"On the night when I identified Count Preslova's associates, I went to the St. Francis Hotel to inform the count. When I arrived, Luka Varvarinski and another man were interrogating Preslova in a most aggressive manner. Had I not intervened, Preslova might have joined his two associates in another shallow grave."

Maxwell addressed the grand jury. "This is speculation on the part of the witness."

They understood.

Mike addressed the grand jury. "Count Preslova had been tied to a chair. Luka Varvarinski and Grigori Balakirev, the other man, had been taking turns punching his face. I witnessed two such blows before I intervened. Grigori Balakirev is still at liberty."

Judge Maxwell allowed this testimony. He asked, "Were there any witnesses as to the deaths of Preslova's associates?"

"None that we have found, Your Honor."

Maxwell looked at the grand jury. "Any connection with those held in custody and the two men found dead is speculation. It has no bearing."

The jurors understood. Some looked at Mike as if he had lost something.

Maxwell said, "Go ahead, Mike."

"Last Sunday, while on a family outing at North Beach, our good friend, Raul Perez, was shot. My wife, our son's governess, and our son were kidnapped."

Raul, Molly, Coira, and Jimmy stood, then sat back down.

"I saw General Krestyanov, a man I have known most of my life, holding a smoking gun, and climbing into a carriage. I gave chase but he escaped. When I returned, my wife, Molly, our son, James, and Coira Macauley, our son's governess, had been taken by two other men. This, according to several witnesses. You have their written statements and they are willing to appear to testify.

"We immediately carried Raul, by wagon, to Saint Mary's Hospital on Stockton, where he quickly recovered."

Maxwell said, "So, nobody, as of yet, has been killed?"

"No, sir. None, other than those two Russians."

"Continue."

"I went down to the White Chapel Saloon, into which Count Preslova had moved, and asked him to stay the night at my family home. When we arrived, we found Raul and Coira in the kitchen. Raul had left the hospital on his own, and Coira had been released by the kidnappers.

"The following day, I received written instructions to come alone to Portsmouth Plaza, if I ever wanted to see my family again. I met there with this man . . ." Mike pointed, "Luka Varvarinski, and Grigori Balakirev. They tied my hands, put a sack over my head, and took me by carriage to a small iron forge down on the Barbary Coast. There, my wife and son had been tied to chairs, and had been forced to watch a man known to us as Duncan Frack, also known as Jack Wick . . . They were forced to watch this man kill and butcher a young child, then cook and eat his liver. You have my wife's statement."

Several members of the jury sucked air and mumbled, as did spectators.

Judge Maxwell gaveled once and eyeballed the room for silence. He asked, "Were all of these prisoners present?"

"When they removed the sack from my head, only Duncan Frack, the Lady Catherine, Luka Varvarinski, and General Krestyanov were present. Sacha Varvarinski and Grigori Balakirev were not present."

Maxwell asked, "Did you witness the killing of the child?"

"No. My wife and son did. I would rather not involve my son further. I fear for his future wellbeing. Such memories as this . . ." Mike shook his head.

"I don't think his testimony will be necessary." Maxwell looked at the defendants, one at a time. He looked at Mike. "So, these defendants were not seen killing anyone. General Krestyanov shot this man, Raul, who has recovered. And, this, Luka, and an unknown man kidnapped your wife, your son, and the governess. And, there are accessory charges, of course." He looked at Mike. "Is that about it?"

"Yes, Your Honor."

"Okay." Maxwell looked toward the grand jury. "Any of you want to ask any questions of Count Mike, or any of the others?"

The jurors leaned into each other, whispering and looking toward the prisoners. The foreman stood. "I think we have what we need."

"Okay." Maxwell gaveled and stood. "Bailiff, return these prisoners to their cells." He turned to the grand jury. "How much time do you boys need?"

The foreman said, "We'd like to toss it around. We'll get back to you as soon as we reach our decisions."

"You have any questions for the district attorney's office?"

The foreman shook his head.

The bailiff escorted the chained Russian prisoners out.

Maxwell gaveled. "This grand jury is now in deliberation." He turned and left.

Chapter Thirty-Five

DUNCAN FRACK SAT AT their small table with Susan Yee and Juanita. From the moment their eyes met, Juanita and the girl had become best friends.

This was bad news for Duncan and his appetites.

The plate of pinto beans, pork, rice, and tortillas tasted fine, but he hungered for more. He needed to consume his pound of human flesh to feed his dark power.

That darkness pulled and compelled him. It demanded obedience, since his first taste.

Juanita's stare poked to the back of Duncan's head. She would fight to protect this little girl.

The China doll's head bobbed back and forth, watching them stare at each other between bites of Mexican pork and pinto beans. She liked the food.

Duncan lowered his head and glared defiantly into Juanita. "Woman, we have a job to do, tomorrow morning. We need to leave here, late tonight. What do you want, to bring her with us?"

Juanita slammed her spoon onto the table, stood, and leaned toward Duncan. "Yes. Why not? She can ride with me!"

China Sue smiled and nodded. She liked it.

Bad news for Duncan's appetite. "I need her power." Duncan stood and braced into Juanita's anger. "I always thought you understood."

Juanita propped both fists onto her swaying hips and sashayed toward him. "You are already powerful, you stupid man. You should not invite this evil into our home. Whenever your royal Russian comes in, I am suffocated by the hate she brings." She spat out a dry breath, not yet daring to actually spit on him.

Duncan smiled and stepped back, reminding himself of how much he needed this woman. He slumped into his chair, amazed by her awareness and insight. *She might be right.* He couldn't afford to lose Juanita. Maybe he loved her, maybe not. He'd never been able to define love. Love her or not, he needed her. Without her, he could never have managed his growth of wealth. Her instincts had proven true, time after time.

There were other things to consider. She always submitted on cold nights, warm nights, too. She craved it. They both did. And, she could cook, and clean, and she seemed to enjoy both.

He said, "Okay. We'll try it your way. Get her ready by three in the morning. I'll take care of the horses. We need to pick up Donald on the way."

HAN WOK AND HIS UNCLE arrived at the council of elders meeting a few minutes early. Han could not hide his exuberance. They had successfully negotiated an agreement with Chiang Po for the hand of Chiang SuLin. Han would pay for the wedding ceremonies at the Tien Hau Temple, in honor of his uncle's Taoist beliefs. This ceremony was to fall on Friday, January 19.

On Saturday, January 20, in honor of Han and SuLin's Christian faith, another ceremony would be held at St. Mary's Cathedral. It surprised Han when his uncle had agreed to a church wedding. The fact that Po would pay for the church wedding must have helped.

Christmas of 1865 was only one week away. Even Chinese, here in America, celebrated the birth of the Christ, maybe another reason his uncle had agreed to a church wedding. Their weddings would be in one month, an eternity of waiting.

They entered the council chamber amid shrieks from a woman. Her twisted face gleamed, soaking wet with tears. Han could only glimpse between other council members and citizens, tightly gathered around her.

The husband of one of Han's cousins pushed his way through the cluster and braced Han's uncle. He spoke in Cantonese. "Your granddaughter is missing. Neighbors say she is taken by a tall American in a white coat."

The honorable hatchet man stepped out of the shadows to face Han and his uncle.

MIKE ZABEL, FRANKLIN Mosby, and Vladimir Preslova led their horses onto the Vallejo Ferry in the quiet darkness of a cold morning, well ahead of the scheduled Wells Fargo stage.

Mike had seen Preslova's mare before, a muscular bay, but he hadn't seen Franklin Mosby's horse. Still too dark to be sure. "Mister Mosby, is that a gelding or a mare?"

"He's a gelded Spanish Mustang. I won him at your faro table, saddle and all."

Mike placed a hand on Franklin's shoulder, speaking softly into his ear. "From where does Abe Warner take his cut?"

Franklin spun to face Mike. "I've already put it in your bucket." He saw Mike's smile and they both chuckled.

The horse carried the markings of a pinto paint, black, brown, and white. It had a proud stance, head up, strong neck. "This pinto looks like you won more than the turn of a card."

Franklin said, "One cannot say. I haven't had an opportunity to ride him yet. He's friendly to feed, brush, and saddle. He's got smart, clear eyes." Franklin knew horses.

"What's his name?"

"Uktena. It's a Cherokee name; or so I was told. I'm not sure if I'm pronouncing it correctly."

Mike stroked Jasmine's neck. She leaned into him, bobbing her head. She liked it. "This is Jasmine, a Kentucky bred mare. I've had her for nine years."

He looked across Jasmine's back.

Preslova stood like a soldier, feet slightly spread, reins held in his left hand, right hand behind his back, detached, but always observant.

"Vladimir's mare is named Whiskey, maybe from her color. He bought her at auction on Pacific Street Wharf, two years ago."

An acknowledging smile came from Vlad. "She is a good horse."

Jasmine flinched, as four horses towed the Wells Fargo stage onto the ferry.

The ferry whistle blew twice, longshoremen tossed rope onto the ferry from the wharf, and the side paddles kicked up a cold, misty spray from the bay.

Three hours later, with sun breaking through the overcast, the side paddles reversed, and the ferry nudged into the Vallejo landing.

They led their horses off the landing and tied them to hitching posts in front of the ferry landing eatery.

The stage rolled past, turned up the steep slope, and climbed away from the bay.

Mike said, "The bacon smells good. Anybody else want bacon and flapjacks?"

SEVEN MILES UP THE road to Sacramento, Juanita had backed their wagon off the road, hiding it behind a thicket of tall pine trees. With the help of China Sue, she'd built a fire, made coffee, and cooked an early breakfast of bacon, pinto beans, and fried potatoes. They finished eating, drank their coffee, and doused the fire.

Duncan Frack and Donald Thorne had tied their horses behind the wagon, leaving everything out of sight from the road.

Duncan pulled three precut flour sacks from his saddle bag, tossed one to Donald, and handed another to Juanita. He tossed his hat into the back of the wagon, pulled the third flour sack over his head, and adjusted it to the eye and mouth cutouts. "Let's get ready."

He broke down the 24", double barrels on his Ithaca shotgun, checked the load, snapped it shut, and handed it to Donald. "Don't shoot unless you have to."

Donald leaned the shotgun against a tree, pulled on and adjusted his mask, and carried the shotgun at arm's length. "Tommy said Wells Fargo carries shotgun messengers now, if they got freight to protect."

"They've got freight to protect today. Let's roll them rocks onto the road. We'll get the drop on any such messengers. We set it up right, only a fool would try anything."

Duncan led Donald down the road to a dry creek bed and rolled a rock the size of a horse head across the road to the far side. "Get to work. It needs to look like a flashflood pushed this stuff. A couple more this size, with some smaller rocks, and some of them dead tree branches tossed in. We need enough to make them stop the coach and climb down to clear away."

Donald tossed several rocks onto the road and Duncan rolled them into place. They scattered some branches and rubble until Duncan said, "That's enough." It looked convincing. "Remember, hide till they start to climb back up, then come out with that scattergun and demand for them to stand."

"Hear that?" Donald hiked the short distance uphill and grabbed the shotgun.

The sound of thundering hooves carried up from the road below.

Duncan jumped down the drop-off on the downhill side of the road and hid behind a fat pine tree. "You'll know when they've finished clearing the road. That's the time to come out. Don't show yourself before. Don't do nothin' stupid."

Donald said, "Okay, already. I got it."

A four-horse team pulled the Wells Fargo stage around a bend, still more than a hundred yards away.

Duncan's position offered a clear view, but Donald's spot across the road did not. Donald wouldn't see the coach until it stopped.

The ground shook with the pounding of hooves, getting close.

Duncan peeked out from behind the tree.

The coachman pulled reins and shouted, "Whoa!"

The horses stopped above the debris. The driver looked at the shotgun messenger seated next to him. "You wanna help with this?"

The shotgun messenger said, "You do it. I'd best stay put. I got a feelin'."

The driver said, "This happens all the time. Get a little rain and stuff breaks loose."

The driver climbed to the ground and walked into the debris. He looked around, bent, and tossed rocks.

After a short look around, the shotgun messenger lowered his shotgun into the boot under the driver's platform and climbed down.

About three minutes later, both men returned to the coach and started to climb aboard.

Donald jumped out of hiding with perfect timing, scattergun held high. "Stand tight, gents." He leveled the scattergun at the messenger's head.

Duncan pulled his revolver and climbed up to the road, about ten feet behind the driver. "Hands up, boys."

Both men spun around, saw Duncan's poised revolver, and raised their hands.

Juanita climbed onto the top of the stage from the rear boot and aimed her rifle at the driver. "Are there any passengers?"

The driver shook his head, "No sir . . . ugh, ma'am."

Duncan said, "Slowly set your pistols on the ground and walk down into that creek bed."

Donald held his scattergun close to the messenger as both men moved slowly, lifting their pistols and bending to put them on the road.

Duncan said, "Go on, now."

The driver and messenger walked downhill on opposite sides of the team of horses.

"Right there's good." Donald moved into position to guard both the messenger and the driver.

Duncan holstered his revolver and climbed up the left front wheel. He sat on the driver's bench and passed the messenger's shotgun back to Juanita. The strongbox sat at the bottom of the boot, under the driver's seat. He bent, grabbed the handles at both ends, and pulled. The weight drove his elbows to his knees, struggling with the heavy trunk. A smile nobody could see bent his face. "Eureka! This here's the mother load." He slid and hung the strongbox off the side of the coach, finding and resting it on the left-front wheel. "Climb down there, baby, and hold this in place."

Juanita laid the rifle and shotgun on the back of the coach, climbed down into the rear boot, grabbed the weapons, and jumped to the ground. She leaned the weapons against the left rear wheel, ducked under the side window openings, moved to the front wheel, and held the strongbox in place.

Duncan climbed down and lowered the heavy box to the ground. He straightened, pulled his revolver, and stepped wide of the horses. "Okay, boys, climb back up and slap them horses on down the road."

Juanita dragged her rifle and the messenger's shotgun off the rear wheel, leaned the rifle against a tree, stepped back up, opened the side door, and levelled the shotgun on the messenger inside.

The messenger tossed his shotgun and sidearm out the opposite window and hoisted both hands.

The driver and messenger climbed onto the driver's bench, the driver picked up the reins, and released the foot brake.

Duncan and Donald stepped up, looked across at each other, and slapped the rumps of both lead horses.

The horses snorted, kicked a little, and pulled the coach down the road at a trot.

Duncan pulled off his flour sack and smiled. "Well done, all around."

Juanita and Donald pulled off their sacks and waited for orders.

"Come on, Donald. Give me a hand with this."

They carried the heavy strongbox up the road, turned off into the trees, and lifted the box onto the back of the wagon.

Duncan climbed up and slid the box forward, half under the seat.

Juanita slid the cradled weapons close to the strongbox and helped Duncan cover everything with a canvas tarpaulin.

Juanita ran to the campfire and hugged China Sue. "You have been a brave, good girl."

Sue smiled and hugger her back. "I go home now?"

"I DON'T MEAN TO TELL you how to do this," said Franklin Mosby, riding on Mike's left. "However, it seems to me, we're not likely to catch anybody robbing that stage when we've stopped for breakfast."

Mike smiled, pleasantly filled with flapjacks and bacon. "We do not want to get shot at, or to get the Wells Fargo driver and guards shot. Whoever might rob the stage will surely travel back down this road. The Oakland ferry has been decommissioned over a taxation squabble up in Sacramento. I already know what Duncan

Frack looks like. He comes this way, we will have him cold, along with whoever else is helping him."

Franklin said, "Doesn't he know what you look like?"

Riding on Mike's right, Preslova asked, "What if they ride upriver and take a boat back from there."

Mike said, "We will still know who is the inside man. It is somebody working for the U.S. Treasury. We can work it back from there."

A single horse pulling a flatbed wagon rounded a corner a quarter mile up the road.

"Why am I here," asked Franklin. "What does this have to do with my daughter?"

"I needed help in case we run into trouble. I hope you do not begrudge me this small courtesy."

Franklin bit down on whatever else bothered him. He already knew why he'd been asked to come.

The woman driving the wagon toward them looked familiar. Mike wasn't sure from where. "That hat."

Franklin lifted a wary eye at Mike. "What?"

"That woman's hat. I have seen it before." Her flattop, black hat with gold embroidery identified its Mexican heritage. "She helped with a train robbery a few months ago. She waited offtrack with their getaway horses."

A little Chinese girl rode on the wagon bench with her.

At twenty yards, Mike held up his hand, ordering her to stop.

She slapped reins and her horse bolted forward, forcing Mike, Franklin, and Preslova to scatter.

Mike kicked Jasmine and leaned forward, rushing after the speeding wagon.

The Chinese child turned and held the back rail of the bench, eyes wild with fright.

Mike glanced back.

Franklin and Preslova rode hard to keep up.

Mike slowly overtook and passed the wagon. He leaned out, grabbed the reins, and leaned back, slowing Jasmine and the wagon.

A gunshot rang out and Mike looked back.

Stopped at the sides of the wagon, Franklin and Preslova trained their revolvers on the woman, motioning for her to drop her shotgun. She set it in back and sank down onto the bench, signaling surrender.

Mike held the wagon reins while he dismounted.

The Chinese girl stood on the bench and shouted at the woman. "I want my mommy!"

Preslova circled to the front of the wagon, dismounted, and took the wagon reins from Mike.

The woman threw both arms around the child. "Oh, please don't hurt us, kind sirs. We have nothing for you to steal." Her accent matched her Mexican hat.

Mike laughed softly and hid behind Jasmine, forcing himself to get serious before stepping out around her. He opened his coat and displayed his state badge. "Sorry, madam. We have no intention of harming you in any way. We need to take a look." He reached into the wagon, threw back the tarp, and exposed the Wells Fargo strongbox. "What is this?"

Chapter Thirty-Six

MOST OF TOMMY CHANDLER'S boarders had shipped out and his downstairs parlor was empty, when Dink Watkins rushed in, waving a newspaper. He slapped it onto the bar in front of Tommy Chandler.

"The Daily Evening Bulletin? I never read that rag." He grabbed it, ready to throw it back in Dink's face, then the headline grabbed him. "WOMAN ARRESTED WITH WELLS FARGO STRONGBOX."

"Why bring this to me?" *How could Dink know?*

"You, Tommy. You once sent me to the Forge with a message. I seen this woman. The man brought stuff here to you. You know how much little Dink watches what's about. Don't you trust me no more?"

Tommy drew a beer and set it on the bar.

Dink smiled and took a swig.

The article reported that state special officer, Mike Zabel, had intercepted a wagon driven by Juanita Sanchez, of this city. The U.S. Treasury strongbox had been taken this morning during a stage robbery, on the road to Sacramento.

The strongbox, believed to be carrying a significant sum of newly minted gold, would be stored in the special officer's home until it could be returned to the U.S. Treasury on Monday.

"I hate that Russian." Tommy's long history with that no-account, Count Mike, went back to the count's first arrival. He'd stayed in Tommy's boardinghouse, built up a debt, and had refused to go to sea as payment. Tommy had, of course, seized the man's property, a stupid fur coat and cap, and a Russian officer's sword and sash. He looked up at the sword and sash, still hanging on the wall above Tommy's bar. He smiled.

When the count had tried to take back his property, Tommy had used his championship boxing skills to beat him down. Thinking he'd accidentally killed the man, Tommy, and this here Dink, had dumped him through a hole in the floor, sinking him into the briny sludge under the wharf. They'd both figured the crabs would eat him.

Months later, when he'd walked into Abe Warner's Palace wearing the no-account count's coat and cap, the no-account had the effrontery to pay Tommy his overdue rent and demand the return of his property.

Tommy had, of course, claimed to have won the coat and cap in a prizefight with a sluggard. The no-account count had demanded a rematch on the spot, to which Tommy had been eager to comply.

I wasn't ready for that.

The count had gained weight, had become fit, and had received some top-level training from heavyweight champ John Drury, and from that dangerous little Portuguese, Raul Perez.

The no-account's speed, his well-placed punches, and the power the no-account count had delivered that night had surprised Tommy. Stunned dizzy, laying on the floor, outraged, Tommy had pulled a derringer from his boot to do away with the no-account once and for all.

That stupid, no-account count had moved too fast. He'd stomped on Tommy's gun hand and the gun had gone off. It had taken a minute for Tommy to realize that he'd shot himself in his left hand. That shot had ended his boxing career, forever.

Now this. That no-account count had spoiled the best robbery yet, one-hundred-thousand-dollars in new gold coin. Tommy would figure a way to make him pay for that.

"Well, look at that." Tommy filled Dink's beer and motioned for him to find a table across the room.

Donald Thorne and Duncan Frack crept up to the bar, blinking and looking sideways at Tommy. It might get interesting. They couldn't know what Tommy knew.

Tommy slid the Bulletin under the bar, smiled, and drew two beers, eager to hear what they'd say.

Duncan lowered his head, took a sip of beer, and spoke softly. "I don't know what happened. The robbery went perfect. We put the strongbox, heavier than any before, we put it on the wagon, and then we sent Juanita to carry it home. We ferried across four hours later. We just got back."

Donald tossed down a mouthful of beer and nudged Duncan aside. "His woman run off with the gold."

Duncan pulled his revolver and lowered it onto the bar, glaring down at Donald. "That's a lie."

Donald said, "She was supposed to bring it to their shack down in the basin. We got there but it looks like she never came back. She had a little China doll with her." He stared up at Duncan, unafraid.

Duncan turned to Tommy. "I thought she might have come straight here."

Tommy grinned, pulled up, and slid the newspaper across the bar. "Either of you morons know how to read?"

Donald read the short article quickly, then passed it to Duncan.

Duncan shied, maybe unable to read.

Donald said, "Sorry, Duncan. I owe you an apology." He asked Tommy, "Who's Mike Zabel?"

Tommy looked into Duncan. "That state copper arrested Juanita and took the gold to his home for the weekend."

Duncan grinned. "I know right where that man lives. We'll get that strongbox back, tonight."

Tommy said, "This smells like a trap to me. Maybe we should let it be."

Duncan picked up and looked at his beer, thinking about it. He looked at Tommy with absolute certainty. "I can't do that. He's got Juanita."

Tommy said, "She's in jail. You got a plan for that?"

Duncan swilled his beer and burped. "I'm working on it."

Tommy said, "If you go up there, end that no-account Russian's stinking life."

Duncan smiled. He liked that. "If he's dead, won't it be hard to keep Juanita in jail?"

"Maybe." Tommy glanced at the newspaper. "The Bulletin didn't say anything about witnesses."

Duncan smiled. "No witnesses, no court case."

Tommy leaned close. "This gets back to me, you'll both meet a very painful end, especially if I'm in jail."

DUNCAN AND DONALD TIED their horses to a hitching post on the corner, three houses down from Count Mike's house, all dark, in and out. Duncan still didn't know exactly how to work this. He'd feel better, had he eaten some Chinese liver, even just in the past couple of days.

Donald stood in the center of the brick paved street, looking up and down both sides. "Which house?"

Duncan pointed. "That one over there. The dark one."

Donald said, "It looks like nobody's home."

"They might be down at the White Chapel Saloon. His wife owns that place."

"His wife owns a saloon?"

"It's a boardinghouse." Duncan walked uphill, crossed the road, and stood in front of Mike Zabel's house. The transom window above the front door showed a flicker of light from deep inside the house. "He's here. Go up and knock."

Donald planted both of his feet, like he might think he's anchored himself to the brick paving. "Me? What for?"

"I'll be right there with you, just a step back. Soon as the door cracks open, I'll rush it, and you follow me inside."

"Then what?"

"We shoot the count, and anybody else. Only, just wound him. Then, we'll find the strongbox."

"Me? Shoot?"

Duncan said, "I know you ain't afraid to shoot a man."

"He's a state lawman and he's supposed to be plenty dangerous."

Duncan glared down at Donald. "He's got a wife and kid to worry about. He don't give me Juanita and give us that box, I'll cook and eat his kid's liver. He already knows that."

Duncan had finally formed a clear plan, a good plan.

"Okay." Donald ducked out from under Duncan's stare and crept up the brick steps onto the brick front porch.

Duncan trotted up the steps, no noise on bricks, and stood two feet behind Donald. He nodded.

Donald knocked softly, three times.

"I bust through that door, you follow me and look for somebody to take down. Don't kill anybody before we get that box."

They waited at least two minutes, but nobody came to the door.

"Knock louder."

Donald knocked louder, four times.

Bright light showed through the stained-glass transom window over the door.

Duncan lowered his shoulder and positioned his feet.

The latch turned, the door cracked open, and Duncan Frack lunged forward. His lowered shoulder hit the door and threw it wide open. He stumbled into the well-lit entry and fell forward. The side of his face hit the query-tile floor, where he painfully skidded to a stop.

Donald rushed in right behind, tripped across Duncan's tangled feet, and landed hard on Duncan's head.

They untangled themselves quickly, Duncan rolled onto a knee, and stared into the twin barrels of his own scattergun.

"Is nice of you boys to drop in." Count Mike pressed the scattergun to Duncan's forehead.

Duncan rocked back onto his butt and threw up both hands. "We're done."

Donald sat on the floor next to Duncan, staring at a cocked revolver held by the little Portuguese he'd heard so much about.

MIKE AND RAUL RETURNED home with Han Wok at 10:05 p.m., Saturday night. Han had been at the police station front desk, reporting another missing Chinese child, his cousin.

Mike and Raul hadn't said anything to Han at the station, just that Mike had something to talk over, and they'd brought him along.

Mike and Han turned into Mike's office. Mike turned up the wall sconce and motioned to the chair in front of his desk.

Raul went into the kitchen without discussion. He knew what to do.

Han sat, dour faced over worry for his cousin. "Was that Duncan Frack you brought in?"

"It was." Mike smiled and sat behind his desk.

"So, why am I here? We need to find my cousin. She's just a baby."

"I understand you want to marry Chiang SuLin." Mike frowned across his desk. He needed to discuss something, anything. "You didn't think it necessary to ask me? I might have something to say about it."

Han's eyes popped wide open. His mouth dropped. "What? You don't . . ."

"Han Wok," shrieked little Susie, rushing toward Han.

Han spun in his chair and Susie slammed into him, throwing both arms around his neck.

Chapter Thirty-Seven

FOLLOWING CHURCH SERVICE on Sunday morning, Paddy took Raul, Jimmy, and the ladies to their Russian Hill home.

Mike took a taxi down to the Barbary Coast. He got out on the corner and took the alley into the kitchen of the White Chapel Saloon.

Martha and Sally worked over their new gas stove, dumping shoestring-sliced beets into a large cook pot.

"Hmm. I haven't smelled borsch in many years." Mike breathed deep, the familiar aroma from his Crimean youth.

Martha smiled. "Good morning to you, Michael. Your friend, the colonel, he's been teaching us. It does smell wonderful, this time."

"This time?"

"We've had a couple of disasters. Sally, here, thought she knew better."

Sally waved a wooden spoon at Martha. "Shush, you . . ." She turned and grinned at Mike.

"Is my colonel here?"

Martha said, "Aye. He's in there, reading last night's Bulletin. Billy's telling him, anyways." She tapped her wooden spoon on the rim of the pot and set it on a plate. "With the smell of this pot, everybody's up."

Mike said, "I love a good borsch. How soon is it ready to eat?"

Sally sniffed and swept a sleeve across her tear-streaked face. She'd been dicing onions. "Ask the colonel to come in and give us a whiff."

Five sailors Mike didn't know sat at the dining room table, randomly scattered between Franklin, Moses, Preslova, and Billy. Chiang SuLin and Chiang Po sat near Molly's old bedroom.

Mike said, "My colonel, the ladies want you in the kitchen."

Preslova smiled at Mike, stood, and marched into the kitchen.

Mike walked to the end of the table, lifted SuLin, and wrapped her in a brief hug. "I heard the news from Han Wok. When were you going to tell me?"

She smiled and looked away.

"When?"

She covered her smile and refused to look at him. "We kneel to Taoist Buddha on Friday, January nineteen. We have Christian wedding on Saturday, January twenty, at Saint Mary's Cathedral. You and your family go worship there, right?"

"Yes, we do. We just left there, in fact." He hugged her tight, then pushed her to arm's length. "Are you happy?"

"Han is good man?"

"I think he is."

"Then we are happy to marry him. You come to church wedding, yes?"

"Yes. We would never miss this one."

A Christmas tree filled the space next to the main stair, decorated to the top with cut-out dolls, colorful paper loops, and unlit candles on small, ceramic holders.

Mike backed toward the tree and addressed the room. "Molly will deliver two large geese for your Christmas dinner. We will try to stop by after Christmas Mass."

Preslova carried in a large serving bowl and set it at the center of the dining table. "Ukrainian borsch is served."

Martha and Sally carried in soup bowls, spoons, and a platter of hot biscuits. Everybody stood and crowded the table. Two sailors pushed to the front and Mike stepped in to block them. He pulled

SuLin to the front of the line. "Ladies?" He motioned for Sally and Martha to follow SuLin.

The sailors eased back, smiling shyly.

After everybody else had filled their bowls and started eating, Mike ladled a bowl for himself and sat next to Preslova.

Mike's memories of home flooded in with the first spoonful. "Very tasty, my colonel."

Preslova said, "This still needs improvement. We are getting closer. It is hard to find fresh beets, this time of year."

Mike finished his borsch, wiped his mouth, and leaned close to Franklin. "Can you and Moses spend some time with me today?"

Franklin swallowed borsch and wiped his mouth with his napkin. "How long?"

"I need to go up to the city jail." Mike shrugged. "They might have some information."

Franklin tapped Moses and they both stood. Franklin said, "Give us a minute."

Moses followed Franklin up the main stairs.

Mike turned to Billy. "There might be a story in this."

Billy wiped his face, stood, and rushed upstairs.

Preslova said, "I am bored. I will also come."

THE DESK SERGEANT EYED Mike and his group suspiciously. He didn't know Mike and Mike didn't know him.

Mike said, "By chance, is Detective Sergeant Angus McFee in?"

The sergeant said, "What's this about?"

Mike lifted his coat to display his state police badge. "I am State Special Officer, Mike Zabel." He pointed. "These are my deputies, Vladimir Preslova, Moses Broadback, and Franklin Mosby." He pointed. "This one is William Cahill, reporter for the Daily Evening Bulletin. Moses is an eye witness to kidnapping and murder."

"Do all six of you need to see McFee?" He shook off his own question. "He's not in on Sundays. Come back tomorrow morning, after nine."

Mike smiled, being patient. "We brought in two prisoners last night. They are being held for U.S. Treasury Agent, Percy Bickford. We need to talk to the prisoners, now."

The sergeant pulled out the desk log, opened it to the daily page, dipped his quill pen into the ink well, and handed it to Mike.

Mike signed in and handed the pen back.

The sergeant asked, "You know the way?"

"I do." Mike led the others through the squad room to the cellblock.

Chunky sat, slumped over his desk, snoring softly.

Mike took the keys from the wall hook, opened the cellblock door, and led the others through the twisting maze of mostly occupied cells, two prisoners over here, three there. Near the back, they stopped at the cell holding Donald Thorne and Duncan Frack.

Frack reclined on the upper bunk, awake.

Donald Thorne stopped pacing and faced Mike. "Why you holding me? I didn't do nothing. This guy come and asked me to help him collect a debt."

Duncan Frack threw his legs over the edge of his bunk and sat, looking angrily at the back of Thorne's head. He silently dropped to the floor. "That's right. I thought your house was the home of James Winters. He owes me money."

Mike smiled. "You kidnapped my wife and son. You held me against my will. There has been a warrant out for your arrest for more than a week, under the name of Jack Wick, for robbing a train."

Frack blinked and shook his head. "Must be somebody looks like me."

Mike pulled Moses forward.

"That's him, Mr. Mike. He took little Mellie and killed Allison Mosby. I know his eyes."

Thorne lurched to the jail bars and reached through for Moses. "What're you talking about, nigger? I ain't never seen you before."

"No, sir. But I seen you."

Franklin cranked Thorne's extended arm backward against the bar.

"Ahh!" Thorne recoiled in pain and grabbed another bar with his free hand.

"Where's my daughter? Where's Melanie? Is she . . ?"

Thorne grimaced with pain, spitting words at Franklin through dark stained teeth. "Mister, I don't know what you're talking about."

THAT AFTERNOON, HAN Wok led one of his waitresses to the corner table, where the fat jailer scooped his third plate of peeled shrimp into his oily, fat face. He sat across from the man and pushed back in his chair, repulsed by his disgusting eating habits.

The waitress set a fourth plate of shrimp in front of him and carried the empty plates away.

Han said, "So, what you think?"

The jailer chewed, and chewed, and chewed with his mouth open, shifting shrimps around in there. He finally swallowed and chugged a whole cup of tea. "I hate that Count Mike. He made me look real bad today. He took a bunch of people into the cellblock without me even knowing."

"So, what you think?"

He scooped in more shrimp, chewed, and chewed, and chewed, and stared at Han. He finally swallowed. "It'll cost you a thousand dollars."

Han shook his head. "Too much!" He stood and started to leave.

"Look here, Han. You're asking me to take a big chance. How can I explain, two guys gone from their cell? Answer me that."

Han slid back into his chair, put his elbows on the table, and leaned forward, speaking softly. "I only need the tall one."

"I gotta unlock the cell door for both of them or it won't look right."

"What time you get off tonight?"

"Midnight."

"Who follow you? Maybe I speak to him, huh?"

The fat jailer said, "Not sure. It'll probably be Tommy Olson. He's just a kid."

"He check everything when he come on?"

"No. He doesn't like going back there, says it stinks." He smiled, chomped shrimp, and slurped tea. "It does stink. I'm the one who trades out the waste buckets and brings in the fresh." He chewed peeled shrimp and thought about it. "Okay, how much?"

"Two hundred."

The fat jailer scoffed. "You silly little Chin. Why, I ought to break your scrawny neck."

"You eat free for one year. Final offer."

He thought and swallowed, took another bite, and chewed. He swallowed and swilled tea. "Plus your two hundred?"

Han set ten twenty-dollar gold coins on the table.

The jailer scooped up and counted the coins. "Okay, then. I'll let them out the back, around eleven thirty."

Han said, "We only need the tall one."

"Gotta let 'em both out. Can't leave one behind to talk. I only hope the other prisoners are sleeping."

Han stood. "You only eat free one meal a day. Is okay?"

The fat jailor thought for a second. "Sure."

Han left the table.

DONALD THORNE HADN'T been able to sleep. He'd been pacing the eight-foot-square cell in the dark, with the sounds of sleep all around. How Duncan could sleep mystified his senses. Evidence against Duncan was strong. All they had against Donald was some stupid nigger's word.

A lamp turned low cast faint light through the bars between cells. The shadows slanted and overlapped as the light approached.

The jailer reached their cell and quietly slipped a key into the lock. He whispered, "Don't say nothin'. Somebody paid good money to get you two outa here." He opened the door. "Get him up and be quiet about it."

Duncan already sat on the edge of the upper bunk. He dropped silently to the floor and pulled Donald out of the cell.

The jailer left the door ajar and quietly led them toward the back. He carefully inserted a flat key into the lock on a large steel door. He turned the key with a loud clank.

Everybody froze and looked back into the dark cellblock.

The soft, steady sounds of sleep had not been interrupted.

The hinges squealed softly as the jailer pulled the door inward. He motioned for them to get out.

Without hesitation, Duncan dragged Donald outside.

Donald shivered and crouched, feeling uneasy. He looked back.

The jailer had left the door ajar. Donald could go back inside.

No.

Moisture slicked the irregular brick walls and brick paving of the narrow alley that followed the downhill slope into dense fog. Moonglow above the fog cast an eerie, blue light, making it easy for them to see their way.

Duncan grabbed Donald's arm and thrust him to the front. He shoved from behind and said, "I told you not to worry. Tommy's got our backs."

Donald slipped and stumbled on wet bricks, barely catching himself from taking a tumble. "Take it easy." He looked back at Duncan but Duncan was looking below.

Thirty yards downhill, at the bottom of the alley, a pale-yellow streetlight winked through blue fog, surrounded by a yellow corona. A small, dark form stepped under the light and turned toward them.

A hard, cold chill gripped Donald's spine and he froze.

Duncan pushed from behind but Donald couldn't budge.

Duncan said, "Well, come on."

Moving quickly from under the light, the black form danced up the alley toward them.

Duncan said, "That's a Tong hatchet man. I should have ate that little Chinese doll's liver. I would of got more power."

Donald said, "Hatchet man?"

The small, dark form danced ever closer, his elbows moving up and down, his legs kicking in and out, skipping and spinning like a cat on a rainy day. His black, flattop hat seemed not to move.

Donald asked, "Is he wearing Pajamas?"

"Downright creepy, ain't it?"

His black form disappeared into the dark shadows of the alley, making him impossible to see. He reappeared, closer, magically floating in the misty-blue glow.

Duncan shouted, "You little Chink. Get up here. I'll eat your liver." He crouched and braced for a fight, instinctively reaching back for a knife that wasn't there.

The little black pajama man in the flattop hat twirled and jumped, hatchet in hand.

"You little . . ." Duncan lunged.

Black pajamas danced to one side and jumped high. He came down quick as a blink, with the thump of metal on bone.

Duncan dropped to his knees. His arms hung limp.

Black pajamas in the flattop hat stepped up and wrenched his hatchet from the center of Duncan Frack's skull.

Duncan flopped forward onto wet brick paving.

The little, black-clad Chinaman in the flattop hat turned toward Donald, bowed at the waist, and brusquely walked downhill under misty blue, shifting into misty yellow light. He turned the corner at the bottom of the alley and vanished.

Chapter Thirty-Eight

TOMMY CHANDLER GOT up with the first cockcrow, stuck his head into a cold bucket of water, and brushed his teeth. He liked the predawn hours, being alone to brew coffee, cook bacon and cornmeal, and to read the newspapers.

When the coffee smelled right, Tommy took the pot off his wood burning stove, poured himself a cup, and opened the previous night's edition of the Daily Evening Bulletin.

"I hate this rag." But the Sunday Times wouldn't arrive for another hour or more.

"TWO MEN ARRESTED while BREAKING INTO MIKE ZABEL'S HOME."

Idiots!

Tommy read the article quickly, reporting how Duncan Frack and Donald Thorne had forced entry into Mike and Molly Zabel's home on Russian Hill. They'd been taken into custody and were being held in the city jail. They would face a grand jury at 9:00 a.m. on Tuesday. *Day after tomorrow.*

They, and Juanita Sanchez, would be charged with stagecoach robbery.

Duncan Frack would be facing charges of stagecoach robbery, train robbery, kidnapping, murder, and cannibalism.

What?

Cannibalism didn't fit his notion of Duncan Frack. He'd always been a reliable operative. Tommy sipped coffee.

Donald Thorne bolted through the front door, stumbled across the room, and lunged against Tommy's bar, out of breath. "He's dead."

"Who ... What're you doing here? You're supposed to be in jail."

"Duncan's dead."

"What? Who killed him, that no-account, Count Mike?"

"No. He was a hatchet man. Duncan said. I never saw nothin' like that. Not even in the war." Donald motioned for a beer, still finding breath.

Tommy dragged a mug off the shelf, drew a beer, raked foam, refilled it, and set it on the bar. He walked back to his stove and slid the cornmeal and bacon skillets to the side.

He turned back to the bar.

Donald set his empty mug on the bar, burped, and motioned for more.

Tommy obliged.

Donald took two swallows and set the mug on the bar. "I figured it was you who got us out. Then, out in that dark alley . . ." He shook his head and took another drink. "I still can't figure why he let me go."

Tommy had read about the missing Chinese kids and the cannibalism with that Russian duchess. It all made sense. "I learned a long time ago not to mess with the Tong."

Donald sipped beer, waiting and wondering.

Tommy said, "I've been reading about a man who called himself Jack Wick, kidnapping Chinese kids and eating them."

Donald's eyes opened wide. He nodded. "That was Duncan. I couldn't watch. He fried and ate their livers. Him and that Russian princess."

Tommy said, "The Tong sent their hatchet man for Duncan. He didn't care about you."

"Who's the Tong?"

Tommy turned to the stove, refilled his coffee, and turned back to the bar. "The Tong control a lot of Chinese slave labor and they run the opium trade. I learned never to tangle with the Chinese. They think and plan everything to the last detail before they make a move." He sipped coffee. It tasted good. "I never learned to play chess."

Donald finished his beer and set it on the bar, waving off a refill. "I never even heard of Chinese before I moved here."

Tommy said, "Look, the police will be coming for you. You need to get upstairs, collect your gear, and get out of here."

"Where am I supposed to go?"

Tommy asked, "Don't You know where Duncan lived?"

"Oh, yeah. Yes. Yes I do."

WHEN MIKE AND FRANKLIN met in front of the courthouse at 8:15 a.m., Tuesday, Franklin asked, "What happens now?"

Mike said, "We need to give evidence before the Grand Jury about our seizure of the U.S. Treasury strongbox and the arrest of Juanita Sanchez. Then, I need to testify about my arrest of Duncan Frack, for various crimes, and my arrest of Donald Thorne for armed robbery and for unlawfully entering my home. Following the indictments, we need to apply for a search warrant. You'll need to tell the judge why you think your daughter is being held at Tommy Chandler's Boardinghouse."

U.S. Treasury Agent, Percy Bickford, climbed out of a taxi and strode up to Mike and Franklin. "Good morning, Mike." He shook Mike's hand and eyed Franklin.

Mike said, "Franklin Mosby, meet U.S. Treasury Agent, Percy Bickford."

They shook hands.

"Franklin, here, is one of my special deputies." Mike faced Percy, "So, what brings you here?"

Percy spread his coat, stuffed his thumbs into his vest pockets, and rocked up onto the balls of his feet. "My little plan worked, didn't it?"

Mike smiled, thinking what to say. "I've still got the locked strongbox. It hasn't even been opened. We'll swear it into evidence at the trial."

"I need it back after? I'd like to keep it in my office back in Washington." He grinned. "You know, kind of a trophy."

Mike couldn't help himself. "No, no. I'm keeping that with my other memorabilia. It's sitting next to a gold chess set I got from the Chinese community up in Weaverville, right next to my mink coat and cap."

"What?" Percy stepped back and spread his hands. "But . . ."

"This is my jurisdiction." He poked a thumb toward Franklin. "We recovered that strongbox, and we made the arrests."

Percy's arms flapped like a seagull's wings, groping morning mist. "What? Why the . . ."

Mike smiled. "Just having a little fun, Percy. The box belongs to the U.S. Treasury Department. If it's alright with them, it's alright with me."

Percy choked out a short laugh and unwound.

Mike put a hand on Percy's shoulder. "I couldn't help myself. The moment seized my better judgement."

Several taxies had, by then, parked in front of the courthouse.

A police wagon stopped in the middle of California Street and Sergeant Angus McFee climbed down, followed by Billy Cahill.

They joined Mike and the others, nodding hellos, shaking hands. McFee said, "I'm glad you're here."

Mike said, "Of course. We have an arraignment."

McFee said, "We had a jailbreak last night. Donald Thorne and Duncan Frack went out the alley door. We found it unlocked, this morning. They got out sometime after midnight. Dunkan Frack's body was found early this morning, laying facedown in the alley. His skull was slit like a melon.

"We're on our way down to Chandler's with a search party." He pointed to the police wagon. "It looks like Frack and Thorne might have had an argument. I've got another squad on their way to the end of Pacific Street Wharf. I thought you two might want to join in."

TOMMY CHANDLER SKIPPED rope near the open doorway to his office, watching his Chinese coolie dish out cornmeal mush and bacon for his seafaring tenants. Even though his fighting days had abruptly ended when he shot himself in the hand, Tommy worked at keeping fit.

The front door burst open and four uniformed police officers rushed in, quickly standing and backing his tenants against the walls. Two more uniformed officers strolled in to block any possible exit.

The no-account count strolled in with Sergeant Angus McFee, that young news reporter from the Bulletin, and that well-dressed gentleman who'd asked about a room. The very one who'd stayed to play poker with Dink Watkins and Donald Thorne.

Tommy never forgot a face.

The no-account count marched up to Tommy's bar like a strutting cock, waving a folded sheet of white paper. "We have a warrant to search this establishment."

Tommy looped his jump rope over a post hook and grabbed the paper. He quickly unfolded and read it. "A man named Donald Thorne and a little girl?" He tossed the warrant onto the bar, happy to watch it land in a puddle of bacon grease. "You know I don't let kids in here."

No-account said, "We will take a look, just the same."

McFee, two uniforms, and the well-dressed gent trotted upstairs.

Tommy rounded his bar and squared to the no-account count. "You want to search my office? They might be hiding in there." He didn't expect a search of his office to take place.

The no-account brushed past Tommy, strolled into his office, and quickly stepped back out.

Tommy smiled big at the no-account. His office was too small to hide even a kid, and his well-concealed floor safe was nearly impossible to find.

No-account pulled rolled-up paper from inside his coat, unrolled it, and showed Tommy a charcoal sketch of Donald Thorne, from before he'd shaved his head and beard. He said, "This is the man we are searching for."

Tommy took a long look, being sure to fully cooperate. He shook his head. "Who is he, anyway?"

"His name is Donald Thorne." The no-account remembered something, stepped sideways, and pulled up the trash door, where he'd been dumped nearly ten years earlier. Finding nobody, he dropped the door back into place.

"Donald Thorne sounds familiar." Tommy held up a finger and looked at the floor. He looked back, grinning. "Oh, yeah. You just told me that. Who is he? What did he do?"

"He escaped jail last night with another man. The other man was found dead, early this morning. His name was Duncan Frack, alias Jack Wick."

"What? Am I supposed to know him too?"

No-account rolled up the sketch and returned it to his inside coat pocket. He turned toward the stairs.

McFee, his two uniforms, and the well-dressed gent descended the stairs slowly, empty handed.

Tommy picked up the grease-soaked warrant and held it out toward the no-account. "If your finished harassing my tenants . . ."

No-account glanced at the warrant, then looked above Tommy's bar. "Ah, my sword and sash. I had forgotten all about this." He squared to Tommy and smiled, confident, and eager to take them by force.

Tommy jumped onto his bar, unhooked the dusty sword and sash, jumped down, and handed them over. "I've been keeping them safe, just for you."

Sword and sash in hand, the no-account turned toward the door and led the search party out.

Tommy grabbed his skip rope and resumed his exercises.

Dink Watkins hurried in from the wharf and rushed up to the bar. "You, Tommy. Was they looking for little Dink?"

Chapter Thirty-Nine

MIKE LED BILLY CAHILL and Franklin Mosby down the alley behind the White Chapel Saloon, through the back gate, up the step, and through the back door into the unusually vacant kitchen.

Martha and Sally sat in the dining room, close behind Moses Broadback, watching him chalk a portrait of Molly. Molly sat in the sitting room, sideways to the light from the bay windows. She did not turn to welcome Mike and the others.

Raul stood and looked into Franklin, anxious for any news.

Franklin shook his head and sat at the far end of the table, staring into his open hands. "Donald Thorne escaped jail. We have no idea where he and my daughter might be. They've already vacated Tommy Chandler's."

Raul said, "I been waiting for you to get here. You remember when I told you how I followed Thorne to that Duncan Frack guy's new hideout?"

Franklin looked at Mike, expecting answers.

Mike said, "Raul, go hail a large taxi."

Raul hurried out the front door.

Mike bent and kissed Molly's forehead. "Please, my love, do not hold the lunch for us." Mike led Billy and Franklin out the front door.

Raul stood on the corner, waving and whistling up the street.

Mike checked both his Navy Colts for load, then followed Billy and Franklin toward the corner.

A two horse, double-bench taxi stopped at the corner.

Raul opened the door for Mike and the others, followed them in, and tagged the driver. "Take us down to China Basin. I tell you where on the way."

The taxi turned onto Front Street and quickly lurched to a lope. After a mile of travel, nearing China Basin, Raul leaned forward and tapped the driver's back. "Stop here."

The taxi stopped, everybody climbed out, and Mike said, "Wait here."

The driver set his foot-brake.

Raul led them down a muddy road between tents and canvas roofed shacks. He stopped about fifty feet from a small, stone and wood building. A colorful, Mexican blanket over the door had been pulled back, probably for fresh air.

What fresh air? It smelled worse than under the planks of the Barbary Coast.

Raul turned to face Mike and the others, speaking softly. "This is where I followed him. He went inside, and I ran to find you."

Mike pulled his shoulder-holstered Colt and handed it to Billy. "He'll recognize all of us. No getting around it. We'll need to walk in there and take our chances, or hide out here and wait. This is not my decision to make." He looked at Franklin. "She is your daughter. She might be hurt."

The others studied their surroundings, looking for places to hide.

Chinese women with babies gawked at them, some doing their laundry, others stooped over cooking pots. No men could be seen. Many places to hide might be possible, with so many tents and shacks crowding each other.

Mike looked from Raul to Billy, and from Billy to Franklin. Nobody wanted to make this decision. "Franklin?"

"Sir, I'm happy to follow your lead."

Mike smiled, unable to stop himself. He jokingly said, "Coward."

"I know." Franklin smiled and waited.

Mike pulled his hip-holstered Colt. "We cannot risk shooting any innocents, especially not Franklin's daughter."

Franklin pulled his weapon and looked toward the stone shack.

Mike blocked Franklin and the others. "All of you should wait out here."

Mike cocked his Colt, crossed the muddy road, and ducked past the blanket into darkness.

Something heavy rammed into his right side and a strong hand grabbed his right wrist, controlling the gun.

Mike's left shoulder slammed into the stone wall at an angle and Mike rolled with the momentum, pulling the other man in front of him and onto the dirt floor.

The man's grip tightened on Mike's wrist, his trigger finger flexed, and the Colt discharged with a deafening boom.

The flash lit Donald Thorne's angry face.

In a frozen moment, a child screamed from the darkness, as Thorne pressed a knife toward Mike's throat.

Mike's left forearm braced against the crook of Thorne's elbow and locked his arm. He rolled slightly and pressed his left shoulder over the flat of Thorne's knife hand.

Mike's eyes quickly adjusted and he head-butted Thorne's nose, not enough. He head-butted Thorn's nose again.

Thorne grunted, with blood and tears oozing from his snarling face.

Mike stretched and twisted, freeing his right wrist. He pressed the Colt into Thorne's left eye socket and cocked it. "Give it up."

Thorne relaxed.

"Drop the knife."

The knife slacked under Mike's left shoulder.

Shadows danced against the wall and a woman said, "What are you doing? Get out of my house."

Standing over Mike and Thorne, Raul said, "I got him, Mister Mike."

Mike pushed off the floor and put his knee on the knife. He withdrew the gun and Thorne's left eye blinked open, looking into Mike. "I told you, I thought we was collecting a debt. I barely knew that guy."

Mike reached inside his coat, found the shackles, and rolled Thorne onto his stomach. He pulled Thorne's arms behind his back and clamped on the shackles. "Is that why you killed him?"

"Killed who?"

Mike stood and dragged Thorne to his feet.

The woman huddled in the corner, protecting a little girl. "Get out of my house!"

Mike said, "Madam, you will need to come with us."

Franklin rushed in, Billy right behind, and both waited a moment for their eyes to adjust.

Franklin turned to look at the woman and child. "Melanie?"

The little girl looked at Franklin for a long minute, slowly climbing to her feet. "Daddy?"

Franklin dropped to a knee and extended his arms.

The child rushed into his embrace. "Daddy! Daddy!" She pushed away and scowled at Thorne. "You told me my daddy was dead."

Thorne looked at the dirt floor.

Mike pushed him toward the door. "Raul, can you bring the woman?"

"WHEN WE TOLD JUANITA about Duncan Frack's death, she refused to believe it." Sergeant Angus McFee placed his hands, palms down, on his desk, wagging his head like a horse with ear mites.

"When I took her to the coroner's and showed her, she collapsed to the floor. Since then, she's been a flood of information."

Billy frantically scribbled notes.

Mike thought about the possibilities. Did they really have a case against Donald Thorne? Could Thorne or Juanita lead him to Tommy Chandler? He asked, "Did she positively identify Thorne?"

"Yes, for two stagecoach robberies, a train robbery, and for the shotgun murder of a guard. She swears her man didn't do that. She says he never killed anybody."

"I doubt her testimony would stand up." Mike shook his head. "I saw the dead body of a Chinese boy, and my wife watched the killing. Frack cut the boy open, took out the liver, fried it in lard, and shared it with Lady Catherine. Juanita was not in the room, at that time."

"Those kids were Chinese. Nobody cares." McFee grimaced. He didn't like having said that. He knew Mike didn't like hearing it.

Mike said, "I care. So does the governor. Do I need to bring him into the chief's office for a talk with the both of you?"

McFee took a sheepish step back. "Come on, Mike. I'm just saying . . ."

Mike forced himself to calm. "Here is the point. Her saying Frack never killed anybody brings the rest of her testimony into question. She might have killed that guard herself. Or, she might just be protecting her dead lover."

McFee said, "After you brought Thorne and the woman in, we searched the shack they lived in. We found more evidence, which is at least part of why she opened up."

Mike sat on McFee's desk to listen.

Billy scribbled notes.

McFee said, "Their wood-burning stove had been recently dragged in there and set over a slapdash layer of flat stones. A curiosity overtook me, so we removed the stove and ripped up that small area of stone floor. Underneath, we found a canvas treasury sack containing five-thousand-eight-hundred and sixty dollars in twenty-dollar, Coronet-Head gold coins, and another sack containing six-hundred-twenty-two dollars and fifty cents in fifty-cent, Seated-Liberty silver coins; all fresh minted, all from the San Francisco mint." McFee sucked air and filled his chest with pride. He'd finally done some police work.

Mike asked, "Are you taking Thorne out to the Presidio, or should I?"

McFee sat and rocked back in his chair, his chin nearly resting on his puffed-up chest. "What for?"

Mike said, "Our only evidence against Donald Thorne is that he was involved with the robberies of U.S. Treasury shipments. This is a federal crime, outside our jurisdiction. We also have evidence that he engaged in kidnapping and murder. These crimes were committed in the State of Georgia, again outside our jurisdiction. According to the girl's father, local authorities down there think he was a deserter from the Union Army."

McFee sat upright, no longer puffed with pride. "Let's get a photographer in here and take his picture for our records. Then, you can take him over, if you want."

Mike said, "Of course. Do what you need to do."

McFee's eyes popped wide. "That reminds me; that lady Russian." He stood and shuffled through paperwork on his desk. He pulled up a business card and handed it to Mike.

The card read: "William Henry Seward, United States Secretary of State."

McFee said, "He wants to meet with you. He's staying at Governor Low's house. You know where that is?"

MIKE AND BILLY WAITED in Governor Low's parlor, scanning his personal library; books by Mark Twain, Charles Dickens, a lot of political writings, and some travel journals had been squeezed in with a wide variety of other published materials.

"Mike!" Governor Frederick Ferdinand Low, a man of endless energy, marched in with another, older man. Low shook Mike's hand and waved at his guest. "Mike Zabel, this is Secretary of State, Bill Seward. We met when I served in the U.S. Congress. He's the one who recommended me to President Lincoln for my Port Collector appointment."

Mike and Seward shook hands and Mike motioned toward Billy. "Governor, Mister Secretary, this is William Cahill, from the Daily Evening Bulletin. I hope you do not mind me bringing him."

"I should say not." Governor Low shook Billy's hand. "Finally, we meet. I've enjoyed your reporting since my return from Washington." He turned to Mike. "He's a fair-minded, honest journalist; a rare thing these days. A rare thing."

The governor turned to Secretary Seward. "Mike and I are trying to put legs under the railroad plans to cross the Sierra Nevada Mountains and hookup with the Union Pacific Railroad."

"Oh . . ." Mike squared to Governor Low. "I have been trying to get with you on that. I am finalizing our investment offer. We are tying in a cost of labor contract as part of our investment. We will supply labor and labor support - You know, housing, food, and a doctor. I am still working up the numbers." He shook his head. "I have been too busy. I wanted you to see this before I submit it."

Low said, "Get it to my desk, as soon as you can. I'll take it to the legislature for possible additional funding."

Seward said, "Get that to my desk, Freddie. I'll take it to the Speaker of the House. We'll get it done." He turned to Mike. "Now, to what this meeting is really about." He motioned to a circle of chairs and everyone sat.

Seward leaned forward, interlocked his fingers, and studied Mike. "You've arrested the Grand Duchess, Catherine Mikhailovna,

General, the Count Boris Romochka-Krestyanov, and Luka and Sacha Varvarinski. You are Major, the Count Mikhail Diebitsch-Zabalkansky, are you not?"

Mike stood, thinking he was being turned over to federal authority. "Not anymore."

Seward leaned back in his chair and blinked.

Governor Low chuckled. "I told you, Henry, this man doesn't push."

Mike glared down at Seward. "I am American."

Seward put up a hand, shook his head, and smiled. "Let me start over." He motioned for Mike to sit.

Mike sat, ready to jump up again.

Seward said, "The governor and I have read the charges and statements. We don't see a case against Sacha Varvarinski. We don't see her connected to any crime, other than working for a very bad lady."

Mike relaxed. "Agreed."

"You do have a strong case against the two men, and at least conspiracy and accessory counts against the duchess."

"Yes, we do."

"You may or may not be aware, but the United States is in negotiation with Czar Alexander for the purchase of Alaska. Their arrest has actually helped that process, provided the Czar's aunt and her party are released and returned to Russia. It's called a quid-pro-quo. That's when one . . ."

"I know what it means." Mike stood and loomed over Seward. "Let me get this straight. You're going to allow capital crimes to be committed on American soil, without consequence?"

Seward said, "Not exactly."

Mike said, "This is America. We are supposed to have equal justice under the law. Social rank and wealth should have no weight. Not in our system of justice."

"You are correct, sir." Secretary Seward stood, smiled, and faced Mike. "Here's the deal. The duchess, the general, and this Luka . . ." He waved his hand over his head, unable to remember or pronounce their last names. "They will all plead guilty to the charges."

Mike stepped back, doubting. "She will plead guilty to cannibalism?"

Governor Low stood and stepped between them. "No, Mike. She won't. The Czar will not consider a member of the royal family even being accused of such a thing."

"She ate the lard fried liver of a baby. My wife and son witnessed this."

Seward asked, "How old is your son?"

Mike shook his head and sat. "I cannot let him testify. He has been through enough."

The governor said, "So, it's your wife's testimony against a grand duchess, a decorated general, and two high-level servants of the duchess. They will certainly deny this ever happened."

Mike leaned back in his chair, frustrated. This was a solid legal position, even though they would be perjuring themselves.

The governor said, "They will be sentenced to the maximum extent allowed under California law. After one week of incarceration, in our state prison system, I will commute their sentences under an exit agreement. They will sign an agreement to leave this state, and this country, and to never return. They will then be escorted to this port and placed aboard a southbound steamer. Should they ever return, their sentences will be reinstated, and they will serve them in full."

Mike said, "What about the other man? He is still at large."

The governor asked, "Do you have a name?"

"Grigori Balakirev. He will certainly change his name, and I will certainly hear from them at some point in the future. They kidnapped my wife and son. They threatened torture and death."

THOMAS HOLLADAY

Mike leaned closer to the governor. "Is there any way to make them supply Balakirev's location?"

Seward said, "This deal is carved in stone, between me, the governor, and the Russian consul. Trying to add anything now might cause a problem."

Name change or not, Grigori Balakirev could be found, unless he sold *Black Swan*. Either way, Mike knew this wasn't the end of his problems with the Romanov Dynasty. He asked, "Can you let me and Billy know when and where to witness their departure?"

"Mister Cahill?" said the governor, shaking his head in Billy's direction. "As part of this arrangement, the Bulletin is to cease any publication concerning the duchess and her party. Just let the story die."

Billy's head shot back, eyes blinking. He did not like this arrangement. "What about the other newspapers?"

The governor said, "I've already contacted every publisher I could think of, including the Police Gazette. They've all agreed to leave it alone."

"It's the Bulletin's story." Billy threw an angry glance at Mike. "Thank you!"

Mike had to smile at this one. He could not help it.

The governor said, "They wanted you to write a retraction, something like these Russians were pretenders, that the duchess never left Russia."

Billy shook his head, not going to happen. "Don't push me. I'll stand on the First Amendment."

Secretary Seward placed a hand on the governor's shoulder while addressing Billy. "Mister Cahill, does the Bulletin want to be responsible for our nation's failure to acquire Alaska? This purchase will block any possibility of future Russian aggression toward the United States. It will also help protect this hemisphere, against any future threat."

Mike recognized the importance. "Russia is always at war with somebody. They swallow territories, wherever and whenever they can."

All eyes focused on Billy.

Billy asked, "Have you spoken with my publisher?"

The governor said, "He's reluctant to do anything, without speaking with you first. You seem to be of great value."

Billy looked at Mike, that *Thank you* look for his education and placement with the Bulletin. He stood with his notepad, turned to look at the books on the shelf, and turned back. "Okay. Okay. I'll write nothing more about the duchess or her party. But the Daily Evening Bulletin will not print retractions for reporting the truth. The publisher would never agree to that. And, in future, you will agree to give the Bulletin a first look at matters of political interest. That's my quid-pro-quo."

Chapter Forty

TEN DAYS LATER, ON December 24, 1865, Christmas Eve, Mike, Billy, Sergeant McFee, and Colonel Preslova followed the shackled Grand Duchess Catherine Mikhailovna, General, the Count Boris Romochka-Krestyanov, and Luka Varvarinski onto the main deck of S.S. California, a three masted, side-wheel steamer bound for Panama.

Sacha Varvarinski waited near the open door of a forward cabin.

McFee handed Mike the key to their shackles and Mike stepped in front of General Krestyanov, staring solemnly into his steel gray eyes. He removed the shackles from his wrists and handed them to McFee. He unshackled Luka Varvarinski, handed off the shackles, and stepped in front of the duchess.

Her angry, green eyes burned to the back of his skull. This once beautiful woman now wore angry creases around her mouth and dark circles under her hate filled eyes.

Mike spoke in Russian. "Look at you. Your hatred for me has ruined your once wonderful face." He shook his head and removed her shackles. "I feel pity for you."

"You are deserter." She glanced at Preslova. "You will both pay the heavy price." She slapped Mike's face. "Pity your widow and orphaned son."

Neither McFee nor Billy would understand the threat delivered in Russian.

Mike handed the shackles to McFee. "Thank you, Angus."

"Any time."

Sacha Varvarinski helped the duchess into the forward cabin and closed the door.

A steward escorted the general and Luka to an adjoining cabin on the starboard side.

Whatever the Duchess had planned would reach fruition. Mike knew not what or when, but he knew it would come.

MIKE SAT ACROSS FROM Jimmy at the small gaming table in the corner of his office. The inlaid white and yellow-gold chessboard and pieces he'd received from the Chinese community in Weaverville, years earlier, had long been a curiosity to Jimmy. Mike had finally decided to teach his son the basics, going through the moves allowed by each piece on the board.

He picked up the yellow-gold queen. "This is the queen. She is the most powerful of all of the king's warriors. She can move across unoccupied squares vertically, horizontally, or diagonally, for any distance. She can stop anywhere, or she can remove an opposing player from the table and take its place." He demonstrated.

Smiling from the open doorway, Molly said, "She will do anything to protect her king."

Outside, carolers started singing, *Hark the Herald Angels Sing*.

Molly turned toward the kitchen and disappeared.

Jimmy jumped up and rushed from the office.

Mike followed.

Raul pushed past and opened the front door.

Mike, Jimmy, and Raul stepped onto the front porch and watched a group of about ten men and women on the street below. They sang beautifully.

Molly carried a large platter of cookies onto the porch.

Raul turned back inside, brought out a small table, and set it on the stoop.

Molly set the platter onto the table and said, "Isn't this nice?"

Mike put an arm around Molly and pulled Jimmy against his legs. "It humbles me."

"What, my sweet?"

"The joy that is Christmas. I have so much for which to be grateful. You, Jimmy, Raul, Abe Warner, Coira, and our many friends in this place. There are so many opportunities." A lump choked his throat. He blinked away tears and whispered, "Thank you, Lord."

Molly asked, "Did Franklin and little Melanie get off okay?"

"Yes. They sailed for Panama, late this afternoon. Moses has decided to stay. He will be selling art at North Beach on Sundays. He has special permission from the city to set up on the sidewalk, Sundays only."

"What about his work at the Palace?"

"He will still be there, six nights a week."

Molly turned closer and stroked his chest. "Jimmy and Melanie sure hit it off. I hope I can give him a little sister, just like her."

The carolers finished *Hark the Herald Angels Sing,* and lined up around the cookie platter.

"Merry Christmas!" Wishes were voiced all around.

Coira stepped out with a large tray of cups filled with hot cocoa. Jimmy grabbed a cup. "Thank you, Coira."

Thank you, Lord.

The End

Also by Thomas Holladay

The American Way
Deliberate Justice
Pursuit: The American Way

Standalone
Treasure
The Birthday Box
Meadowlarks
Comes the Call: For God and Country

Watch for more at www.thomas-holladay.com.

About the Author

Thomas Holladay writes from a Christian conservative world view, never preachy, never teach-me, always clean, almost never sweet. He creates riveting images through the senses of his vividly drawn characters to create fast-paced action, drama, and suspense that make his stories hard to put down. Read more at Thomas Holladay's site.

Read more at www.thomas-holladay.com.